*P*raise for
THE COUNT OF CONCORD

"Like Thomas Pynchon's *Mason & Dixon,* or John Banville's *Doctor Copernicus,* this brilliantly written novel—by turns wrenching, antic, and deep—marvelously illuminates a complicated scientist's life and times." —Andrea Barrett

"What a story. Benjamin Thompson, aka Count Rumford, is one of the great American characters—like Gatsby, but before his time, he reinvents himself, then sets about inventing everything else, including soups, fireplaces, social welfare reform, landscape architecture—you name it. Our hero has a certain problem in regard to loyalty, and virtue is somewhat alien to him, but he is a real character, a man of stature who, as a near-fiction himself, belongs in a novel. Nicholas Delbanco has done us a wonderful service in finding and recounting this American's life for us. And it's all true! Or not."
—Charles Baxter

"*The Count of Concord* is a true original, as unexpected, as multifaceted, as restlessly vital as its protean hero. What begins as a romp (an American *Tom Jones,* if you will) deepens into a tragedy of talent, not so much unfulfilled, but rather insatiable. Delbanco's trademark wit and sophistication, his exquisite prose, have found a perfect subject. This is the bravura performance of a maestro." —Peter Ho Davies

"Historical fiction about a figure as grand and capacious as Count Rumford demands a writer whose abundant gifts, virtuosity, and importance equal Rumford's own. Fortunately for him (and us), he has found the perfect dramatist for his life in the always dazzling Nicholas Delbanco, one of our most elegant prose stylists and a master storyteller. With *The Count of Concord,* Delbanco, a true man of letters, once again generously enriches our literary culture."
—Charles Johnson

THE COUNT OF CONCORD

Library of Congress Cataloging-in-Publication Data

Delbanco, Nicholas.
The Count of Concord / Nicholas Delbanco. -- 1st ed.
p. cm.
ISBN-13: 978-1-56478-509-1 (cloth : alk. paper)
ISBN-10: 1-56478-509-2 (cloth : alk. paper)
ISBN-13: 978-1-56478-495-7 (pbk. : alk. paper)
ISBN-10: 1-56478-495-9 (pbk. : alk. paper)
1. Rumford, Benjamin, Graf von, 1753-1814--Fiction. I. Title.
PS3554.E442C68 2008
813'.54--dc22
2007042288

Cover art: Thomas Gainsborough
Sir Benjamin Thompson, later Count Rumford (1753-1814), 1783
Oil on canvas; 75.7 x 62.7 cm (29 13/16 x 24 11/16 in.)
Harvard University Art Museums, Fogg Art Museum,
Bequest of Edmund C. Converse, 1922.1
Photo: Imaging Department © President and Fellows of Harvard College

Partially funded by a grant from the Illinois Arts Council,
a state agency, and by the University of Illinois, Urbana-Champaign

www.dalkeyarchive.com

Printed on permanent/durable acid-free paper and bound
in the United States of America

THE COUNT OF CONCORD

A NOVEL

NICHOLAS DELBANCO

Dalkey Archive Press
Champaign and London

for ELENA
my darling wife

THE COUNT OF CONCORD

Being an account of the remarkable life and illustrious career of
Benjamin Thompson, Count Rumford of the Holy Roman Empire,
born in Woburn, Massachusetts, in 1753, of humble origin, thence
established in Concord, New Hampshire, where his fortunes were
enlarged, an informer to General Gage, thereafter destined to be
confidante of Princes and of Potentates, Secretary to Lord George
Germain, Knight of England and the order of St. Stanislaus, scientist,
Founder of the Royal Institution of Great Britain, together with an
accounting of his devises and inventions, his divers campaigns, his
public writings and his private letters, his wives, his daughters, the
vicissitudes of nations, his philanthropy, his fame, his failing health,
his numerous and scandalous amours, the whispered intimations of
his envious detractors, the folly of ambition and occasion of his death
outside of Paris under siege, in the suburb of Auteuil, 1814.

PROLOGUE

1814

They laughed at him. They watched him pass. Fond mothers drew their sons to the embrasure of the window and, peering, pointed him out. "Formidable," they whispered. "Extraordinary. It is something to remember and tell your children's children you have seen. Look!"

Around the corner, rattlingly, the Count appeared. Along the Avenue des Ternes and stopping to collect his glass beyond the Place des Ternes—around the corner, well concealed and from French spies disguised—the beakers and alembics privately prepared for him, the necks in their tight spirals blown according to his secret and exact specifications, these coded in his assistant's German so that the envious incompetent calumniating locals could neither copy nor take the credit; from Boulevard du Bois le Prêtre, along the Avenue de Clichy and out at its high gate; from Malesherbes, along the Boulevard des Batignolles, or to the north—Berthier, Bessières—he made his great processional: one coach.

The women stared. They smiled and cradled their young sons and kissed them on the cheeks. "You must not forget this, darling, what you see." And little Jean or Claude or Michel or Philippe would approach the window, greatly daring, and promise to remember and press a cold nose to the glass.

They called their daughters also. "Come and watch this. Remember," they said. The worldly ones—the eligible—gazed boldly down at his carriage; the modest averted their eyes. No window was unoccupied, no doorway empty where he passed. Old women peered through the folds of the drapes; old men muttered sagely or shook their powdered heads. Servants caught a glimpse, or tried to, jostling for position by the garden wall; the brazen ones braved passage in the street.

There his horses thundered: four white stallions draped in white. They did not require blinders; their manes and tails were clipped. Air escaping from the matched team's nostrils plumed; black hooves struck sparks from the cobblestone paving. The coach doors bore his crest. His wheels were thrice the width of wheels on any other *équipage*, the felloes broad and stable, this effected to his satisfaction and by his own particular design; while clattering round the corner, in mud or snow, on hill or ice or thoroughfare, his conveyance did not lean.

The Count wore white. It is seemlier in winter, he maintained; it gives back the sun's irradiating heat. From head to toe, from cap to boot and cape to glove he clothed himself entirely in that glacial hue; both he and his horses advanced.

Wherever mad brilliant famous ancient Count Rumford went that season was a sensation: all Paris observed him; all gaped. He moved as if impervious through clamor and derision and applause and whistling fuss. At times he doffed his cap, then tightened the fur at his neck. For what was extraordinary to the populace was, to the object of their wonder, simplicity itself. He smiled and waved and bowed from the waist. Or he paid *la foule* no notice and drove on.

SALLY

Or that, at any rate, is how I imagine it—an old man in the avenue, the carriage and horses and perfectly white clothing and the serving girl and jostling crowds who gather where he goes. These streets are the streets of the Paris I know. Knew. Remarks the Instructor, clearing her throat. Few cities, Class, so clearly demonstrate how the long-established and more modern structures can coexist, their glinting contiguity and outward aspects intertwined like those of the aforementioned old man and young woman or, less frequently (as I have learned to my sorrow, for all knowledge is sorrow since Eden), the reverse.

In which case the dark city of light may represent for us that productive juxtaposition of opposites grown apposite, a marriage of convenience, call it intimacy even—his blue eyes and her auburn hair, her pure heart and his teeth. His height and her coloring, their fatal smile. What I *mean* is on occasion you still see them cheek by jowl, the recent and the ancient, the narrow alleyway extruded from a boulevard—*extruded*, would that be the word?—and the only real problem with street maps of Paris is that Baron Haussmann redesigned the city after Rumford died. Our hero did depart this vale of tears Anno Domine 1814, yet the oldest chart I could locate—given my limited resources, the constraints not so much of fiscal as of physical opportunity —is dated one year subsequent. So my beautiful Prologue's a fake.

But this is a novel, not history, and in our godforsaken town (not Paris, I mean, but Rumford's youthful locus, his true provenance and starting point) with its shabby Historical Society and little Public Library, I can't do any better for maps. We shall eschew anachrony in these our pages, Class. No willed inaccuracy here, nosiree Nabob's your uncle.

Except, to tell the truth, the architect of Paris was Napoleon's nephew, the Third not the First, with his grandiose intentions, his Empire-building pretensions, his self-vaunting renovation of, let's say, the city gates. Further, *Les Maréchals* Berthier and Bessières were cronies of the First Napoleon, the one who wasn't finished until Waterloo, so maybe where the Count drove clatteringly their names festooned no portal. Berthier was defenestrated in 1815, his colleague died two years before that, and which of us may hope to be so honored while alive?

It doesn't matter, really, all I wanted to establish is that Benjamin Thompson, Count Rumford, gets on his high horse and into his carriage and Cliphippityclippity cloppop goes mad . . .

Not unlike his natural son's granddaughter's granddaughter, or the lady who styles herself that. Me. Yours truly, reader, the last survivor, the final bud—if withered, if a trifle dessicate—of the cadet branch of the family tree and grafted stock *(that productive juxtaposition of opposites grown apposite,* etc.*)*: Sally Ormsby Thompson Robinson at your service, my various dears. On the *Who Goes There? Qui vive.* Who has been, I don't see why I shouldn't *use* the term, positively *haunted* by his unrelenting ghost and daily discovers his books on the shelves, his invasive presence on the Baking Powder can. Who sits in her front parlor with a Rumford Roaster for company, who dines off his cold soup. Who cannot fall asleep at night without the old man visiting, his face half-hidden by the curtains or stepping forth from *the embrasure of the window,* his wig in the glare of the light.

All right. Let's start again. Last night and this morning it snowed. "Mornin', Miz Robinson," said Alex—after he had plowed me out. His blue Dodge pickup with its lifted blade is running, engine thrumming, headlights on, its exhaust a thick white spiral. He's standing in the doorway on the shoveled stoop, stamping his boots and rubbing his gloved hands together, wet steam escaping from his mouth, the utterance dispersing into air so that we may see how much of what we say is mere exhalation and complicated vapor *(Dick the Shepherd bites his cuticle)* for all the world in his red padded jumpsuit like some shy unabashed if possibly southern retainer but using that long-voweled drawl of his that signifies a native of Concord and nonetheless comes clipped.

"Mornin', Alex," says I in return.

"Cold enough for you, is it?"

"A witches' tit," says I, "a bitch's wit."

Well I don't really *say* that, of course, I wouldn't, I'm not such a fool. So witlessly we nod at each other and smile and steam and I offer him a cup of tea or to hot him up a coffee and he says, "No thanks."

"Much obliged," says I, as always, and as always he touches his cap. Then he turns and lumbers off again and I am alone.

John Fowle served as Thompson's first teacher; I have examined his books. *The Universal Spelling Book* was the text in these parts at that time—which is to say, two hundred and fifty years ago—and it's remarkable how tortoise-like our language changes, day by century, how slow and small the alterations but how largely the changes accrete. Consider the example of the stream. This valley I inhabit on the cold north of the hill, these deep-cut cliffs were once a level—*a glacial, an antediluvial?*—plain. When ploughman Alex's ancestors first scampered—*scarpered, is it scarpered?*—after elk or mastodon or whatever gray beast they were hunting back then, when the first tribes stalked their supper, this valley was a height.

I'm an old woman mad about writing who huddles for warmth by the stove. I sit all day in the one chair and try to remember who wrote that before and verily I say unto you I cannot remember: it runs together, quite. It is the flowing stream.

So Benjamin Thompson, late of these parts, and I, Sally Ormsby Thompson, (who cleaved by marriage to the Robinsons so dear to Alex's heart, so consequential once in this New Hampshire town, the family that ran the Coal and Lumber Yard and whose names are

17

legion on the slabs above the church, overlooking the black river, fading, crumbling, by the wind effaced, which fact suffices to explain the habit Alex has of addressing me as the widow of his cousin's boss, but of whose actual corporeal presence—his cousin's boss, I mean, my husband and *hah!* one true love—I have no proper recollection: a formal encounter, a brief twenty years, a habit of pipe-smoke and tapping his nose and nighttime importunities of which this account will take no notice) flow together sweetly. The man who was Count Rumford and his surviving legatee conjoin as do cities or water: now I am he, he me.

And why do I write this, you ask? Why take the trouble here? Why should I vex myself and, by extension, you with this fact-fraught invention; what may we each discover in the dark backward of place from a long-vanished time? (Oh critic, ah gentle reader, even now I see you underline for purposes of paraphrase or perhaps direct quotation these very questions and uncertainties; *why take the trouble,* etc.)

The answer is simple; *he matters.* Mattered. I have been writing for much of my life and always before for money: this for love. My ancestor was famous, infamous, and is forgotten today; I herewith claim and reclaim him.

"Mornin', Miz Robinson."

Aye, that it is. Seven o'clock and the dark starts to lift, the first faint suggestion of dawn in the east, and with it the promise that maybe by nine we'll turn off our headlights and porch lights and watch unassisted the way the snows drift. The slow moon wanes, the long day climbs, the many voices shrill at me to stop this parakeeting and get to actual work. Tea. Paper. A carrot stick. *Ben.*

18

Rumford, His Book

Part One

The cow was done. Ben slapped her flank and moved his head back, hot. The warm milk's streaming stopped. Flies settled by her tail. She shat. The barn cats licked the gutter when he raised the pail. He disliked the smell of it, the heat of it, the ripe spread new-mown hay and the pigeons in the rafters where they shifted, ullulated. Light spilled thickly through. October, and the split-leaf maple flaming by the toolshed and the tamaracks beginning to go yellow by the fence-line, the oak at the crest of the hill; it was as if—he wiped his wet cheek, lifted, turned—the light above were pouring from the spigot of the sky.

Smoke from the kitchen chimney rose, mingling its aspect with haze of the sun, and for a moment ruminant young Thompson watched its coned dispersal into air. There were horses in the meadow —Aristotle, Amos, and the chestnut mare they pastured for his father's cousin Samuel who had gone to sea. His fingers ached; he rubbed them on his smock. From somewhere in the house he heard the sounds of music, and that meant his uncle played, which would mean he had a lesson and would have to practice; from tit to fiddle, his uncle declared, that's how a gentleman goes. *Hiram,* said his mother. Well, it's true, said Hiram, I call a spade a spade.

Now that Ruth Thompson had married again his uncle seldom visited. He smoked a pipe at table and left his beard unclipped. He himself owned too much land, he said, to mind or be affected by the notions of his kin. When Ben's mother had been left a widow by the death of his dear father, she tilted her cap jauntily and married Mr. Pierce. Then they left Grandfather's house. Josiah Pierce is not a bad man, Hiram said, and he gives you a good home, my boy, but there's no music in it so I bring the violin.

Hiram played it well. He could hear a tune just once and later on repeat it; he played the "Song of Winter" and you shivered in your seat. Ben went to Mr. Fowle's school first, and then to Byfield down the road, and then to Mr. Hill's in Medford. All of them were dull. Mr. Fowle taught Latin and had been a taskmaster but was sleepy, ancient now, and nodded at his desk. Loammi Baldwin knew as much about *The Universal Spelling Book* as did Mr. Fowle; he could do a sum so quickly in his head that you were busy copying while he had the answer, and the answer was correct.

Woburn Aug 16th 1769

Mr. Loammi Baldwin

Sir

Please to inform me in what manner fire opperates upon Clay to Change the Colour from the Natural Colour to red and from red to Black &c and how it operates upon Silver to Change it to Blue

I am Your most Huml

& obedient Servant

Benjamin Thompson

God Save the King

His bookplate bore his crest; he fashioned it himself. He engraved a set-square and dividers, a vessel under sail, then drew a stout tree with a broken trunk and an eye suspended in the top right corner and a radiating sun. A lion lay beneath. He drew an open book, a sword, a closed book, and a shield, which latter object he had learned to call escutcheon and bore the name B. Thompson.

His mother was Ruth Simonds, the eighth child of the union of James and Mary Simonds; Mary was the daughter of James and Mary Fowle. His father had been born the son of Ebenezer and Hannah Convers Thompson; Ebenezer was the son of Jonathan and Frances, Jonathan the son of Elizabeth and James. His father and his mother had been joined in matrimony on May 30, 1752, and he himself came crying forth next 26th of March. His father died November 7, 1755, at the age of twenty-six.

Love is a Noble Passion of the mind. That was what he copied in his schoolbook: LOVE. He drew a set of bosoms and the head of a donkey upon it; *I'm fashioning my idol in the likeness of an ass.*

Each spring they planted squash. He broke through the rough, stony soil and set cabbage seeds and turnips and onions and potatoes down and covered them again. Josiah Pierce said there's nothing better than potatoes for new ground, but Ben Thompson hated it—the hard cold earth, the grime beneath his fingernails, the reek that in his nostrils flared of cautious penury while he dreamed himself a gentleman. At table he desired to be served. Instead he poured the broth himself— the gristle floating in it, the stock-boiled shreds of meat. He asked his mother once what food the wealthy ate, and she said, Ben, the wealthy eat their food for sustenance, they swallow just the way that we do and to the same purpose. Use your spoon.

Ben got sixteen shillings every year and would get that sum, his uncle said, until he was fourteen; your grandfather was generous, my boy. Ebenezer Thompson had provided for his children, and his children's children too. There was an arrangement for your mother till she married; she had one half the garden at the west end of our house. And I supplied her wood. Now she has a husband to do it, so I save myself the trouble to my back.

Hiram laughed, then lit his pipe. In addition, eighty weight of beef, eight bushels of rye, two bushels of malt, two barrels of cider, three bushels of apples to keep: your grandfather was generous indeed. Old Ebenezer, if I ain't much mistaken, bequeathed you fifty acres on the north side of the hill. Count yourself among the fortunate, said Hiram, and make certain you can count.

"What doth it profit a man," Josiah Pierce inquired, "if he lose his own soul and gain the whole world?"

"We wasn't talking scripture," Hiram said. "We was talking testamentary arrangements."

"It's not a fortune," warned the prudent Mr. Pierce, "and it won't make your fortune but will start you off. You have to be less laggard at your chores."

Josiah was a farmer and his mother was a farmer's wife, but Ebenezer Thompson had owned a house in town. Milking, Ben would dream of it—the drawing room, the dining room, the visitors from Boston who had been to see the world. Uncle Hiram saw the world. He had business in Wilmington and went to Salem often and proposed that Mr. John Appleton, Merchant, teach young Ben the trade.

His mother doted on him; he was her blue-eyed boy. She declared he looked the spit and image of his father, who had died untimely, and was growing into just as tall a figure of a man. "Why, Ben," she said, as he set the pair of milk pails by the kitchen stoop, "we were saying how we'll miss you here."

He was leaving with his uncle who brought the apprenticeship papers; it was October 14th. They would set out together for Salem in the morning; it could not come too soon.

"We will," said Dinah, wheezing where she stood beside the stove.

His mother's breath was sweet, her cheeks were pale.

Hiram clapped him on the shoulder. "He'll go far. But he won't be leaving Massachusetts, sister, nor not go far away."

"No?" She had been crying, Ben saw. Women have that habit; on the smallest provocation, women weep.

"John Appleton's a worthy master," Hiram continued. "A gentle-man, to hear of it, and in commerce and scripture equally learned. Too, his shop's well stocked. You'll return in triumph, won't you Ben?"

"Return I will," he promised.

"You'll send us—often—news?" That spring his mother had pro-duced a second son, Josiah Pierce the Third, and by this new arrival her attention was diverted.

"I will."

"You won't forget us?"

"No."

Farmer Pierce had entered. He stood listening; he was standing in the doorway to the hall. He had that quiet way with him; you could not hear him in the woods or see his baited trap. "And your lessons?" asked Josiah Pierce. "And your prayers?"

"No, sir."

"No?"

"No, sir, I won't forget them."

"We want to hear you play your scales. Give us some music, nephew."

"Gladly." He picked up the violin and smiled at Uncle Hiram who put rosin on the bow. Yet in truth his heart was elsewhere, down the shining path already that would lead him from this place.

"And meantime don't forget"—Josiah Pierce insisted—"your duty to your mother."

He promised he would not.

But once in Salem's bustling town, under the eye of Mr. John Appleton, he was too busy for worship or music, too gainfully engaged. The Appleton house was big as his grandfather's, with sleeping-quarters for the shop's 'prentice up on the third floor. Ben learned to greet their customers with "Good morning, Sir, good afternoon, Madam," and "Good evening, Miss. May I help you?" he inquired, and they told him yes.

He took pleasure in the twill and various buttons and ribbons and the bright bolts of cloth. They ordered what they wanted, and observed with great particularity while he brought it to them, and then they said how much. He studied the proud bearing of the quality, and by his bed at night Ben Thompson practiced bowing, heels together, palm across his heart. He did his sums and read his verses and improved his written hand; he learned to gauge expense in leather, coat and carriage, and could recognize distinction by its cut. While he arranged the shelves and worked at the display he carried measures and a rule and shears and pencil, no longer axe or pail. Clothes make the man, he saw. There were spermaceti candles, calico and a fine assortment of patches; the Stamp Act was repealed.

Soon, patriots appeared. Arguing their politics they leaned across the countertop and pounded it for emphasis; upon arrival, evenings, they fastened the shutters behind. They were soft-voiced when they started but loud by evening's end.

John Appleton entered into a most solemn engagement not to engage in further commerce with Great Britain and to order no more goods with import duties on them. He had signed the document although custom must suffer thereby. His brow was furrowed, worry-lined, yet he said I have no choice: there are certain things a man must do, I'll honor our agreement, boy, and you can stay on if you wish. My books are yours to read. You would be advised to study and then sweep the floor and scrub.

So he fell to doing chores again, as if this were the farm. He admired Mary Appleton, who had turned seventeen. Snow blanketed the yard. The shop was rarely frequented, the house a quiet place, for Salem grew less prosperous; men with muskets walked the streets and gathered on the green. John Appleton instructed him: there's much to do with powder now, and if we sell these fireworks you may keep a quarter of the profit for yourself. Young Thompson fashioned fireworks with powder, sulphur, saltpeter and charcoal; he built compound rockets and recorded the procedure in his book.

The Composition for middle Size Rockets may Serve for Serpents and for Raining Fire. When you have filled the Rocket within abt. 2 Inches of the Top, he wrote, *thrust down a piece of Leather abt. the bigness of*

the hole of the Rocket & punch it full of holes in the middle with a bodkin
then Strew a little Dust of powder Grownd fine and fill the rest up with
unground powder & Stop up the remaining part with Leather or paper.
This was how to build a rocket, and it worked.

He ground the powder fine. Mr. Appleton and family were elsewhere visiting for tea and therefore the apprentice labored on his
own. It was a warm late afternoon: new spring. He busied himself at
his task. A curricle rolled past. The scent of apple came to him, and
somewhere on the breeze a hint of cloves. He would never be quite
certain how it happened, why it happened, but one minute he was
measuring saltpeter, considering the way that Mary Appleton had
said to him that noontime, Ben, you're growing mightily, but you're
the proper man—and the dimple when she said it, the bright eye, the
imperious fashion she swept from the room before he could marshal
his tongue-tied retort, before he had imagined what to tell her even,
Miss Mary, but aren't you the proper lady to say so, to notice, I'm delighted
by your notice—and the next the spark had taken, flared, the powder
hissed, exploded, and he was blown up.

He remembered the loud light. He remembered the red acrid
whiff of it, the high-pitched humming in his ear, the furry vision
of his hand above the yellow bench. Before the blood there was no
pain, and there was very little blood: the pain was elsewhere coursing
through a body not his own. It was separate by burning; it was heat so
absolute he thought it chill. Pain was dissevered, rampant, on the ceiling and the floorboards and the wall. Before he fainted Ben was sure
he spied a figure in the smoke, a beckoning demon with pitchfork,
except the tines became a hoe and the hoe was white hot, wand-like,

and transmitted flame; it was only when he touched it that he knew he had been burned. He cried out; he must have; the people on Essex Street heard. There were shouts he could not answer, and the frantic disapproving solicitous bustle of schoolmaster and merchant, and water pails and blankets and the poultice they applied to him until the doctor came. There was time he could not measure, and the long slow ache of recognition: I survive.

Mary Appleton was kind and bent down to his bed. His mother Ruth lay prostrate in Woburn; her husband rode alone. He who plays with fire, said Josiah Pierce—but collected himself and did not speak the rest of it—*has compacted with the devil and gets burned.* He leaned above Ben carefully: I've come to fetch you home.

The wounds took weeks to heal. Convalescent, he slept day and night in the downstairs parlor. Uncle Hiram tuned the fiddle for him, but he did not play.

Once he dreamed he met his father, who helped him with his sums. His father had the clearest eyes: a fine, straight nose, red hair.

"Don't be frightened," said his father. "You must not be afraid."

"I cannot help it, sir," he said. "I wish you were alive."

"But I am with you always."

"How so?"

"A bright lad," said his father. "A questioning intelligence." He faded. "How indeed?"

Ben listened to the chatter of Dinah in the kitchen, or the sounding silence of Josiah Pierce, or the loud bravura humor of his uncle. When he rehearsed the accident he blamed himself for carelessness and dreamed of the harnessed explosion and perfect arching flight.

What he had seen in Salem were men engaged in large endeavor, the business of politics and passion of attainment, the speculative bustle of invention and the trimmed sail of concession to a prevailing wind. Day by week as he grew hale once more the patient plotted his escape—for Woburn could not hold him now, its life was not his life.

He improved. The powder burns on his right forearm healed, and the scar above his eye. You're filling out, said Dinah, you're on your feet again and too much grown to be so underfoot all day. His brother, young Josiah, was too young. Loammi Baldwin was his friend who lived across the hill. Loammi was nine years older and planned to see the world. That had been his intention, but the Baldwins needed him at home and had no second family to send him on his way. His father was a carpenter, and Loammi helped.

When not engaged in study, Thompson wielded saw and plane.

> Sir: Please to give the Nature, Essence, Beginning of Existence, and Rise of the Wind in General, with the Whole theory thereof, so as to be able to answer all Questions relative thereto.

And when Loammi answered this he asked again.

> Sir: Please to give the Direction of the Rays of Light from a Luminous Body to an Opake, and the Reflection from the Opake Body to another equally Dense and Opake; vizt. the Direction of the Rays of the Luminous Body to that of the Opake, and the direction of rays by reflection to the other opake Body. Yours &C. Benj.

Thompson   N.B. From the Sun to the Earth. Reflected to the
Moon at an angle of 40 degrees.

And when Loammi answered this they raced each other to the
pond, and it was a perfect tie, and they swam across it and Loammi
won.

"I have great expectations of you," Ben announced.

"I thank you, sir." Loammi bowed.

"Mine was no idle compliment. You must not take it so."

Loammi smiled. His smile was modest, affable, and his teeth were
good.

"I plan to go to Boston."

"When?"

"As soon as ever Mr. Hopestill Capen takes me in. I am promised
to him and his dry-goods by October."

"Yet again," Loammi mused, "you leave us in October."

"'The Sign of the Cornfields,' it's called. I had far rather see a sign
than the actuality. Come with me. You'll find work."

"We've got the Grange to finish roofing," said Loammi. "And after that the library."

"There's libraries enough in Boston. You come too."

Loammi did not join him, as he had known would be the case,
but Ben set off for Boston nonetheless. His mother wept more openly,
less long. Uncle Hiram, whistling but otherwise silent—a country cap
upon his head, a country blend in his carved pipe—drove him in the
trap. On the outskirts of the city, they had to ask the way.

Mr. Hopestill Capen was a Royalist, not patriot, and therefore his shop prospered as to stock. It stood on Union Street, just off Dock Square. The house was brick, two story, and Ben enjoyed his private bed at the turn of the back stairs. He wrote to Mr. Appleton to thank him for the reference and ask for his few furnishings—the trunk, the desk and chair—to be forwarded to Boston; *I am most sincerely grateful for all your kindness shown. Never shall I live at a place again that I delighted so much as at Your house nor with a Kinder Master.*

Mr. Capen did not seem as kind. He had a high-pitched voice, a stutter, sparse red hair. There was tallow on his waistcoat and powder on his collar and his boots were imperfectly clean. He had business in London and had been to visit there, and he spoke of Boston with a weary querulous impatient condescension, as if he were condemned to life among the savages while across the ocean society flourished. "T-T-Thompson," he would say, "you simply f-fail to understand, you have imperfect understanding of the w-w-world."

"I am here, sir, to improve it."

"Mind you do, b-b-boy. Mind you do."

Ben drew "A Council of State." There were thirteen heads—one talking, one sticking out his tongue, one looking like a dog. Further, he drew boats and bottles and close renderings of pistols and crossed bones. He drew "Harry Modiste," an old man with a cane and hat; the jester points and calls to him, "Ha, you red nose, how will you sell your wig? by the Cord?" Down the street there was a school for fencing and for French. Mr. Donald McAlpin was the master; he catered, said his advertisement, "to lovers of the noble Science of Defence."

For ten shillings a month he provided instruction in the Back-Sword; he called it an "Art." He also taught French "in a most concise Manner and on reasonable Terms."

Ben enrolled. He drew pictures of the proper posture of defense, and practiced with the sword each morning in his room. Mr. McAlpin had one eye and a piratical swagger and swore great rolling oaths in French while he thrust and lunged. "*Sacre bleu!*" He parried: "*Parbleu. Charognes des gosses!*" He had fought the French in the last war, and claimed they had no equal in the Back-Sword but would sometimes falter in conviction; you can beat them through endurance, boy, and with that strong right arm of yours, but not in skill. You may practice conjugation but must enlarge your wrist.

His understanding enlarged. In his rare free hours or at night he walked the streets of Boston, seeing everything there was to see in the teeming waterfront: the ships and purveyors and sailors and the grog-shops by the docks. He watched soldiers at parade and heard men argue politics, protesting the inequity of tax. He met clergy and a black man with a parrot on his shoulder, saw a one-legged infant scuttling where the daylight beggars slept. Ben moved among the tinkers, grocers, red men, blacksmiths, cooks, attenuated shapes that breathed upon the paving blanketed in rags; they sang, they moaned and muttered so he knew they were alive. By the chandler's dory he saw commerce: dice and bulldog, fighting cocks.

"Young sir," a woman called.

He went to her.

"Got a copper, darling?"

"That I do."

She bit it, then lifted her skirt.

McAlpin took him roistering to bawdy house and brothel; twice, McAlpin paid.

One girl had the coloring and guise of Mary Appleton; Ben fancied her particularly and visited three times. On the third visit she was gone, and he found himself disconsolate and drank strong ale till morning who had been abstemious, and his head felt like a bladder and his hand shook at the counter so that Mr. Hopestill Capen asked him if he were unwell, if he had contracted palsy in addition to the pox.

"No sir."

"I have written to your m-mother. I have t-t-told her you must m-m-mend your ways."

"Yes sir."

"I find you more often under the counter, with gimlets, knife and saw, constructing some little m-machine or looking over some book of science, than arranging c-c-cloths behind it."

"Sir."

"We have c-c-customers here, Thompson, we have custom to attend to."

"Sir."

"You may go now, Thompson. I had rather you sleep lying down than upon your f-f-feet."

So he was dismissed to Woburn and returned there yet again. This was a falling off. He was seventeen years old and had no real employment and cut wood to pay his debts. Josiah Pierce grew more severe, his mother less indulgent, and his hours in the forest were put to proper use; he cut and loaded logs and stacked and sold what Ebenezer Thompson had bequeathed him on the hill. He learned a saying as to wood: it will warm you thrice. Once when cutting, once when splitting, once when burning: in each of these three processes good wood provides us heat. Add to this the exercise of loading, dragging, hauling, stacking, and every tree is severally productive.

Ben noted how the saw-teeth bit according to the log. The locust branch was hotter work than apple, the apple than maple, the maple than oak. He told Loammi Baldwin he could gauge the kind of wood he cut by how hot the blade. In June he and Loammi wrote a plan for "forming a Society amongst us for Propagating Learning and usefull Knoledge, by means of Questions to be Proposed to a Certain Number of Person's and each Person to bring his answer to said Quest propos'd." Loammi studied engineering, and they disputed together with profit and read Boerhaave's treatise on fire admiringly out loud. He described for his friend's benefit his revels in the city, the worldly lures of Boston and the soldiers in the streets. There had been a massacre; he heard reports. Four citizens were shot. Loammi knew no French.

They went fishing to Nahant. They made a party with Abijah Thompson, his cousin, and Loammi and Dr. John Hay. It was a clear day, and a pleasant one, and they engaged in scientific observation and banter and caught quantities of mackerel and cod. Ben went to fetch the horses and left Loammi cleaning fish; Dr. Hay and Abijah Thompson left too. At the inn they shared a meal, and Dr. Hay said, "Thompson, you should study with me, I will teach you what I know."

They discussed this eagerly, and Dr. Hay impressed upon him the advantages of medicine; they contracted then and there for Ben to start his studies and take lodgings with the doctor at forty shillings a week.

"It's an excellent career," said Abijah, "there's always someone sick or dying," and they drank a toast to celebrate the new physician's future, and only back in Woburn did he recollect Loammi at Nahant still cleaning fish.

It's betrayal, said Loammi, it is callous disregard. I was gutting them and wetting them and making myself nauseated whilst you three were drinking and disporting; I brought back all that fish alone and in a hired trap. I am most heartily sorry, said Ben, I should not do what I did. Your apology, Loammi said, if heartfelt, is sufficient. It is heartfelt indeed, Ben insisted, pinching himself cruelly so as not to laugh.

"Why does the flame of a candle tend upwards in a spiral?"

"Why is the sound of clicking stones transmitted and not instead dispelled by water?"

"What is the reason the tides rise higher in the bay of Fundy than in the Bay of Delaware?"

"Why does ice diminish in its volume melted; what loss of water in steam?"

"Does the same proportion hold for tea?"

"Whence comes the dew that stands on the outside of a tankard that has cold water in it in the summer-time?"

So he moved to Dr. Hay's house and resolved on a career. Each day he devoted to study and Sunday ate at home. He worked hard. He contrived a learning schedule:

Monday--Anatomy, Tewsday---Anatomy, Wednesday---Institutes of Physic, Thursday---Surgery, Fryday-- Chimistry with the Materia Medica, Saturday---Physic 1/2 & Surgery 1/2.

Mrs. Hay was kindly, bustling, busy with her household and three children and their clamorous necessities: food, clothing, cleanliness, heat. Benjamin perceived the order of the day. In emulation of the Hays he set himself thereafter to abide by order also, and made himself a schedule that he pinned above the desk:

"6 a.m....Get up, wash hands and face

"From 6 a.m. until 8 a.m Exercise and study

"8 a.m…10 a.m. … Prayers and breakfast

"10 a.m….12 noon … Study

"12 noon…1. p.m…Dine

"1 p.m….4. p.m….Study continualy

"4 p.m….5. p.m... Diversion or exercise

"5 p.m….11 p.m... Follow what my inclination leads me to.

What his inclination led him to was Abigail the children's nurse who slept behind the nursery and took him in at night. He doted on her legs. They were long and white and fine and when she raised them for him he felt himself wholly a man. She flattered him, gasping, convulsive, and gave him his first lessons in the lexicon of pleasure and anatomy of love. This was what he studied Mondays and Tuesdays in the book, Anatomy, and when the children were asleep and Dr. and Mrs. Hay had retired yawning to their quarters, Ben took off his shoes and tiptoed up the attic stairs and knocked twice, lightly, and once hard, and was let in with no candle and took off his trousers and his shirt. She lit the candle, barred the door, and turned to him on her incomparable legs and said, "It hurts here, doctor, touch this swelling. Here's a sweet soreness you can examine; will it please you, press this breast."

He started at her toes. He kissed her metatarsals and the joinings of her ankle and her calf and knee and thigh. He delighted her entirely, she said, and he delighted in her also and repeated her name often, since this was his first woman with a name. They had great times together but one morning she was sullen, sallow, and by evening had departed and he never did learn why. He made inquiries but could not ask too often for fear of troubling Dr. Hay, who had turned a blind eye to his nightlong revels and his daytime torpor. He did not know if Abigail went willingly or had been dismissed; from their attic whispers he had known she came from Cambridge but did not know her family's address. He confided to Loammi who said best stay away, friend, what you don't know will not injure you and ignorance is bliss. We've lived our whole life, Ben protested, disdainful of that proposition, and you tell me now to embrace it. Loammi said, I do.

Once more therefore he found himself perplexed by limitation. He lay in his cold single bed and failed to find the reason she left him thus disconsolate; he blamed her, then the world. She was carrying his child, perhaps, or the baby of another, or had tired of their pleasure and had found employment elsewhere or been summoned suddenly and would one day return.

Taking comfort in this last, he exercised and prayed. He applied himself to surgery and drew the picture of a fetus and studied its strange attributes minutely. It was a male, club-footed, with the toes growing by pairs. A stump grew from the sternum and the heart was visible and lungs did not inflate. This monstrous child was born in Woburn on April 16, 1771.

John Winthrop's fame was wide. In June he spoke at Harvard College, and Loammi planned attendance, so Benjamin went too. Employing a day for the trip they walked together companionably and by the time the noon chimes rang were striding past brick buildings, gleaming spires, vaulting domes; horsemen and carriage clattered down the teeming streets. There, having obtained the directions, they entered a high hall. John Winthrop spoke of natural philosophy, the nature and the *modus operandi* of the earth. His electrical apparatus came from London and had been sent by no less a colleague than Benjamin Franklin; he spoke extempore, as though at his worktable, but to great effect. The gentleman in front of Ben wore a scarlet coat.

To the inquiring mind there was abundant matter for debate, and discussing great Winthrop's discussion the two young men walked back. Although he had intended to, Ben made no search for Abigail in town. He left Cambridge ruefully, dreaming and desirous, but not on her account.

One day he played the bugle with the bronchia of a hog. Dr. Hay was much perturbed; he thought a hog ran squealing in the room. He rumbled up the stairs and flung the door ajar. "What are you up to, Thompson?" he shouted. "Whatever are you doing here?"

"Examining the hog, sir, for its tympanic properties."

"Are you mad, boy? Joking?"

Ben blew again, less loudly now.

"And what is your vocation?"

"Sir?"

"Your purpose, Thompson, blatting so."

"Pure inquiry," he said.

"Pure foolishness," said Dr. Hay, and slammed the door again.

Ben folded his bugle. It stank. He who dreamed of high adventure was forced to scrimp on wire for his kite. The light poured through his window as once above the barn: cow's teat, cornfield, tree stand, pig's lung—the lineaments of country life he longed to leave behind. He had no greater interest in medicine than drygoods, no reason to remain with Hay, nothing to keep him at home.

For Phillis Walker he prescribed tincture of asafetida. The primary ingredient of B.T. Nerve Oil is Spirit of Wine. He wrote this in his day-book, and he traced the emblem of the woman with the donkey's ears, then rocket, swordsman: LOVE.

That winter he left Woburn to teach school at Wilmington, and thereafter he taught school at Bradford for two months. He met the Reverend Samuel Williams and through him the Reverend Timothy Walker; they supervised his teaching and declared themselves well pleased. They suggested he visit in Concord, and there his life was altered, lightning-struck.

Ben walked from Salem School; he carried both satchel and hat. Low creatures scattered helter-skelter at his progress, and the fields around him steamed. It was a late spring morning, mild and newly dry. Whistling a tune of Uncle Hiram's, a snatch of song he could not name, he made for the white farmhouse by the river; meanwhile, the mist dispersed. I am, dear lady, universal, so to speak an open book. He had an introduction to the widow Sarah Rolfe.

The Universal Spelling Book: he rehearsed it yet again. Conjugation, spelling, syntax—these describe what depends upon what; they require observation of the world. To take but a single example, a subordinate clause of its own nature argues mastery; it modifies or amplifies but does not in essence alter the noun phrase to which it belongs. Therefore walking he grew casual—indifferent, even, in his leathers—as to mud. As when himself a student and bored by Mr. Fowle, Ben displayed the yellow volume to his charges and by way of an example kept it at his desk. But where in class he might insist on orderly instruction, outside and on this April day in the year of our Lord 1772, his nineteenth spring just underway and music in his head (and redwing blackbirds and the robin redbreast and the jay, their startled birdsong, the wind in the leaves), he could not keep that earnest mien befitting a young scholar; he could do nothing with the title but repeat it while he paced. "*The Universal Spelling Book*": iambic tetrameter, dull.

His bearing if not station was assured. His carriage was his own two feet, and they bore him rapidly. At Wilmington they spoke of him as a prodigious gymnast, at Bradford much the same. He did not own a horse but knew well how to sit one and had cut sixteen cords of wood in barter for his cloak. It was a Hussar cloak, bright blue, and many the compliment he received as to its color; his eyes were also blue.

He studied where he walked, though the parish was half Woburn's size and the surrounding farms—not poor but not yet prosperous—looked raw. Concord was a village still, mere palisade and possibility: fresh-named, beginning to grow. The trip from town through shady lanes took Thompson thirty minutes: *Universal Spelling Book*. The Indians had only recently been driven north, or killed. Felled trees formed the fence-lines, and cleared rock was piled but not as of this early season ordered into walls. Now there were apple blossoms underfoot; poplars rustled in the breeze that wafted from the Merrimac, and willows tumbled greenly by its banks.

Sarah Rolfe had been a widow since the previous December. She was thirty-three. Her husband, Colonel Benjamin Rolfe, had been of considerable means and uncertain health; in view of the latter condition, perhaps, he took a wife at sixty and by their shared exertions they produced one son and heir. Too young as yet to go to school, young Paul required a tutor; he was supposed to profit from the occasional lesson and regular example a journeyman scholar might set.

Ben learned all this on Tuesday. After lessons in the schoolhouse, while he was correcting sums (that number which, when multiplied by itself, produces sixteen is neither six and ten nor eight and eight nor sixteen times one, Class, but *four*, and this same principle applies throughout, so that the root of four is two, of nine is three, of eighty-one nine), he had been to his surprise approached and interviewed by the Reverend Timothy Walker. There was thunder outside: the first spring storm. It rained.

The Reverend Walker had an ample stomach, a snub nose; his eyes were brown-flecked green. His wig was large, well-powdered; his shoes had silver buckles and he wore a three-cornered hat. He clothed himself entirely in black. He and the dead Colonel Rolfe had been friends and were, albeit self-proclaimedly, the two leading citizens in town.

"Might I be permitted, dear sir," he inquired, "though your labor is of consequence, ever so briefly—and with view to an employment similar in nature though particular and personal—to interrupt?"

Benjamin put down his pen.

Timothy Walker was grateful. "It is, I trust, an opportune moment, what though the weather be intemperate, a cloudburst kind only to husbandry, and—since properly considered no such expression is accidental, I seem to see a form of instruction in that choice word, *husbandry*—for us to conduct this discussion." Arranging his coattails, he sat. "There is mutual advantage—nay, universal profit—should we come to terms."

He cleared his throat. He spoke as though from a traveling pulpit, orotund in discourse and prodigal of emphasis. Having styled himself a student of humanity, he had persuaded others of his excellent discernment; his opinion was local law. His flock were sheep.

"It is a matter of some urgency," Reverend Walker confided. "Some delicacy also. Nerves. The shock of bereavement: so recent, so harsh.

She does not deal with deprivation as well as her fond father—your humble servant, sir—might have been permitted to expect."

He proceeded to describe the nature of the post. "It is of the utmost importance," the Reverend asserted, "that a seed so tardy sowed be nurtured promptly, prudently. For want of proper tending, if I may so describe it, full many a crop has been lost." He consulted his watch, then took snuff. He entertained a particular and, he was persuaded, a pardonable interest in this case. The widow was his daughter, after all, and Paul Rolfe his grandson, and therefore no two citizens of Concord could be more near or dear to him; none required such close care.

Ben listened in silence, nodding at intervals, clearing his throat; this last sufficed as speech. Having four or five times pronounced himself content, the Reverend suggested that next Saturday young Thompson pay a visit to the widow. "Talk to her," urged Walker. "Use just such conversation as we have enjoyed. Enlarge her understanding, as you have with profit my own. Note how the boy behaves."

The Rolfe estate was large. Eleven surveyed lots fronted the Merrimac River, and there were well-tended barns. Attention had been lavished on the lawn, as though the outward show and circumstance of things might make manifest the inward, and the portico (both inviting and formal of aspect) was a strait gate. In his one cloak, approaching, the schoolmaster readied himself.

By all standards of the place and time, Sarah was a wealthy woman, and alone. She owned a negro and a curricle and plate and livestock valued at above two hundred dollars. The deceased—so Reverend

Walker had informed him—held every responsible and remunerative office a citizen could hold. Now, shaded by her parasol and attesting her condition by the black lace at her wrist and black ribbon at her neck, the lady who might offer him advancement waited by the fence.

The man who studies fire must prepare himself for burning; he who deals with powder must anticipate the charge.

"Mr. Thompson."

"Mrs. Rolfe."

"Your given name?"

"Is Benjamin."

"My husband's name was Benjamin."

"So I was informed, Madame."

"Benjamin Rolfe. You would have liked him."

"Certainly."

"Why so certain, if I might ask?"

"Because of his reputed generosity of spirit. His personal largesse. His bravery. His excellent taste."

"His candor too?"

"Of that I heard no evidence and have encountered no witness, Madame."

"No. Nor learned as example."

"I will try to teach Paul candor."

"Do."

"He is attentive?"

"Very."

"Quick?"

"He resembles his father in that."

"If fair, he resembles his mother."

"Candor, Mr. Thompson. Teach him truth."

"I would teach him nothing less than candor, Mrs. Rolfe, in so saying. Should he prove fair."

"You may call me Sarah."

"Madame?"

"It was my husband's wish that we observe small ceremony in this house. And his strong persuasion."

"Yes."

"No ceremony here."

"Then I will call you Sarah."

"You are very welcome."

"And you must call me Benjamin. I hope to be of use."

"We'll use you in this house."

The usage that she put him to was rapid and abrupt. No sooner had Thompson contracted with her—bringing his books, his joint-stool and his writing desk—than she invited him to dine. He would be welcome at table; he must be hungry, thirsty, and therefore, as she put it, she might watch him at his work.

Paul Rolfe was two years old. He had an old man's wizened visage and thin hair. His antics, however, were childish; he had been much doted on, applauded and indulged. His mother spoiled him shamelessly, for young Master Rolfe was—she confessed to it, dimpling— the apple of her eye. He could not be expected yet to pursue the skills of language or arithmetic, so she desired him to participate in discourse and observe the art of mannerly procedure and how to use a fork.

The schoolmaster complied. He spoke, though guardedly, of his time in Salem and his time in Boston and the lectures attended at Cambridge. He improved on his acquaintance with John Appleton, he invented a friendship with Mr. John Winthrop and mentioned as though but a fishing companion and equal in such pastimes the excellent doctor John Hay.

The Widow Sarah Rolfe had traveled little, it appeared. She paid him close attention. Paul did not. Banging his spoon and rubbing his eyes, he rearranged his food. Ben spoke of his dear father dead at roughly the same moment in this his one son's childhood and how his own mother had married again; he conferred prosperity upon Josiah Pierce. He praised the Sunday dinner: a game bird, a pudding, red wine. He discussed philosophy and politics and, he hoped, altogether contrived to give the impression of a man widely versed in though not tainted by the world.

Her nose was sharp. Her eyes were pink-rimmed, watery, and the pinkness of her cheeks owed less to nature than art. Her cap revealed reluctant curls, and her nether lip a tooth more yellow than white. Her ears were large. Her fingers were long, her hands broad. She was no beauty, but he had not come for beauty, and a certain vivacity prompted by wine gave to her features a pleasing arrangement. She flattered him; he, her. The expression of the Widow Rolfe was mobile yet attentive, and she followed her new lodger with close if distracted attention. Having emptied a flagon and then its successor, she drank his conversation in as if she had been parched for it; she told him they had missed a man about the house.

"To enlarge our understanding. Oh, Benjamin, how hard that is!"

"How necessary, Sarah."

"Yes."

"Else how may we remedy our relation to this planet, our standing upon it as creature? The cog that does not fit the wheel is forced into adjustment and must be ground down."

"But forcibly?"

"Not always, no."

"By friction? By attrition?"

"Or mutual advantage—the mesh of cog and measured gear."

"Yes, *doubly* yes."

Young Paul fell asleep in his chair.

That very night she came to him, on the pretext that she needed to make certain of his comfort. The Rolfe home had a center hall; a dining room and drawing room gave off it to the east, a ballroom to the west. Above this ballroom he must lodge, since—so his hostess smilingly confided—he would be undisturbed. They gave no dances now. Few visitors came calling; in the evenings none arrived. His hostess pressed his hand. She would, she said, deny him nothing: not the library nor stables nor access to the kitchen or the music room; Sarah trusted that she need not say this and that he—so capacious in his courtesy, his scholar's understanding—understood.

"You have what you require? You have everything you want?"

"I am most grateful."

"Everything?"

"On my travels," he declared, "I often made do with rude quarters and am used to deprivation. This is abundance, Sarah."

"Good." She sat. "Paul has grown so fond of you."

"Already? You predict him, surely."

"A mother can tell."

"I shall enjoy him as a student. Those in my schoolroom are not, not always—how shall I put it—not always so well-mannered."

"He will be your willing student soon."

"He seems alert."

"He profited from what he heard, I have no doubt. And now he sleeps. The household sleeps."

Intending to adjust the sash, Ben leaned across her to the window and said, "Close. It's close in here."

"These April evenings . . ."

"Yes."

"You have your daytime duties. You have the morning's class to teach . . ."

He moved to her. She welcomed him.

"Yet let me be your pupil in the night."

It is an old, old story, as he would later learn. The May-December marriage—for she had married Colonel Rolfe—becomes December-May. The man who summons youth to warm his bed is partnered by a woman who, when old, may summon youth. Nor was she yet, at thirty-three, an altogether ancient or soon-sated partner; she had more of Abigail's enthusiastic appetite than he would have guessed at table from the way she picked at food.

The widow Rolfe discarded modesty when she took off her clothes. She did not toy with him, nor play the reluctant matron; she

49

was starved for affection, she told him, with no stomach for delay. She would tell him later that she chose him at the moment of his first arrival at the garden gate, on the instant of approach had made her choice. Though she treated her young lodger in daylight with propriety, she embraced him with abandon in the dark.

Such hunger grows with feeding; she wanted him in daylight soon enough. When Paul was at the river in the company of playmates, or visiting a cousin, or taking his afternoon nap, while Timothy Walker's congregation sat attentive to his sermons or meting out its charity or deciding on repairs for the scorched spire of the church; once a neighbor's call was finished or promised arrival delayed, if Benjamin corrected lessons or the school were at brief recess—his mistress arrived at his door. She gave him no notice, no respite. He was pleased at first, and flattered, then surprised by her hot urgency, and finally impatient with her importunings; she came always to his garret and—though avid there, extremely fond—denied him her own room.

"What we do," said Benjamin, "we do as adults."

"Yes."

"As equals."

"Yes." She smiled. "Although you master me." She touched his cheek.

"We are discreet."

"I hope so."

"I do not display you in public."

"No."

"Your neighbors know nothing. Paul suspects nothing."

"So it would seem."

"Why then should I be shameful in your quarters? Why will you never greet me there and keep me so completely here?"

"You are my secret," Sarah said. "You are my private pleasure."

"I have little time in private. No chance to study, no hope of advancement."

"None, unless . . ."

"I require independence."

". . . you marry me," she said.

The principles of order may seem various. The split log or the fruit fall into their component halves at a decisive stroke. A triangle is altered by the addition or subtraction, at that figure's apex, of just one single degree. Those who paid Thompson scant notice before now flattered him, attentive, and he became the object of universal curiosity in that particular universe where Sarah Rolfe loomed large. All Salem came to call.

Reverend Walker havered mightily and gave them his permission who could scarcely have done otherwise, then described it as his blessing. He had grown forgetful. He complained about his slaves: Prince, Luce and Violet. They were lazy, shiftless; they fouled his linen, he was sure, and failed to shine his brass. They misplaced his silver and his walking stick and books. He too had hailed from Woburn, and the coincidence of Benjamins—that his daughter married two of them—exercised the Reverend greatly; he referred to young Thompson as "Colonel" and reminisced about their trip to London as if his future son-in-law were his original friend.

He said, "Ha, Benjamin. Well met. Well married and well done!"

Indeed, he and Colonel Benjamin Rolfe had traveled to England together in 1753. That their journey took place in the year of Ben's birth made no impression on Timothy Walker; he nodded, blew and doddered on about the rigors of travel by water, and who better withstood the foul weather, and which of the two voyagers had been more ill.

"You are aware, I take it, of our nomenclature's provenance. I may in all due modesty aver that the late Colonel and your interlocutor were of some—indeed, considerable—consequence in setting matters straight."

"How so?" inquired Benjamin, who had heard the story often.

"Politics," said Walker, "is the art of adjudication. It is self-interest selflessly administered." He paused to admire his nails. "You know the history perhaps. This place was first called Penny Cook or Penacook, then Rumford, in honor of that Essex town from which its founders hail. In the English town of Rumford, it has been reliably reported to me—though I claim no first-hand certainty—they brew a first-rate beer. Once the border between Massachusetts and New Hampshire was agreed on as the River Merrimac—a process of negotiation, I might add, both long and obdurate—we christened Rumford anew."

"And called it?"

"Precisely. This place." He waved his hands. "This shining little city on a hill. Those who were wont to live in Rumford at present pay taxes to Bow; they have become to our collective satisfaction the citizens of Concord. Thus was resolved and by name acknowledged a boundary dispute." He sighed and tapped his nose. "Would we had concord again."

Young Paul was indisposed. He kicked his feet and squalled and flung his food and overturned his cup. Benjamin ignored this; Sarah Rolfe did not. She feared that what he suffered from might be a mortal fever, and would not hear of nuptials till the storm had passed. So son and mother huddled to the nursery, he complaining and she comforting; she changed his bedding daily and prepared his poultice and hot soup. This went on for five weeks.

Meanwhile the schoolmaster considered his condition, for it was insecure. He walked the lanes in his old boots and fished the Merrimac and speculated on the nature of ambition: what depends on, is subordinate to what. While Ben pursued his courtship's goal, the tongues of gossip—ceaseless and calumniating—wagged; his dream of brilliant fortune depended on a cough.

At length the boy improved and, on his third birthday, danced. Perhaps he vauntingly believed himself to have vanquished the intruder, this tutor in his mother's house who sat with them at table and carved the Sunday joint. Perhaps he did not notice or, busy with his own campaigns and conquests (the setter pup, the pony, the regiment of soldiers massed to charge along the bookshelf), did not care. At any rate Paul Rolfe grew weary of his supervised confinement and went to the river to play. This proved beyond dubiety that she need not fear judgment, and in proportion to her son's health Sarah's ardor too recovered; arriving in the library and fastening the door behind, one finger to her lips and one undoing ribbons, she favored Benjamin again.

The pair drove to Boston for clothes. He had worn nothing till that season but the costume of a scholar. The future husband of the richest widow in Concord, however, could not properly disport himself in one blue Hussar cloak. The tailor showed scarlet shaloon. "I am yours to command, sir," he said.

Ben stood six feet tall and held himself erect. Mirrored, there were several of him, and he admired the view. Two experienced attendants paid attention to detail in button and sash. They spanned his paired wrists with respectful concern—the right one being larger from the sword. Mock-spangle metal buttons were the order of the day.

He had learned to recognize distinction in his days at Salem, and these tailors and their cloth were a cut above John Appleton; they sold imported goods. They fitted their new customer with hat and cape, with leather of the finest quality in belt and glove and boot. He had latterly acquired the habit of command, and it afforded him great pleasure to give orders to such men; Sarah took her gratification in watching him take his.

On their return from Boston they drove to the Pierce farm. It was Benjamin's intention to introduce his bride-to-be to her future mother-in-law. His mother and John Pierce were home but had not seen such horses nor so elegant a curricle, and on first viewing they mistrusted his companion and new clothes. When he knocked upon the door, his mother had no greeting but reproach.

"Why Ben, my son, how could you go and lay all your winter's earnings in Finery?"

"I am to be married," he told her. "And this is Sarah Rolfe. It is not a tithe of what we bought, nor any of my earnings. Congratulate me, mother!"

She fainted dead away.

There was no lawful impediment. The Governor was kind. John Wentworth was a man of parts, surpassing any other sponsor that a man might claim. He had been born in Portsmouth, wealthy and well-favored; he attended Harvard College and helped repeal the Stamp Act and returned, as governor, to New Hampshire in 1766; there he was also named surveyor general of His Majesty's Woods in America, in which capacity he ascertained that all trees of the diameter of twenty-four inches and upwards were to be reserved for masts, yards, and bowsprits for the Royal Navy. John Wentworth loved the wilderness and made excursions and found respite there from Portsmouth; he undertook to survey the White Mountains' highest peak.

When approached about the marriage, he told Sarah he approved. This was important news. On the day before the wedding, the Second Provincial Regiment of New Hampshire mustered at Dover; the wind was high, and the regimental colors, the flags and plumes and pennons snapped smartly, and the horses, wheeling, neighed. Clouds scudded down the sky as though also on parade. The cannon sounded thrice; three times the bright rifles volleyed. Then the ranks presented arms.

Governor Wentworth and his retinue surveyed the scene; the local notables had gathered in attendance. Benjamin in his new cloak was of that retinue, and called to the Governor's side.

"You are welcome with us, Thompson."

"Sir."

"You are expert with the broad-sword, I am told."

"Not expert, no. I handle it passably."

"Mind you, to a soldier this argues expertise."

Benjamin inclined his head.

"The amateur," continued Wentworth, "is boastful, not modest. The true soldier knows his own worth." He cleared his throat. "I knew the Colonel, your bride's former husband. A disputatious person."

"Sir?"

"Quarrelsome. He might have been a lawyer, he so enjoyed an argument. You take a wrangler's seat."

"A wrangler's bed," affirmed Jamie Edwards, who was a known wit.

"I heard it reported," the Governor said, "that Philip Eastman told his wife, 'Well, Abiah, I have been to a meeting of the proprietors today and have not had one word of dispute with Colonel Rolfe.' When she told him she was gratified, he answered, 'There was a good reason for it, for he died this morning.'"

Benjamin chuckled. He took no offense.

"His commission must be filled. Think on it, Mr. Thompson, you may wish to join."

"You ride the same horse nightly," said Edwards, but Governor John Wentworth frowned, as if to say, Thus far, but go no farther, and turned, giving Edwards his back.

What he gave by contrast to Thompson was official smiling favor. He was open-handed to his protégé, and—so whispered the town gossips—as rapidly enamored as had been Sarah Rolfe. Whatever the true motive of the Governor's indulgence, whether he attended to the nuptial pair from policy or reasoned judgment or concupiscent self-interest, the bride and groom on the day of their wedding sat as fêted intimates at Wentworth's own table. Knee to knee they thanked him, then they danced.

Once having "conquered Concord"—a phrase repeated often by Jamie Edwards over ale—Ben styled himself a soldier. He was made welcome in the governor's council at Portsmouth, and he joined the entourage that planned to climb through Crawford Notch, thence from that lofty junction to approach the Western Pass. Mount Pleasant loomed above these soldiers and surveyors, and its aspect was benign.

The first weeks, Sarah seemed as flattered as was he to have been made so privy so quickly to what others called the court. Then she grew querulous. It is the tongue of envy, Benjamin assured her, not plain truth; we men around John Wentworth are not his servants, not at all. By every means at our disposal we must celebrate his courtesy and make known to those who question it how his intention stands to benefit the province; the Western Pass will offer fair passage for every citizen and not the chosen few. I doubt it not, said Sarah, I doubt you in no way. But this is a strange honeymoon, for you to climb a mountain and leave me here at home. We enjoyed our honeymoon, said Major Benjamin Thompson, before the nuptial night.

He and the Reverend Samuel Williams and Loammi Baldwin prepared for the ascent. The Governor had offered him the run of Wentworth house at Wolfeborough, not thirty miles from the mountains. Ben urged them to arrive. "Is not this a sweet gentleman?" he wrote. "One exactly suited to our taste, and how charming! How condescending!" They would share a tent. He wrote Samuel Williams that the Governor possessed "a number of Mathematical instruments (such as two or three telescopes, Barometer, Thermometer, Compass &c) at Wentworth House, all which, together with his library, should be at our service."

Then he played his trump: "But stop! I will not tell you any more till you come and see me as you promised; then we will lay the whole plan of operation, and I will tell you a charming secret—something you would give the world to know. 'Tis nothing about Magnetism, nor Electricity, nor Optics, nor Evaporation, not Flatulances, nor Earthquakes. No, but 'tis something twice as pretty! something entirely new; but it can't be revealed except in the town of Concord. And I do solemnly protest by the third joint of St. Peter's great toe, that unless you come and see me this winter, you shall never know this grand Arcanum."

The treasure was two globes, fashioned for John Wentworth in London by James Ferguson. One was celestial, one terrestrial, and they ascended to an equal height, suspended in matched wooden rings and excellently made. James Ferguson was also the author of a book of thirty problems for the terrestrial globe, and eleven concerning the celestial; these problems delighted the mind. To a student of mechanics and experimental philosophy, the arcana of topography were here displayed if not revealed, and Benjamin spent hours doing computations and considering aspects of volume and density, distance, the span of the spheres. John Wentworth urged him, "Study this," and left behind the objects and his promise—unless detained by matters of the most pressing importance—to join him in the field. "I count on you," said Wentworth, "to do the counting, Ben."

His span had increased, sphere enlarged.

Come walk with me down by the river."

"Shortly."

"And why so shortly answered? What keeps you at your schoolbooks when you keep no schoolroom?"

"What keeps me, Sarah, is desire."

"It is a perfect afternoon. Desire once to come with me."

"These books contain most complicated matters, they need close scrutiny."

"The river crests, the trees begin to bud."

"I am glad to hear it."

"Only see it. Come and look."

"I will, Wife, as I said."

"Ben, you make me jealous."

"How?"

"Of your glad company. Of that day not ninemonth since when you hung waiting for my invitation to share just such a promenade."

"We'll walk, then."

"Excellent."

"With Paul?"

"Alone. I have something to tell you."

"And why so secretive this afternoon?"

"I have a secret."

"Out with it. You'll have me in the garret—for I do believe, wife, you preferred me private. You would have me keep close quarters."

"In which case you might notice."

"What?"

"And have you noticed nothing, dear?"

"I have been busy noticing. I have done nothing else all spring."

"Not so. You bend your eye on distance and neglect what is most near."

"Out with it, Sarah. I weary of riddling."

"We look to have a child."

Later, in his letters, he justified himself. He was wealthy by association, not by birth. For the years he did her bidding, she was more Sarah Walker than Rolfe, and more of both than Thompson; she had formed her character and was disinclined to change. She wanted him for pleasure in the bedroom and an elbow at the dance; she wanted him to teach her son and provide her with a second child and then to be a soldier but not engaged by war.

In the end, however, he failed her expectation; the war required service and he turned twenty-one. He could not stay at home. Had he not labored hard and long to earn advancement, and did he not require the kind countenance of Governor John Wentworth? He studied in secret and courted for show—the reverse of what had been their courtship's actual case. No doubt his wife wished him glory —covered with medals, brought back on a shield; she would have mourned him all her life had he been dead at the charge. Yet he who is not born to it must forge his own estate.

Sarah Thompson, never slender, burgeoned during pregnancy, and grew shrewish too. She complained of Ben's association with the Governor, of his study and experiments, his inattention to Paul. She called him cold, inconstant; she had been, she insisted, bewitched. Had he been trafficking like this some years before, they would have called it witchcraft; how else could he have gained such widespread access to affection? She accused him of alchemical potions, necromancy, spells.

No matter how he reasoned with and tried to offer comfort, no matter how he explained his scientific instruments and the benign— nay, Benjamin assured her, innocent and profitable—purpose envisioned, her irritation lingered and would not be dislodged. It drove him from his consort's side who hoped to draw him near. Alone he dreamed of mountain peaks and measurements and fame from armed engagement and the renown bred of discovery; in her presence he dreamed of escape.

She married him, not he her.

SALLY

This last phrase is Ben Thompson's own. Well, let me be entirely accurate, reader; the phrase that he himself composed was "She married me, not I her." And my own early claim that "I am he, he me" proves less than entirely honest; I write at a remove. So do we all, we all. In 2007, in Concord, New Hampshire, and in spite of global warming the winter snow lies deep as then, the river runs more or less equivalently in its ice-clogged channel through. The cliffs and the maples remain. The long day wanes, the slow moon climbs, etcetera. But not much else looks similar, and my brilliant boy from Woburn with his one cloak and eager ambitiousness would find things different now.

It's also true, according to report, that Ben's mother fainted dead away when she learned from her son what he'd done. Imagine: he sets off to make his fortune and comes back, the fortune made. In a curricle, no less. But how may we interpret that shocked maternal faint, her *Ben, my son?*; was it induced by horror or pleasure or simply a ruse to gain time, a feint, while severe Josiah Pierce raised her from the kitchen's floor and she tried to collect herself for a response; smelling salts, would they have had salts at the farm? Was she delighted or aghast, his mom; how did she take the news? Mrs. Thompson knew a full-filled bed and then the widow's outcast state and then remarried, after all, and even in the presence of her second husband might perhaps have had some sympathy for her rival's quick decision; what other suitor than her son could possibly come courting on so well-turned a leg?

Strange that I, his daughter's step-granddaughter's great granddaughter, should find myself taking his part. Or, more generally, that of the young persons, I in my sixty-ninth year. Still, my heart's with Ben and Abigail—not Sarah Rolfe. I hoped for all wrongs to be righted and Jack to have his Jill. In another draft and version Abigail might be a princess or perhaps an heiress or at least have great expectations and reveal herself to the medical scholar because of his surpassing courtesy, his refusal to take liberties with her indentured state. In secret she's of noble birth, and when she doffs her gladrags our hero spies alabaster perfection, her adamantine flesh. And then they all go to the seashore and live happily ever after.

But who expects that nowadays, or thought it plausible back then; what serving girl would not expect—whether made to do so by rude force or in willing compliance—to serve? Far more predictable the downward than the rising path, the slow or rapid sinking into gutter or hayloft and soon or late the all-obliterating earth. Perhaps the Widow Rolfe, though ample both of waist and fortune, would have seemed a kind of serving girl to Thompson in her own way also. What was she but the second rung, a step on the ladder he set out to climb? Instructed by Governor Wentworth: *Here, put your foot on it, here.* Did Sarah, at the garden gate, have any foreknowledge or least hint of what would come to pass beyond her own imperious desire; did she lower her high station while unfastening her gown? The truth is I distrust them both and in my nighttime imaginings requite them with each other: they were equal adversaries in the lists of love.

And do you hear, dear reader, how the rhetoric invades me, how Sally Ormsby has been *bound,* nay, *violated, seduced, compelled, made rapt* by how they parleyed then?

Talk English, kid, I'm dying here. In this dull town, alone. In my old house not half as old as the one down on the Merrimac that Thompson lived in as tutor then master. It burned, they tell me, years ago.

Who tells me, how do I know?

I show Alex the picture: the willows, the dirt road, the white picket fence.

"Ayup," he says.

"You recognize it?"

"Ayup."

"Their house, is it still standing?"

He shakes his head.

"What happened, do you remember?"

"Ayup"—his little litany, his single-size-fits-all.

"What happened?"

64

"Fire," Alex says.

Two, Class, can play this waiting game. "Oh?" I rock back on my heels. I twitch, I stare. My silence echoes his. If there were candy to suck I would do so, if there were a cigarette, light it.

"Some time ago," he says.

"When?"

"Sixty-six or thereabouts."

"That so?"

"Ayup."

I nod my head. I sigh. And then, as I had known it would, my patience trips a switch and—like a cold engine coughing, turning over, kicking in—Alex starts to talk. He puts his finger in his ear, corkscrewing it, and discourses on the Thompson homestead, the place that had been Rolfe's before, them forty acres on the Merrimac and what they farmed and what they sold and who raised which silo and how they passed the jug too soon with that sprung barn on the northern slope, the one that his grandfather carpentered, which is why it juddered so along the roof-line if you looked. He pulls his index finger out, examining the nail for wax, and then inserts it again. He talks about the trouble with the sleet-storm back in '56 and what it did to willow trees—trash trees, your willows are—and how when they tipped over there was a whole horse skeleton upended in the roots; what Alex means was, is, the old grey mare was buried and then the roots surrounded it, great spreaders, willows are, and when the storm brought down the tree it brought the carcass up. Well, they'd made a home there for runaway girls, for (he won't dare wink at me, not yet) girls who had no place to go and needed a roof and an honest day's work to mend their ways and, if I take his meaning, needed some—what would you call it, Miz Robinson?—protecting, watching over.

Then he stamps snow from his boots. From the factory down by the river we hear the siren sound. I ask about the owners and he says he wouldn't know. Except what he's heard is the one from the city installed a lightning rod, not on the barn or the high trees but right there on the kitchen chimney and grounded it the wrong way 'round and what it worked like, mostly, was a magnet for the storm (like them girls, says Alex, making the connection, making what he thinks of as an intelligent remark, well it was something wonderful once they got locked away down there, the way the boys drove idling past, just happening to use the River Road, just stopping a minute to smoke); he isn't saying so for sure, it's too chancy to be definite, he's heard how lightning can reverse an electrical entrance when it hits, so maybe the grounding was proper but what they found there af-terwards—after the fire, understand, when everything was burned so bad you couldn't tell the marble stoop from window-frame, the living room settee from somebody's toothbrush or hairbrush—was nothing left alive or worth the saving, finally, except the portrait that came through untouched. It was eerie, matter of fact, it was just the strang-est thing, you step across what used to be a doorway into what used to be a parlor or a music room and no way to tell the difference and there's nothing left but the old man in his gold frame staring out.

"The old man?"

"Ayup."

Who's that, I ask, Count Rumford? and Alex nods his head. Safe.

That's why I called it haunted, Class, repeats the writer in her dotage and soft chair. And do please pay attention to the rhetorical device deployed, the linking of dissimilar components (*dotage, chair*) in one prepositional phrase; note how we assume, by dint of mere proximity, (or earlier, *eerie, matter of fact*) that the two belong together, he and me. Or how, because I used to teach, I call this piece of paper "class" and profess instruction still. I haven't taught in years. In point of historical truth the thing that failed to burn is not the actual painting but a copy he sent home, and there's one in Woburn too. The original—*that's my last Rumford, on the wall*—remains on display in the Fogg. The way that in this modern age we have a photograph copied if the likeness pleases us, then mail it out to relatives or high-school friends or newspapers, so Benjamin Thompson paid the famous Thomas Gainsborough once for a single sitting and had the portrait multiplied and sent it sailing back. The copies aren't as good.

Since 1983, I've called this house my home. Not three miles from the farm that Alex tells us burned. "Ayup." The glottal stop of it, the half-hiccoughing noncommittal affirmative (it might mean "Maybe," after all, or "No," or merely that he listens), the way he clears his throat. And I have undertaken to write the old rogue's life. Because of what he did to her and she to him and they to each other and therefore to us. Because of their conjunction and its issue: me. Because of the choice that Ben Thompson must make: to stay or run away.

Therefore we find ourselves, reader, at the rising dawn of this nation's great day, gazing out upon the tide upon those shifting sands that might have stranded, undermined or drowned the rude colonials we call our heroes now. Or kept them steadfast royalists or turned them back to loyalists (*rhyme, rhyme, the drumbeat's ta-dum, the view halloo and the beaten tattoo*)—as was our Ben, who loved if he loved anything the hierarchical arrangement of order, the logic of authority, and so his good King George.

He's not the only soul I know in town, is Alex, by no means. Nosiree Betty and Bob. Due to a certain, how shall I put it, position in this inbred place, my private views though public do not entirely prohibit commerce. People call to sell me things. They offer me vacations in the mail. I'm a registered Democrat and attend no house of worship and am in consequence exceptional, though this is not construed by other elders of the town to be a happy singularity; it limits social range. I'm familiar with Miss Harriet Winthrop of Winthrop's Beauty Salon, one of her regular customers; I have a nodding acquaintance with Brian Palmer of Palmer's General Store, with Abraham Fetter from Ace Hardware. I know Dr. Allen, of course, and lift my hand acknowledging the men who haul the trash. At three-thirty Tuesday mornings from the bottom of my drive. "Mornin'," I say to Miss Harriet Winthrop, "Mornin'" to Abe Fetter and he consults his Mickey Mouse and answers, "Afternoon."

For twice twelve years and for my sins I've stayed in this cold place, transported here by my own prince—with his two-hundred-twenty-five horses, his two-tone Chrysler Imperial and habit of wearing a hat while he drove. "A man needs his headroom," Husband averred, and what he said he had the habit of repeating; for him repetition was the essence of assurance, assurance the essence of wit. "A man needs his headroom," he said of the car, the open air, the house, and pronounced it every time he entered the W.C.. Whether he did so in my absence I am of course unable to affirm, but in my presence or that of our guests he said it three, four times a day.

What else did Arnold Robinson repeat? "A bird in the bush is worth two in the bed." "A stitch in time saves nineteen." His coy little variant on the old theme, his prideful assertions that rubbed me entirely wrong. To wit: "I'm not an expert, of course, but if you ask me." Or, "I'm just an ignorant country builder, but if you want my opinion."

Why did we marry, you ask? The usual reasons: exhaustion, sloth, desire, the sense it might make sense to die with someone by your side. Someone you predecease. Husband did so, anyhow, but by how long an interval it's not yet plausible for his widow to determine; I've outlasted him, as of this writing, four years. Eating biscuits and cheddar and drinking his gin, scraping sardines and tuna from tins. Eating fresh fruit from the orchard and produce while the garden yields, and emptying the cellar of its put-by beans and jam.

The night he died I came back from the hospital, and there was this stench in the kitchen, this reeking blood-soaked odor of the abbattoir I understood on the instant meant spoilage. The kitchen tiles were wet with blood, the grouting turned a darker brown, and the freezer-compartment yawned open; what failed or broke or which cleaning person had been careless I never could determine, but all his meat had thawed. His precious tenderloin and sirloin and duck and venison and his racks of lamb. His pork and prime ribs and veal. All gone, all maggoty and wrecked and soaked right through the wrappings, expensive carrion all of it; I have not touched meat since.

Enough. Let us imagine, reader, colonial New Hampshire just before the war. Let us put our hero to the test and judge him passed or failed. In the back of my brain a puppet is having hysterics and what I hear now are the fife and drum and pipes, Major Thompson, *the pipes*.

ᕯ III ᕯ

Great day in the morning; Benjamin sat his white horse. Fourteen hands high and spirited and one else to master him, none other who could ride him at parade: Blaze, the steed was christened, heat and light. At regimental muster he pranced and nickered and flicked his thick tail and rolled his large blood-marbled eyes; all the men were envious and admired Major Thompson and drilled at his instruction when they met. From his estate on the Merrimac to parade ground at the Village Green was a twelve minute canter or sixteen minute trot. Blaze did not break a sweat.

On October 18, 1774, he had become a father; young Sarah was born. As every night that week, that month—for he was bent on celebration, and offered brandy to the doctor, and they shared a toast to the girl's future, then to the mother, then Governor Wentworth—Ben drank himself insensible. He was woken by the chambermaid, an ancient squint-eyed hireling scarce calculated to inflame the mastering passion or urge after rising the *droit de seigneur* (which had itself no doubt been part of her prudent mistress's premonitory calculation), who flung the shutters wide and raised the sash and informed him prissily that it was ten o'clock.

That year, for the first time, he farmed. He who had had no interest in toiling for Josiah Pierce took considerable pleasure in planning the harvest at Concord. He rode his lands' perimeter to survey what the men cleared, then measured and had the fields fenced. It was rolling bottom land. He ordered seeds in quantity—as did every proper gentleman—from London. He required one hundred pounds of the best red clover seed, and two additional clovers, three varieties of grass, five of cabbage, four of turnip, six of peas, five of oats and barley and fifteen of wheat. He pursued his mathematics and posed questions to Loammi Baldwin, as before: "A certain Cistern has three Brass cocks—one of which will empty it in 15 minutes—one in 30 minutes-and the other in 60 minutes—Qu: how long would it take to empty the cistern if all the Cocks were opened at once?"

Escape was what they plotted in the parlor; revolt was how they shouted in the street. It is tyranny's cruel yoke, they cried, King George's trifling pleasure to give pain. We will not bear it, not endure it; we will throw old England off and surrender nothing but taxation's heavy weight. We are the Sons of Liberty, free men!

From pulpit and in conference he heard the same: the God that gave us life at the same time gave us liberty. The old men and the young concurred, the women and children agreed: We are those who know no liberty, we are but slaves to London. They tapped at his waistcoat or pulled at their chins; *Ben, Benjamin, Major Thompson, Mr. Thompson, boy, friend.*

Such sentiments were uttered by the elders, gray beards gravely wagging, fingers shaking as they punctuated speech. Independence is the recourse of the desperate, they said, and we have been rendered despairing. Now even the Reverend Timothy Walker declared himself a patriot and perorated at table: We are citizens of a new land, delivered out of bondage as were the chosen people delivered out of Egypt when He divided the sea. Thus was Pharoah chastised by our Lord. Please pass the relish, Sarah, and I believe I'll have a second portion of those dumplings there, they are excellently spiced. King

George shall weary, falter, and the strength of his legions give way.

These were the legions, their strength. The fifteenth regiment of the New Hampshire Militia culled soldiers from the following Towns and Parishes: Concord, Canterbury, Epsom, Bow, Loudon and Chichester in the County of Rockingham; Boscawen, Salisbury, Hopkington. There were Henniker and Hillsborough, New Almsbury and New Britain in the county of Hillsborough. *The Exercise or Discipline Ordered to be observed and practiced in this Regiment is that composed for the use of, and practisd by the Militia of the County of Norfolk in Great Britain. By the order of his Excellency. John Wentworth. Esq. Captain General. Feb. 15th, 1774.*

Major Thompson kept his peace and kept the Regiment's books. Field Officers of the First Company of Concord were as named: Andrew MacMillan, Esq., Colonel; Thomas Stickney, Esq., Lieutenant-Colonel; Benjamin Thompson, Esq., Major, his commission dated January 20, 1774. Thomas Walker, Sergeant-Major, served as non-commissioned officer. This is what they wore. *The officers to wear Red Coats, cuffed, lined and lapeld with sky-blue, sky-blue waistcoats and Breeches, all Trimm'd with white. Black hats with Silver hat-band button & loops without lace. White stockings. Cockade sash and white gorgets. Swords with silver hilts. Captains & Lieutenants to carry Fusee's. Field Officers to wear Silver Shoulder-knots.*

The commissions of Captain Joshua Abbot, Lieutenant Jonathan Stickney—brother to Colonel Thomas Stickney—and Ensign John Shute were dated February 21, 1774. The four sergeants Richard Hazeltine, John Chase, Dan Stickney and Nathan Kinsman held warrants dated the 24th May.

On 19 May, John Wentworth *Ordered that the Commanding officer of each Company, as soon as he shall have appointed any Sergeants or Corporals to Serve in his Company, shall certify the Name and Rank of the Persons so appointed, together with the time of their Appointment to the Major of the Regiment. And a record being made of their appointment as aforesaid, shall be full sufficient to all intents & purposes, to Authorize them to act in their office, as much as if they had a Warrant under the hand & seal of their Captain or Commanding Officer.*

Might a man serve two masters or be of two minds? What idea worth entertaining does not prove mutable? By its very entertainment will not an idea alter; is behavior not subject to change?

There were additional questions. What gentleman of consequence contents himself with just one suit of clothes or set of principles or passion for the week? What, for instance, might fidelity entail if a man choose to be faithful to more than one mistress at once? What is integrity if the number be itself a fraction of the whole: *fides, integer?* These were the words in his head, and these were the matters he pondered, riding, alone with his thoughts and his horse: *loyalty, oneness, good faith.* The man who holds one standard of behavior, and to that standard only, is an honorable stalwart man, yet the honorable stalwart man is cousin to the bore.

Loammi said our system of behavior must not change: respect is due to all. I must treat my old and wealthy uncle as I do a schoolboy, or I fawn upon the one and underprize the other.

Not so, said Benjamin, treat your uncle like a schoolboy and the schoolboy like a patron: there lies wit. Mere constancy is lack of humor, and the absence of good humor makes for mournful countenance. The constant man is self-deluded, possibly, but not the dupe of others, and there lies the secret of balance: poise and counterpoise.

So he strove to be cheerful at home, where the presence of young Sarah made every day a holiday, where nothing she desired was denied. He strove to be cheerful with Governor Wentworth, who required shoring up while what he called the edifice of government was crumbling, day by week collapsing. As a sailor trims his sail to wind, and tightens and makes fast the sheets, Thompson strove for equanimity in the high tumbling tide of the times.

"The answer to your question," said Loammi, "is eight minutes."

"What question?"

"The keg with three cocks. And fifty-seven seconds if the spigots be not clogged."

Colonel Andrew MacMillan had fought in the French and Indian Wars. Lieutenant Colonel Thomas Stickney was an old campaigner also; they were twice Ben's age, men who rioted at table and swore in their deep tankards that order must be kept "I love the peace so much," joked Thomas Stickney, drinking, "that I fight now to uphold it. I love this land so dearly I will not yield an inch. I prize these colonial children"—he wiped his mouth with his broad hand—"and will not let them go."

It fell to Thompson's charge therefore to organize the ranks, and he did so with precision. His list was as good as a warrant; he authorized each particular office and wrote down every name. In the Second Company there were mustered these men of the region: Jeremiah Clough, David Merrill, James Stephead and Archelaus Miles. Captain Henry Gerish reported to 3rd Company, and to the 4th in Hopkinton belonged Captain Jonathan Straw. There were Lieutenant Joshua Bagley and Ensign Joseph Chandler, Captain Abiel Chandler of the 6th Company, and Ebenezer Virgin, Lieutenant, who signed on 26 February, 1774.

There were Jonathan Eastman, Ensign, and David Campbell from Henniker, and Josiah Ward and Aaron Adams, Lieutenant. Aaron Kinman, Captain, was listed on the 2nd of March, from Bow; so too was Ephraim Moor, Lieutenant; there were Nathan Bachelder, Captain, and Nathaniel Bachelder, Ensign, from the 11th Company; there were mustered Ezekiel Straw, John Hale, Stephen Hoyt and Joseph Flint. Moses Gould and Jacob Tucker and Daniel Flood and Jacob Waldron were of that company, as were William Emery, Abba Brown, David Knowlton and Jonathan Leavit, who joined on March the 9th.

Who goes there?"

"William Bowdidge, sir."

"What brings you to me, Bowdidge?"

"Orders, sir."

"From Boston?"

"Sir."

"And by whose hand?"

"The General's, Major Thompson sir. Our General Gage."

"Then hand them to me, Bowdidge. Why so slow?"

The soldier cleared his throat. He coughed. He looked significantly at the window, then the door.

"We are alone. You may speak your mind freely."

"These orders, sir, are not writ down. They are for your ears only."

"Speak."

"I am to be your foreman, Major. And to hide this uniform. I am to work your fields and watch the men who work there and urge them to return to arms and bring them back to Boston when they run."

"You will pay them bounty?"

"Sir." He clicked his heels. His bearing was a soldier's, and it did not matter if he wore a uniform.

"Thus we reward desertion?" Thompson asked.

"It is cheaper, begging your pardon, than recruitment. And they have been trained as fighters and we would not have them fight against us. They are much prized by the rabble and we must prize them also."

"True."

"I bring you two men even now who think you a firm patriot. Who want to work in freedom and for freedom on your farm."

"And what of my commission? I serve in his Majesty's army."

"They believe in secret, sir, you serve against it. On their side."

Benjamin laughed. "We shall so contrive it, Bowdidge, that the army will be—will look to have been—a holiday for those who come to Concord. When I finish setting them their barnyard tasks, King George shall appear a gentle master by comparison."

"I understand you, Major."

"Then we understand each other. My compliments to General

Gage." He was recovering from fever; he spat in his handkerchief. "That door will see you out."

Great day in the afternoon: he brought Blaze to the Merrimac and they waded in the shallows where the horse might drink. Since they had traveled hard, however, and for fear of over-watering, he would not let Blaze drink his fill but hauled back on the reins.

The horse complied and stood in the loud rill. A trout broke the water, then two; flies swarmed about the rock-pool and mosquitoes at his ears. The stream was rapid here, deep-channeled, and the eddies at his feet rewarded study: a spiral, a wide-spreading cone. Where there were rocks and a felled tree the pattern of current reversed.

Major Thompson cut a switch. Idly, he peeled it—the knife slicing sharply, the bark ribboning back to his thumb. His boots required cleaning; his coat too. Thick gobbets of mud grimed his knee. He was making up his mind. He had done so, riding, *that side, this side, that.* In the maple on the farther bank a woodpecker resumed: a drum-roll, the rapid tat-tat.

Other men altered allegiance; turn by turn they deserted or joined. There were men who had been soldiers he hired for the farm. When he worked them now as field-hands eighteen hours at a stretch they recollected the army as heaven and wondered why they ran from it and wanted to rejoin. Thus he encouraged the deserter—most changeable of creatures—to shift allegiance once more.

Ben sheathed his knife; Blaze drank. The sheer elation of it, the glad release in action—their long fluid gallop through Concord, the high white clouds, the early autumn afternoon, the gleaming obedient hot musculature beneath him, the muscles of his arm—he whistled a low snatch of song. A kingfisher swooped, soared. It held in its bright beak a silver wriggling morsel: captive thing. He took it as a sign.

For it had come to Thompson now that this must be his testing-time and he must make his choice. He could not truly understand—or, having understood, admire—his kinsmen and his countrymen, those savages bewigged. They called themselves, though subject to temptation, free from sin; they took for inward measure the lineaments of outward bearing; with their frock coats and homilies they thought themselves devout. In their offices and by their works they claimed themselves redeemable, thus saved.

And this self-invented nation declared itself complete. Like children self-persuaded of bravura independence who wander not a mile from home and think themselves abroad; like sons who, aping fathers, say they have grown more civilized than those who went before; like all derivatives who vaunt themselves original, the men of Massachusetts rallied to the cause. The rabble of New Hampshire cheered; from representation to separation appeared but a small step to take.

These radicals were clever men; they dressed themselves as Indians and had a party with tea. What need have we of England, the rebel leaders dared to ask, why must we follow its lead? So they toddled into liberty, teetering out from the fold. They broke and argued over laws and swore they had as good a right to rule as kings. This notion, once agreed upon, seemed ancient and inviolate; why should we not stay separate from those who cast us out? A lie thus widely broadcast and universally acknowledged counts—so Thompson came to recognize—as truth.

But it was not his truth. He was servant to established rule and would ascend and be himself advantaged by the proper maintenance thereof. To withdraw from high entitlement is foolish where not vain. He could improve himself, admittedly, but never by pretending that the master is the man. They must be patriots without him; he chose to follow, not lead. At twenty-one he now assumed his manhood in full flower, an ordered profusion blooming, and he would not harvest it to serve these rough colonials. He had attained authority and did not choose to lose it; King George remained his King. Therefore he must turn informer; he had flourished in the system because there *was* a system, and he could not countenance rebellion but would instead ride it out. The man sits the horse and the horse hauls the cart, which it cannot do behind-hand but must go before. Such arrangements are susceptible to change, perhaps, but cannot be undone; Major Thompson turned Blaze easily—a light booted kick, a flick of the reins—and made his way for home. He would cast his lot with order where disorder reigned.

He saw his mother often, Hiram too. Uncle Hiram had no hair, and his right eye wandered, and he limped as a result of an argument with Struther's bull. Hiram had not forfeited, however, his sanguine disposition; he smiled and showed his teeth. Struther's bull, he said, had won that particular argument but had been afterwards shot. He who laughs last laughs the best.

"What think you, Uncle, of rebellion?"

"How, Ben?"

"Of our chances. Of the quality and bearing of our army?"

"I am too old to think of it."

"You are not fifty, uncle."

"Forty-seven. Old enough."

"They call us, I am told, the wild colonials. They do not rate us highly."

"Us? You are commissioned by and subject to King George. You are loyal, are you not?"

"I am. But would not wish mere loyalty to put me on the losing side."

"Depend on it. These are children crying out against authority." Hiram lit his pipe.

Major Thompson made contact with General Gage and, because he feared discovery, wrote with gallo-tannic acid—a yellow sympathetic ink—on yellow folded paper. He described the disposition of the rebel troops.

Thompson used an infusion of nutgalls, these nutgalls soaked in water and gathered from the oak tree leaves behind his house. It was an ancient stratagem that he had learned from John Hay. Such an infusion also served to ward off diarrhea, and he took the precaution of writing a friend, "Since I left Boston I have enjoyed but a very indifferent share of health, having been much troubled by putrid bilious disorders." This explained the nutgalls' presence by his desk.

The message came to light in Boston only after treatment, ferrous sulphate bringing back the script. With that secondary application, the matter of the message would appear. Otherwise, and to the untutored eye, the cover letter—written on Saturday May 6 and in black carbon ink—said simply what it seemed to say: *Pray send me a receipt for papers which I left in your care. You will much oblige your Humble Servant, etc.*

Thus he proceeded all summer and fall, ranging freely through the ranks. He furnished information on the rebel army, its preparedness and number and—where he could—named names. There was much to do in the militia, both to maintain order and to insure discipline. He commended himself earnestly to the General's attention and carried letters to and from the Whig informer, Benjamin Church.

Dr. Church was a respected citizen, a member of the Provincial Congress and the Committee of Safety. His wife required a mansion, however, and his mistress enjoyed lavish presents. "The patriot is poor," said Church. "And pleasure, young man, is expensive."

"So it appears."

"In consequence I take—I am compelled to accept, or else my creditors take all—quarterly retainers from the payroll of General Gage. I do not do it lightly."

"Of course not, no."

He offered Ben fine claret. "We play a high-stakes game."

The stakes increased: men died. There were Riflemen at Lexington and Concord and rumored to be part of the attack on the hill at Breed. The boasted riflemen, however, wrote Thompson in his hidden script, were not so accurate as feared: "Instead of being the best marksmen in the World, and picking off every Regular that was to be seen, there is scarsely a Regiment in Camp but can produce men that can beat them at shooting." This pleased the English General, who hoped that it was true.

He gathered information from Loammi Baldwin, "a Field officer in the Rebel Army, if that mass of confusion may be called an Army." Loammi was no gossip; he dealt in matters of fact. But later Ben would wonder if his old friend too—who knew him well, who sounded him as though a flute—had played a doubling game. They gave each other intelligence, making certain it was wrong; they smiled and clasped each other's hands and laughingly, frankly, openly, in tavern or Grange Hall or meadow, at parade ground or town meeting or by the river, they lied.

Major Thompson spent what time he could on business in Boston. He hoped to furnish uniforms for the rebel ranks, and the purveyor Hopestill Capen was obsequious towards him now, for he spent freely, frequently, at the old Sign of the Cornfields. Donald McAlpin was dead.

His intention was to join the revolutionary circle and to become its leaders' intimate and report their plans, and in order to promote this purpose he took fine lodgings in Hanover Street. He frequented the house of the engraver Paul Revere, and the office of Isaiah Thomas, printer. Thomas had a wife he married in Bermuda—Mary Dill. The printer was a fiery man, an ardent revolutionary, and he it was who set and published *The Massachusetts Spy*. Ben courted Mary Dill.

He did this for three weeks before his first success. She pretended virtue, and helped her husband move the press to the safe haven of Worcester forty miles away, then settled her two children in Watertown nearby. That very night, returning, Miss Dill arrived at Hanover Street, and without his importuning removed her hat and coat and dress and shift, walking naked through the rooms. She knew his game, she said, she recognized his ways. In Bermuda she had entertained the garrison, having there a bastard son, and had been prostituted to many more soldiers than one. She offered him her service, and he paid for it to start with but she soon refused his coin and declared herself amply rewarded. Like Ben's wife she was his senior, and her ardor unconstrained; rather than give him up, she said, she would roast in Hell. While Thomas printed, Thompson pressed, and she answered in her transports everything he asked.

As Major, Benjamin became the foremost of his family; he brought fiddlers to the house and called the tune. He sent the curricle to Woburn to collect his mother for an evening's celebration, next day to drive her back. The house was brightly lit; the silver and the candelabra gleamed, the floors had been well waxed.

His mother and his wife were famously polite. They treated each other with that deference due to station, in the fashion of a warring truce; they agreed only on Sarah, and only that young Sarah was the darling of the universe, its sun and moon and stars.

She was perfect, Mrs. Pierce declared, and with a brilliant future. She had ten toes and fingers and her father's bright blue eyes. Other members of the family must languish in her orbit; when she left the evening paled. She was swaddled by her nurse and taken off to bed: fat, dimpling, earnest, fine. By comparison with such a splendid light,

Ben's mother told him softly, Paul Rolfe the elder brother was sublunary and dull.

Sarah Thompson showed her teeth. "You are welcome, Madame, for your own son's sake. But would be wise to remember that I also have a son."

"I am sorry, Madame. I did not know you listened."

"It was not my intention."

"Nor mine to offend you. I gossiped in private."

"All gossip, Mrs. Pierce, is public in its nature. Or it is not properly itself."

"I did not mean to slight your son, praising your daughter."

"He will not be slighted. Rest assured."

The musicians began their performance with Italian songs. They were expert with their instruments and maintained a rapid pace, completing the first movement in perfect unison. The man who played the violin had too much powder in his wig; when he nodded—and he nodded vehemently, often—white powder sprayed in the air. Benjamin was drinking, marking time, admiring the candlelight reflected and thus multiplied by chandelier and sconce, was considering the angle of refraction when patriots appeared.

He knew them: Phillip Russell, William Tidd. They stood at the door to the hall.

"Gentlemen, welcome," he said.

"Not so," they said. "Not here."

Phillip Russell was the elder. He stepped forward first. His hands were raw from the December wind, and he rubbed them noisily.

"It is a family gathering," Benjamin explained. "None other was invited." He gestured at the drawing room. "You are most welcome to join us, however. Come and dance."

"We are not here for dancing, mister." William Tidd was portly, his left leg stiff. He puffed and blustered, but nonetheless kept his voice low. "We have business to transact with you. The business of state."

"A cup then, for your trouble. The night is a cold one. You'll not refuse that."

"Not in this house," William said. He held their two greatcoats. His cheeks were red.

"You surprise me, William. Why so solemn suddenly?"

"It is solemn business."

"Concerning? Surely you can tell me."

They were silent, long-faced.

"You are in my parlor, I remind you. You have arrived in my hall."

"It is not by accident," said Phillip Russell, obdurate. "We come for our transaction."

William Tidd nodded, unsmiling.

"I enter no transaction"—Major Thompson struck his palm for emphasis—"no business arrangement, without a discussion of terms. What, friends—for so I thought you until just now—are we discussing?"

"Come tomorrow to the tavern. We meet there at eight o'clock, and you have our charge to answer."

Major Thompson straightened. "And how if I do not? If I choose not to?"

Phillip Russell blew his nose. "Then we return in force."

"Force?"

"This is by way of warning, mister. You are summoned to explain yourself to the Committee of Correspondence."

"How? Explain myself?"

William Tidd leaned in so close that Thompson smelled his breath. There was acid in it, onion also, small beer, cheese. "A William Bowdidge, farmer, has been seen in Boston. He was in the uniform of a British Army Regular."

Now it was Russell's turn. "He and his commanding officer—you who have pretended, sir, that he was merely your foreman—are rebels to the state."

The musicians paused, uncertain. He waved them to continue. Sarah came to join him, and he took her by the waist. "You know my wife?" he said.

Phillip Russell bowed. William Tidd inclined his head.

"You knew her husband, Colonel Rolfe?"

"I did," said Phillip Russell. "Good evening, Madam. We happened by."

"The prospect of music . . ." began William Tidd.

"They mean to arrest me," said Ben.

To Governor Wentworth he wrote: "I am formally to be declared a *Rebel to the State,* and unworthy the benefits of Civil Society, and a vote is to be pass'd in this and the neighbouring Towns forbidding all Persons having the least connection or intercourse with me. And my Name is to be posted in this, and the Province of Massachusetts Bay, after which I am to be solemnly Anathemised and consign'd over to the fury of the enraged Populace, to receive punishment equal to the blackness of my aggravated Transgressions."

To General Gage he petitioned: "The people of this and the neighbouring Towns by some means or other have gotten some inteligence of my applying to your Excellency for a Pardon for some Deserters, and I hear are about to send to Boston to find out the certainty of the affair. And it is of the utmost consequence to me to have the matter kept a secret from them: This is most humbly to beseech your Excellency to give such orders as may effectually prevent their receiving any information from the Soldiers."

And yet the soldiers came. They were drunken men, mere rabble, who made their camp in taverns and their war with words. They arrived at Concord with their knives and pistols and their loud insistence that he join the cause; they called themselves the Minute Men but came twelve hours late.

By then he had decamped. Blaze needed exercise, he told the family; he would visit Woburn and send for wife and daughter once the way proved clear. The patriots followed next day, marching shamblingly to Woburn, where he visited his mother, and they planned a shivaree. He hid inside the house.

"Come out and join the party, Ben," they cried. "Come view your regiment and show us how to fight. Come with us willingly or else we storm the door."

Loammi Baldwin stepped outside and told them to go home. "I

know the man," he said. "I would recognize him anywhere. He is not here tonight."

"His horse is here," cried William Tidd. "None other in the stable."

"Yes, but not the Master," lied Loammi loudly. "I inquired of his whereabouts just now from his poor mother. He leaves his horse here stabled, so Mrs. Pierce informs me, and is away on business. You know me as a patriot, I recognize you all."

Major Baldwin had great credit with the mob, who dared not shout him down. They shuffled in the street.

"Let's look for our true enemy," Loammi said, "not someone like Ben Thompson whom I warrant for a friend and have known since childhood. Now put aside this business and help me raise my barn."

"What for?"

"Neighbors, I thought you were come here to help. I was hoping for your company."

While Benjamin watched from the window embrasure, they stood there a moment, uncertain; they leaned upon their muskets and spat and scratched their heads. Then Loammi cried: "A barrel of good cider for the Minute Men who join me," and the gang dispersed. The smoke from their bright torches rose more slowly, spiraling, and then it too dispersed.

To his father-in-law he wrote carefully, at length. "Mine enemies are indefatigable in their indeavours to distress me, and I find to my sorrow that they are but too successful. I have been driven from the Camp by the clamours of the New Hampshire People, and am again threaten'd in this place. But I hope soon to be out of the reach of my Cruel Persecutors, for I am determined to seek for *that Peace* and *Protection* in foreign Lands and among strangers which is deny'd me in my native country."

Major Thompson loved his country but remained a Loyalist; he professed fidelity but did not say to what. "Whatever prudence may dictate, yet Conscience and Honor, God and Religion forbid that my Mouth should speak what my Heart disclaims. I cannot profess my sorrow for an action which I am conscious was done from the best of motives."

On Christmas Eve he wrote once more. The discerning reader might well read a message here eluding Reverend Walker, who had but faint discernment. "I must humbly beg your kind care of my distressed Family: And hope you will take oppertunity to alleviate their trouble, by assuring them that I am in a place of safety." Where it was he would not say, but "this you may rely & depend on, that I never did, nor (let my treatment be what it will) ever will, do any action, that may have the most distant tendency to injure the true interest of this my native Country."

Well-meaning men may disagree and honest adversaries quarrel as to the true nature of true interest in a country; there would be patriot and loyalist in the years to come. But all such argument would henceforth be conducted in Thompson's absence; our adventurer was gone.

Mother, I must leave this place."

"Why, Ben; do we not suit you?"

"Not lately."

She put down her needlework, placing the pattern on the shelf. "You are unkind to say so. How is't we have failed to please—in which particular?"

"In no particular, mother. But in general."

"You refer, I imagine, to General Gage?" Her bonnet had been loosely tied; white curls emerged unkempt.

"What makes you say so, why mention the man?"

She wagged her head. "They say you are his hireling and that you report to him."

"And who are they?"

She pursed her lips and looked beyond him, blinking.

"The Committee knows my name," he urged. "They will try me, then convict me on no evidence. They are envious."

"But honorable also," protested Ruth Pierce. "They are, are they not, honest fellows? Would you not have yourself considered in the ample light of day by those who hunt the truth of things, who wish for full disclosure?"

"No."

"This speaks a guilty conscience, Ben."

"It speaks no more than knowledge, mother, of the venal proceedings of justice, and the way truth in these provinces has come to be routinely traduced. I have nothing to hide or declare."

Her eyes were red. With her red fingers, she rubbed them. "You mean they would convict you?"

"But will not have the chance."

Great day in the evening: he walked Blaze to the woodlot that grandfather Thompson bequeathed. That day there had been snow. The trail grew steep. Beneath the pines, however, and the latticework of oak and ash there lay but little powder here to cover the cold ground. Blaze made his way through brush. The moon was low, and the new growth where he'd cleared the old impeded easy progress; branches prodded at his elbow and tangled with his sleeve.

Ben required clarity; his gloves were thick with burrs. Exhaling, he watched his cold breath. The last time he had walked this hill he had been penniless, in debt, and skidding felled logs down to earn his keep. Then he had failed with Hopestill Capen, who had sent him home. Now, just four years later, he was one of the principal men of the region—the Governor's close confidante and owner of fine bottom land. His marriage and position were assured.

Blaze rolled his eyes inquiringly; he pawed the frozen track. Ben smiled, then rubbed the creature's neck. He must not, he warned himself, lie. To delude another is expedient at times; to delude one's self in disputation is by contrast dangerous. The Minute Men had left this once but surely would return. He had survived the scrutiny of the Committee of Correspondence, but might not be so fortunate next day. Major Loammi Baldwin was his good friend but not credulous; they fought on opposite sides, and though Baldwin condescended once to save him from the mob he might not prove so generous again. Major Benjamin Thompson, Esq., was but an informer to General Gage. If caught, he would be hanged.

And so, he told his horse, things change: I chose the side of order but chaos reigns instead. He continued up the hill. He would make his way to Boston—where the snow was trackless because so thickly trodden—and escape. His position was assailed. Having been driven from the house he took decreasing pleasure in it and did not know when he might next embrace his wife and daughter. He did not greatly care.

Far rifles sounded: a volley, an echoing roar. He had grown out of compass in the provincial sphere; true interest had been yoked to false, and Thompson could not long remain in this his native country. He had made many enemies and they were now ascendant; Fortune's Wheel had turned.

ᔥ IV ᔥ

Racked upon Fortuna's wheel for the Atlantic crossing, our voyager grew weary, sick at heart. He could not find his sea-legs and lay groaning in his berth or, having dragged himself aloft in order to breathe fresh salt air, went stumbling through the rigging and convulsed above the rail. They joked with him belowdecks about his soldier's stomach and lack of sailor's ease. They called it a smooth crossing and said Thompson should be grateful, for these were but moderate winds. It is tempest sufficient, he said.

Where he lay was a torment, a cauldron of griefs. His old ghosts came to call. John Appleton his gentle master and Abigail his mistress and Loammi Baldwin and his uncle Hiram—all those who used him kindly once proved cruel. He had failed them, they said, he had failed. They reproached him with long faces or beseeching cries: he had left them for no reason or betrayed them wantonly, had squandered what he should hold dear for mere ambition's sake. Sarah his wife and Sarah his daughter invaded the cabin like smoke. How could you leave us, they whispered, how could you do such treachery? —dear father, husband, love.

Old Timothy Walker preached brimstone and fire; Thompson turned his back. But he found no comfort, turning, and could not shut his eyes. That demon he first spied in Salem when the fireworks exploded came to visit, wreathed in red, and perching on his basin— one leg hoofed, the other clawed—would not be dislodged. The monstrous fetus from Dr. John Hay's returned as his familiar, grinning. The maimed and the deformed and the beggars from the Boston

94

docks thronged to join him where he tossed. He thought them happy by comparison: blessed stationary creatures on the constant shore.

Even John Wentworth reviled him: he had failed to chart Mt. Pleasant or continue the ascent. He had enjoyed the confidence of many but retained it now of none. His father's dear imagined gaze and mother's dear remembered were stone-cold, unforgiving; all his once-glad companions scorned the bed.

The collapse of the army at Boston had been rumored but not witnessed; he alone could tell the tale. His was important news. His notebooks were informed. Yet he had embarked in secret and must disembark in England uncertain of his welcome, for he knew no one at court. The messenger is often punished for the message, and the news was bad.

Unaccustomed to grief, Thompson wept; though attempting to pray, he could not. His tears provided salt sufficient to make the pillow reek of brine, and what he tasted was gall. In his narrow hammock arcing to and fro beneath the deck he lay for seven days and nights in a fever of recrimination: fleeting, perjured, guilt-tormented, lost.

By slow degrees, however, our traveler revived. With that part of his intelligence neither appalled nor fearful—that scientist's dispassion which permitted him to note reaction even in its throes—Major Benjamin Thompson determined on revenge. He took his first swallow of broth, then kept a biscuit down. Tentative at first, but every day more confident he ventured forth upon the deck to pace it with a rolling motion, breathing brisk Atlantic air. He held counsel with himself, and there were those on board who believed him distracted

—or, perhaps, a poet—for he clenched his fists repeatedly and knit his brow and muttered imprecations at the wind.

> Benjamin Thompson, Esq., having been forced to abandon a competent Estate in the province of New Hampshire, from whence he was cruelly drove by persecution and severe Maltreatment, on account of his Loyalty & faithful Efforts to support the Laws and promote the service of Government, took refuge in Boston, Where as well as in the Country he has endeavour'd to be useful to His Majesty's service, and is therefore to be considered as deserving of Protection & Favours.

So wrote General Howe on his behalf to Lord Sackville, George Germain, and—albeit driven like a whelped pup from his own entitlement, his lands and family—he had other such letters to show. Because it was of consequence in Concord, the Committee knew his name; the minutemen had found him out and hounded him from town. For service to his sovereign, he had been threatened with tar and with hanging; for having done his duty, he had been reviled. His was the cup of exile, that bitter draught to drink.

Now he would make others drink deep.

"You're feeling better, Major?" A ferrety fellow approached him.

"Yes."

"You were quite unwell, it seemed."

"An indisposition merely. I thank you for your interest."

"You have business in England?"

"Yes."

"London?"

Thompson nodded.

"It's good to see you once more eager to transact it."

Thompson bowed.

"And might a fellow passenger be of assistance, possibly? Might I inquire its nature?"

Frowning, he shook his head.

"The nature of your business in London?"

He withdrew.

Once landed at Southhampton, this attitude endured. It made him steady at the docks who might have been irresolute, took him rapidly through streets both rich and various. Disregarding the loud babble of the port, the hubbub of greeting and trade, he held firm in the face of importunate strangers—those who make a living off the pockets of the innocent and prey upon the new arrival, hawk to gull.

The cutpurse and the whore fell back, the wharf-rat scuttled free. Major Benjamin Thompson of Concord, New Hampshire, undertook as his first business to demonstrate his loyalty, and he would have no commerce with distraction nor play festive Jack o'Shore. He carried his papers himself. He closely supervised the dispatch of his trunks. When his 'tween-decks interlocutor appeared yet again at his elbow—still curious, still helpful—he shook the fellow off.

For anger provided direction and it clarified resolve. It conferred its high authority while he journeyed up to London and Lord George Germain.

Germain was the King's trusted servant, and yet his supporters were few. Ben made inquiries of several in the town, learning what he could beforehand: how Lord George was impulsive, mercurial, and how he took an instant liking to or dislike of a man. As Secretary of State for America, of high birth and exalted rank, he stood second to none but the King. His protection and his favor came and went as rapidly as summer rain; it showered and then traveled on.

In his presence soldiers trembled; they called him wise and brave. In his absence they called him the Coward of Minden, where he had disobeyed orders and insisted on court martial, or reviled his present conduct of the war. He had not known, for example, that rivers froze in Canada; he proposed to sail the St. Lawrence although it iced over in winter, and in this mistaken fashion had planned to send a convoy to Quebec.

They praised him and curried his favor. They were flatterers in public and in private his detractors. He was sixty years old, arrogant and tall and stout and prideful and pious and surrounded by inform-ers who, in their privy correspondence or when not within his hear-ing, called him cold. His affections were a Catamite's, and hot.

Thompson heard it whispered further how his lordship's wife and their two daughters were depraved. Of libertine society these women were the darlings; licentious London rang with news of their lewd games. They gave great feasts at which they made their appearance on dishes, with sauce, and once upon the table guests were urged to lick them clean. Or the trio emerged instead naked and gleaming, wearing only ribbons, from the soup tureen. They brought courtesans to Pall Mall and provided male and female guest alike with practiced dalliance; then they passed around the chamber pot and poured it on the fruit. These ladies joined—so Thompson heard it rumored within two days of arrival—at Lord George's nightly revel with his lusty boys. They vied in their debasement for who could outpace whom.

Lord Sackville's nose was round. His eyes were watered blue. His wig was white, and the rings on his long fingers glittered; the silks he wore were of the choicest quality and cut. The buckles on his shoes alone would furnish a king's ransom, were Lord George inclined to pay.

He was not so inclined. It was his custom to receive a gift, not offer one; his coffers bulged with that respectful tribute the tongue of envy calls a bribe. It is more statesmanlike and prudent, he told his American visitor, to receive than give. What brings you here, my boy? do tell us what you brought and who it is that sent you, what you want?

In the event, the interview went well. As though again in Concord, and considered for the post of tutor, Ben knew that by this meeting he might be ruined or made; therefore he strove mightily to please. Lord George proved gracious, affable, and the excellent impression made by Major Thompson was remarked upon that night in many an establishment. He was shown in through the entry door with no mark of special favor, and then—more than an hour later—by Sackville himself escorted through the hall.

Thompson was fair-spoken and fair-skinned. He was tall and assertive and precise; having entered a petitioner, he withdrew acclaimed. The young Tory from America (with his information on the number and the nature of the troops, their training and prepared-ness, the evacuation of Boston and lack of proper signal systems in the fleet, the tactics of the victory at Breed Hill now already known as Bunker, and the cost of such a victory to morale and life, so that three further successes might spell failure in the war) established on the instant how he might best serve Germain. His eagerness of man-ner must have charmed an old campaigner, and the scandal-mongers soon had a new scandal to purvey. They discussed him high and low. What are the marks of his favor, they asked; which stripe does the Coward of Minden cause our hero to bear on his back?

"Bare on his back, you mean," they said.

"On his bare back."

"And trumpeting, I warrant."

"And serving under Sackville. "

"Or riding his cock horse."

Thus did they calumniate the friendship sprung up between two men—the one in need of solace and the other of advancement. The elder wanted information and the younger gave it; Lord George re-quired energy and Major Thompson had it; he needed a protector and Lord George a protégé. He who had two daughters embraced a full-grown son; he who knew no father returned the paternal embrace. Thus does the tongue of gossip gauge true silver as false brass.

You have not met my wife."

"I have not had the honor."

"Nor my daughters."

"No, milord."

"Come 'round again tomorrow. You must meet them. Tell them stories of America: sea monsters, the vast trees."

"I'm afraid I have no skill at such invention."

"Three-headed men." Lord George chuckled. He sneezed. "Tell them tales of red-skinned savages who daub themselves with bear grease and wear only the breech-clout in winter. Or perhaps you should omit this last."

"Omit the breech-clout, do you mean?"

"The mention of it, Thompson."

"They would be safe there, surely."

"But speak of naked savages and I'll have to furnish transport in the morning. There would be bedlam at the docks; all the great ladies of London would vie to get on board. No; best discuss the perils of the weather. The rough, ill-favored climate, the rude food."

"The food I can attest to. Its insufficient nourishment, its lack of proper preparation."

"Do so. Come to supper. Praise the cook."

"A happy prospect, Lord George."

"Do you dance?"

"As we are taught to in America. Only passably, I fear. Provincially."

"We'll have you caper for us. We'll have you do the colonial reel, the Gouverneur Morris dance."

Germain laughed loudly, ringingly, at his own witticism—as if the prospect pleased him and the joke were good. And then, once more, he sneezed.

So Ben became an intimate of wife and family, ranging freely through the house. They made him welcome in the great halls and the drawing rooms and library, as had his mistress Sarah when first his horizon enlarged. He endeavored to repay their kindness and render what service they wished; he did indeed go dancing and he praised the cook. He partook of the choice morsels and the leavings of the feasts. Telling stories of the battles of Lexington and Bunker Hill, of cavalry engagements and French privateers assailing English ships, he enlarged the number of his regiment at Concord; the King's Dragoons with whom he'd fought grew well-subscribed and brave. With such an audience attending, such exalted ears to hear them, his accomplishments flourished mightily, for Thompson chose to substitute invention for the deed. He who reports the story, he assured himself in private, is witness to an action if only by dint of the telling, and it did not truly matter if he was not truly there.

They made him welcome also in their private chambers, in the high heart of the house. He carried and extinguished their flambeaux. They indulged him particularly. He who had worn broadcloth, then a scholar's, then a soldier's garb now wrapped himself in garments of their choice—the shepherd's robe they swathed him in at midnight, the cod piece or bear-pelt they removed from him at two. He admired the pictures, the carved mirrors, the statuary and the rocking horse in the likeness of a rooster by Lady Elizabeth's bath. Its beak was fashioned in the shape of a prodigious penis, and it faced the saddle. He helped the daughters sate themselves upon that saddle, rocking; he was thought to be the favorite of father, mother, and both daughters turn by turn.

It was a busy time. Thompson met with loyalists in London who wanted reparations and came to ask for help. King and Crown had claimed their service and they therefore filed a claim. They gathered in the anterooms of the colonial office and at nearby counting houses and coffee houses and taverns to press their several suits. They had lost estates in Boston or in Hartford or Philadelphia or New York, and thought to be rewarded for their loyalty, growing bitter at their treatment and perplexed by this new poverty; they had not dreamed the revolution might succeed. Departing they made no provisions for failure, and found themselves now wholly dispossessed.

"You must help me with his Lordship," one of them told Thompson.

"Help you? How?"

"You are his favorite."

"Not so."

"You have his ear."

"From time to time, his Lordship may indeed incline to listen."

"Please fill it for me."

"With?"

"My case. My just cause. This."

And he handed Thompson the purse.

Another, Mr. Jeffries, offered Thompson Mrs. Jeffries, who visited him readily at night. Mr. Jeffries waited for preferment; he lingered by the door. Mrs. Jeffries was ample and buxom, with a good-natured and endearing fashion of sneezing in the crisis.

She procured for her young gentleman some letters from Benjamin Franklin and Governor Pounall and Reverend Cooper concerning the state of affairs in America in 1774. These he bound in gold-tooled red morocco and presented to the King.

There were expenditures also. The Secretary of State dispensed three thousand pounds a year—not out of charity but caution, for fidelity is best assured by the well-placed reward. So he purchased information from those who might otherwise turn on him, faithless, maintaining a network of spies. He explained to Thompson that in this economical fashion the right hand may investigate the left, the left the right: put Peter in the pay of Paul and you have perfect disciples. He was, he said, concerned there be no least cessation of control. Control is the art of enclosure, the baited trap and snare; be certain of your party, that they dare not deny you at dawn.

Major Thompson undertook the role of private secretary to Lord George Germain. Taking lodgings in Pall Mall, he honed his courtier's skills—for here, he came to understand, was his academy and 'prentice-shop, a chance to observe and thereafter emulate the mannerly ways of the world. Flattered, glad to be of service and to study statesmanship, he attended his master in conference and carriage; they dined together mornings and again at night.

Germain was practiced in the use and maintenance of power; his text was Machiavel's. He was secretive, then candid, and planned down to the last detail what appeared to be mere whim. Those who serve you, he maintained, must never take for granted whom they serve. He taught Thompson the advantages of carefully managed caprice. Let me remind you, he said, that there are many in America—and they have friends in London—who would like nothing better than to see you hanged. They know you as Gage's informer and have measured you, Ben, for the rope. You were outfitted in Boston, were you not, and such tailors record to the inch, nay to the very centimeter—here, tenderly, regretfully, he reached down to stroke it—the size of your neck.

Whether this was truly so Thompson was uncertain; whether he was marked or no he could not take the risk. Unlike those loyalists who thought themselves but briefly gone, hoping monthly to sail to America, he had no intention of returning, and nothing to return to that he preferred to luxury: the marbled halls and chandeliers and mirrored ceilings, the silk sheets.

In London he made a new friend. The household in Pall Mall was large, and there were many retainers, and among them the American discovered a young Kentishman—Jonathan Leigh by name—who steered Thompson through the tortuous maze of free-spirited dependency. An adept of labyrinthine ways, of dark turnings and the hidden door, he served as Thompson's guide.

Young Jonathan was comely, tall and fair. It took no skill to see what George Germain had seen in him: his shoulders were broad and hips slim. His cheek was smooth, his skin without blemish, neck long. Though bruited everywhere as Sackville's catamite, he also served by everybody unremarked as spy. Of an equivalent stature, Leigh looked Thompson in the eye; his sanguine disposition and evident enjoyment of his present circumstance gave our traveler hope of a future as lavishly provided for as had been the case in the past.

Now the Kentishman was twenty-four, grown wise in the ways

of the court. They exercised together, with Indian clubs and épée. Last season's favorite made his successor welcome in an open-handed manner that bespoke true brotherhood and dismissed mere rivalry; what's good for the goose is sauce for the gander, said Leigh.

Ben acquired English manners. He learned how to dress, when to smile. He had not known—for which of us may know without instruction and by instinct, not example?—what moment to be bold and where demure. He practiced drawing, dancing, how to bow. As so many years before when but a stock boy at John Appleton's, he studied the proud habits and the bearing of the rich. He learned when "certainly" means "no" and how, by contrast, "not at all," could come instead to signify "absolutely, by all means."

When he remembered, however, he grieved. "I did not come here willingly and do not plan to stay. I miss the gentle Merrimac, my pasture and my lands."

"'By the waters of Babylon,'" Jonathan teased him. "You are no prisoner and must not bewail your state."

"But you belong here."

"Not so. I come from Canterbury, Ben. It is a world away."

They traveled to that world. The young pair rode to Canterbury, at Germain's behest and on collector's business, spending three days on the journey. It rained. At the Leigh home (a low brick warren of barns, a rose-covered cottage, a dovecote) Ben felt so keen a pang of loss that he feared indigestion. He doubled over, rocking, then turned pale.

"You are unwell?" asked Jonathan.

"My wife and daughter," Thompson said. "My dear old widowed mother. The companions of my youth."

"They thrive in your ascendancy, be certain. They take pleasure in and comfort from the news of your success."

"I cannot help it," Ben confessed. "I do feel alone in the world."

"But there are those who care for you, who supervise and will not let you languish."

"No."

"A second glass of port? A pipe?"

He waved such comforts off. He could not tell his friend how this old house, so full of threadbare relics and the well-worn regalia of childhood, had made him miss as not before the farm in Woburn with its cramped familiar spaces and daily dull routine. The corners of the room—the miniatures and drawings, the dolls and jars and rusted grate and embroidery and herbs and flowers under glass and candle-sticks and torn brocade—reminded him so forcefully of his mother and her brother, Uncle Hiram, of Josiah Pierce the elder, and his half-brother, young Josiah, of all that he had left behind, the father he had never known, that Ben gave way to grief.

He raised his head and knew he had been crying. It took no great discernment to establish root and cause. He had made his way through trackless seas yet must continue journeying; his name was writ in water though he'd hoped it hewed in stone. He was a pilgrim, and alone.

Then Jonathan embraced him and licked the salt rime from his cheeks.

His Lordship next conferred the position of Deputy to the Inspector General of Provincial Forces. Thus Thompson was responsible for clothing and accoutrements sent from England to the colonies. He concerned himself with saddles, swords and uniforms, their fabric and design, and in the role of Deputy made a small fortune in cloth.

By December, 1776, he had been commended to the King's attention as register of records for the province of Georgia. King George approved. The tongue of gossip wagged again and called him Under-Secretary and envied his reward. On the day of his appointment Germain caressed him lingeringly, and said, "Our trusty and well beloved Benjamin Thompson."

"I thank you for your kindness."

"Able. Loyal. That's how I put it to the King."

"I am very grateful. You know that. "

"Then show your gratitude."

"How further, milord?"

"Come hunting with me Wednesday. The women wait at Stoneland. I want sport."

Stoneland Lodge near Tunbridge Wells afforded a sportsman's variety. Shooting, they rode through the green hills of Kent, traversing thickly wooded lanes, the deer park and the copses stuffed with grouse. Germain appeared well pleased. He commended his steward and bearers and beaters, meantime inspecting his gardens with care. The park had been maintained with just that hint of wildness that gives flavor to the hunt, a piquancy of danger made domestic.

When they each had killed sufficient fowl, and the first carts were loaded and sent back to Stoneland's kitchens, his lordship called a halt. He and his Secretary continued on alone, abreast, for the elder of the two desired conversation. He thought powder was improved in its velocity when wet, the explosion augmented by steam. And better than water was gin; a bullet impelled by powder dampened prudently with alcohol would increase both in impact and rate.

Thompson disagreed. He begged respectfully to urge instead the adage: keep your powder dry.

"An old wive's tale," scoffed George Germain. "Advice from those who do not shoot. Mark me: gin and powder, that's the thing."

He had been born at Knole, the Sackville seat, and this country-side was anciently familiar. He reminded his young protégé that he first had served as Member of Parliament for Dover—a borough in his father's gift—in '41. Among his father's titles was Lord Warden of the Cinque Ports. "Dear boy," concluded Sackville, "since long before your birth I have been shooting here."

Thompson bowed his head. His early interest in matters scientific had been allowed to lapse. He who once pursued his studies now pursued advancement merely, and it galled him to be far removed from instruments and desk. He had—he assured himself, posting, urging his horse to a canter—a restless disposition and an inquiring mind. He needed proper work.

The weather, fine early, had turned. Rain threatened; then it fell. They came upon a ruin recently installed, in the emergent fashion, with fallen timbers in the roof and long grass at the door. Germain examined this construction, then dallied at the window and invited Thompson to seek shelter from the rain. He winked.

The younger man dismounted. A muscle in his right thigh twitched and fluttered; his knee ached. The night before, he had enjoyed both Lady and Lord George. After supper they retired to her chambers, as had become their custom. She was hungry, Lady Elizabeth declared, for fare not there at table. Of fruit and cheese and dainties she had sampled a sufficiency; of foul and guinea hen and fish and game-pie and oysters and broth and pudding and partridge and Rhenish wine and lemon and claret and treacle she had had her fill.

The woman bade them both disrobe, then joined the two men in the bed, securing them with scarves. Ben studied the carved cherubim and the hanging tapestry of Pan with nymphs and pipes. Soon enough his Lordship dwindled and—no matter how the other two attempted to revive him, exhorting him to greater heights—turned his face into the pillow and, shading his eyes with the coverlet, snored. For her own part her Ladyship first emulated the tapestry's topmost right-hand nymph; then she assumed the attitude of—in the bottom left-hand corner of that sylvan illustration—the spotted dog.

Lord George appeared inured to scorn, indifferent to ridicule. So great a man could greatly dare to contravene, as long as he did so in private, the law. But his young partner did not like it. He had been reading pamphlets and had heard abusive rhyme:

> Sackville, both Coward and Catamite, commands
> Department honourable, and kisses hands
> With lips that oft in blandishment obscene
> Have been Employed.

The rain abated; Thompson shook his cloak. "Like that powder

110

you prefer, milord, I am but barely damp."

"Yet come inside."

"It slackens, the rain."

"Come."

Now he was coy. "I need that gin you spoke of 'ere I shoot."

In July, at Stoneland Lodge, Thompson settled down to work. He undertook to determine the most advantageous situation for the vent in fire-arms, and to measure the velocities of bullets, and the recoil under various circumstances. He had hopes, also, of being able to find out the velocity of the inflammation of gunpowder, and to measure its force more accurately than had hitherto been done.

He was assisted by the Reverend Mr. Bale, Rector of Withyham, who lived in the neighborhood. The weather proved remarkably favorable for their experiments, being settled and serene, so that the course of Thompson's labor was not interrupted for a whole day by rain or any accident. The mercury in the barometer stood high, and the temperature of the atmosphere was very equal and moderately warm for the season. In order that each experiment might, as nearly as possible, be conducted under similar circumstances, they were all made between the hours of ten in the morning and five in the afternoon; and after each experiment the piece was wiped out with tow till the inside of its bore was perfectly clean, and as bright as if it had just come out of the hands of the maker. Great care was taken to allow as much time to elapse between the firings as was necessary to render the heat of the barrel nearly the same in each experiment.

Applying himself to the question, he worked nine full days without rest. He found it wholly pleasing to be absorbed in study, to lose himself in measurement and speculative inquiry and occupation of the intellect, constructing equations and charts. The two men used Lord George's coach house and hung a heavy pendulum as target at one end of the open room—the doors remaining open so that smoke might neither cloud nor thicken air nor in any way impede the velocity of bullets—and a cannon at the other. Thompson then determined the recoil of both the target and gun.

The distance each swung back was measured by securely fastened tapes; these were run through friction slots to hold them at their maximum extension. The proper parameters of the momentum of the pendulum might therefore be recorded. He and the Reverend Mr. Bale—a silent man, yet competent, and anxious to be of assistance, for had not Lord George Germain himself expressly commended the venture, from time to time appearing in the coach house with a restorative cordial to oversee their progress?—completed one hundred and-twenty-three experiments in that nine day time.

He examined the position of the firing vent, reaching the conclusion that it made no appreciable difference to the force of the explosion. He tried to shoot fire, and failed. He discussed the composition of the powder and the virtues of his cannon as an éprouvette. He perorated also on the value of iron ordinance for field artillery or naval guns, not brass. He noted the increase of heat in the gun barrel after firing and would have measured it precisely had not his thermometer cracked. Being so far from London he had it not in his power to procure another and was obliged to content himself with determining the heat of the barrel as well as he could by the touch.

No human invention of which we have any authentic records, except perhaps the art of printing, has produced such important changes in civil society as the invention of gunpowder. Yet, notwithstanding the uses to which this agent is applied are so extensive, and though its operations are as surprising as they are important, Thompson thought it not to have been examined with that care and perseverance which it deserves. The explosion of gunpowder is certainly one of the most surprising phenomena, and he was persuaded it would much oftener have been the subject of the investigations of speculative philosophers, as well as of professional men, were it not for the danger attending the experiments; but the force of gunpowder is so great, and its effects so sudden and so terrible, that notwithstanding all the precautions possible, there is ever a considerable degree of danger attending the management of it, as he more than once found to his cost.

His eyes watered. His ears rang. The smell of cordite and its acrid after-odor stayed with him at night. Although their ladyships Germain rode up to Stoneland for the sport, he demurred when they asked him to mount. "You are grown dull with shooting," sighed Lord George's daughter. "I am off to London, Ben."

Now Thompson came to understand what he had seen in Salem when he first played with rockets and had been blown up. He had believed it satanic, demonic, a sign—yet the figure in the workroom smoke was an encouragement, not warning; the fire urged him on. It was an orange, fork-tongued flame, an eloquent consistency of discourse to translate. It gave him a changeable language to learn—a secret to acquire and proclaim. The heat of the barrel revived him, and its controlled explosiveness afforded hot delight. Removed, his fingers shook. As with those messages conveyed by means of sympathetic ink, it was his code to crack. Such shooting did not make him dull, as the foolish daughter feared; it sharpened him instead.

He was at ease with fire, that gift of the renegade Titan made fast to the fierce rock. Our young inventor laughed; he pitied poor Prometheus for ancient limitation. It would be his own gift to men to measure and then harness heat.

Once more the wheel revolved, for Lord Germain grew feeble. From a surfeit of pleasure comes pain, and now his life of unremitting excess took its toll. His pulse went weak, his color poor, and he had fainting spells. He who had enjoyed rude health turned sickly now, and delicate; strength failed. Keeping close to his hushed chamber, he did not leave the bed.

It was predicted everywhere that Viscount Sackville must soon resign; his influence was waning and his enemies conspired. They clustered to him greedily and struggled for succession, easing the robe of leadership down past his shrunken shanks. They wrested the affairs of state from him who conducted them weakly. As when a great beast wearies from long seasons of command and leaves the pack to lie apart and lick his wounds and pant for breath, so did the jackals circle the old lion in Pall Mall—sitting back on their haunches and wetting their chops, awaiting the chance to attack.

He called his Secretary to him, saying, "Go."

"I will not leave you, George. I cannot go in conscience."

"The least relevant of words," said Lord Germain.

"My place is at your side," cried Ben.

"You don't believe that, surely. I am not yet dead and when I am you should be elsewhere."

"Where?"

The high-pitched voice was low. The words came slowly, haltingly. "They will hang you here for treason."

"How?"

"They will try you with that fool LaMotte, as having served the French. Go home, I tell you."

"My home is here!"

"Go back, then, to America. Reduce them to your purpose and be by that action enlarged."

"I know nothing of LaMotte. I have not trafficked with him, not at all. I have served England faithfully."

"You are my servant, Thompson."

"Entirely." Ben fell upon his knees by the wide bed. He grasped his lordship's hand and kissed the shapely fingers and cold knuckles and the rings. "I cannot continue without you."

Germain went white. His lipstick and his rouge set off the pallor of the cheeks, yet there was something of the old command in his lordship's visage: "Then do as I tell you: go back. Poor innocent, you would not last ten minutes in this government without me."

Ben buried his head in the sheets. Again he wept, convulsive; again he tasted salt. His first Atlantic crossing was years behind him now, and he was a made man. But only with the prospect of departure did he learn how much he yearned to stay, how much he owed Germain. By his hot tears and his submission he acknowledged what he cherished here: a father who had brought him forth in tender fornication, a teacher who revealed to him how passion and protection may be joined.

In fact his lordship did not die, although he dwindled mightily and withdrew to Stoneland Lodge. His creature went forth in the world.

SALLY

Well it's a bitter world he goes to, Class, the one he thought forever to have left behind. But that's the value of a wheel, its circularity, a turning to completion: what goes up must come down. *M'sieurdames, faites vos jeux.* In case you're curious about my French, I taught the language once. But this is what *les croupiers* say, not what we learn or teach in school: roulette as Fortune's wheel. The leaden sky has lifted now (how may lead lift but feather-lightly, loweringly?); the winter's snow begins to thaw beyond my south-facing window and, by the mud-room overhang, thick icicles thin in the sun. *Les jeux sont faits. Rien ne va plus.* I sit here by the fire and reread our boy:

> No subject of philosophical inquiry, within the limits of human investigation, is more calculated to excite admiration, and to awaken curiosity, than FIRE; and there is certainly none more extensively useful to mankind. It is owing, no doubt, to our being acquainted with it from our infancy, that we are not more struck with

its appearance, and more sensible of the benefits we derive from it. Almost every comfort and convenience which man by his ingenuity procures for himself, is obtained by its assistance; and he is not more distinguished from the brute creation by the use of speech, than by his power over that wonderful agent.

Thus Benjamin, Count Rumford in the book I own—the second of his volumes of collected essays, leather-bound, end-paper torn on the right top, rear verso lightly damaged (this the Third American Edition from the English Third), dated 1799. He wrote these things for money, Class, but also to establish reputation and in the hope of widespread fame, for his was the homespun high style. He described himself as follows: *Knight of the Orders of the White Eagle, and St. Stanislaus; Chamberlain, Privy Counsellor of State, and Lieutenant-General in the Service of His Most Serene Highness the Elector Palatine, Reigning Duke of Bavaria; Colonel of his Regiment of Artillery, and Commander in Chief of the General Staff of his Army; F.R.S. Acad. R., Hiber, Berol, Elec. Boicoe, Palat. Et Amer. Soc.* Not bad, not bad at all.

But what does Sarah Ormsby Thompson Robinson, b. 2/11/38, make of her ancestor's effort? Staring out at the icicles, down at the page, then out, then down again. For her own part of her own free will she chooses a verse to recite:

> The honeywind blows, and the warm days dwindle
> The butterfly spins a silk cocoon on a silver spindle.

Let us ignore, for a moment, the fact that the poem's a song. Let us disregard its sentimental pairing, its questionable end-rhyme and insistent trisyllabic of the second word. The jingle remains in my head; I cannot get rid of it, Class. *Dwindle, spindle.* Let us construe as irrelevant the fact that it evokes not late winter—as in the weather this morning—but fall. The song has other rhymes as well, other moons and Junes and silver spoons: *I sit alone, and the Good Lord knows, I miss you so, when the honeywind blows.*

There are several things to say.

Primo, the very word "class," Class, had a different import then, and what George Germain did with his little boys or Lady Germain with her large was no one's particular business but their Lord and Ladyship's. Until, that is, arrests were made and the perpetrators brought to book; to be proved a Sodomite then gave capital offense. So Thompson sailed close to the wind. He would not have had protection like the mighty of the realm, who were beyond the reach of envy or consequent reproach. What of Governor John Wentworth's interest in and admiration for him; had that early and fond notice been salacious also; did Ben work his way up through vile play?

My instinct tells me no. Not this calculating man. The *arriviste* arrived is not quite the same as the one on the make, the gift conferred less valued than the article withheld. He was a beautiful young fellow, according to report, a person people noticed where he rode and strode. But the promise of seduction is more seductive, often, than the goal achieved. That scene of failed recognition when he asks for Sackville's blessing and gets sent back to America seems to me a crucial one, the young pup weeping by the side of the old dog. Although I put them all in bed I'm not sure what they did there, and possibly the tender-ness was real. For in any case he could have flattered Wentworth and Germain and others by his simple presence; the act itself might well have been unnecessary.

Here Sally Robinson ventures an epigram, Class: *Those who gain the world's advancement cannot advance on their knees. Though sometimes on their backs.* Was it the estimable Rochefoucauld who said fewer women would engage in sex if they received compliments standing? Wrong, wrong. It's the kind of observation old men make—sniggering, simpering—and it's entirely wrong. Let us admit to desire; we are the only animal that drinks when less than thirsty or ruts while out of season. Thus averred Buffon.

Secundo, how vivid they appear, these folk, how much more alive then than now. I'd trade every anchorperson on the nightly news from Nashua for one lecture on anatomy from Dr. John Hay; every time I eat an apple I taste Loammi Baldwin, and the mailman in his Taurus reminds me of Jonathan Leigh. When he delivers a package or postage-due or certified letter and from time to time I sign for it, he brings, alas, the news of war, and wouldn't it be wonderful to pen the answer in code? Imagine, reader, the sheet spread out in front of you, the gallo-tannic acid or lemon juice and essence of nutgall passed twice across the surface lightly until—hey presto!—characters appear. The blank space blackened as we watch: what a paradigm of writing as illustrative art!

Tertio, I think I understand now why heat was Thompson's chosen mode. Of the universal four—earth, air, water, flame—this last is his defining element, the only one to which he paid continual heed. He disliked the earth and quit the trade of farmer as soon as he could manage to; he was seasick on, suspicious of the deep. No man less airy in demeanor, none more pragmatic in inquiry. So perhaps he was chosen by fire instead.

"It is owing, no doubt, to our being acquainted with it from our infancy, that we are not more struck with its appearance, and more sensible of the benefits we derive from it." Remember his first letters to Loammi, his experiments with powder and his plan to build a rocket? Or his research and data at Stoneland and the flambeaux he bore for Lady Sackville, the sacrifice required of the wizard and Black Mage?

Mornin', Miz Robinson."

"Morning," I say.

"Cold enough this mornin'?"

"Ayup."

"Sap's runnin,'" says Alex.

I smile.

"Good sugarin' weather."

"Already?" I ask.

He nods. Ayup Ayup. He has the pails with him, of course; he knew I'd give the go-ahead for those six sugar maples on the west-facing slope. But while we're standing here together the strangest thing occurs, and the strangest thing of all is how it feels familiar: he, my present visitor, goes incorporeal, and what I see instead is that ramrod-upright English soldier, Lieutenant of the King's Dragoons, vaulting from saddle to stoop.

Ben clatters up the side porch stairs, his boots fairly polished and gleaming, his uniform spruce-brushed. With his left hand on his sword's bright hilt he sweeps off his hat and bows low. He has that piercing blue-eyed glare, that orange hair, the tensile strength of someone I remember that I know I never knew; is this what they mean by possession?

By all means, I whisper, *Proceed. Be my guest, please, Lieutenant-Colonel Thompson. Tap.*

ৡ V ৢ

Now he set sail from England to do service in the war. He knew it a lost cause: there was nothing left to win. Yet a man may serve his country by returning to subdue it, and he had old scores to settle and accounts to square.

This time the weather proved brutal. They left Cork Harbor in October, on a bright, brisk autumn day, his Majesty's navy in force. Not three days into the crossing a whelming gale blew the convoy apart, and his ship, the H.M.S. Rotterdam, continued on alone.

Thompson's sea-legs were uncertain, and he waited for his illness to return. To his relief, he stayed hale. The other vessels were not lost, the Rotterdam's captain assured him, but only lost to view. Captain Knowles had wooden teeth. These had been, he complained, ill-fitted, and they gave him greater trouble than the present wind.

But then the wind increased. It bore upon them ceaselessly and came from the northeast and fed on itself, doubling back, tearing apart the mizzen sail and in the fore topgallant and main topgallant staystails accumulating force. Soaked sailors fought for purchase on the rain-sluiced decks.

Lieutenant Colonel Thompson observed with equanimity torrential rain and heavy seas and gusts that made a nightly howling in the sheets. Wind whipped and lashed and tore. When the bowsprit snapped like kindling he helped with the repair—feeling well, exultant even, in the storm.

Eight hogsheads were washed overboard, together with the livestock, and our traveler took the precaution of securing himself with thick rope. His predecessor in this stratagem, according to blind Homer, had survived the sirens' song—enjoying it, enduring it—and in just such a manner Thompson weathered the first weeks. As fixed in purpose as in place, he spent the nights on deck. It had been his plan to study cannon and to pursue his inquiry of powder, since the Rotterdam was copper-sheathed and equipped with fifty guns. The roiling sky, however, made experiment impractical; lightning and attendant thunder played about the mast.

He watched the great waves crest and trough, the blown spume and the seabirds and the leaping fish. He learned the use of sextant, telescope and chart, and when the skies grew clear at last he learned celestial navigation from an obliging mate. Studying astronomy as at Concord years before, he enlarged his old awareness of the patterned constellations and configured stars; believing that his own might prove again ascendant, he plotted its new course.

The moon grew full, then waned, then filled again. The other ships appeared. By comparison with his first trip—when he had been immoderately ill although the breeze was moderate—this western passage seasoned him; the sailors praised his stomach and cool head. For now Ben Thompson's mind was easy and intention fixed. Landfall was his every thought, and the debt he had determined to collect for all his old indignities: derision, expulsion, the high cost of exile, loss, scorn. He would fall on his first countrymen like an avenging angel or red ghost.

Their convoy, however, had been blown south; on the twelfth week of the voyage out, at seven o'clock in the morning, they came in sight of land. The men gave thanks to God. They spied a welcome light-house but then pine trees, palm trees, sand, an unfamiliar sea wall and then cobblestone and brick. The Rotterdam weighed anchor in Charleston, not New York.

Thompson was unsatisfied and urged the northern route. He and the ship's captain disagreed. Now Captain Knowles proved contrary as the prevailing wind itself; he held conference with messengers and would not tell his passenger the substance of dispatches or the nature of the orders he received. For there was much uncertainty and rumor-bred confusion: Cornwallis had surrendered, or so the gossips claimed, and there were tales of treachery, of plans and forts and armories breached, of traitors and informers; at Yorktown two months earlier the British had collapsed. The white-whiskered harbormaster said the Rotterdam was not to leave; he ordered all baggage ashore.

Thompson had brought cannon, several horses, and even a milch goat; in New York he planned to raise a regiment of horse. But that was many days away, and the New York harbor—so the captain asserted—was blocked. He would not say how long their vessel must remain in its safe haven.

"I cannot in conscience determine," said Knowles, "upon a course of action that leaves you unprotected." Here the captain examined his thumb. "You know General Clinton?"

"I do."

"You have made his acquaintance?"

"Not personally, no. I know the man by reputation."

"And caution's the watchword, correct?" Knowles laughed. His eyes were red-rimmed and his buttons dangled from a tunic in need of repair; for the last several days he had applied no razor to white stubble on his cheeks.

"Correct," said Lieutenant Colonel Thompson.

"I have my orders."

"Whose?"

"The General's. General Clinton. He writes particularly from New York that you are not to venture there, you are too rich a cargo." Knowles laughed again, mirthless, and rubbed at his teeth. "It is in any case the harbormaster's instruction: we disembark."

"You will not sail without me?"

"No."

"You wait for further orders?"

"But of course."

The Captain's caution did in truth seem warranted; his was a precious freight. The four pieces of artillery and a quantity of ammunition had been consigned to Thompson by King George himself. It would have been improvident to release them to the enemy or suffer quarantine. Therefore—having obtained the promise that he would be given ample warning of any change in plans—Lieutenant Colonel Thompson disembarked.

Under the captain's watchful eye, he made a great show of unloading. This procedure was elaborate; slaves and sailors grappled with the horses and the goat. Each cannon required a dory; his trunks, too, filled a lighter and were ferried with close care. Since he had been so long at sea and was now grown unaccustomed to the shore's stability, the ground beneath him seemed to sway and the cobbled paving lurch. It rained.

Ben marshaled his belongings on the dock.

Then the Rotterdam raised sail.

"I find," he wrote Germain, "I shall stand in need of all my prudence to steer clear of all the snares and lures that will surround me." There were factions and betrayals in the fleet. They stranded him, or tried to; he was abandoned in Charleston and left to winter there. They had left him, certainly on purpose, and hoped by this contrivance to keep him from the war.

But he had come for war, and wanted it, and would not be denied. He was a man, not stripling now, and had acquired both cannon and horse. There is a time for computation, a time for calculation, and a time to fight; that last at last had come.

It was January, 1782, yet the Carolina winter felt warm as an English July. Orange trees and myrtle flavored the soft air. Lieutenant Colonel Benjamin Thompson was received at headquarters with deferential courtesy; here, Germain and his orders held sway. Lieutenant General Alexander Leslie made him welcome, as General Clinton had not. He was assigned a detachment of five-hundred infantry and two-hundred horse; his men were volunteers of Ireland, who had been organized in Philadelphia and served under Lord Rawdon. They made a seasoned crew, and this was fortunate as well as needful, for their task was not a simple one: they were to capture Francis Marion, known as the Swamp Fox.

The garrison at Charleston weekly expected a siege. They had languished in this attitude and had grown disheartened, idling the autumn away, so now they are better at drinking and dicing than war,

General Leslie complained. And besides—he rubbed his large belly, emphatic—we have nearly nothing to eat. It is imperative, my friend, to seek out and defeat the Swamp Fox or, failing that, lay waste the countryside. What rice you cannot forage you have my instructions to burn.

The Swamp Fox had disposed his forces twenty miles outside the city, along the Cooper River. Marion was now a Senator at Jacksonborough, drinking and disporting with the Congress there; his cavalry went unopposed from Jacksonborough to Strawberry Ferry, and from the Santee to the Wando Rivers. They commanded all land routes to Charleston, and all access but the sea.

Colonel Horry was positioned to the north of Wambaw Creek. Colonel Maham was not feeling well and had gone to his plantation for a rest. The rumor of the British force—a rumor bruited then outpaced when Thompson marched his soldiers thirty-six miles without halting—fell on indifferent ears. Major Benison was eating dinner and would not be disturbed, for there were shoats and venison, coffee, cheese and cakes. Colonel McDonald too sat at table, though he was playing cards. The soldiers of the Swamp Fox had grown comfortably lax; they had not tasted combat in too long.

So when the Royal mounted militia fell on them it was as wolves on sheep: the Americans bleated and ran. They had not expected British soldiers in such numbers nor so fierce a troop. Some of Colonel Horry's troops did rally and attempt to fight—yet these were late and scattered and soon killed. The majority raced pell-mell back to Wambaw Bridge, and there were soon so many upon it that the span collapsed. With a rending of timbers, it cracked.

They fell into the water, screaming, and they floundered there. Only a few knew how to swim, and the moiety of these were heavy-loaded or injured, so the turmoil was astonishing, attaining fever pitch; to a man who cherished method, the principles of order, such extravagant disorder in these his quondam countrymen neither could nor need be brooked. Men wailed and beseeched him and all unavailing fled.

Lieutenant Colonel Thompson stood upon the farther bank and fired in at leisure, watching the Americans writhe, flail, sink. The water boiled with blood. He reloaded at his ease. It was as if he fished once more with his companions at Nahant, but what they caught were traitors now, not cod. They had lost all discipline, all proper management. Till his pistols grew too hot to hold, he slaughtered rebels with them and enjoyed the sport.

You are married, Colonel Thompson?"

"Lieutenant Colonel, milady. I may not as yet lay claim to the exalted rank of Colonel."

"I have no doubt you will attain it."

"You would enlarge me?"

"Were it in my power." She smiled.

Thus he avoided the question. He was married and his wife and child were no longer an ocean away. But he did not choose to write to Sarah nor announce himself as husband, and the Charleston ladies failed to press him on the point. They flattered him instead. He was the vaunted hero of the fight at Wambaw Bridge, who had been blooded there. Mrs. Elsie Cotesworth—whose ballroom he was dancing in, and whose husband was away on business in Savannah—placed her white hand lightly on his cheek.

"They say had not the bridge collapsed you would have killed them every one."

"It hampered our pursuit."

"Indeed. An involuntary drawbridge." Mrs. Cotesworth shuddered. "They pulled it back behind them, I am told."

"It did rather more damage than we did, perhaps."

"You are too modest, Colonel."

"Again you have promoted me."

"And you press the advantage. I am defenseless, Colonel, you may triumph as you choose."

Her bodice heaved not a handsbreadth removed from his own half-raised hand, but whether from emotion or exertion he was unable to tell.

"I take it, Mrs. Cotesworth, you are willing to negotiate?"

"I do desire it, yes."

"You will receive my emissary?"

His hostess curtseyed. "At midnight," she whispered, "I will surrender privily. May it please you to come back."

Thus Benjamin proceeded. When he later broached her in her bedroom filled with flowers, she sighed, "I am your prisoner, soldier. Impose what terms you will."

He next conceived a plan to capture General Greene, and once again he hoped to profit from surprise. The general was quartered in St. Andrew's Parish, at Ashley Hall; the Ashley River might be forded at Bee's Ferry. Thompson asked for and received permission to form a raiding party and beard that sleeping lion—the bravest of the enemy—where he wintered in his den.

General Leslie approved. "We might yet turn the tide."

"We have the advantage of secrecy, sir."

"How many battles, Thompson, does it take to win the war?"

"Sir?"

"How many battles does one need to be declared the victor? This is the secret of success; I give it to you freely."

The Lieutenant Colonel pondered, or appeared to, since he well knew the answer. It was Leslie's favorite riddle, and he posed the question often. Always, Thompson strove to look surprised.

"That depends, sir, on the nature of the conflict. The duration of the war. It might be half a dozen, half a hundred . . ."

"One."

"One, sir?"

"Yes." The General clapped his hands, delighted. "Providing only that it be the final one. The last."

So he set off again for battle at the River Ashley, ten miles outside of town. He took Major Fraser with him, and one hundred men. Their secondary purpose was to secure provisions, and they brought in one-hundred-forty head of horned cattle, and goats, yet their progress was hampered by marsh. The tide was at low ebb. On the miry banks he called a halt and gathered his dragoons.

"What say you, Major?" Thompson asked. "You know this country well. Here we ford?"

"It cannot be done," Fraser said.

"Why not?" he asked. "'Tis but a stone's throw, surely."

"Three hundred feet," said Fraser. "And treacherous water for swimming."

Again it rained. The rain was cold.

"Had I my proper horse, good Blaze," said Lieutenant Colonel Thompson, "we would ford it on the instant, taking pleasure in the swim."

Major Fraser was a stubborn man and would not be persuaded. He spoke of Wambaw Bridge and how the Americans died; he said these waters were like those of the River Santee—shallow, then suddenly rapid and deep—so those who did not stick in mud would surely drown. He said General Nathanael Greene could snore or revel undisturbed at Ashley Hall, for he would win and they must lose this fight without a single skirmish. No man among them might contrive to cross the Ashley River without risking powder and mount.

At length they formed a plan. They would take one of their number—the strongest, bravest swimmer on the finest horse—and have him ford the Ashley or fail in the attempt. This experiment would demonstrate if they should continue or turn back. Thompson chose a volunteer. His horse was proven and he could swim; he gave his name as Atkins. He conferred with his superiors and declared himself content, for they hinted at promotion and promised an increase of rum.

"You understand," said Major Fraser, "there is great risk involved."

"Great glory also," Thompson said.

Sergeant Atkins saluted and made for the river. Nut-brown from the winter sun, he was wide-framed, tall and fit. The officers withdrew to higher ground, where could be seen a grassy knoll sufficient for two men, and upon this elevation Lieutenant Colonel Thompson with his second-in-command dismounted, then tethered their horses to graze. The rain increased. As once on his own eastward crossing, when he first set sail for England and whatever waited there, Thompson watched with forced dispassion while the scene played out.

The troop fell silent, all. An active death awaited him who crossed the river, a passive death yawned here behind—for which among them might expect true clemency from the rebel forces, or hope to return home unharmed? Sergeant Atkins urged his horse. He spoke to it, then whipped it, and they entered the wide stream.

For the first minute all went well, the steed appearing at ease. Atkins sat lightly, his heels and soon his booted foot submerging, his knees and then his waist in water, and next his trailing hand, until the horse gave a great shudder and began to swim. This too proceeded apace, or might have, had not the current grown suddenly rapid and brought with it a log. Major Fraser shouted, "Man, look out!" but above the lethal water he could not have been heard.

As though volitional, intentional, the roiling log bore down on horse and rider. It was black and broad. It reared and tumbled, speedy, pitching, in the grip of force far greater than a swimming beast might contravene, and the angle of approach could be measured by geometry, a line drawn to a point.

Thompson closed his spyglass, having no need to see. He could hear with perfect clarity the slapping sound of wood on flesh, the splintering of limb and log, the despairing cry of Sergeant Atkins as his horse was struck. The animal died on the instant, its skull crushed. The man fell back, submerged, and only at length floated lifelessly free. Major Fraser galloped to the river bank to aid the salvage procedure with rope, but Lieutenant Colonel Thompson stayed aloof. In the distance he imagined the derisive chuckle of Nathanael Greene, the doleful cries of Atkins's widowed wife and child, the dirge for sailors drowned at sea—and all such lamentation as attends a failed adventure.

The rain was loud. The captured cattle mooed. What he heard was his men shouting and the desperate bustle of rescue, the foredoomed and bootless flailing of those who would escape their fate; what he sounded was retreat.

So he set out for New York. He had been commissioned to raise a regiment of King's Dragoons, not languish by magnolia and stream. General Leslie did not attempt to keep him, but sent dispatches north. Neither could the Charleston ladies keep him, though they sweetened his departure and salted it with tears.

This journey proved uneventful. He set sail with his four cannon and two negro body-servants and his complement of horse, but Lieutenant Colonel Thompson left his milch goat behind. He was favored with a healthful breeze, a following sea, a gentle and persistent sun, no privateers or challenge from the shore. Having landed unopposed, he marched from Ireland Heights the three days and the forty miles to the outpost at Lloyd's Neck; then he made camp on Long Island, at Huntington, New York.

It was early autumn, warm; the war was nearly done. There had been no fighting since the surrender at Yorktown, and all eyes were on the future and the sight of peace to come. Thompson's negroes served him in the tent.

What is certain, however, is war and not peace; he continued to recruit. Men who had been royalists he found once more, men who had no funds or prospect of employment, men who owned a horse or sought to leave the country and fight for King George elsewhere—all these flocked to his table, and he signed them on. They wrote their names in a trained hand, or signed laboriously, or scrawled with a proud flourish or simply scratched an X. They were young and breathless, old and wheezing, fat and swart and short or thin and tall. They had lost fingers, some of them, and teeth, and one an eye. They spoke patois or pidgin or English indifferently well, and from this avid rabble he marshaled his dragoons.

"I am going," he wrote George Germain, "to carry on a little war of my own, the only war permitted here, against the rebel whaleboats which absolutely swarm in the Sound. I have raised a company of boatmen from among the Lloyd's Neck people and I intend fighting them with their own weapons. Nothing but a whaleboat can catch a whaleboat. If they come on shore I shall be ready to receive them. If they put to sea my boats will have play with them."

One man came from Woburn and appeared to know his name.

"You are mistaken," said the Lieutenant Colonel. "You mistake me, fellow."

"Ben Thompson, am I right? Ruth Pierce's boy, correct?"

"For my part, I know you not."

In hailing distance now of old wife and young daughter, he weighed a visit to Concord: whether surprise or announced. He sat down to write to them but could not determine what to say or which was the wise course. The years had treated him well—so said his admirers—and he was not yet thirty now, in the prime of martial health. Elsie Cotesworth had extolled his youthful vigor and salt heat.

But it had been a decade since he first encountered Sarah Rolfe, and he was less persuaded of the beneficent effects of time on her autumnal self: he pictured his wife unaltered, then withered, then stout. This last seemed most likely the case. She was fourteen years his senior, and a shrew. Whether pink or gray, ample or pinched, he had no doubt that she was angry and thought herself abandoned—no doubt that she spoke ill of him and would do so, shrilly, to his face. The charms of domesticity had paled in his long absence; to dandle children on his knee seemed insufficient exercise. Nor could he counterfeit subservience again to that demanding widow who made of him a gentleman and helped him on his way. Young Sarah must have been so changed as to be a total stranger, a girl he would not recognize, and he had known strangers enough.

Thompson walked the streets of Huntington in private, debating with himself. He wondered how best to proceed. He was troubled, restless in his mind, grown weary of inaction and the ceaseless petty squabbles in the camp. To have tasted the high wine of combat and be thereafter reduced to the brackish ration of inertia is galling to the active man, a bitter draught indeed. As the farmer must attend his crop, the mason his mortar and weaver his cloth, so must the soldier fight.

"Young sir," a woman called to him.

He stopped.

"A word with you, young gentleman."

"What?"

"Young gentleman," she said again.

"I know your voice," he said.

"It's not my voice that matters," the wench responded saucily. She wore a scarf.

He could make out only the shape of a face, only the outline of limbs.

Indifferent, he walked on.

"How's Doctor Hay?" she called to him.

"Excuse me, who?"

"Dr. John Hay of Woburn. And Loammi Baldwin, your great friend."

Once more he stopped. Once more she retreated to shadow. "You know me?" Thompson asked.

"That spot on your left shoulder, Ben. The mole on your right arm."

He peered at her, uncertain, the while she raised her skirt. It was the gesture of a prostitute, of many he had boarded, but he recognized her legs.

"You know me now?" she asked.

"Why, Abigail!"

She dropped her skirt and returned her right hand to her scarf.

"I hunted you," he said. "I asked repeatedly. They would not tell me where you went. What brings you here?"

She laughed.

"What brought you here, I mean." He faltered. "Did you go directly? I asked in Cambridge, everywhere."

"That scar above your eye—the burn from the powder, it's healed. You wear a British uniform. By the look of it, a Colonel's."

He did not correct her. He would be one soon enough.

"A proper gentleman," she wheedled, "a man with money in his purse."

"Might we walk some way together? Can I offer you refreshment?"

"You asked what brought me here. The answer is commercial, Ben. The ring of silver, soldier."

Now he touched her on the arm. "Agreed. But take me to your quarters, for I cannot bring you to camp."

Again her manner coarsened. "But I have been there often, Colonel, and they told me their commander's name." Her laugh was mocking, practiced. "I thought it must be you."

"Only let me see your face," he pleaded. "I would know it anywhere."

She held the scarf more tightly. "Come."

He followed where she led. They walked through a low warren, in the reeking alleys of Huntington where he would not otherwise and on his own recognizance have ventured, more doubtful than the Boston docks he'd frequented when young. Now he clutched both sword and pistol but knew himself protected, rather, by the unwritten law of commerce which governs the nightly transactions of women, keeping their customers safe. They doubled back, it seemed to him, and circled and made their slow way. She had not lost, it seemed to him, that compelling grace in motion, that long-legged, straight-backed gait. We are creatures of first passion, all, and though his better judgment urged Thompson far from Abigail, his memory of early nights now clouded clear perception and he was in her thrall. He knew he must knock on her door yet again—twice lightly, and once hard.

She would not speak. She crooked her finger only, and maintained her loose-limbed pace—half-swallowed by that darkness to which her kind belongs. At length, in utter blackness, she stopped before a house. She touched her finger to his lips, then touched his tunic-buttons and signaled he should come behind; the door creaked open groaningly and gave on a hallway within. They mounted narrow steps, with neither a remnant of carpet nor rail, and now the stench grew thick and close so that Thompson held his breath. At the third turning to the left she disappeared, and he waited a moment, confused.

Then he saw a candle's glimmer and heard her say, "Young sir." She whispered it hissingly, as in the street. "Young gentleman, come here."

He entered her low room. He stooped to cross the sill, then, straightening in the dim light, he let his eyes adjust.

"Did you complete your studies?"

"How?"

"Are you a doctor?" she asked.

"A soldier, as you see me."

"But were you ever a doctor?"

"Not properly, no."

Upright, and with a practiced motion, she released her shift. As was the case a dozen years before, in Woburn where they both began, Abigail stood naked.

"It hurts here," she reminded him. "Feel this swelling. Press this breast."

The sight appalled him now. Her breasts were worn dugs, drooping, and her whole body was covered—nay overlaid, impacted, gessoed—with sores. She turned for his inspection while he stared. Her back was a map of raised blisters and welts, her stomach a red lacerated griddle, and now she dropped her scarf and raised her pullulating lips to him and within her toothless mouth obscenely flicked her tongue.

There was a washstand, a basin, a bed. There was no window and no circulating air. "Do you remember, Benjamin?" she asked. "Do I delight you still?"

"I remember," Thompson managed.

"Everything?"

"Everything," he said.

"Then kiss my toes," she commanded. "Kneel down and begin with my feet."

At the foot of the bed there was also one chair. He sat. "You must excuse me."

"Why?" she asked.

He could not speak.

Now Abigail showed impatience. "I'm a busy woman, Colonel. It was you who brought me here. Was it for conversation, then? All right, sir, let's converse."

He could not manage it. She asked after the Hays, their children, the household in Woburn and why and when he had left. She loomed in front of him, her profession proclaimed in the tilt of her hip, her shamelessness his shame. She was taunting him, he knew, compelling him to witness how her own fortune plummeted while his was on the rise. She had lured him to this wretched place to tax him with betrayal, and she toyed with him and punished him as if it were for punishment he'd come. She bore him no good will but kissed the rancid air instead, her racked familiar frame revealing the last stages of disease. She told him they had had a son, but that the boy was monstrous and had been dead at birth and left within a pickling jar for students to describe. Then she leeringly invited him to try his luck again.

"Is that why you left us?" he managed to ask.

"Why?"

"Because you were with child?"

She cupped her breast. Black pustules ringed the nipple that he had adoringly sucked. "I tired of them all," she said. "You innocent, you never guessed."

He looked at her. She shivered. "Cover yourself," Thompson said.

And as though with this assertion he had regained a customer's authority, Abigail complied. Coughing, she gathered a sheet and draped it from those shoulders that to him once seemed a chill perfection, albeit warm, and that once appeared marmoreal, now chalk.

But then she weaved such a story of seduction and ill-usage, of Dr. Hay's brutality and Loammi Baldwin's custom, of how they sold her daily and would fornicate together or would pay to watch her entertain the village, of how corruption bloomed where all appeared most pure, and the women and the children too were of the devils' party—such a skein of accusation woven with bright malice, so cunningly embroidered a history of whoring that he could not be certain what was invention, what truth. Their dead son abandoned in Woburn, for instance: was he actual or imagined, a piercing shared sorrow or jibe? Abigail was lunatic; he saw it in her eye. Yet had that glitter come from what she saw unblinkingly, what she endured and asked him now to see? Or was it but the progress of a fever, the febrile dream of circumstance improved?

He could not tell. He stayed with her until she fell asleep and then left money at her side, emptying both pockets. She stirred but did not wake. To the root of his being, he quailed; those things he had taken for granted were no longer his to take. He would not know— although he tormented himself asking it, for years uncertain, decades torn, along the narrow stairwell and down the winding stair, through streets still unfamiliar and the warren of a city insubstantial now as air, wandering all night unguarded, and wondering returned to camp—if Abigail had lied to him or rather to herself. They did not meet again.

When news came to the camp next day that Abby their camp-slattern had at last succumbed to pox, had died in her hot sleep and been limed already and dispatched to Potter's Field—yet the slut was hoarding silver, there was silver by her bed—Lieutenant Colonel Thompson was, to outward appearance, unmoved. To casual or close scrutiny he looked unconcerned, for he was fashioning a model ship and bent back to his work.

Everyone tells me that I cannot go on except I drink wine. I drink water notwithstanding (mixed with a little brandy or rum) and take as much exercise both of body and of mind as would kill a dozen of the lazy wine-bibbers that preach to me; and often laugh at them while they are quivering and shaking with ague.

Now he embraced annihilation and made of it a mistress. He lay in his tent like a despot of old and had his harsh justice dispensed. His negroes trembled and his soldiery obeyed. The town of Huntington grew hateful, and all of its inhabitants. His first principle was rigor, his second ruthlessness. He made them pay and pay.

He had winter barracks built, for which he needed wood. The First Presbyterian Church stood on two acres of cleared land, and here he planned his campground, burning apple trees for firewood and all the chestnut rails. He collected three-thousand-five-hundred rails, the pride of the Huntington farms. Penned livestock therefore wandered loose, and he had these sheep and cattle butchered for the troops. If a whaleboat failed to raise his flag, he had the whaleboat sunk. The wooden chapel served his purpose also, and he tore it down. When a pious sergeant faltered he ordered thirty lashes; when a corporal refused to raze this house of local worship—claiming the scruple of conscience—he had the corporal shot.

Next he broke up the burial ground. He ordered its destruction and supervised the transfer of the jumbled bones. He had one-hundred tombstones used for fireplaces and for baking ovens; they served as tables too. The bread was baked on tombstones and the populace ate rolls and loaves festooned with their relatives' names;

their friends and dear departed family inscribed the lower crust. He kept one tombstone at the entrance to his tent, in order that his heels stay clean and he might step on marble in the mud.

In time and times to come the citizens of Huntington would call Thompson the red devil, warning their children to behave or else the traitor would discover them; in hushed tones in the humming dark they spoke of his demonic compact—the glee he took in desecration and thick tail at his britches' rear, the horns beneath his curling hair, the way he warmed his hands before the hot mouth of the fireplace and his sepulchral ovens. He taught them till he sailed for home the truth of homelessness. In memory of his own pain he rendered heart-break general and showed them soldier's justice, the ravening visage of rage.

RUMFORD, HIS BOOK

Part Two

Our story, reader, concerns itself with greatness, the very pith and marrow of a life. All life when rightly seen deserves close scrutiny, but this man's history—it may be rightly argued—is both notable and strange. Until the time to which we turn, the career of young Ben Thompson—that parvenu, that *arriviste,* that adventurer for whom the English tongue knows no description so sufficient as the French—proceeded up the ladder rung by rung. Yet now he dared a leap. The social climber jumped.

> Per Fess Argent and Sable, a Fess embattled, counter-embattled, counter-changed between two Falcons, in chief of the second beked, membered and belled Or, and a Horse passant in base of the first. And for a Crest on a Wreath of the Colours, A Mural Crown Or, thereon a Mullet of six points Azure, and between the Battlements four Pine Buds Vert.

This improved upon the shield he had designed when young; this was conferred by the King. For divers acts of valor, Colonel Thompson was rewarded; for his unstinting labor he was honored by the Crown. Nobility is a condition of the mind, and it did not therefore matter that his particulars and representations were less than entirely true. They would come true soon enough.

In Woburn Ben had drawn his own imagined crest, but now the Garter King of Arms had that ennobling task. The Grant of Arms described his status and attainment. He was Sir Benjamin Thompson, of "St. James's, Westminster, Knight, Colonel of the King's American

Regiment of Light Dragoons, and Fellow of the Royal Society of London, late Under-Secretary of State of the Province of Georgia, and Colonel of a Regiment of Militia in the Province of New Hampshire."

Commensurate with this new state, and in order to render it seemly, he improved upon his old. In science one must be precise and, embracing the particular, avoid the inexact; in matters of style, however, selective precision is best. So he borrowed an island called Thompson and discovered it to have been from the very beginning ancestral. The family of David Thompson owned an island proximate to Boston, at the harbor's mouth; they had done so for one hundred years. That Benjamin and David Thompson shared no lineage seemed—from the vantage of the crossed Atlantic, a wide ocean away—immaterial. The varnish on the canvas lends its own highlighting luster to the image there contained.

Do we not dream ourselves princes? does not the ugly duckling translate itself to swan? We come crying squint-eyed to this world and must perforce imagine what it is we left behind; the mists of ancestry are hard to penetrate and harder still to dispel.

So Benjamin offered his claim. As "Son of Benjamin Thompson late of the Province of Massachusetts Bay, in New England, gent., deceased," he maintained "that an Island which belonged to his Ancestors, at the Entrance of Boston Harbour...still bears his Name; that his Ancestors have ever lived in reputable Situations in that Country where he was born, and have hitherto used the Arms of the antient and respectable Family of Thompson of the County of York, from a constant Tradition that they derived their Descent from that Source."

What is ancient once was young: the great oak grows out of an acorn, the thick limb from a twig. Therefore, and with no fear of contradiction, he warranted the past. Long-vanished members of the respectable family of Thompson in the County of York, England, made him welcome in the lists. Into their august company he recruited himself as cadet, and they opened their parchment-clad arms.

Such a tradition depends on its claimant, and he maintained it constantly. The barn at Woburn acquired the stature of stables, the home of his grandfather Thompson became a manor house. So may leaf and branch commingle, derived from the one root. His mother's Osnabrig apron was reported by him finer cloth than that of English ladies; his father, dead untimely, was elevated to the post of mayor of the town.

There were those who did not look upon his great good fortune as their own, and those who failed in courtesy but succeeded in complaint. They greeted him with honey-tongues that soon enough spilled bile.

"Welcome back, Sir Benjamin."

"I thank you."

"Well done, Sir Benjamin."

"I thank you kindly, friends."

"Congratulations on your military appointment. Your promotion and your pension as full Colonel."

Thompson bowed

"The other loyalists, it seems, have not proved so successful. They seek advancement painfully. Penuriously, I am told."

"The settlement goes case by case."

His hosts were unimpressed. *Sir* Benjamin, they called him, with ironic condescension. Their titles were inherited, not earned.

"We were discussing your particular case, Thompson, were we not?"

"We were."

"Your rapid and most notable success."

Again he bowed.

"Yet it was a provincial appointment, correct?"

"Correct."

"As *full* Colonel? However did you manage it?"

"Manage?"

"I mean, *until* a Colonel's pay assisted you to scale so arduous a ladder. And to such dizzying heights."

Now he straightened. These two were fools; fools are rampant everywhere, and in London fops are legion. These chittering magpies, these apes.

"Well, never mind," said one of them. "A provincial appointment suffices. Do not let it trouble you."

"I do not. Not in the slightest."

"You will be a balloonist, soon. In the court of some aerial Queen."

"*Honi soit qui mal y pense.*"

"The Order of the Garter," one of them translated. "In case your French ain't up to it."

"Gutter." They laughed.

"I am His Majesty's servant," said Ben. Turning, he gave his back to all such titled rabble.

150

"Delightful. Yes, I'm sure you are. 'In the court of some aerial Queen.' That's who will promote you next. Great Catherine . . ."

"You would dispatch me?" Thompson asked. He turned to face them both once more and pulled his glove.

"No need, sir. Have a drink."

Sir Benjamin Thompson, Knight, was thankful for his newfound honor. Yet as so often on this earth, the prize, once attained, diminished; it had looked brighter while beyond his reach than now within his grasp. He did consider, briefly, a trip to rich wild Russia and its salacious Empress and whether he might manage fresh favorable notice from Catherine the Great. It was rumored that the Empress dallied daily with her lovers, if not in a balloon, then on table and trapeze. He had ascended so successfully from commoner to knight that he entertained the prospect of promotion once again; the ladder of advancement contains no topmost rung.

Yet his mother and his wife and daughter did not know. Perchance, he told himself, they would have disapproved; they might not esteem his knighthood as they should. Equality—that flattering illusion of the lowly and the second-rate—was America's rallying cry.

Nor did his second father receive Thompson's proper gratitude or raise the naked penitent from dust. He could have gone down on his knees and begged forgiveness and been welcomed and absolved. He owed this title—as so much else, as everything—to the kindness of Lord George Germain, yet he and Viscount Sackville would no more play the prodigal or kill the fatted calf.

He mourned the loss. From all reports Germain lay languishing, near death. New-succored by religion, the Viscount grew reclusive and renounced all company, retiring to Knole. In pain in that great country house he ceaselessly prayed for surcease. It was as though the title conferred were his last mark of favor for Thompson; Ben's letters went unanswered and, quite possibly, unread. He drove to Stoneland Lodge but found its gardens oppressive, its carriage house abandoned and its steward grave. There were rabbits on the lawn. London was an earnest town without that gaiety Lord George engendered, its pleasures stale and flat; all celebration seemed mere mockery and laughter insincere.

He tarried this way for some months, engaging in his wonted round without his vigorous and customary zeal. Lady Elizabeth and the two daughters were roses wholly blown; though they invited him to dinner, he begged to be excused. He visited the court, of course, but King George disdained to notice him when not by Sackville's side. The English look with scorn on all those not born English, and they remain suspicious of honor earned abroad. The loneliness of cities is keener-edged than country isolation, and harder to endure.

He made friends with Sir Charles Blagden and then with Mary Palmerston, who consoled him charmingly—teasing him from his dark humor and his solemn ways. They played at four-hand piano and he tinkered with the violin while she played the flute. He resumed his sexual exercise but took little pleasure in it; often as not, of an evening, they talked. He turned thirty and took stock.

Might a man serve two masters or be of two minds? He asked himself again what merited allegiance in an era so provisional, a time of such sea-shifted tides. Sir Benjamin Thompson, Knight, knew himself much envied now, much suspected and despised. The constant man—so he remembered saying to Loammi Baldwin—must learn to serve inconstancy, to marry mutability or else be swept aside.

His family were women, and a continent away. He wept in a whore's sleeping presence, then wiped his boots on tombs. Upon the stage of the great world he had played several parts by now, had worn the uniforms of farmer, doctor, teacher, spy, then soldier, courtier, scientist, and he not unreasonably feared his face might seem—because mutable—inconstant. He had his portrait done.

Lady Palmerston said her friend Tom Gainsborough would be the man to do it, less expensive than Joshua Reynolds and more amusing to know. She arranged a meeting with the two men at her home. At the appointed hour Thompson came; the painter had arrived beforehand and stood by the bay window: feet planted widely, hands clasped.

Mary made the introductions. "All society admires you," she said. "You are praised by *le tout Londres*." She fluttered her eyelids and fan. "I am honored and delighted to have you in my home." She paid this compliment to neither man but to the middle distance so that both were pleased.

Both bowed. Gainsborough wore black. Thompson observed him narrowly but nonetheless could not retain an image of the artist's features; in later years he tried, tried often, and as often failed. Gainsborough was older; it was hard to say how old. He thought the painter short, then of an average stature, then more than commonly tall. It was as though the face—as Thompson feared would be the case with his own visage otherwise, and thus had commissioned this portrait—were changeable, uncertain. A mirror held to mirrors reflects the witness-eye.

At times he seemed plump, at times lean. The artist's nose looked sharp, then flat; his cheeks were red, then white. His pupils were of a color indescribable by Thompson, and everything about him was refractive, mere transmission, a recording apparatus as inconstant as the light.

"He does everyone," said Mary. "He did me."

"But I did not match your splendor. No one could."

"You flatter me," said Mary.

"On the contrary, my dear. I did not do you justice."

"But that atrocious shawl."

"We shall improve it, I promise."

"You should see the shawl, Ben. Purple, and with the most disgusting fringe. Not a color one would wear."

The painter was in fact society's darling that season, and had come down from Bath. Having just arrived, and weary, he begged to be excused.

Mary Palmerston refused. She enjoyed a complacent good humor and she told him, "Tom, what nonsense. Make the time."

"For you, my dear . . ."

"For Viscount Sackville," Thompson said. "I would send it to him."

"Down to Knole?" inquired Lady Palmerston.

"Indeed. I would send it there by way of a keepsake. As remembrance."

"Come see me Tuesday fortnight," said the artist. "Bring your cloak."

So he sat for Thomas Gainsborough in Schomberg House, Pall Mall. A springer spaniel welcomed him, then settled back to sleep. There were landscape studies on the wall, hayricks and cottages and many faces of women. Paint, paper, canvas and charcoal lay piled in easy reach. Coal burned in the brazier fitfully; a dressmaker's dummy loomed beside a magic lantern on the desk.

Thompson wore his white cravat, his gold-trimmed coat, and held his black hat balanced in the crook of his left elbow. His wig was gray and thick on top, brushed straight back from his forehead, then curling at his ears.

It was not a full-length portrait. The canvas was rectangular, and within that rectangle the painter set an oval. Within this framed interior roundel Thompson's face and chest emerged—so that the effect was of a cameo, the head its own medallion. The background wall was russet, the oval darker brown. They both had been painted lightly, in advance, and there was no attempt at furniture or landscape, no secondary figure in the scene. Thomas Gainsborough provided him with neither hands nor lap nor legs. It was faster that way, cheaper too. He drew neither horse nor hunting dogs nor cannon nor flowering tree.

At the two sides of the canvas, however, in addition to the lower edge, the oval was truncate. This suggested space beyond. It was as though the King's Dragoon might burst into the world outside the frame's perimeter—a trick of composition, Thompson saw. Had the canvas been three inches larger, the secondary form of the medallion which contained him would itself have been contained. Instead—and therefore life-like—it escaped confinement. Perspective rendered circular the slope of his shoulders, the arc of the lapel and corner of his hat. His buttons too were circles, and they echoed the motif.

The perpendicular bisector of the canvas was a plumb-line dropping from his nose to mouth to chin. He studied his own visage as though through the painter's eyes. They were narrow and expressionless; they watched. No one could have been more affable than Gainsborough beforehand; his manners were assured and he had theatrical friends. In Lady Palmerston's drawing room he had been conviviality itself. He would alter, he assured her, the offending shawl. He was lively and good-humored, yet had quarreled latterly with the Royal Academy of Painting and in consequence withdrew his membership. By God, he said to Mary, the fools wanted to hang portraits everywhere except at eye-level, *under*neath a landscape and a church and sheep in sunset, over trees, paying no attention to the sight lines or his urgent protestations; he'd be damned if he'd set foot in those dull halls again. By God, he said, they'll not exhibit anything *I* do.

So saying, he had laughed and clapped his hands. He was full of gossip, compliment and chatter; he accepted tea and cakes with seeming-relish, happily, and moved among the notables with insouciant ease.

But in his high white room indulgence fell away. The painter sat and stared. He made no attempt at conversation and would not answer questions if addressed. He neither ate nor drank and offered no refreshment but expected from his subject a soldier's perfect immobility. He himself seemed half-asleep; he nodded his head, moved his lips without speaking, and narrowed then widened his eyes. Thomas Gainsborough examined Thompson in a way that argued neither interest nor disdain, approval nor suspicion: a set of shapes, an arrangement of color, unmediated sight.

What he saw—and Germain if he chose to would see on the wall, and Thompson ordered copied later for his daughter and for sundry friends—was a man no longer young. The nose and chin were strong. The forehead high and white, the lines about the mouth, the hint of hardships weathered in the texture of the skin: all these the painter caught. As is the case for those who labor in the craft of portraiture, he sought to fashion of impermanence its opposite: a permanence, a dissolution stayed. The gaze was clear, unwinking yet abstracted; a half-smile—as of some private joke, some inner rumination—played about the lips.

The King's Dragoon displayed his costume well. He bore himself erect. He was resting, not irresolute; he waited for the impulse and then for permission to move. He was fixed in the passenger moment and would travel on.

For there were colonies to visit, wars to fight, and such an appetite aroused is hard to sate. He considered the West Indies, Nova Scotia, India. England was no country for a loyalist to make his way; without Germain to anchor him, he felt unmoored, adrift. He remembered those two intricately fashioned globes—one terrestrial, one celestial— provided for John Wentworth by James Ferguson. Long years before, in the province of New Hampshire, Ben Thompson had delighted in the problems thereby posed: how often he landed in water, how various the contours of the land! He had traversed the ocean thrice but had not yet crossed the channel or seen the fabled capitals and northern parts of Europe. Dreaming of Flanders, Strasbourg, Ulm and Munich and Vienna and Berlin, he undertook a tour. He promised Mary Palmerston that he would write her often, and would miss her very much, and he extracted in exchange the promise of long letters on the gossip of the day.

He took three horses with him from Dover to Calais. These were Tancred, Fawn, and Lambkin, and they suffered mightily in the channel crossing. So did their owner, Sir Benjamin Thompson, who felt again the whelming inward turmoil and the convulsive revulsion of his first Atlantic voyage. He relieved himself over the rail. Edward Gibbon the historian stood nearby at the railing, though he sniffed the salt sea air with gusto and did not appear uncertain either in spirits or stomach; he engaged the silent Thompson in animated discourse as to matters of philosophy and history and the advantages of travel as an aid to education and the consequential broadening of vistas and the virtue of a comprehensive understanding of the continent, its past predictive of the future soon to come—both for amusement and improvement such a tour as they embarked upon was all the present rage. Is not adventure, he inquired, the advent of circumstance necessarily unknown, yet in retrospect not prospect foreordained?

Thompson rinsed his mouth. He shut his eyes, then opened them. He wiped his chin. The historian continued. Advantageous indeed for the adventurer, with precisely that reward afforded by perspective—here Gibbon pointed at the white mist-shrouded cliffs receding behind them—precisely the prospect of event and eventuality considered, of vision and, if one may be permitted so predictable a doubling, revision, is the pleasure of travel untrammeled, the purpose of secular pilgrimage since time long out of mind. Why else would we embark on journeys protracted or brief, assured or uncertain of purpose, philosophical in nature or scientific in intention (uprooting our root system, as it were, from friendly and familiar soil), consigned to new acquaintanceship and companions such as—here he paused and, beaming, bowed—that man who has the honor of addressing these particulars to you, Colonel, though I do so to your only partial and wavering attention, it must be admitted, and your at best imperfect enjoyment of the topic now addressed. He who feels himself so buffeted by circumstance is not the keenest judge of circumstantiality, Edward Gibbon felt constrained to add, but by your reputation, sir, as Natural Philosopher you are or should be nonetheless sufficient to the day.

The day was wet. The spray was cold. Bending his head once again to the rail, Thompson suppressed a groan. The historian bade him farewell and favored the next passenger with his generous attention. Thompson rubbed his eyes. On the screen of his shut eyelids the cliffs of Dover danced. When he reached Calais he lay abed till horses and rider recovered, and then he traveled to Strasbourg where his good humor returned.

On market mornings, in the clear October light, there seemed to him no city more convivial than Strasbourg, no commercial center as inviting. Walking the cobbled streets, Ben fingered lace and purchased it for Mary Palmerston; incomparable chocolate and truffels and pâté were his to sample, strolling, and compare. The hurly-burly charmed him, and the jumbled fare. These alleys were crowded with enterprise: hats and pistols and ribbons and brocade and chickens and chronometers and knives and fish and every kind of flower and woven basket and pitchfork and spade and spice and bauble fairly leapt at him from tables or the vendors' eager hands. There were cartloads of pigs, honking geese. Sheep bleated at him, and the caged birds sang. Goats capered in their halters; calves waited, docile, ruminant, and dogs scrambled on the paving for tossed offal, cats for cream.

Thompson walked past beggars, soldiers lounging on patrol, and musicians and jongleurs. In corners they jostled and danced. Ladies of an easy virtue haggled for quick purchase with farmers come to market who sold what they arrived to sell and now prepared to buy. The more expensive courtesans did not patrol the square but positioned themselves in lit windows, displaying their lewd wares. These he sampled like the cheese. His appetite returning, he would purchase bread and coffee and fruit at a stall or café, then climb the stairs and bargain with the ripe blonde who had summoned him, all lace and rouge and high-pitched happy cries. Or there were darker women, Romany and Moorish, with glass gems at their bodices and perfume on their thighs. In remembrance of Lord George Germain he also purchased boys.

With rain the city cleansed itself, the gutters running freely, the cobbles turning brown. Then too Thompson wandered, purposively aimless, hearing church-bells and the muffled clatter of laden cart and carriage, the rumble of prayer and trade. He exercised his horses daily—Fawn, his favorite. He rode past steaming kitchens, fountains, tinkers, tanners at their work, as well as scribes and carpenters. Men in counting-house and grog-shop hailed him where he wandered, and children ran alongside till they tired or lost interest. Monks told their beads and mendicants besieged him as he passed.

His French improved. He studied German also, in preparation for his visit to Vienna. He liked the geese of Strasbourg and the cackling, gabbling washerwomen, and the languorous mornings abed with his whore, and the coffee and strong port. He knew no one in the city, and nobody who knew him could say with daily certainty where he passed the night. He enjoyed the feel of foreignness, of paying for his pleasures in a straight commercial way. He liked the northern light.

Prince Maximilian of Deux Ponts—Zweibrücken when in Germany —reviewed the garrison at Strasbourg; Colonel Thompson donned his uniform and rode forth to see. As when a decade previous he had been noticed by Governor Wentworth, in his Hussar Cloak at Portsmouth, so now again the King's Dragoon was singled out, resplendent in his scarlet coat and sitting in the sun on his imposing horse. Field-Marshal in the service of France, young Maximilian commanded his troops on parade. He had the English soldier brought forward to his side.

"Your name?"

"Is Benjamin Thompson, your Highness."

"Your rank?"

"I served as Colonel of the King's American Regiment of Light Dragoons."

"Ha! So you come from America!"

"I fought there, yes, your Highness."

"Brave man to wear that uniform in Strasbourg." Maximilian pointed smilingly to those who formed his entourage. "They fought there too. Against you."

Thompson asked for permission, received it, and replaced his hat.

"These my officers," declared the prince, "belong to the Royal Regiment of Deux Ponts. They acted in America under the orders of Count Rochambeau."

"Gentlemen," said Thompson. "You were honorable adversaries." He hazarded his French. "Happily the war is over. *Heureusement que la guerre est finie.*"

Prince Maximilian laughed. "*Das zweifl'ich,*" he said. "I doubt it. That particular war is over, perhaps, but general war has a future, my friend. Do you speak German also?"

"*Ein bischen,*" Thompson said. "A little, and with difficulty. *Péniblement.* I have engaged a tutor, however, since I plan to visit great Vienna, and then perhaps Bohemia, Berlin."

"Come drink with us this evening." The prince was suavely gracious, clean-shaven and keen-eyed. He swept his arm again at the surrounding officers. "We will discuss our battles and tell lies."

All that night and the next afternoon they did indeed drink, roistering. In Maximilian he met an adventurer of exalted rank, and though their standing in the world was of course unequal he recognized a kindred spirit and admired his new host. The prince showed impeccable bearing yet a way with his inferiors that put them at their ease. His prodigious use of tankards and liberal distribution of silver might have turned a glum campaigner gay and brought the flush of reckless youth to grim and wizened cheeks. But since these soldiers all were young and needed no encouragement, the prince stood— swayed, it must be admitted, and from time to time he tottered—in a circle of enthusiasts who sang and danced and scored the table with their whetted knives.

Ben enjoyed the officers of the Royal Regiment of Deux Ponts, Maximilian's entourage, also. They swapped stories and brave deeds. They boasted of heroics and invented fierce encounters where they might—beneath the smoke of battle, in the din and carnage—earlier have met. They studied and drew maps. They were sure they had seen Thompson astride his prancing stallion three months before he had in fact first disembarked at Charleston; he did not correct them or prove over-scrupulous as to his actual participation in campaigns won and lost.

It is in the nature of the soldier and the lover to exaggerate attainment, to swear great oaths in darkness that will not survive the light. They had fought each other, surely, in ditch and hill and town. They remembered in persuasive detail what they had not done, and by way of celebration commandeered the serving girl and caressed her unbound bosom and traced upon her buttocks the line of the cavalry charge.

By the third night these soldiers were old friends. Prince Maximilian insisted that his close and valued comrade Sir Benjamin

Thompson, Knight, must visit his dear uncle Karl Theodor in Munich. His uncle the Elector Palatine ruled all Bavaria; surely he could find a place for Thompson and provide some occupation to enliven the traveler's stay! Maximilian wrote letters commending his boon companion, the English American Colonel who planned to see the world.

First, however, he went to Vienna. He met Jan Ingen-Housz and discussed alternatives to gunpowder; he met Sir Robert Keith, the British Ambassador there. He admired the great palaces and gardens, the ladies at the opera and dance. He studied the deportment of the erect pale horsemen and their liveried teams trotting past. That curricle he had so prized in Concord was an oxcart merely by comparison with the meanest carriage in the Ring; Strasbourg, too, appeared provincial when measured by the grandeur of Vienna, the scale of the wide boulevards and height of the tree-lined allées. Proud nobles in lavish regalia frequented the court, and to begin with Thompson thought their servants to be notables, for page and footman dressed as grandly as the first citizens of Boston or even London town.

All things are relative. He had come from farm to glittering mansion and would continue on. He visited Trieste. He next paid a visit to Munich and was received by Maximilian's uncle with every mark of royal favor. Karl Theodor was, like his nephew, gracious; he perused the prince's letters and laughed and called him "Scamp."

Soon Benjamin Thompson was offered the position of Colonel in the Elector's army, as an aide-de-camp where unofficially he was to tutor Count von Bretzenheim, the Elector's unofficial son. He promised Robert Keith that he would be of service to His Majesty in England though he offer seeming-service to Karl Theodor. "I made a bold stroke and it has succeeded," he wrote.

The ambassador concurred. By this means (it being between them understood they would remain in privy contact) Thompson was released from his allegiance to King George's Royal Dragoons and formally enlisted to serve Germany instead.

Now in truth he had arrived. He studied this new nation with attention—his third and welcome land. Having solidified his standing in the court, he surveyed the squalid circumstance and the lamentable condition of the Emperor's soldiery. He considered what they ate and drank and how they drilled and were rewarded and where these troops were billeted and what they wore. Experiment intrigued him, and he settled down to work. He examined silkworms closely and the likelihood of industry engendered by spun silk, and in the course of these investigations he employed an instrument maker of skill and precision, Charles Artaria. Together the two men built an apparatus for collecting and then measuring the quantity of gas released by silk; they built thermometers to measure the propagation of heat in various substances, and Thompson availed himself of the vacuum pump at Mannheim. He reported to Karl Theodor on all these matters faithfully, to Ambassador Keith less and less.

Not each of us, however, has the gift of rapid progress or may make our way so quickly in the world. Count Bretzenheim proved slow. The child spent hours over problems—arithmetic of the simplest variety that Ben had once provided for his schoolboys back in Bradford—big eared, split-lipped, drooling in the goblet he carried with him always, as if that gold-tooled chalice were collecting Christ's own tears.

"*Lacrimae rerum,*" he mouthed—and, this completing the extent of his Latin—"*Ibi sunt.*"

The young Count limped; he walked with a queer lurching gait, and often he stumbled and fell. He was goatish in his appetite for cherries, and he ate them voraciously; all other fare appalled him, and he turned from it and wept. He trailed his broad sword in the dust, neither attempting to lift nor to brandish it, then stared with rapt inattention as the tennis ball bounced past. After ten months of such tutelage, the Count was removed from the Colonel and prepared for a career not in the army but church.

For his efforts on Count Bretzenheim's behalf, nonetheless, in July of 1785, and having been appointed Chamberlain to His Most Serene Electoral Highness, Sir Benjamin Thompson further received—at The Elector's request, and conferred by Stanislaus II, King of Poland—the Royal Order of St. Stanislaus. This pleased him mightily. He wore the medal everywhere, and the ribbons, and the chain. His lodgings were large and lavishly appointed, befitting his new rank. He shared his residence with the Russian Ambassador; they met in the courtyard, nodding, bowing, exchanging pleasantries about the weather and the quality of horses and the health of their respective monarchs, George III and Catherine the Great.

He acquired a retinue of servants—a family called Aichner principal among them—and of blooded English horses; he acquired mistresses in the nobility and married to men of high station. The

Countess Baumgarten, for instance, was a lady he presumed to share not merely with Count Baumgarten but with the Elector himself. They made a night-time ministry—conferring in private, or with Karl Theodor's confessor and the other favored Chamberlains—on matters of court consequence and pressing arrangements of state. He sent one final letter to Lord George Germain:

> I can say with truth that I hardly know what there is left for me to wish for. Rank, Titles, Decorations, Litterary distinctions, with some degree of litterary, and some small degree of military fame I have acquired, (through your availing Protection), and the road is open to me for the rest. No man supports a better moral Character than I do, and no man is better satisfied with himself. Look back for a moment my dearest friend upon the work of your hands. *Je suis de votre ouvrage.* Does it not afford you a very sensible pleasure to find that your Child has answered your Expectations?

Germain could make no answer, however, for he at last lay dead. The work of his hands traveled on.

SALLY

What do you need to know of me, reader, and why I write this book? Which are, as Thompson might have asked, the relevant particulars; how much must I explain? Since he's gone now forever and ever from the New England I call home, perhaps we should start here. By providing, as it were, my local *bona fides*. I attended Radcliffe College, which was as close as a woman could come to matriculation at Harvard in the late 1950s, and a good deal more than young Ben Thompson managed two hundred years before. He attended lectures for an afternoon or three, I took the full four years. Our author and your 'umble servant lost her prized virginity—though the misplacement was intentional—in Winthrop House, on the third floor, in what I think was entry K and during parietal hours. The word means nothing now, but then "parietal" meant opportunity, a time to be alone together behind the bedroom door.

Who I was alone with, a boy called Billy Proctor, had pimples all over his back. We met in Art History class, Class, and by the sixteenth century were cuddling in the sixteenth row while the professor used his lighted pointer to illuminate the finer points of Brunelleschi's stairwell or Mantegna's Christ. By the time he spoke of Rubens's nudes and traced Titian's fleshly drapery or Gainsborough's American we two were playing pat-a-cake in the instructive dark. It was an education, and the Astronomer John Winthrop whose lectures roused Baldwin and Thompson could not have had more excitable an audience than we were in Cambridge that spring.

I loved the place, the taste of hot corned-beef on rye, the look of the Commons in snow. I can conjure with no trouble the musty book-thick smell of stacks in Widener Library, the sound of traffic on Linnaean Street. I loved the Square, the lights of the Agassiz Theatre at night, the banks of the Charles River, the First Congregational Church Cemetery, its ancient rain-slick stones, its honored dead, the coffee cooling in Hayes-Bick while we smoked our cigarettes. I gave the habit up, of course—smoking, not coffee—once they proved beyond doubt how lethal it was, but now when I remember college I see an ashtray, a matchbook, a smoldering cigarette tip.

We had long, earnest arguments about society and politics, nature versus nurture and free will versus determinism. In secret I wrote poetry, those ballads and sonnets and villanelles on which we cut our eyeteeth then; the vocalic distinction of promise and premise—its single, simple variable—seemed to me profound. I studied French and German History and Literature and, under supervision, read Max Weber and Albert Camus. On my own thereafter I discovered— and was sure I'd done so on my own—Simone Weil and Simone de Beauvoir.

169

My tutor was a nervous man who knew that he'd not receive tenure; in April of our senior year, according to the story, he shot himself by accident while cleaning his pistol in Maine. Somehow when we learned of this it seemed an admission of weakness, a gesture in poor taste. Astride a bicycle, with a green book-bag stuffed in its basket, I felt as though I'd learned the password to some secret kingdom— or, if not secret, privileged—where the chosen few could meet and wrangle with the chosen few.

My thesis was a comparison of two poems on the same subject: Rainer Maria Rilke's *Geburt der Venus* and José Maria de Hérédia's *La Naissance d'Aphrodité*. How's that for pretension, gentle reader?—I'd fallen under Rilke's spell and thought his *Letters to a Young Poet* were written directly to me. All that business about the lighthouse, the maiden and the castle wall—those breathy self-dramatizations and paeans to love as "bordering, protective solitude"—all that romantic posturing rang true. The other poem, on the birth of Venus on the Half-Shell, was written by a justifiably obscure French Parnassien poet, Hérédia, who had been raised in Cuba and wasn't even French. But I analyzed the texts, translated them, and labored over what I called, portentously enough, "Birth and Death of an Object." Is it any wonder that I found myself one raw March afternoon in Winthrop House, unbuttoning Proctor's white shirt?

He himself was a student of Physics. He'd been enrolled in a seminar on "The History of Science" and I remember his high-toned disquisitions on Copernicus and Kepler and Tyco Brahe and the rest; I remember also his roommate's sniggering compliance, the sudden appointment he had—or so Billy reminded him—in Boston, the abrupt solemnity with which we pulled down the shade. My lover's future and my own were, to use his language, asymptotic. That's as much as I learned about solid geometry, ever; asymptotes are parallels that cannot converge in the Euclidean plane but may in space intersect. Not so for our young scholars, Class; though we met in our little infinity the parallel lines we inscribed on his bed were slated to diverge. He went to Brookhaven, I think, and later into business; a class note for our 25th Anniversary Report said he had had two children, grown, and one grown-old divorce.

But it was Billy Proctor who first pronounced "Count Rumford" in my presence, and that's why he enters this narrative—taking two sorts of innocence away from the untutored girl I'd been. I left him with a bloody sheet to send to Laundry Service and he left me to finish up a paper on "phlogiston" that was three days overdue. "What's 'phlogiston' anyhow?" I can remember asking, and he said it was a bad idea but one that served its purpose for a while. He couldn't explain it—he zipped up his pants—but had to get over to Widener and finish the damn thing. "Do you mean me?" I asked him, and he said, "What are you talking about?" and I said, "When you said it was a bad idea." "It will be better the next time," he said. "It always is, the second time." Then he pulled on his loden coat and held out mine, for me. I shrugged myself into its arms, attempting not to cry.

We do tend to take these things personally, don't we; we remember them quite clearly though it's very long ago. I knew about the Parnassiens and love as a "bordering, protective solitude" but didn't know why Billy talked about "phlogiston" as an idea whose time had passed. All that stuff he was trying to tell me about the nature of transmitted warmth and boring the Emperor's cannon in Munich and how heat could not be substantive—his whole mumbled explanation (to a girl who wanted nothing more than that he'd say "You're wonderful, see you tomorrow?") seemed, if not an evasion exactly, a form of veiled reproach. And it took more than forty years for me to come to understand how he had been a virgin too, (cf. young Ebenezer, of the 6th Company, p. 76) and desperate to cultivate an attitude, ("It always is, the second time.") and needed some premeditated something cool to say.

I borrowed his scarf, I remember, and remember bleeding badly and hating Count Rumford and the Rumford Professor at Harvard who had assigned the text. Parietals were over; it was time to pedal home.

When next we meet our narrator, it's 1969. I'm older, Class, and wiser now and living in the hills. Those were the years, remember, of what we called the "counter-culture," and yours truly entered same with something of a vengeance; I'm standing at the kitchen sink of a farmhouse in upstate New York. It has four chimneys, it's built out of brick, and me and my companion are heating it with wood. I'm thirty-one years old. I do the cooking and she does the cleaning and neither of us does it well; my soups are indistinguishable, one from the other, my loaves of bread rarely rise. The woman that I live with, Adriana, has an abiding respect for the natural world and wouldn't dream of dusting it. We've been together nine months.

I love the long white curve of her throat, the thick blonde hair she wears in braids, the comfort we provide each other in the double bed. We heap the mattress high with quilts bought in a local Antique Shop called "Hen 'n Chick," and the brass headboard could profit from polishing, and the box spring's a disaster, but neither of us care. There are baskets of rank-smelling wool. Adriana is a weaver who takes her inspiration from the spider webs that—when the sun slants through the room—display themselves intricately along the bookshelves and the curtain rods, elaborately linking wall to wall. I'm shivering; it's cold. Beyond the kitchen window, on the poor pasture that belongs to our poor neighbor, there are Holstein cows.

What cash we require for day-to-day living I earn by teaching French. In the intervening years I've traveled and improved my accent and learned to scorn Hérédia and given up composing ballads, sonnets, villanelles. Now I work as adjunct tutor at the local prep school—though what those kids were being "prepped" for it's difficult to say. Mostly they're delinquents, the children of the middle-class who've been thrown out of Hotchkiss or Concord Academy, the ones who have dropped too much acid or stolen the Porsche once too often, but whose parents aren't quite ready yet to relinquish the idea of Bryn Mawr or Yale. My own degree from Harvard has impressed them all no end, and the two years spent in Europe at what I not untruthfully claim was the Sorbonne. I did spend some time on the Rue des Écoles and once was caught in a riot with an architecture student whose arm the *flics* twisted and broke.

So that qualifies me, more or less, and the schedule is undemanding: twice a week, after field hockey practice, I come in and conjugate verbs. I teach idiomatic expressions to and fail to improve the pronunciation of a bunch of spacey Space-Age adolescents who all are doing drugs.

Well, anyway, I'm standing at the stove. There's a knock on the porch door, and I say, "Come in, it's open," and in comes a man we know. His name is Michael Saunders; he runs the Real Estate Office on Main Street, and he sold Adriana the farm. She has money, understand, which is why she can afford to be so insouciantly a weaver, but her trust fund hasn't helped us to establish solidarity with the suspicious locals; they wonder what we're doing here and how long we'll remain. At night, in the cold smoky rooms, we ask ourselves the same. So Michael has been driving by and thought he'd stop and say hello and ask how things are going and suggest, not incidentally, that if we want a buyer he's got somebody who'll buy.

Was it Spengler who observed—*wasn't* it Spengler who observed?—that we will know the Decline of the West has been completed when the children of the bourgeoisie turn to handicrafts? The answer, Class, is yes. But we turned in that direction, most of us, those years; we played the shakuhachi and wore bracelets with metal from downed fighter planes and shouted "Up the Pigs!" We were convinced of Armageddon just around the corner; the times they were a'changin' and we had to raise the food we ate and withhold that portion of our taxes that was ear-marked for Defense and warm our homes not with petroleum products but with the wood some honest yeoman cut.

The living room fireplace smoked. That's the point of this discursus; I couldn't make it work. It was tall and wide and shallow and elegantly faced, and no matter what I did with it the smoke poured out into the room. It was doing so just then, and Michael Saunders took a look and said, "Hey, that's terrific, you've got a *Rumford* fireplace!" I shrugged and said so what.

Adriana came into the kitchen, wearing one of her sarongs. He had a thing for her, I think; they all did, really, she was beautiful. He said, "That fireplace, it's valuable, original, it's an extra added attraction," and I said it didn't work. He looked at me with the veiled condescension we reserve for ignorance, or maybe he was showing off for sexy Adriana (unable or unwilling to accept that she was bored by men, by just such macho preening), and announced it wasn't deep enough for the kind of fire we'd been setting and, here, ladies, let me help.

Beside the tool-rack for the fireplace we kept asbestos gloves. Michael checked the flue. *That* ignorant I hadn't been, the flue was open wide. Adriana sighed, then smiled at me her secret smile that meant, let's tolerate this fool for just a little longer, OK? OK, I said, and turned back to the bread that I was kneading, setting out to rise in pans, and then something astonishing happened in Count Rumford's fireplace. Michael put on the gloves, I remember—rolled up his sleeves to demonstrate a tattoo on his forearm of a mermaid and an anchor—and reached (oh bravely, manfully!) into the bed of ash and stood the smoking logs *upright* and the cherry-wood and maple and the red oak slabs burst, hey presto, into flame, and everything was heat!

My parentage, my parents. I should start with childhood—should tell you how I started and thereafter came to this pass. But not today;

the far smoke furls, the barn-cats lick the gutter (cf. p. 21). October, and the split-leaf maple flaming by the tool shed and the tamaracks beginning to go yellow by the fence-line, the oak at the crest of the hill.

As tedious Rilke was wont to observe, when discussing his own captive state, *You must change your life.*

Mary Nogarola was the younger of the sisters—celebrated not so much for beauty as for wit. She was lean and quick and bright-eyed and precise. She became his mistress when her sister, Countess Baumgarten, grew otherwise preoccupied and too plump to comply.

The Countess was a lady famed for dancing and her passionate behavior who attached herself to Thompson for a year. They strewed the bed with roses and drank toasts to sweet romance; she smiled at him beguilingly across the goblet's rim. She urged him to performance with a vigor that belied his age and, at year's end, conceived.

Once pregnant with their love-child, however, the Countess resumed her station and no longer drove to his lodgings at night or summoned him after the ball. Instead she said, "My sister, now. She'll suit you far better. Use her."

Mary claimed he did so merely as a substitute, yet the substitution satisfied them all. She possessed an inquiring mind. As was the case with Mary Palmerston—to whom he continued to write, remaining on excellent terms—Thompson's pleasure in his mistress had much to do with pleasures of the intellect. They spent long hours together, playing whist and rummy, engaging in and disengaging from alliances at court. She helped him with his writings in German, Italian, and French.

The beautiful sister, the Countess, delivered herself of a daughter. Her husband did not seem to care, affecting the opinion—more plausible in prior years—that the child was the Elector's; the Count in any case preferred boar-hunting, sweet white wine from his vineyards and the company of dogs. "Let's call her Sophie," Mary said. "Sophia means wisdom. And she's so unwise." The Countess and Thompson agreed.

He worked out problems to amuse the women, based on his research in silk. If a silk gown worn by a lady weighs twenty-eight ounces, he wrote, it is very certain that she carries upon her back upwards of two thousand miles in length of silk, as spun by the worm. A man might actually carry in his pockets a thread long enough to reach around the world. It would require four million, two-hundred and thirty-nine thousand, one-hundred and fifty-three threads of raw silk to form a solid rope or cylinder the area of whose transverse sections should be one inch.

Mary Nogarola laughed. Athletic, she joined Thompson on his morning canter through the avenues of Munich, and on his excursions from town. Lambkin was her favorite, whereas he retained his preference for Fawn. They roamed the Isar Meadows and the Elector's farm; they had free reign in the gardens of the Residenz and out at Nymphenburg. He planted one hundred lindens in a row in his child's honor; Mary planted fruit trees in a circle, in honor of her niece.

He was happy with the Countess and young Sophie, their beautiful illegitimate; he was happy with his sharp-tongued mistress too. She showed charming disrespect. She taxed him with his pedantry, his earnest speculation: she said order and disorder require each other like blossom and thorn, and she would therefore have to be disorderly sufficient for them both. Mary said he seemed so German it's a wonder he was born in America and not Wurzburg or Tübingen or, God forbid it, Berlin.

She liked to wear his riding boots and the order of St. Stanislaus around her neck, and nothing else. She anointed herself with lavender water or his bottle of Eau de Cologne. She had—astonishing in one so thin, and he warned her that it would not last—a great appetite for marzipan and every sort of chocolate. "What will not last?" she asked. "My adoration of chocolate or"—here she spanned her hands around it, her index fingers touching and her hip tilted—"my waist?"

"The latter, my darling. Your waist."

"I understand you; it's shameful what you're saying. *Schande*. You mean your adoration will not last."

"Not so." He kissed her navel. "I am constancy itself."

"Yes," Mary Nogarola said. "That's what my sister tells me. That's what she complains of in your case."

They discussed the situation of the poor in Munich. It grew daily graver, requiring redress. To clear the country of mendicants—the number of whom in Bavaria had become quite intolerable—it would be necessary to adopt general and efficacious measures for maintaining and supporting those who, for lack of an alternative, were thieves and vagabonds. In his capacity as Chamberlain, Thompson devised a plan. The number of itinerant beggars, of both sexes and all ages, as well foreigners as natives, who strolled about the country in all directions, levying contributions from the industrious inhabitants, stealing and robbing and leading a life of indolence and the most shameless debauchery was quite incredible. So numerous were the swarms of beggars in the capital, so great their impudence and so persevering their importunity, that it was almost impossible to cross the street without being attacked. And these beggars were in general by no means such as from age or bodily infirmities were unable by their labor to earn a livelihood; but they were, for the most part, stout and strong and healthy citizens who, lost to every sense of shame, had embraced the profession from choice, not necessity, and who not infrequently added insolence and threats to their importunity, and extorted that from fear which they could not procure by their arts of dissimulation.

These beggars not only infested all the streets, public walks, and public places, but they even made a practice of going into private houses, where they never failed to steal whatever fell in their way; and the churches were so full of them that it was quite a nuisance, and a public scandal during the performance of divine service. People at their devotions were continually interrupted by them, and were frequently obliged to satisfy their demands.

In short, these detestable vermin swarmed everywhere; and not only their impudence and clamorous importunity were without any bounds, but they had recourse to the most diabolical arts and most horrid crimes, in the prosecution of their infamous trade. Young children were stolen from their parents by these wretches, and their eyes put out or their tender limbs broken and distorted, in order by exposing them thus maimed to excite the pity and commiseration of the public. In pursuit of this well-intentioned but, Thompson was persuaded, misplaced benevolence, every species of artifice was made use of to agitate the sensibility, and to extort the contributions of the humane and charitable.

Some of these monsters were so void of all feeling as to expose even their own children, naked and almost starved, in the streets, in order that by their cries and unaffected expressions of distress they might move those who passed by to pity and relieve them; and in order to make them act their part more naturally, they were unmercifully beaten when they came home, by their inhuman parents, if they did not bring with them a certain sum which they were ordered to collect.

But the evils arising from the prevalence of mendicity did not stop here. The public, worn out and vanquished by the numbers and persevering importunity of the beggars, and frequently disappointed in their hopes of being relieved from their depredations, by the failure of the numberless schemes that were formed and set on foot for that purpose, began at last to consider the case as quite desperate, and to submit patiently to an evil for which they saw no remedy. The consequences of this submission are easy to be conceived.

Mary said the poor were shiftless, notoriously lazy, and had only lax morals to blame. "It is impossible," she said, "to light the flame of virtue in the close quarters of vice. Good behavior must have open air—as well as ventilation, *natürlich*—to breathe."

Thompson disagreed. He himself had risen out of anonymity, and he had reason to expect that others might manage the same. Since he had proved so able to improve his circumstance, why should not men and women everywhere enjoy just such enlargement; by dint of ambition and unsparing labor, who cannot scale the ladder of success?

This was a difficult position to argue, however. Candor contended with pride. He had settled in Bavaria as Sir Benjamin Thompson, Knight, not a farm boy arrived from a shop; further, he now claimed noble ancestry and dressed as though accustomed to the company of kings. He could not therefore use his own career as an example of advancement, since it might occasion restiveness in those less well advanced. Full disclosure of the case would prove unwelcome, possibly; frank discussion of his history would not have been germane.

Too, he was in private convinced of his special endowment and talents. Had not a multitude praised him, from Sarah Rolfe to George Germain to Mary now astride his lap, fondling his manhood, athwart it, her mouth engorged with marzipan that had fitted itself gaspingly not three minutes before to the shaft? It could not, surely, be an accident of circumstance that had brought him so far and so fast; it had to be some special providence, some form of signaled intention that had thus singled him out. His career was as a comet's, with its attendant fame. While Mary sought and fought for and found her release, pitched forward on him wetly as if at the completion of a ride— "Horse," she whispered, "Lambkin"—he mused in the great rumpled bed as to his high calling and the nature of the task.

The Elector's soldiers had required his assistance; so too did the mendicant class. Bavaria would profit from his supervision and his organizing competence, for he was determined to help. He would feed and clothe the poor, thus rendering them useful, not useless, and thereby transforming liability to gain. He himself had flourished mightily, had risen into prominence; he would shower benisons upon a grateful populace like rain. Mary brought him to his climax, using her bejeweled hand and then her intelligent mouth. He had been appointed Minister of War, Minister of Police, Major-General, Chamberlain of the Court, and State Councillor. Now his mistress reached across him and plucked a chocolate truffle from the box.

All that autumn, unrelentingly, Thompson drilled the troops. He would dispense not charity but aid, for the happy man and woman pose no threat. Thus happiness may prove its value for the individual and, by extension thereafter, the commonweal. Reformation may prove arduous; plain comfort is by contrast simple to provide. He readied an abandoned building in the outlying suburb of Au, and inscribed above its portals, in gold letters, HERE NO ALMS WILL BE RECEIVED. For Thompson dealt with probability, not chance. He counted on his high authority, his great thoroughness and—with reference to those whose lot he planned to meliorate—the element of surprise.

Each beggar must be registered and his or her particulars described. These would be taken to the Workhouse, then numbered, scrubbed and fed. Here a modicum of force might perhaps prove necessary, since the dirty man fears water as though it were the flood. He would remove Munich's poor.

And what if they don't want to go?" asked Mary Nogarola.

"They will be grateful," he said.

"But what if they prefer the street?"

"I prefer them off it."

"Does the Elector share your preference?"

"He does."

"I saw young Sophie yesterday."

"How is she? And her mother?"

"They send you fond regards," said Mary, "and their respectful love. I am deputized to bring it. They complain of some neglect." Suggestively she pursed her lips.

"How terrible," said Thompson. "I must remedy that straightaway."

"You may begin," said Mary, "with their deputy. Your servant, sir." And lightly, lingeringly, she placed her hand on his knee.

"I am a very busy man."

"Ten minutes of your time."

"If you require it," he said. He liked to make her ask. This also she had taught him: the pleasures of reversal, the game of feigned indifference, the quarry self-ensnared.

"I do. Ten minutes. Starting now."

To make vicious and abandoned people happy," Thompson wrote, "it has been generally supposed necessary first to make them virtuous. But why not reverse this order? *Why not make them first happy and then virtuous?* If happiness and virtue be *inseparable*, the end will be as certainly obtained by the one method as by the other; and it is most undoubtedly much easier to contribute to the happiness and comfort of persons in a state of poverty and misery, than, by admonitions and punishments, to reform their morals."

His soldiers would patrol the streets, arresting the mendicant class, for there were ten thousand at least. He rehearsed his plan for months. "What exquisite pleasures then must it afford, to collect the scattered rays of useful science and direct them, united, to objects of general utility! to throw them in a broad beam on the cold and dreary habitations of the poor! spreading cheerfulness and comfort all around!"

An orderly assessment of things requisite, he explained to Mary, is one hallmark of the scientific mind. It improves the likelihood of an experiment's success. Further, it lessens the chances of failure, and in so original an enterprise as his, an effort—if he might be permitted thus to describe it—wholly without precedent, the likelihood of failure is substantial. Caution would be therefore the watchword of the day.

On New Year's dawn, 1790, he walked to the Marienkirche, where Munich's poor convened. The wind was raw, the streets were dark; there had been a light dusting of snow. He wore his greatcoat and black gloves and had ten soldiers with him, twenty paces back.

"For the love of God, sir, help," a cripple cried.

Thompson paused.

"It is New Year's," pled the beggar. "And you see me here in rags."

"I will clothe you," Thompson said.

"*Sei dank der Liebe Gott.* And I am very hungry."

"I will feed you," Thompson said.

Another called for alms. A third said she was starving and had no milk left to offer and that her son must also—unless there be some charity this morning—starve. A fourth said nothing, tongueless, extending a brown palm. A fifth, a sixth requested help until he drew a crowd; "*Hilfe!* Help," they cried. The maimed, the broken and the bent approached him, swarming to largesse like flies to something rotten or ants to something sweet. The old advanced their palsied hands, the young clung to his boots.

Then he opened his greatcoat and showed his high rank and placed them all under arrest.

They drew back, shocked, attempting to disperse. But Thompson had given his signal and the soldiers had meanwhile advanced. Such resistance as was offered was simply overcome. He placed his own hands on the shoulders of the first to be arrested; his soldiers claimed the rest.

All morning long—all afternoon and evening and well into the night—this procedure was repeated. From dawn to dark, the Minister of Police and Major-General and Minister of War and Chamberlain and Councillor of State—so many titles for one man that he perforce seemed multiple—swept ceaselessly through streets. His lieutenants followed suit. The Civil Magistrates did likewise, dispersed within the city, and field-officers and soldiers everywhere in groups of ten collected the idlers, the mendicants, and registered and conducted them to the Town Hall and thereafter safely away. He herded thousands off. They made a royal fellowship: the halt, the blind and lame.

My Chamberlain," said the Elector. "My excellent right hand."

"You flatter me, your Highness."

"Only as the arm and wrist flatter and extend the fingers, Councillor. We have a great deal in common."

He bowed.

"Countess Baumgarten, for instance. And the complaisance of the Count."

He bowed again. Karl Theodor was proud and fierce and capricious and vain and arrogant yet cunningly seemed none of these; he ruled his kingdom with a negligent-seeming attentiveness, a fist disguised as glove. They think me an old fool, he said, and that suits my turn exactly; they gossip in my hearing because they think me deaf.

"And your charming daughter Sophie?" The Elector took snuff, then sneezed. "How is she?"

"Well, I trust."

"We should have a house here for the incidental children of nobility. The by-blows and proof of romance. The accidental consequence of champagne and dancing, *nicht wahr?*"

"*Certo.*" With Mary, he studied Italian.

"See to it, Chamberlain—a place where the unwanted will be cared for: fed and taught."

"Little Sophie is well cared for, I believe."

"Not so. Her mother is light-headed—idle, frivolous."

"It's possible. *E vero.*"

Karl Theodor tapped his nose. "The children of the poor," he said. "You are dealing with them ably. But the children of the high-born too require help."

"*Votre altesse.*" He clicked his heels.

"Your great friend, my nephew Maximilian"—the Elector sneezed again. "Why he alone could furnish half a house."

The beggars were conveyed—for the most part without force or protestation, with no unseemly incident—to the Military Workhouse that Thompson ordered readied in advance. Here fires burned brightly, warmly. The tables by the kitchen offered tureens of hot soup and great high-heaped platters of bread. Here too had been arrayed beds with adequate linen in rooms neither draughty nor close. There were tunics of various sizes and cut, that all might be properly clothed. A priest, a physician and an apothecary were established in attendance; barbers waited also, and a surgeon hovered near. The whole had been arranged on the model of a barracks, but with provision made for families and the particular necessities of the very old and young. He completed his arrangements with meticulous painstaking attention, and no kindly office was spared.

The good effects of cleanliness, or rather the bad effects of filth and nastiness, may be satisfactorily accounted for. Our bodies are continually at war with whatever offends them, and every thing offends them that adheres to and irritates them; and though by long habit we may be so accustomed to support a physical ill as to become almost insensible to it, yet it never leaves the mind perfectly at peace. There must always remain a certain uneasiness and discontent—an indecision and an aversion from all serious application, which shows evidently that the mind is not at rest.

Those who from being afflicted with a long and painful disease suddenly acquire health are best able to judge of the force of this reasoning. By the delightful sensation they feel at being relieved from pain and uneasiness, they learn to know the full extent of their former misery; and the human heart is never so effectually softened, and so well prepared and disposed to receive virtuous impressions, as upon such occasions.

With a view to bringing the minds of the poor and unfortunate people he had to deal with to this state, Thompson took considerable pains to make their new situation painless by comparison. The state in which they had been used to live was certainly most wretched and deplorable, but they had been so long accustomed to it that they were grown insensible to their own misery. It was therefore necessary, in order to awaken their attention, to make the contrast between their former situation and that which was prepared for them as striking as possible. To this end everything was done that could be devised to make them comfortable.

A man may cross a line, not knowing he has done so, and recognize this only when he chooses to look back. A casual decision may in retrospect seem crucial, a mere rivulet as prospect prove the Jordan once we ford. Thompson wandered through the Isar Meadows, the Elector's Hunting Ground. Today he rode alone. Coming on a clearing scored by deer-prints and the scat of some clawed predator he failed to recognize, he found rushes by the muddy bank that had been trampled, broken off. There were feathers, a gnawed bone. Here before him—perhaps as recently as that same morning, perhaps the night before—had transpired the time-honored sequence of hunter and hunted: a thirst slaked, a hunger aroused.

He dismounted and let his horse drink. The wind off the water carried with it, faintly, a hint of the broad Merrimac, the river he had walked beside when young. A vision of his daughter Sarah swam before him suddenly, as though she too enjoyed the Isar Meadows and was sitting by the bank.

Head averted, she offered her back. A picnic basket (or, perhaps, a sewing basket; in the light he could not tell; he squinted, tried to focus, but the glare was in his eyes) spilled its contents to the grass. A dog lay in her lap, a yellow ribbon fluttered in her auburn hair. Her neck was as a swan's. He called to her, or started to, but the girl—if girl it was, and not, as even on the instant he half-knew, a shibboleth in siren's guise—denied him her attention. She held her face inclined and stroked the sleeping dog; her presence was beguiling, sweet, and she moved within the charmed enclosure of the air.

The Isar burbled gently where it ran. Here bull rushes and cattails stood green and thick and high. His daughter enlarged and then, shimmering, shrank; she wore a white bonnet and trailed a white hand in the stream.

Thompson shook his head. He blinked. Something scuttled in the brush. That was my life before, he thought, this my life hereafter, and here the turning point: my Sally does not know me, living in America, and I cannot return to her and am no longer young. The figure in the reeds is but my mind's composite—a compound of imagination and yearning remembrance: mere art.

He tethered Fawn. Birds called and did so, he knew, in alarm. He waited by his grazing horse while their shocked music subsided. When the Minister of War looked up again, he saw no daughter opposite, nothing composed of or in the bright shade. All abstraction, distraction was gone.

The building in the Au had been remodeled and repaired. A large kitchen and an eating room and commodious bake house were added to the structure; work-shops for carpenters, smiths, turners and other mechanics were established and furnished with tools. Large halls were fitted up for spinners of hemp and flax, for spinners of cotton and wool, and for spinners of worsted; adjoining to each hall a small room was fitted up for an inspector or clerk. Halls had been likewise established for weavers of woolens, for weavers of serge and shalloon, for linen-weavers, for weavers of cotton goods, and for stocking weavers; work-shops were provided for clothiers, cloth-shearers, dyers, saddlers, and rooms for wool-sorters, wool-carders, wool-combers and knitters.

A spacious hall, with many windows on both sides, was fitted as a drying-room; here tenters were placed for stretching out and drying eight pieces of cloth at once. This hall was one-hundred and ten feet long, thirty-seven feet wide and twenty-two feet high. A fulling-mill was constructed upon a stream of water which ran by one side of the court; the courtyard in the middle of the building had been paved, and the approach from every side was leveled and covered with gravel. To those who last lay on the paving or wedged between cobble and gutter, breathing the rank exhalations of their own filth and decay, degradation their habitual companion and contumely their lot, dependent on the passersby for charity—if slops and offal may be so described, if the leavings of a kitchen (that skin and bone flung down for cats, the rancid intestines and eyeballs of sheep) may properly be called a meal, the wall a roof, the rag and torn discarded blanket adequate as vestment—this must have seemed like paradise indeed.

And in that paradise instruction waited also. Those who would avail themselves of the chance of self-improvement found ample opportunity and wherewithal at hand. Useful labor is a form of education, transforming idleness and sloth to profitable industry, and which of us might not be grateful for the chance to help? The inmates of the workhouse were taught to spin cheap hemp. Flax and wool were likewise provided, and some few good spinners of those articles were engaged as instructors; the children sat—inattentive to begin with, then bemused, then rapt—and watched. By far the greater number of the poor began with spinning of hemp, and so great was their awkwardness at first that they absolutely ruined the materials that were put into their hands.

Little by little, however, they learned. Improvement registered upon the hemp entitled the spinner to undertake flax; the more dexterous the spinner the more valuable the wool. But what was quite surprising, and at the same time interesting in the highest degree, was the apparent and rapid change which was produced in the manners of the poor, in their general behavior and even in the very air of their countenances, upon being a little accustomed to their new situations. The kind usage they met with, and the comforts they enjoyed, seemed to have softened their hearts, and awakened in them sentiments as new and surprising to themselves as they were interesting to those about them.

"Good morning," Thompson said. He made a daily visit, and often he brought guests.

"Good morning, sir," the children chorused. Then they doffed their caps.

"Did you sleep well?"

"We thank you, sir."

"And have you said your prayers?"

"Yes."

"And was your breakfast filling?"

"Yes indeed, sir. *Herzlich dank.*"

"And you have not been idle?"

"Not at all sir, no. We have been doing lessons."

"Good." He turned to his companions. They were a deputation from Alsace.

"What we have here, gentlemen, is progress. I think of it as reclamation: what was lost is found."

"Well done," they murmured, and moved on. He gathered the fruit of the loom.

Munich pleased its newfound master; its walls were well-defended and its churches clean. Clocks struck the quarter hour, and the carillon and cow-bell made music all day long. At night he liked the chimes. He enjoyed the market, its variety of wares; he watched the thick-limbed farmers and fine-fingered artisans, the blue eyes of the serving maids beneath their flaxen curls. He sampled fish and silks and spices and cheese and bread and fruit and grain for sale beneath the Marienkirche. It delighted him to saunter through the market square, down alley and wide avenue without the importuning press of beggars at his side.

Bavaria was the third country Benjamin Thompson called home. This present one, he told himself, was admirably suited to his taste.

Though not of course a native, he felt nonetheless at ease: his work here was worth doing, and well done. His neighbor the Russian Ambassador invited him from time to time for caviar and conversation, and the two of them discussed this quality of obedience, this habit— so alien to the America from which Thompson hailed, or the Ambassador's Russia with its wild steppe and ill-tamed Cossack—of ungrudging acquiescence to command. When he gave an order here it would be followed promptly, cheerfully; when he offered an opinion it was seen to be correct.

Only Mary Nogarola maintained her independence. She toured the Military Workhouse and refrained from praise. His love of order, Mary said, was fitting for a soldier—except this was peacetime, not war. Hers was the quizzical amusement of a high-born scamp. She teased him, taunted him; she said he liked the factory because of all those children spinning in their muslin frocks; she'd seen him inspecting their knees.

"Of course," he said. "I want them clean."

"What is your English expression," she asked, "to be beneath reproach?"

"Beneath contempt," he told her, and she said, "Below reproach?"

"Beyond reproach," he said, and she said, "Yes, that's it."

Lately, her passion for chocolate had had its predicted effect. Her thighs began to swell, her buttocks droop. In an effort not unlike his own with Gainsborough, she wished to render permanent a form now newly mutable; Mary offered him her portrait, wearing black.

"It's an excellent likeness," he said.

"Don't say that, *du*. It's awful."

"No."

"Those lines beneath my eyes. That pointed nose."

"I am happy to have it," he said. "The painter is an expert."

"The hands are all right possibly. I'll grant you he does hands."

"You're fishing for compliments, *Liebchen*."

"With a long line." Ruefully, she smiled. "In this, at least, you resemble my husband. You do not pay them often."

"It's an excellent portrait," he said.

An industrious family is ever a pleasing object, but there was something peculiarly interesting and affecting in the groups of Bavaria's poor. Whether it was that those who saw them compared their present situation with the state of misery and wretchedness from which they had been taken, or whether it was the joy and exaltation which were expressed in the countenances of the poor parents in contemplating their children all busily employed about them, or the air of self-satisfaction which these little urchins put on at the consciousness of their own dexterity, while they pursued their work with redoubled diligence upon being observed, that rendered the scene so singularly interesting, he knew not; but certain it was that few strangers who visited the establishment came out of these halls without being much affected.

Nothing is more extraordinary and unaccountable than the inconsistency of mankind in every thing, even in the practice of that divine virtue, benevolence, and most of our mistakes arise more from indolence and inattention than from any thing else. The busy part of mankind are too intent upon their own private pursuits; and those who have leisure are too averse from giving themselves trouble to investigate a subject generally considered as tiresome and uninteresting. But if it be true that we are really happy only in proportion as we ought to be so—that is, in proportion as we are instrumental in promoting the happiness of others—no study surely can be so interesting as that which teaches us how most effectually to contribute to the well-being of our less fortunate yet nevertheless fellow-creatures.

Councillor."

"Prince." Thompson bowed.

"You have done very well indeed. You have made an appreciable difference in these our Munich streets."

He clicked his heels.

"And we are grateful. We acknowledge this. We take pleasure in that promenade which once was vermin-clotted and unsafe. We breathe freely now again in the uncontaminate air."

"So do your subjects, Prince."

Karl Theodor smiled. His lip had cracked; he rubbed it. "I have considered how to thank you, how best to acknowledge your service. The Order of St. Stanislaus was adequate before, perhaps, but now we think it insufficient."

"Your acknowledgement is thanks sufficient, Prince."

Karl Theodor brushed away this courtesy as if it were a crumb. "But you are foreign-born. You know the obstacles attendant on ennobling in Bavaria a citizen of somewhere else, a servant to some other Crown."

"I am the Elector's servant. Entirely."

"Indeed." For the first time in their acquaintance, he offered Thompson snuff.

This was a high honor, and the grateful Thompson bowed. There were others in the room. He watched them watching him.

"The Holy Roman Empire," Karl Theodor pronounced—surveying the ceiling idly, slowly, as though considering aloud, as if he had not long since made up his decisive mind—"can use another Count. And will make no objection if I present a candidate. I might—indeed, I intend to—sponsor you for that."

This outstripped expectation. Thompson stared.

"It will not happen overnight. We must wait the occasion."

"Prince."

"Consider, my very dear Councillor, what name you will choose when a Count."

He kissed his master's hand.

⁂ III ⁂

That night he rioted with Mary Nogarola in her chambers by the river. She showed an unfeigned astonishment at his success—his triumph, as she put it—and he was glad to share the fruits of his hard enterprise, working above her in the bed as though again a boy. He plunged but could not cool himself within her liquid loins. He probed and battered at her, while she in her turn yielded heat. What will you call yourself, she asked, Count what?

"I have been thinking. Count Rumford."

"Who?"

"Rumford." He spelled out the name.

"*Und Wass bedeutet Rumford?* What means the word?"

He explained its import to her—how the town of Concord, New Hampshire, had once been called Rumford instead. He had been happy there, beginning his career, and since he now must change his name there was a kind of symmetry in the sobriquet of Rumford. In this manner what was past retrieving might be nonetheless recalled, and a small vanished township endure in his renown.

It has not happened yet, she warned, but he said done and done. The Elector keeps his promise, and a promise had been made. "The Holy Roman Empire," said Mary Nogarola. "Imagine. *Du.*"

Countess Baumgarten, her sister, could claim no greater title; little Sophie would be proud. In his mistress's voice there was—for the first time since he'd known her, in the course of their long amity—respect. She stroked his palm; she fondled it; she cradled her neck in his arm.

"Rumford," Thompson said again, and she said, "Absolutely. Though not yet."

With an expression of contentment, a sigh as of those sated cats that, having drunk a bowl of cream and commandeered the counterpane, will stretch out by the pillow and arch their backs, purring, luxuriant, she turned from him and slept.

Now the Chamberlain worked without respite, setting himself for the next weeks and months and—should his promotion require it—years to answer whatever Karl Theodor asked. The Elector asked often, and much.

Thompson dammed the Isar River where it wandered through the meadows, and persuaded the Elector to permit of cultivation within the fertile park, those woods where once Karl Theodor had hunted flesh and fowl. He mobilized a corps of the Bavarian Army for this reclamation project, and they worked there one whole year. Having constructed earthwork fortifications, they tore them down and built them back again. What the troops protected were lettuce and onions, but it proved excellent practice for warfare, and training for his military engineers.

The soil was rich. Each man received a plot. The soldiers of the garrison took turns at planting, cultivating, harvesting, and because they were given their seed *gratis* gardens flourished where he fenced them by the Isar Meadow walls. What had been reeds and marshy weeds soon gave forth ordered nourishment, and those who earlier relied on requisitions from the town now grew their own healthful provender. Working in the open air they harvested what they themselves had sown, being spared the temptations of sloth. The more assiduous and skilled at farming could sell their superfluity at market and keep a profit-share.

As nothing is so certainly fatal to morals, and particularly to the morals of the lower class of mankind, as habitual idleness, every possible measure was adopted that could be devised to introduce a spirit of industry among the troops. Every encouragement was given to the soldiers to employ their leisure time, when they were off duty, in working for their own emolument; and among other encouragements, the most efficacious of all, that of allowing them full liberty to dispose of the money acquired by their labor in any way they should think proper, without being obliged to give account of it to anybody. They were furnished with working dresses (a canvas frock and trousers) *gratis* at their enlisting, and were afterwards permitted to retain their old uniforms for the same purpose, and care was taken in all cases where they were employed that they should be well paid.

In this way soldiers were encouraged both to produce and save. Those members of the garrison who were the heads of families could billet them nearby; in the enterprise of husbandry their women and children could help. The citizens of Munich wandered gaily, gratefully, through the Isar meadows and down the green allées. He planned for a Chinese pagoda and a temple on the hill, then lined the watercourse with jetties where the poor might fish.

The length of the grand promenade was fully six miles long. A private domain of the Elector was thus converted to the public charge, its utility established and value fivefold increased. Thompson stocked

his "English Garden" with thirty of the finest cows that could be purchased from the Tyrol and Switzerland and Flanders. In a thick wood
behind a coffee-house he concealed a stable, elegantly fitted up and
maintained with close care. Nearby farmers came to gape. Connois-
seurs traveled to Munich with the express and particular purpose of
examining these horned cattle, and by the process of examination to
improve their herd.

In addition, and on his own initiative, he undertook a multitude
of tasks—no project too lowly or hard. Thompson studied the potato
and the nutrient value of soups. He continued his experiments with
silk. He considered the nature of cloth and its color, its relative value
in dress, and of these values he established a hierarchical listing: blue,
then brown, then black. He made drawings for a kitchen, its arrangements and utensils, and began to implement efficiency in stoves. He
considered the matter of smoke, then invented a portable stove. He
made notes on the use of steam heat. He wrote of the salubrity of
warm rooms, of the salubrity of warm bathing, of the management of
fires in closed fire-places. He experimented on the use of steam—as
opposed to open fires—in the manufacture of soap.

Further, he attended to his duties as the Minister of War. He
established a foundry at Munich, and neither pains nor expense were
spared to make it as perfect as possible; a most excellent machine
was erected for boring cannon, with work-shops adjoining to it for
the construction of gun-carriages and ammunition wagons. Restless,
questing, constantly engaged, he resumed his old experiments upon
gunpowder, and he labored at improving the Elector's arsenal.

Now the Councillor stayed in the foundry sixteen hours at a

stretch. His assistants grumbled and muttered; three left. Two that remained were blinded by powder, and one blew off a leg. When the time came for his elevation to the Holy Roman Empire (that time deferred by Karl Theodor, not consciously perhaps but negligently, insouciantly, and in any case and for whatever reason delayed through 1790 and 1791 and then the early winter of 1792, what though court gossips whispered that the Empire was irrelevant, mere titular pomp), he planned to have deserved the prize beyond all contravening. As he told Mary when she urged indifference upon him, a title is inherited or won.

It frequently happens that in the ordinary affairs and occupations of life, opportunities present themselves of contemplating some of the most curious operations of Nature; and very interesting philosophical experiments might often be made, almost without trouble or expense, by means of machinery contrived for the mere mechanical purposes of the arts and manufactures.

He had often had occasion to make this observation. The Chamberlain was persuaded that a habit of keeping the eyes open to everything in the ordinary course of the business of life has more often led, as it were by accident, or in the playful excursions of the imagination, to useful doubts and sensible schemes for investigation and improvement, than all the intense meditations of philosophers in the hours expressly set apart for study.

While superintending the boring of cannon in the workshops of the military arsenal at Munich, he had been struck with the very considerable degree of heat which a brass gun acquires in a short time in being bored, and with the still more intense heat (much greater than that of boiling water) of the metallic chips separated from it by the borer. The more he meditated on these phenomena, the more they appeared to him curious and interesting. A thorough investigation of them seemed even to bid fair to give a farther insight into the hidden nature of Heat; and to enable him to form some reasonable conjectures respecting the existence, or non-existence, of an igneous fluid—a subject on which the opinions of philosophers had in all ages been much divided.

A cannon to be bored was placed in a container of cold water. The boring proceeded steadily, at a rate he could control, and the water surrounding the cannon became warm, then hot, then boiled. This water was removed and replaced by cold water once more. Again the water was brought to a boil, as quickly in this instance as at first.

According to the then-prevailing theory, the force between two bodies in friction squeezed caloric fluid out of the material. But this failed to answer the case. The length of time it took his cauldrons of water to boil, when starting from room temperature, was always precisely the same. Hence the quantity of heat produced did not di-minish—as might the heat, say, of a horseshoe when hammered into shape. His great bubbling cauldrons were proof.

If one immerses a sponge in water and then hangs it from a thread, the liquid will evaporate and the sponge go dry. When one strikes a gong, by contrast, the sound of the bell will continue as often as one strikes. There is no perceptible loss. Thus Thompson reasoned; he riddled it out. Water is a substance; sound is not. It is of course well known that two hard bodies rubbed together will produce continuous heat. If heat in the form of liquid were flowing from the cannon, why did it not evaporate or come to be exhausted finally? If heat were a substance, phlogiston, then it should behave as does water and not insubstantial sound. Since heat behaves not as the former but the latter, it has to be instead a variety of motion—of energy transferred and not a concrete entity diminished. Thus was the problem posed and this the question's answer, a key in a bright lock. Often he brought visitors to watch.

It would be difficult to describe the surprise and astonishment expressed on the countenances of the bystanders on seeing so large a quantity of cold water heated and actually made to boil without any fire. Though there was, in fact, nothing that could justly be considered as surprising in this event, yet it afforded the scientist a degree of childish pleasure that, were he ambitious of the reputation of a grave philosopher, he ought most certainly rather to have hid than to discover.

Mary Nogarola warned him to be moderate; a candle cannot stand upright while burning at both ends.

"You will destroy it, Ben," she said.

"What?"

"Your health."

"*Es ist vollbracht*," he said. "It is already finished."

"Don't exaggerate. You're healthy, strong."

"Not any longer. No."

"Then renew yourself," she urged him. "Take the waters. Take a rest."

"Not now," he said. "Next month, perhaps, next year."

And yet his sweet physician denied him that same cure. Endlessly she spoke about the benefit of silence; immoderate, she counseled moderation in all things. She made repose impossible by prattling at him nightly about the need for rest, for now her children were away and her husband worked in Mannheim, fortifying that city. So the lady Nogarola redoubled her attentions; he was only rarely and briefly alone.

She brought him rosewater in vats. She gave him glass bouquets and figurines of shepherds in china and music-making inlaid globes and tall celestial clocks. She brought him maps and traveler's accounts of the marvels to be witnessed in Umbria and Tuscany, the healthful waters and the bracing air of Appenine and Alp. She brought him drawings and engravings of the River Tiber and the River Arno meandering through fields. Brain fever was her greatest fear, not bodily collapse. He needed to amuse himself, she said; he should lose himself amongst the splendors of antiquity. Unremitting labor of the body may be remedied, yet brain fever bleeds us dry.

"We could travel. We could perhaps go together."

"Where?"

"Baden Baden," Mary said. "Wiesbaden, Montecatini. There are so many places you should visit."

"Count Rumford will travel," he promised.

"And you?"

"I am not Rumford yet."

The fashion of Karl Theodor had been to change his favorites, and in this at least he proved constant—summoning Thompson only rarely now, rarely heeding his advice. The reader will no doubt recall how quixotic in the early years had been Sackville's sponsorship, how that devotee of pleasure embraced the principles of the Italian Machiavel. Karl Theodor did much the same, but he himself was nearing seventy, and fat. Now the Elector loved a princess, not twenty-one, vivacious, and rumored to be pliable and soon to be his wife.

On this matter the Chamberlain kept silent; he tried to keep apart. He pitied his dear sovereign but could not express that pity lest it be construed as scorn. The Prince and several of his retinue—so Thompson heard—had sampled the young coquette's wares. They were worth the purchasing, Maximilian assured him, and in view of the quality cheap: a diadem sufficed, a trinket or a serenade would lay the lady flat. From the crook of the Elector's arm she ogled Thompson brazenly, then winked.

Nonetheless he held his tongue. Where old Bavaria had hovered on his every breath and quailed before his angry eye, new courtiers seemed indifferent to the counsel of the Chamberlain, for a foreigner in service risks mistrust. They bowed to him, not meaning it; their courtesy was sham.

At night, when no one supervised, he stole to his laboratory and continued his experiments with stoves. Where others used the passage to enjoy forbidden charms, taking a dark secret route to a complaisant bed, he used it for those labors he could not complete by day. He focused on matters domestic and continued his experiments on soup. He improved the field-pot and the soldier's boiling pan.

As with his study of rockets when but a boy in Salem, or his eager parsing of Boerhaave's treatise, so now he paid attention to the kitchen stove and as before, unceasingly, strove to be of use. One fire could be made to heat a variety of boilers. Hot air and gas should yield as much heat as possible before escaping; it was a question of enclosure, of recirculating air. In his House of Industry there were two rows each of four boilers, each encased in brickwork and heated by a single fireplace. By means of dampers and a register he could reduce the cost of fuel by ninety-nine parts in a hundred, since the wastefulness of the prevailing system seemed to him a sin. The standard kitchen chimney was contrived, it would appear, for the express and single purpose of devouring fuel. Often more heat would be used to boil a kettle on a kitchen range than it would take to cook a dinner for fifty hungry men.

With redoubled dedication, Thompson worked. He constructed a photometer. This was a platform in front of a white screen, with two round cylinders of equal height embedded on the platform. Their shadows could be measured with respect to two light sources, these set about eight feet apart. If the shadows were identical, then so were the sources of light; if not, the candles could be moved forward or backward along a calibrated line until identity were reached. He used as the standard of measurement a candle of first quality, eight-tenths of an English inch by diameter and which, when burning with a clear and steady flame, consumed one hundred and eight grains troy weight of wax per hour. Since one of the light sources was a known quantity, he could accurately measure the other along a scale of light. The power and intensity of candles might be thus compared.

He built a "passage thermometer." Having mounted a conventional thermometer in a glass tube which could be sealed, he packed the tube with fibers to discover their effect. He tried and assessed a variety of fibers—those normally used for clothing, and those that were unusual. Fur and feathers, he discovered, had better insulating qualities than did wound silk thread. He speculated accordingly that a component of good insulation was the air; air layered and entrapped kept cold things cold, hot hot.

Then, happening to notice a container filled with spirits of wine which he had set in a window to cool—and through which the sunlight came in such a manner as to illuminate the particles of fine dust trapped within—he studied the dust's motion in the wine. Those particles at the beaker's glass rim were traveling down; those in the center rose up. Liquid, he observed, is constantly in motion—and the heat thereof is best maintained when motion is reduced. As in liquid, so with air; the insulating qualities of fabric must therefore depend on close weaving. Obstruction and impediment, all that which keeps the air enclosed—or so he informed the cloth workers at Au—will keep our soldiers warm.

He considered, always, how to meliorate conditions for the poor. He worked on light and clothing, heat and food, then studied the nature of shelter, the chimney and its aperture, the distribution systems of sustenance and fuel. He took no money in exchange, applying for and receiving no patents on his work but wanted gratitude as payment; it would be its own reward. He wrote and the Elector signed a Proclamation of Thanks. The City of Munich was grateful— so Thompson expressed it—for his unceasing efforts on its citizens' behalf. They wished, he was persuaded, to celebrate his name.

The City Fathers had not been consulted, however, and they balked and grumbled, refusing to sign. These contentious brute uncivil citizens complained. The Town Council, they insisted, should issue its own proclamations and they, the chief men of the city, should not be coerced into praise. Therefore he had them dismissed.

A letter arrived from Woburn: Sarah Rolfe Thompson was dead. The widower had guessed it, somehow, and been long prepared. For the general pity of it, however, the condition of mortality and for their transient pleasure he wept.

Loammi Baldwin sent his sympathy; he feared for young Sarah's well-being. She was growing up ungoverned and required education, but he, Loammi, could not hope to replicate a father's fond attentiveness or help. He enclosed a note from Sarah—the first she'd written Thompson—commending herself to her father and hoping at his leisure and should it give him pleasure to hear back.

Loammi urged his old friend also to respond. *Comfort and happiness,* he wrote, *seem to have deserted that once delightsome place. I pitty the little daughter Sally. She suffers for want of an education; she is a hope full branch but I fear will be ruined if she is not transplanted, I think her father wont neglect the first offspring of his body.*

Then Baldwin changed the subject. He inquired as to apples and requested a sampling of seeds: a cutting from Bavaria might thrive in Massachusetts, and he would be grateful for stock. He hoped to see his childhood friend and trusted all was well.

It devolved upon Thompson, therefore, to write letters to his daughter. He did so with some care. He did not wish to lead her— though he assured her of his love—into false suppositions of earthly grandeur or false expectations of wealth. Since he himself was entirely free from that foolish predilection, or rather weakness, which makes parents blind to the faults of their children, she must gain his affection by meriting his esteem. He urged her to be well informed in all the common branches of science, not indeed to enable her to dispute with Doctors and Professors, for he hated the pertness of Philosophy in Petticoats, but in order that her mind might be enlarged. He wished her to be modest and with gentle manners and a real unaffected goodness of heart. He wanted her to be distinguished by the simplicity not richness of her dress; he asked for a lock of her hair. He promised her a likeness of himself and told her to employ a Limner— one of the best in New England—for a half-length likeness in return. He had his portrait done again, in ermine, wearing medals, then had a version sent to Mary Palmerston and one to Sally at home.

His letters from his daughter were a source of some confusion. Her filial devotion seemed all that one might wish. She wrote once a month at length. Her sentiments were pious but her attainments few and her syntax original, her spelling erratic at best. Her education displayed itself as rudimentary, her sense of the world incorrect.

Yet Sally was no fool. She appeared to share his own uncertainty as to the form of rapprochement; they had lived so long apart they could not decide how to meet. He could not tell precisely if she wanted him to visit, or to visit him instead. Nor did he know—unusual in one so firm of purpose—what he himself preferred.

Those circumstances which he described and with which she grew unhappily familiar made it difficult for him to communicate with her—or, indeed, with any of his habitual number of correspondents. These diminished; they shrank and withdrew. Where once he wrote to many and for multitudes he found himself of late alone and out of countenance; the very paper shook at his approach. The characters—as if he used again his old expedient of sympathetic ink—looked timid, quavery. Two years before he had written a thirty-two page letter to the Elector of Saxony, wherewith he might instruct his son; Thompson did not falter once. He flattered himself that Bavaria had profited from such instruction and that the penmanship was bold, symmetrical and pleasing as the precepts it expressed.

Now there was a falling-off; the winter in Munich grew cold. All effort wearied him, it seemed, and though the approbation of so distinguished an audience as the Elector must constitute a kind of cordial, putting momentary warmth in blood and voice, it also cooled in time. Still, the Chamberlain proceeded and was rarely idle and on the page he queried what she did and did not do.

How does Loammi Baldwin fare, and how is Samuel Williams? Has the bottom land lain fallow or borne crops? What is the yield? What of those pease and turnips I imported; did they take? Tell me what you study, what you read. Tell me which music you prefer, and what you play, and with whom, and who provides the lessons? Distance is a function of mere geography; I have ever held you near, and your concerns are mine. Learn languages. They will stand you in excellent stead. Think kindly, dear, of your father, who sends you his warmest good wishes and his unaltered devotion.

Although Thompson had provided them with separate quarters and a sufficient apartment, his servants the Aichners made noise. They were a large family, in constant need, and the prattle of the children and the guttural and sometimes happy and (to judge by intonation, the mutter of the dialect) often argumentative discussions of old Aichner and his wife, the ruckus of duty performed—all this reminded their employer of his solitary circumstance. He was lonely and hoped for a friend.

Children gave him pleasure; he saw them when he could. He held and tickled toddlers on his lap, joining in innocent revels and laughing at their games. He had the workhouse maidens weave their own white uniforms. They carried choice bouquets of flowers from the English garden, tended by his soldiers and culled by soldier's wives.

Young Sophie was his favorite. Though clearly she would be a beauty like her mother the Countess, she was difficult, said Mary Nogarola, and growing up headstrong and spoiled.

"All children are that way," he said.

"No. Only those who have the opportunity."

"She seems so happy," Thompson said. "So utterly alive."

"So were we all."

"But I mean vivid. What is the word for it, *Lebhaft?*"

"You've grown sentimental, *der Herr.*"

The same could not be said of Mary, who grew harsh. She called him "Your High Holiness," scoffing, when he told her of his plans to help the poor. "You've done enough," she said, "you put them into uniform and took them off the street."

"They are grateful, are they not?"

"So it appears. So you tell me."

"Have some charity," said Thompson. "Be just a little kind."

"'And the greatest of these three,'" she mocked, "'is Charity.'"

212

"I'll see to it," he said. "I'll take an interest in her education."

"Good."

"Will that content you?"

"No."

She offered him a sweet confection: nougat and beaten chocolate in a swirl of lemon pastry, the whole powdered lightly with almonds. He refused.

When his daughter proposed a reunion, Thompson temporized. He was not well enough, he wrote, to change his domicile and undertake a journey so taxing to his health, nor could he promise that the transatlantic crossing would be soon embarked upon; his doctors harbored doubts.

For similar reasons, of course, he could not promise a welcome; he himself lived like a hermit now, in absolute retreat. She might not find society in Munich well suited to her taste. Why should Sally travel to the gilded court in order to be caged; an old man's weary company would fail to compensate for storm-tossed weeks and months, and he must warn her in advance that all her hope of bright adventure would be hope deferred.

He entertained at home or was entertained by others. On the occasion of his birthday, he gave himself a fête. The children in their smocks who appeared and sang to him, young Sophie at the center, smartly coiffed and sweetly fresh—their remarkable display of gratitude, his worth proclaimed, his value and valor and importance attested, the charming arrangement of rubies and lilies which Mary Nogarola offered him that evening, wound around her ankle and fastened with a black silk garter at her thigh, the protestations of devotion, music and *feux d'artifices,* sweet cordials and the finest wines, a silver medallion of Venus and Mars, a gift from Charles Artaria of a glass glockenspiel, the dancing and the banter and the pleasures of the bath: this earthly garden of delight looked fallow and wintry to Thompson. He knelt. He bent his head.

For he could take no solace now in what had pleased him earlier. The royal fellowship of death would claim both King and Councillor, and nothing in his power could oppose that claim once lodged. There general must meet with common soldier, and Chamberlain with beggar, and cutpurse with Chief of Police. Distinction falls away. This world so occupied with rank gives over to decay. Though not of a religious temperament (no man less inclined to worship, to credulity untrammeled by the evidence of sense, to acquiescence in the unproved threat of judgment or its verdict if delivered by suspect authority), Thompson found himself once more upon his knees.

He shut his eyes but could not keep from sight. Vanity, the preacher saith, and the banquets and the fountains and the gorgeous lineaments of Nymphenburg, the vaulted smoke-dimmed ceilings of the Residenz—all beauty and the evidence of arching high ambition turned to dust. The armor worn by heroes looked crumbled and corroded, the gauze of female finery became a spider's web. He was forty now, and frail. Staring, he saw his history: a folly built by George Germain behind the leeching field.

Thus did he break his health. He put away his drawings and his beakers and alembics; he had a nervous crisis and would not leave his room. On the membrane of his eyes and in the theater of his skull strange dramas played themselves out. The bread he ate—or this was how the Chamberlain imagined it, wide-eyed, staring, sweeping the crumbs from his plate—had been prepared in ovens built from his comrades' tombstones: broken, cracked. The name of his dead father had been incised in the crust.

He dreamed. Turning his face to the white wall, Thompson watched while it grew populous: tubers gaped at him from graves, and he was forced to separate their maggot-raddled roots, then made to harvest potatoes in the charnel house. The silk industry collapsed, and what he heard was chewing: the incessant high-pitched click of jaw on leaf, the voracious hum of worms. From all that industry he kept a single winding sheet, from the arsenal one metal shaving, and pressed it to his cheek. Often in the night he woke sweat-soaked and shouting—of farm and cannonade, of monstrous concoctions and fiery thick drink, his old familiars in the flame and Munich's beggar-legion unredeemed. He could not shake them off. Nor could he tell the moment when he slipped unquietly from wakefulness to sleep.

The reward of rank and privilege is constant care, continual fear, and the rich man sickens quite as rapidly as does the poor. When the trumpet sounds resoundingly, no man may stop his ear. For what may each of us expect but a narrow final resting-space and deep bone-rattling chill? The Wheel of Fortune rolls beneath both ox-cart and the gilded coach; the reaper's scythe scythes all. All are leveled by that harvest—whether rose or grain or weed.

Within his spread and sweating palm were visions and grim auguries, and inclining now to prophecy he had his fortune told. A gypsy summoned for that purpose to his drawing room proved cautious:

old and bent and brown. Feigning reluctance, she stood by the table; she reeked. When he urged her to respond she bent above his hand, then withdrew from it, shuddering, saying, "Excellency, you will leave this place. Great success awaits you, but danger attends travel also. Beware."

Now doctors came. They were sent by the Elector as his personal physicians, but seemed to stand by Thompson's bed clothed only in their bones. These skeletons bled him and rattled their hands. They asked him what he ate and what he drank and which scabs he had fornicated with in Munich, Strasbourg, London, as if he could remember or had ever known their names. They asked him the name of his horse. They muttered in the anteroom of cholera and dread typhus; they measured the size of his head, then told him he must rest, that his nerves had suffered and his constitution been weakened by too-constant labor. They prescribed leeches and tea.

His neighbor the Ambassador appeared to Thompson also, clad in living fur. A bear and mink and bloody writhing fox commingled at his throat, yet he had brought the Empress Catherine with him, and she condescended to dance. When Thompson raised his arm to start she said, in what he knew was Russian though he could not understand it, "No, you disgust me. Go home."

That he could not understand the language but made sense of intonation puzzled him a moment; he wondered at the universal gestures of compliance—her lips parted, her legs raised—then how she turned her back. Her hair was richly ornamented, a diadem woven of snakes. She raised a flute of cold champagne, wiggling her fingers and tongue.

But then the Empress disappeared, looking coal-eyed at him over her shoulder, and he was left alone and woke to the glad certainty his fever had broken and he would recover—for had he not engaged in speculation? had he not reasoned things out?

The doctors still stood near his bed. It was not the Empress Catherine but his own mistress Mary who bent above him sweetly, breathing cloves and marzipan. "I'm better now," he said, "that's better," and she answered, "Yes."

For they had conferred the high title of Rumford; they had named him Count.

He foreswore the name of Thompson and was thenceforth always Rumford and had his crest embossed on carriage and gateway and plate. He signed his letters "Rumford" and his essays would thereafter be published with that name. He had drawn his own imagined shield when but a boy in Woburn: the book, the broken tree, the calipers and eye. Now all such wild imaginings had been rendered actual, and Thompson claimed a coat of arms in truth.

In truth, however, Count Rumford was unmoved. The honor failed to interest him, bestowed. Perhaps this was a function of his own uncertain health, or how long he'd had to wait since first he sought his title, for the Elector's promise had been some time deferred. As when an anxious father waits the birth of his first heir, and confers a name upon it and endures the lengthy interval (for there are false alarms and unlooked-for delays and still-born sons and daughters), so had the name of Rumford been chosen for its usage years before. When finally that day arrived—though long-awaited, dearly desired and to the nicest detail planned—the ceremony seemed to him mere ritual observance. Under the sun of Bavaria there was, he feared, nothing new.

He had been too long a courtier to be impressed at court. He had met too much nobility to grow vain about his own. For Rumford's restless questing came, he came to understand, from that period of sickness when he'd sweated in his chambers and the wet wide solitary bed, poised between horror and horror, unable—no matter how closely attended or watched, how expensively maintained his convalescence or monitored and celebrated his recovery—to vanquish grinning bone-clad death: *Timor mortis conturbat me.*

For it was not the same as earlier, not what he had dreamed. A fantasy enacted is mere fact. To have become a Count of the Holy Roman Empire was, the Elector's entourage insisted, remarkable; few foreigners might claim as much and no one could claim more; it was a signal honor, was it not? They needed the assurance that he was gratified, the certainty he recognized how much he was rewarded and how splendid the reward. He assured them this was so.

Yet the life of the courtier disgusted him now, the folly of ambition and cupidity's vain dream. He had seen the chalk face of corruption, the grinning image of concupiscence. He huddled in his thick wool blanket, shivering; his return to the palace took time.

"Rest, *Du*," said Mary Nogarola.

"I don't belong here," Thompson muttered. "My home was never Munich."

"Don't talk about it, please."

Thompson told her he had glimpsed the light where all had been a darkness, and that he would devote his life or what remained of it—"Rest now," she said again. "Don't speak that way,"—to selfless-ness and charity, to bringing a measure of comfort to the deserving poor. "You've done so much, *liebchen*," she offered, but he said, "Not enough."

What he wanted next was fame. What he needed was glory, not rank. And fame lies in good works and glory in beneficence, and he would therefore strive to be famous in Munich and throughout the Elector's dominions and the extravagant world. It was a kind of con-version; Rumford prayed for help.

Now slowly in his fearful dark a dawning hope brought comfort: not all achievement fades. His Chinese Pagoda, for instance, gave pleasure in the Garden and would do so till the crack of doom to those who walked beneath. His cows would be admired, no matter how brittle the flesh. Thus Count Rumford found a way to counter mere oblivion. Kind memory—-the gratitude of generations—must endure.

SALLY

My parents. I'd promised you their story—a full and fair accounting of my own childhood, then theirs. And of my father's father's and my mother's mother's childhoods, receding thence by certain stages to the vast backward of conception in the bedroom at Auteuil. Conception, the great word of art and life. What did it feel like, I wonder, that little implosion, the release and conjunction of intimate opposites from which they and I derive?

But it all seems predictable, doesn't it, too modern a description of the way things work. It's not who they were or failed to be that tells me what I am. Remember how I wrote a thesis on the birth of Aphrodite, our Venus on the half-shell and those two poetic versions— by Rilke and Hérédia—of her entry in this world? Well, more and more I find myself preferring neither of those stories but the one about goddess Athena and her chaste genesis—she who sprang full-blown out of Zeus's fathering brain. Born carrying her spear, and with a helmet on; what a headache the girl must have been!

For Thompson was his own invented creature, after all: a self-made man. An *ab*-original. A true American in this regard, even if a traitor, and it's no accident that as his years of exile pass he finds himself dreaming of home. Still, that line of his astonishes, in his first letter to Sally: *Since he himself was entirely free from that foolish predilection, or rather weakness, which makes parents blind to the faults of their children, she must gain his affection by meriting his esteem.* No knee-jerk inclination here to family feeling in my famous ancestor—*the pertness of Philosophy in Petticoats,* indeed.

And who can say if his own father—by early death disservered from Ben's childhood in Woburn—had any real effect upon the person he became? No doubt he missed dear dad but was able to replace him with John Wentworth, George Germain or the Elector Palatine; each time he required protection he found a protector at hand. And when our boy found consolation with his mother-surrogates—Sarah Rolfe and Mary Palmerston and Mary Nogarola and the rest—what he told them in the teeming dark had little relevance, I'm certain, to his childhood on the farm. He kicked off the mud from his shoes. What we call, Class, the shit from his heels.

Then after he fled from the New World to Old his partners could indeed have proved susceptible to country matters, confessing to a pastoral enthusiasm and smearing their bodies with mud, vying in depravity—ah, let us name it inventiveness rather—as did the mother and daughters Germain, and because of their exalted station permitted to indulge—*nostalgie de la boue* indeed!—in jolly reindeer games. And so they play milkmaid to rooster, Phyllis to Strephon, Robin Redbreast to Cock; so Mary Mary urged him on to use her as his

221

spaniel, or perhaps with her ribbons and wood herder's crook disported with him gaily as both shepherdess and sheep.

All right; what do I remember? What do you need to know? We were a family like others: poor, hard-hit after the Depression years but never really starving, living in New Jersey and then Connecticut, in the back streets of once bustling towns where you could rent part of a house. The theater of my childhood was a side-porch and front-stoop. I remember hopscotch, jump-rope, a dog named Tim with only three legs and the queerest rolling gait (à la Count Bretzenheim perhaps?)—how he lurched after what I called squirrels and now think were probably rats. I was an only child. Well, that's the way it seemed to me although I had a much older sister who got married as soon as she could to a man as far away as possible; he had a job in California and they drove there on their honeymoon and died in a car-crash en route. Since we kept it on the mantel, I remember the telegram's text: BETTY IN AN ACCIDENT STOP CONDOLENCES STOP DIED WITHOUT PAIN STOP FULL EXPLANATION FOLLOWS STOP.

What remains for me is absence, a set of black-draped photographs and a teddy-bear gathering dust. Of my elder sister's presence I have precious few reminders: a pair of shoes abandoned in the closet, a lavender sachet beneath a yellow sheet. There's the sound on the side porch of laughter when her suitor arrives with his flowers and flask, the creak of the rocker the two of them sat courting in and how she shooed me inside. There's a flouncing down the stairwell while she practiced for the wedding, and my mother's silent disbelief and then shocked screaming horror when the news of the accident came. I was seven years old at the time. It made me feel important and gave me a reason to stay out of school, but I can't really say that I missed her; when Betty died it was—for me, at any rate—as though she dropped off the earth. Just the way Ben Thompson did when he set sail for England, never returning to Woburn or Concord and only alive through the mail. She disappeared with Jack by heading west, and the telegram was just a confirmation: out there the world was perilous, and you could get killed in a car.

My father was an accountant, a thin pale earnest man. When he was out of work—which was often, those years—he styled himself a "Factor." He liked to read the paper and listen to the radio, adjusting the volume, eating soda crackers and drinking ginger beer. He had a wart on his neck. My mother was the vivid one—loud laughter and loud weeping and an occasional outburst of song; she broke things (not by hurling plates out windows or shattering them on walls, but by simple inadvertence, stepping on them, dropping them) as if she couldn't be bothered with the domestic routine. "Get a handle on it, Rose," I can hear my father saying, "get a handle on it, please."

This was as close as he came to reproach, or dared to in my presence, and my mother turned her back on him or fixed a stray lock of my hair. Perhaps they loved each other, though as a child I doubted it, and their marriage seemed to me a warring truce. It was as though she waited for her husband to complain that she was being careless—so that she, in answer, could tell him she just didn't care. As if there were no reason to, after my sister died.

At the age when children dream that they're adopted I dreamed

it every night: I had been kidnapped by gypsies and was only passing through. I was a princess sent packing on the southbound train
to Bridgeport, the love-child of Ingrid Bergman, the niece of Anas-
tasia. But in all my wild imaginings and fantasies of origin I know I
never thought that Benjamin Thompson, Count Rumford (I'd never
even heard of him, remember) would have spawned me with a serving girl so many years before. Remember the Elector's concern for the
nobility's "by-blows," his desire to educate bastards and teach them
to dance and fence? His instructions to Thompson to build such a
house and provide for all their sons? Well, our hero did so with a vengeance, from the boy in the glass jar in Woburn to the garden where
he helped produce (while the Countess hiked her skirts, bidding him
come to her under the lindens) little Sophie Baumgarten.

These nights, I've not been well. I sweat and shiver and wake up at
three o'clock and cannot fall asleep again or, if so, only fitfully. These
nights I write nonsense, I know. And talking to myself out loud I
mouth the language, tonguing it: *Kind memory endures.*

When they took him from the city, thousands mourned. They lined the Munich thoroughfares and massed at his mansion's closed gate and then, when he departed it, they followed his horse-droppings and the mud-track incised by his wheels. The little girls curtsied; boys bowed. They stood by the hedgerows or underneath trees, waiting at corners and doffing cloth caps. It had been raining steadily, a cold March rain, yet the people stood bareheaded while he passed.

A long sigh escaped them, a high voiceless cry. Count Rumford sank back in the cushions and peered through curtained glass. The poor of Munich grieved—as when a dog perceives its master will depart, and lies at the foot of the bed; there the hound waits inertly, dejected, yet with its eyes scans the least detail and with its ears hears everything: the lightest footfall in the dressing room adjoining, the rustle and susurrus of fresh shirts and folded sheets. No reassurance reassures, nor the promise of return. Each packed trunk is a sorrow, every valise a reproach. How the news of his departure reached them Rumford did not know.

Yet the people had gathered at dawn. From the four corners of the town they poured forth in a constant stream; from shop and hall and stable they drew near. They knelt in silence, watching, and stretched out empty arms. Some offered fruit, or bread. Some—to judge from their pursed lips, imploring eyes—were fearful, as if when he entered his carriage they must abandon hope.

Still others seemed content and smiled and nodded, watching, and waved him on his way. They clapped their outstretched hands for him or bent their heads to pray. These last, he understood, had understood his need to leave and spurred the pilgrim on. A shaft of light broke through the clouds, illuminating the road south; rain lessened and then ceased. Sunlight irradiated briefly the stone wall of the city, its crenellations and portals, while from the Marienkirche and the modest church, from steeple and chapel equally, he heard the tolling bells.

Rumford huddled in his seat. The horses quickened pace. A great supplication went with him, a universal *Vale:* the people wished him well. Go in health, they seemed to say, god-speed.

For company he took his dwarf, the youngest Aichner boy. They traveled in some style: a carriage for himself, a carriage for his servants and seven baggage carts. He clothed his page in velvet and choice Flemish lace and draped his own person in fur. His *équipage* and horses were of the first quality, and there were relays waiting at planned stages on the road.

On March 16 he had received his passport; *il Conte Benjamino di Rumfort* might make his way to Italy. Riding south, the Count was in no hurry to attain this goal but passed two months in Switzerland beforehand, surveying both glacier and lake. Interlaken pleased him, with its unequalled vista and the looming Jungfraujoch; the weather was impressive and a blizzard blocked the pass. Here the cold was absolute and though he took the measure of the depth and catalogued the colors of the snow, it proved impossible to go by carriage or on foot, implausible to lead his horses on the ice-slick track till thaw. Although Hannibal and elephant had managed these same mountains, our voyager turned back.

His retinue were billeted in the hamlet underneath. They used the serving girls and caroused in the Weinstube and played at cards and darts. The Count paid for their pleasures but was elsewhere occupied—lodging seven days and nights in a snowbound chalet.

The owner made him welcome and would take no payment but requested, in exchange, a friendly game of chess. They played each night that week. They were equal adversaries, and Rumford found himself absorbed by the strategy and gambits of the contest—his opponent nodding sagely, the fierce wind howling at the wall, the windows piled with powdered snow and filigreed with ice. His hostess was a woman with white hair so finely spun she reminded him of his dear mother, new-widowed once again; he queened his pawn then lost it to black's rook and sacrificed his bishop and achieved a mate in six. The men shared pipe tobacco and a bowl of buttered rum. Next game, for it was early still, old Hans took the offensive with a discovered check.

These symmetries of chess compelled the Count; they were military, nearly, in the stratagems and angles of attack. He learned patience in defense. When he went to bed he studied (eyes shut, focused, replaying the sequence) his blunders and his coups. Beneath an eiderdown that had been fashioned from the farm's own geese he rehearsed the argument for strong-side castling, a pincer movement of paired knights or the alignment of pawns at his flank. Had he brought his bishop to Queen four, he might have avoided checkmate.

When at length the day arrived, he bade old Hans and Gretchen the fondest of farewells. In the Engadine he gathered edelweiss and berries, and in the Ober-Engadine he sampled cheese. He listened to the melancholy music of the sounding horn, the cow-bells and the shepherd's call, the carillon resounding in the Kammermusikhalle of the rocks.

For the first time in his adult life, Rumford's fancy was mere whim. He dallied and delayed where mountain peaks soared brilliantly and pastures gleamed with streams; if snowmelt glistened in the cupped palm of a boulder he bent to it and drank. Where he went was where he pleased, and his spirits lifted in proportion to his distance from Bavaria, its populated cities and the scheming court. Having no fixed intention or schedule, his progress was on purpose leisurely and he gave contrary orders—proceeding for an hour west or east or north one day, for eleven in a circle on the next.

The meadows south of Munich had been frozen, brown and sere. The sky seemed always gray. His mood at first was bleak, yet as they made their way past village and fortified castle—through dark wood and distant valley, the horses wet and steaming, the carriage wheels encrusted first with snow then slush then mud, the branches rimed with frost, then bare, then lifting into bud and leaf—a brightness came upon him that he had not known in years. For he was no one's creature now, in no one's debt or retinue, and master of his own.

As the weeks wore on, Rumford improved. The potato would be marvelously suited to this stony mountain soil, and he commended its general use. A milkmaid in green Grindewald received him on her knees. He admired the meticulous precision of the farms, the expertise of blacksmith and tanner, the racks of cheese, the cleanly arrangement of stalls. It was as though he rode beloved Blaze again, as half a lifetime previous, and rambling in the countryside for exercise and fun. A prelate in Geneva offered an interesting speculative expectation of the Day of Judgment, since one of the thieves had been saved and one damned, yet both were crucified adjacent to our Lord. He and Rumford argued doctrine as a function of the theory of probability; as with a tossed coin and the two men on Golgotha, so our souls. According to St. Augustine one must neither presume nor despair.

The apple trees in blossom on the broad verge of the roadway were a white marvel, rising, and the Count festooned his carriage with their gathered branches, then strewed petals where they drove. The Duke of Burgundy's young sister had a fondness for raw food; the smell of cooking disgusted her, per contra, and she swallowed nothing hot. He took her standing up. Wood carvings of the hinterland were excellent, and he considered how to replicate them elsewhere: a manufactory might perhaps be established in Munich, and the saints and elves and demons sold throughout the Elector's dominion. This could be accomplished with economy and profit; he sent samples back. The little Aichner boy—hump-backed, big-lipped, silent—proved surpassingly dexterous with knives, and could whittle likenesses from any sort of wood.

Now news arrived from France. It was not good. Bloody Robespierre was guillotined, Marat murdered in his bath, and still the full tumbrils rumbled past. The salubrity of bathing would receive a local—yet, the Count trusted, a temporary—setback; according to the rumor, Paris gutters streamed with blood. The chemist Lavoisier was killed, and this was the world's grievous loss; it had taken civilization so many centuries to produce that noble head, so little time and thought to cut it off! When they addressed the president of the tribunal on Antoine Laurent Lavoisier's behalf, tearful, urging clemency, adducing great protestations and divers irrefutable proofs, brute Coffinhal replied that knowledge was not wanted here and the Republic had no need of clever men: *La République n'a pas besoin des savants.*

The cider by Lake Konstanz tasted achingly of Woburn's, and he wrote Loammi Baldwin that the apple trees of Switzerland would flourish back at home. He missed the boon companion of his vanished youth. He wrote his daughter often but expected no reply; he planned to visit Milano thereafter, and Florence and Naples and Rome. He informed the Countess Baumgarten and Countess Nogarola of his whereabouts by letter—though he stressed in these letters to Munich his continued weakness and not increasing strength. He begged for continuing furlough from his arduous duties at home, feeling weary as he wrote and short of breath. In Lugano he danced for an hour with the mistress of a general, but contrary to his old practice and her practiced expectation declined her whispered offer that they continue upstairs.

"It is time," he told his servants, "to press on."

They saluted. They curtsied and bowed.

"I have engagements elsewhere. I am behindhand already."

"*Jawöhl, der Graf.*"

"*Morgen früh,*" he told them. "Tomorrow morning, early."

They exchanged glances, concerned.

"We've idled long enough," he said. "Go tell your sweethearts *Wiedersehen.* Make them promises. Then pack."

Late May and June in Italy proved, for Rumford, a delight. The glinting silvered olive trees, the terraced hills, the ancient aqueducts and Roman roads and vineyards, the marble statuary and the fountains and the trellised gardens where a man might, reading, rest—all these enchanted him. The soft air soothed his skin, the warm sun burnished flesh. The ample unbound breasts of nymphs bemused him once again, and the painted boys on ceilings with their quivers full of darts. He ate choice bits of milk-fed veal in a peach brandy glaze, and sampled both game-cock and thrush. His appetite awakening, he dined lavishly in banquet rooms with negresses to serve and peacocks in the courtyard and a blind fine-fingered harpist by his chair. Those he had entertained in Munich now returned the favor, and he was rarely bored.

Rumford visited the kitchens and oversaw improvements in the public halls. He listened to the fiddle and clavier. The traveler to Italy—like so many others before him, and since—was beguiled by beauty, the sensual music of the breeze above the soughing pines.

He went out into society each night. He met Sir Joseph Banks and they disputed amiably as to convection currents and the nature of color in light. The Count studied the rainbow's components and, deploying his photometer, attempted to measure the intensity of sunbeams when refracted by water: he enclosed the water severally in a glass beaker, then a silver cup and a stone bowl. He bought a humpbacked whore for Aichner and sketched their respective convexities, then left them to their sport. Remembering, of a sudden, that monstrous child in Woburn he had drawn for Dr. Hay, he was seized by the desire to return, and he wrote Loammi Baldwin with a view to the purchase of land. Buy something for me, Rumford wrote, and set aside a monthly sum to give my mother, please; build us a home across from yours where she may take her ease. I wish we might be neighbors once again.

In July he joined Charles Blagden and Lord and Lady Palmerston; I am an exile, he told her, doomed to roam in the wide world without a home, and without a friend. Mary said, I am your friend, I was and will be that. Don't think I have forgotten you, he said, nor charge me with neglect. I haven't done, she said, no more than you need blame me.

With a certain hesitation, a punctiliousness born of his regard for Palmerston, he made her his mistress once more and resumed their old affair. In Milano she received him while Lord Palmerston conducted business in Rome, and though they joked about Italian ways, the seduction of the southern clime and the invigorating attributes and beneficent effects of peppers and garlic and oil and red wine, though they pretended to shared passion, there was something pale and circumspect about their first embrace—a shadow of old age and sickness by the bed.

"Be gentle, Ben," she told him, when he waxed vigorous, and there were tears of gratitude and sweet recrimination; they had been too much apart. Tom Gainsborough was dead.

Next the Count traveled to Pisa, and he missed her greatly, and wrote that he was spoiled but it was all her fault. He had been so long used to her agreeable company that he really felt quite awkward when deprived of it, and leaving Mary Palmerston was like being forced to leave home. He was melancholy, lonesome; his mind was filled with sentiments to which it had grown unaccustomed. Lady Bolingbroke in Pisa—with her charming daughters, her aged and infirm father—engaged his lively sympathy, and he really did not know, he wrote, how he might have been otherwise tempted to cheat away her tedious lingering hours. The French had lost a boat at Leghorn, with upwards of four hundred casualties, and there were rumors that the English and the French engaged each other at Toulon; he hoped that this was so. He trusted that the family and Viscount Palmerston prospered; he hoped his mistress thought of him, as he himself thought only of her always and each minute of the day.

In Verona he repeated his experiments with kitchens. His introduction of the workhouse model and the Rumford Roaster proved a great success, and he was applauded by all. At Desenzana, on the shores of Lake Garda and by prearrangement he met Mary Nogarola —who had taken her own good advice and journeyed south. Her Italian needed practicing, and her husband was in Mannheim still, and the Munich court grew stale. The Countess was wearing silver at her neck and in her hair. Her dress was deepest blue, moiré, and her arms except for silver bracelets bare.

She was staying with her children in a villa by the water; her balcony was shaded by fruit and almond trees. Olive trees gleamed softly on the hillside just beyond.

"You're looking well," said Mary. "You are perfectly recovered?"

"No."

"You missed your old companion?"

"Yes."

"But I was with you where you went?" She touched his knee, then thigh and then above.

"*Selbstverständlich*," Rumford said. "Self-evidently. See?"

Their reunion was extravagant; it lasted all that night. He measured her dark frenzy by the blonde decorum of his English Mary—musing meanwhile on the happy accident of names. He remembered Mary Appleton, the daughter of his first employer, aloof at seventeen. He remembered, also, his informer—the rebel printer's consort, Mary Dill. This coincidence impressed him, as did the span of years; I will always love my Mary, he declared.

What remained for him in Italy; how while away the time? He wrote essays on his history and speculative enterprise and kept notes, should they prove useful, on the movement of the troops. He found further opponents at chess. His game improved, but no expert proved so utterly his equal as had been the Swiss farmer in the snowbound chalet. Rumford marveled at that natural philosopher and remembered him more fondly every month, since his host had had the manners of a natural aristocrat—refusing all payment but their nightly contest, content to win and equally to lose. Although bounded by his house and land, that homespun citizen had been lord of a domain; his smiling white-headed wife (with her tuneless whistling, her proffered tray of nuts and fruit) had proved sufficient company. They did not leave their hillside and the miniscule metropolis of Interlaken, yet their role in the expansive world seemed to the Count more noble than those by contrast played upon a spotlit stage.

Rumford told himself he missed old Hans and Gretchen far more than the Elector or the grandees of the court. The mountains and the open sky furnished a perspective lost to the palaces of Munich or halls of Nymphenburg. At times the smell of pipe tobacco or the taste of buttered rum brought tears to the traveler's eyes; *Einfach,* he wrote in his journal: give me the simple life.

Lady Palmerston grew jealous and demanded his return. He temporized, informing her that he had great experiments, a course of private study to complete. In truth what he studied was love. His German Mary had displaced the English one entirely, and he found himself besotted by the lake where they swam and rowed. He was happy once again with Countess Nogarola and her heedless headstrong ways; they went riding through the countryside, as earlier in Munich, and the pleasures of the exercise in meadow and bedchamber were keenly reminiscent of their courtship years before. She drew pictures of the sky. She adored Italian chocolate and (as the weather turned and summer settled in) the cool interiors of churches where, while he admired frescoes, she might pray.

"What do you pray for?" asked Rumford.

She stood.

"Is it proper to inquire?"

"No."

"How may I phrase it, then; what do you seek?"

"Salvation. Guidance. Mercy."

"For what transgression?" Rumford asked.

Mary made no answer. Her gaze, however, spoke volumes and that day they read no more.

It had the look of symmetry, the feel of chess; while she advanced upon him he drew back. But now the pattern had reversed, and the pursuer was instead pursued; when Countess Nogarola shrank he pressed himself upon her in attack. An excess of devotion overcame him by the lake; he asked himself why had he been so careless and dismissive of her feelings in the past? Rumford puzzled for some time as to the riddling nature of romance—widower now, and free to wed, he courted only women who would not be free till widowed to invite him to their bed. They did so nonetheless, of course, but at the risk of scandal and at night; he longed for daylit company, the open espousal of vows.

She could not—would not—come with him to Rome or thence to Naples. There were those who thought it in their interest to prevent the journey; they found means, though feigning to approve it, to keep Mary from his carriage and his side. Her husband missed the children, he informed her by his courier, and would return from Mannheim and expected her at home. Countess Baumgarten wrote her sister that she should not be foolish; the Elector had expressly asked about her lengthy absence and required her at court. Karl Theodor was marrying and wished her to attend. He sent his compliments to Rumford also and hoped that all was well; he did not wish to trouble his dear Chamberlain, however, with the taxing imperatives of travel or so heavy a charge on poor health. Count Rumford might remain.

"There is nothing here to keep me," he complained. "Where you go my heart goes with you."

"Nonsense. Come back when you're ready."

"And will you be waiting?"

"As before."

She sat naked on her balcony; the children were asleep. She displayed the old insouciance, the aristocratic ease of their first nights; she had, he understood at last, no interest but her own. Pleasure was her principle, and self-indulgence ingrained. Like her sister and their circle, she was raised to seem obedient, whereas in fact the Countess exercised the habit of command. Now he had served her purpose and was growing tedious and must avoid self-pity in her presence; she was fingering him idly and her robe lay on the rail.

For one moment he persuaded her that he would miss her greatly; she looked so sweetly sorry that he thought his heart must crack. "My Knight of the White Eagle," Mary said. "You continue on without me. I go home."

Thus the wanderer took leave of Countess Nogarola and heavy-hearted and alone resumed his journey south.

He solaced himself with white grapes. They were suited to the climate and the time, for now the heat of Italy grew burdensome, the sunshine relentless: white light. A dry wind swept before him like the breath of Hell itself. He stayed some days in Florence with Mary Palmerston, but she could track upon him the spoor of infidelity—not so much the body's traces, since he was washed and perfumed, and in any case she would not care and laid no claim on continence—but that true faithlessness in love: a preoccupation of mind. His attention was elsewhere and not upon hers. This, she said, was true betrayal and this she could not brook.

Count Rumford traveled on. The hills of Rome exhausted him;

the great square of St. Peter's provided a reminder, merely, of Mary Nogarola's faith and how she could not marry twice or cancel nuptial vows. August proved even more fierce. Though he had not thought it possible, the heat increased. The Tiber seemed the Styx, the Campidoglio blistered—although he wore fine leather—the soles of his shod feet, and the monuments and chapels and remnants of the Empire tormented him acutely with the ruin of his hopes. His second carriage broke, and he left a coachman and three baggage carts behind. They were instructed to return to Munich, once repairs had been accomplished; his heart was in Bavaria, so why not his effects?

Into the teeth of September heat, the mouth of the Inferno, he drove south. Here the landscape was barren, boulder-strewn, and the few wilting fig trees and the stunted olives offered neither shade nor comfort; the mantle of the standing pool lay greenly thick with slime. His horses dragged and hacked. He reached Naples at month's end and settling there disconsolate asked himself repeatedly why he had merited such exile and how had he come to this pass?

He spent the winter alone. He perfected his experiments on color and the pigmentation inhering in shadows; by the open ground-floor window of his palace on the faded park—with no breath of air to make his candle gutter—Rumford wrote. He wandered up and down or labored at his desk. A pretty boy with mandolin passed by that station nightly, and one night Count Rumford summoned him and, struck by the configuration of his slim hips and curling hair, called the musician "Mary" and fell upon his neck. He used the boy dog-fashion and next day paid his successor to oblige in the same manner, but it all seemed poor distraction, and Naples could not hold him any more than mighty Rome. In the springtime he turned home.

"*Wacht auf!*" he told young Aichner. "We go back."

The boy had grown a moustache. He rubbed his eyes, then lip.

"You don't mean that you want to stay?"

He blinked.

"In this *verdammte* country?"

"*Nein.*"

"You want to see your family? Your brothers and sisters. Your playmates?"

"*Jawöhl, der Graf.* But of course, Count. *Natürlich.*"

"Then hurry," Rumford said.

It came to him, returning, that his life had been spent in the service of heat—that this was his great subject and his particular skill. Had he not studied rockets in the storeroom at John Appleton's; had he not learned munitions in the service of Germain? Did he not show the doubting world how heat is transmitted in water, how phlogiston must be reckoned as the merest foolishness, an answer to no question one need ask? The theory of caloric was his to claim, then to refine; he had perfected pot and roaster, fireplace and stove. In pursuit of his hard inquiry he had endured both heat and cold, the tropic and arctic extremes.

Rumford ate and dressed accordingly, in summer silk or winter fur, and monitored his health. He resumed his daily exercise with broad-sword and epée. He felt well, returning, and ready to perform whatever the Elector might require of his servant.

Karl Theodor opened his arms. Where the year before he had appeared indifferent, or in any case preoccupied, now the Elector hailed the Count's return. They discussed the healing waters and the balm of mountain air and spoke about the virtues of retreat. For it became apparent soon that Karl Theodor had met his match, and needed help and comfort; he had married in a hurry and had leisure to repent.

The court was now a haven for the worldly young, a place of midnight revels. The Electrice loved to dance. She was agile and tireless and merciless and gay. She kept her consort standing in the center of the floor—since, married, she would take no partner but Karl Theodor himself. All else was beneath her, she said. So the Elector nightly powdered and prepared himself and wore his velvet leggings and silk waistcoat and his dancing pumps. Below the chandelier he stood, pale hand outstretched, feet rooted, turning slowly, heavily, thick wattled neck abobble, sweating, eyes half shut.

Then his nineteen year old darling would perform her pirouette. She dipped and rose and waved her arms and bent her jewel-bright neck. She twirled and leaped and curtsied and received the room's applause. "How marvelous," they cried. "How graceful and how fine!"

Yet the gallants were less gallant once alone. When she said that other partners were beneath her dignity, they swore that she had danced beneath them often and often before. Karl Theodor would need their help, and she would want their service, to acquire a new heir. Behind their hands the suitors muttered and made jokes; they whispered how the lady planned to kill her husband standing up, then whispered how she wore him out as well by lying down.

"*Das ist genug, Schatz,*" the old man would breathe. "Darling, it's enough."

But she lifted skirts and heels and called out to the orchestra, "Louder! Again!"

"Let's go," Karl Theodor would plead, and she'd say, "Just one more."

The orchestra would hear her and obey.

What we return to, Rumford found, is not what we have left: Bavaria had changed. For though the Count recovered from physical infirmity, in that part of the body the faithful call "soul," he quailed, and to the very depths. What awaited him in Munich was drudgery, stale repetition, a thankless old age. The Zweibrücken faction was weak. The intricate maneuvers of the court—those questions of power and influence and primacy that had so engaged him once—seemed a dance performed by strangers, in strange ways.

Nor could Rumford take much pleasure in the presence of his mistresses; they simply shut him out. Mary, back in Munich, was the Countess Nogarola and otherwise engaged. She helped him with translation still, since his German was imperfect, but denied all else. No longer his companion of the balcony at Garda, the naked sylph upon his knee, she played the part instead of dutiful mother and wife, swathing herself in propriety as once in her perfumes and silk. The passionate commerce between them was done; she told him, simply, "No."

Her sister the Countess had meanwhile grown fat. When Rumford made his overture, she said with the conviction of the truly sated that he ought to be ashamed. It would be embarrassing and foolish and no fun. It was hot and too much work. She'd had no lover in two years who provided her with the sharp pleasures of a pork chop in horseradish sauce and soubise, no lover in a decade who could equal the delight of a warm rising chocolate soufflé. The Countess Baumgarten speared a pickled gherkin and ate it appreciatively. Or—she licked her fingers—a lemon pudding or cherries jubilee or an *omelette à l'anglaise.* Not even you, my dear, she said, could make me feel as satisfied as a first-rate meal. All those tears and protestations, those busy nighttime rendezvous and daylight assignations, those schemes and dreams and stratagems now seemed merely stale to her: the undigested remnants of a banquet long consumed; her new fashion was fidelity, and she embraced restraint.

Little Sophie also constituted a reproach, seeming giddy and foolish and wild. She had neglected her lessons, he feared, and such fear proved warranted: when he asked her to multiply seven and nine she got the answer wrong. Her French was nonexistent and her English a disgrace. If he mentioned Galileo or Copernicus she looked at him, her round face blank, her blue eyes brightly vacant.

"And who are they?" she asked.

She could not draw. She dashed the violin he gave her to the floor impatiently. "I despise this music," Sophie said. "We hire musicians at home." When he taxed her with ingratitude she asked, "What do I owe you anyhow?" and he could find no reply.

She did not know, Count Rumford knew, his true relation to her—and he was loathe to claim it. Let the girl remain, he reasoned, as ignorant of this as in all else. For her official protector, Count Baumgarten, was rich and would provide a dowry so munificent that

Sophie's faults might well be disregarded; her father on the other hand had little to give but advice.

The months dragged on. He wrote to Lady Palmerston that Munich had grown old. *The little dear Sophie,* he wrote, *is as charming as ever, and often comes and dines with me. But the Prophecy of her Mothers Mother that her father and her Aunts Lover would renew an old connection with her younger Daughters elder Sister, is not likely to be verified.*

Still, he went into society. He maintained his place at court and strove to stay amused. In order to effect this last, he assumed the grandee's role; his expenditures were lavish and entertainments large. He gave concerts in his house to which a hundred ladies came, and there was sparkling punch and wine between the acts. His three drawing rooms had Turkish sofas lining the four walls.

Rumford gave a great fête also in the English Gardens. Thousands danced where once alone by the Isar he had dreamed and fished. The poor of Munich sang his praises, and he walked gratefully among them and praised them in return, being more at ease with laborers, as he told his servants the Aichners, than lords. He missed America and his dear widowed mother more from day to day.

"I'm leaving," he told Mary Nogarola.

"Oh?"

"I need to enlarge my acquaintance. There's nothing to keep me in Munich."

She bent to her book.

"Not any longer," he persisted. "Not what I had hoped for."

"The Elector will miss you."

"*Und Du?*"

"*Natürlich,*" Mary told him. "We all will, all of us."

"Will you come with me?"

"Count!"

"Your *caro sposo* forbids it?"

"I am my own mistress entirely."

"Then come," he said. "My darling."

"No." She turned the page.

❦ V ❦

He wrote about his kitchens and armaments and soup. He argued for economy in charity, and computed the state's savings when the poor become productive; it is wiser far, he reasoned, to give assistance than alms. The Count composed those essays that reported on his findings in the management of beggars and of heat. He asked Loammi Baldwin to arrange for Sally's visit and remitted monies for the cost, booking passage for his daughter on the S.S. Charlestown out of Boston bound for London. Having arranged to have his essays published in that English city, he determined, therefore, that it was in London they should meet.

He left without regret. His papers were crucial, were with him, and they would make his mark abroad that here was writ in water. Language lasts. He bade farewell to Mary and her sister and his daughter and the Elector and Electrice and others of the court; he made a solemn promise, after six months, to return.

Count Rumford took his dwarf along, and Anymeetle Aichner to serve as Sarah's maid. Mindful of the snares that wait, the bait that lures the wanderer, he made rapid progress from Munich on main roads north and west. It was October weather: brisk and fine. He did not stop at Strasbourg or that bloody city, Paris, but made his way directly to Calais.

At Calais, however, he indulged himself and tarried before boarding—with results of which the reader will be acquainted hereafter; this time the ferry had favoring winds, and the crossing was easy and mild. Gulls rode the updraft lazily, and our traveler counted their wing-beats and studied their system of flight. Seeing the white chalk cliffs rise steeply out of mist, the shore of England waiting, he thought how strange were his life's turnings, how intricate the circling path that brought him back once more.

London air was thick with coal, wasteful as well as unclean. A vast dark cloud hung over the metropolis, and the surrounding country lay blighted by it also; this dense pall, Rumford knew, was almost certainly composed of unconsumed coal, which, having stolen wings from the innumerable fires of the great city, had escaped by the chimneys and continued to sail about in the obscuring air. Then, having lost the heat which gave it volatility, it returned in a dry shower of fine black dust to the ground; bright day became Egyptian dark beneath this universal descent.

Lady Palmerston's town house in Hanover Square had rooms so sooty and odorous with fireplace discharge that she bought no new furniture, for it would be ruined by smoke. She asked him, as a favor, to improve her domestic ventilation, since he was world-famous as an expert in these matters. He could not well refuse. "A smoky house and scolding wife are two of the worst ills in life"—so ran the verse. The Count applied himself to open fires, as before to closed.

If the room were a box to be heated, then the issue of escaping heat must be as important as that of heat introduced, and insulation would prove paramount; the walls of the room must not leak. He narrowed the aperture of the chimney, so the down-draft might not enter freely with its smoke-laden air. Where the chimney opened out again the cold air waited, uninvasive, as if by masonry forestalled. This management of smoke on a retaining shelf proved crucial to success. Rumford lessened the depth of the fireplace also, and beveled the two sides, thus transmitting more heat to the room. He found out and removed those local hindrances which forcibly prevented smoke from following its natural tendency to go up the chimney. "Less wind," he said to Mary. "We will control the wind." She was grateful and breathed freely and was warm.

There were those who made mock of his efforts—who drew pictures of a bare-backed "Rumpford" toasting himself by a stove. There were those who claimed that Benjamin Franklin had used much the same design. Innovation is, as ever, misunderstood and scorned. Greatness is, as ever, attended by ingratitude and fame by calumny, yet he took all such insults in stride. His Fourth Essay had the title "Of Chimney Fireplaces, with Proposals for improving them to save Fuel; to render Dwelling-houses more Comfortable and Salubrious, and effectually to prevent Chimneys from Smoking." All this he had accomplished for the benefit of others, no matter who whispered to whom.

Then Sally came to London. His fears of being blinded by paternal affection made him cautious, apprehensive even, and he prepared for their meeting with care. That girl he dandled on his knee and last remembered as an infant was twenty-two years old—older now than he had been when driven from their home. The being whom, he was persuaded, Heaven destined to reward him for all he had suffered and endured, arrived in March.

Sally had enjoyed the trip—what though the weather was prodigious, with high running seas, and they had been so battered that they anchored for three weeks outside the Scilly Isles. Unearthly calm succeeded dreadful wind. The Charlestown was commanded by young Captain Oliver, and he proved attentive—flirtatious, even—to his charge. He taught her and they played the game of loo. Her protectors were a Captain and Mrs. Bennet of Boston, and a Mr. Frasier of London; she was to meet her father at the latter's home.

Rumford passed through the doorway alone. At the far end of Frasier's hall, she awaited his arrival, and their host withdrew. Hard to conceive and difficult to describe the so affecting scene; hard to imagine, impossible to convey the perturbation in his breast when Sally took his hand.

She did so with becoming modesty. Her dress was adequate. Her gaze, downcast, was nonetheless direct. In time to come he would admit that this first meeting tested him, but he took her in his arms and kissed her cheek.

"My child," he said. "At last we meet."

"How are you, father?" Sally asked.

"Content again. Well satisfied."

She smiled at him, or attempted to smile.

"Your trip was uneventful?"

"Yes."

"And your arrival?"

"Equally."

"Not so," he said. "For we have met."

She burst into bright tears.

Those copious tears, she later confessed, were produced by disappointment not relief. She had imagined a soldier, with sword and gun and military bearing, the habit of command—a hero, a Baron, a model for all other men and template of the times. His treasured profile on her wall in Concord, being black, made her suppose him dark in complexion, possibly sunburned—in stature, size and looks, the perfect warrior.

But he was thin and pale. His considerable frame was wasted by long illness, his height unprepossessing since he stooped. Her mother often spoke of him as carroty, his hair being red, a very pretty color. Now there was white in his sparse hair, and the remnant thereof was brushed back.

Nor did his voice entrance her, or the questions he asked. That very evening he began a process of instruction, of disapproval voiced, for he complained to his young visitor about her dress. He said that it was suitable for Boston, possibly, but would not do in London and she should purchase better to go out into the world. In consequence, next morning she and Anymeetle bought a cloak. This garment required additional lace, and she returned to Rumford with some of the most elegant the city afforded, they having by chance gone to a very dear and fashionable shop.

Nothing could equal her father's surprise except Sally's shock at his. Next he came upon the full regalia of her shoes—a dozen pairs just purchased, in shade and contour various but all of them expensive and well made. His look was black. He shook his finger at her; his whole body shook. He did not complain, he said, about the cost, but could not bear and would not countenance the waste; three pair must suffice.

Then she curtsied to a housemaid and he disapproved entirely; it was a great mistake. He was, he told Sally, amazed. Was it not common politeness? she asked, and he said all too common, it betrayed a lack of breeding she must look to remedy. One does not curtsey to a housemaid as if to a great lady, but must distinguish rank. In America, said Sally, we believe all men are equal, and Count Rumford said you are not in America and a housemaid is not a lady and you must learn, my little savage, to tell the two apart. I am not little, Sally said, I am full-grown and my own mistress and twenty-two years old. All the more reason, said her father, it's well past time you learned.

Nonetheless he took her to the Italian Opera. There were high fashionables in the company, and this was her first evening in a party of such elegance. She was to make no remark; whatever her impressions of the music, Rumford warned, she was to hold her peace. Sally wore her lace-trimmed cloak and her new pair of lavender shoes. She undertook to be a credit to him and to pay attention and not fidget in her chair.

Yet the other ladies whispered and fluttered their fans and rearranged themselves continually where they sat. Lady Banks seemed attentive, immobile—but that was, Sally saw, because she slept. The room was hot. The opera was long, and Sally not enchanted. She said to Sir Charles Blagden that, for her part, she much preferred music which was natural, liking for instance to hear old Black Prince's fiddle, of Concord—particularly when a rosy lad, leading to the floor of the dance his still more rosy partner, looked at the simple musician and said, "Make your fiddle speak!"

Several ladies heard her speech. They smiled and nodded amiably and asked her what she thought of this particular performance. Sally said that the soprano was too fat and her high notes shrill and her feather hat ridiculous and the baritone with his hand on his breast, yowling, made her think of nothing so much as a cat in heat. Or a cock in the barnyard at dawn.

The ladies laughed. Her father, approaching, inquired if he might share the source of their enjoyment. Sir Charles Blagden said, "Your daughter expresses herself very frankly, Count, very vividly."

"How?"

"And with such fresh opinions." Sir Charles repeated what she'd said. "Is that not perspicacious? Is it not a witty simile?"

The Count was unamused.

So she went to Barnes's Terrace, under the supervisory tutelage of the Marquise de Chabanne. Sally stayed there for some time. Rude ways may be amended with hard work, and little by little she acquired those procedures of etiquette, those patterns of behavior her father feared she lacked.

An American Miss of certain pretensions, approaching or accosting a superior, places the feet in position and, drawing them back, makes a low courtesy. The English custom is, to draw one foot carelessly back, making a courtesy, not near so low a dip, not going back far enough to lose hold of hands mutually given for the celebrated shake. Nor with real fashionables is there any dip at all, going bolt upright, giving the hand, sparing even the epithets, Madam, Sir, or Miss. In France the young person approaches slowly, with apparent diffidence, with a slight motion of the head, looking steadfastly with a smile at the person they are to meet; and when the other with open arms comes forward, as when receiving a child first running alone, and much in the same manner, bestows caresses, with the difference of a degree more ceremony towards the miss than the child, it being thought indecorous to express the same warmth of feeling. The forehead of the young lady is destined to receive the caress. In these trifles are to be seen the characteristics of the three nations—the humility of the Americans, the dignity of the English, and the graceful good-humor of the French.

Sally attended riding school also, where there was much to be learned. She was surprised at the sidesaddle and the English manner, having thought herself sufficient in the art. The mounting, dismounting, sitting, holding the reins, the whip even, walking the horse, putting him on the gallop, the trot—all these were managed otherwise in Ashley's school than had been the case at home. Majority opinion acclaimed this English mode as graceful, but she begged leave to differ: the new way was dangerous, and Sally rode sidesaddle only when the Count was at her side.

It was not reasonable, Rumford knew, to expect of this provincial girl the manners of a lady. She lacked language skills. In order to present her schooling in the most favorable light, Loammi Baldwin, it would seem, had over-praised Sarah's attainments. Her needlework proved poor. Her arithmetic looked scarcely better than that of Sophie Baumgarten—the simplest sums requiring time to puzzle out. Fourteen times twelve divided by six, for example, made her scratch her head and scowl.

Her curls hung slackly, he observed. Her right eye wandered; her nose was too long. She reminded him, not happily, of Sarah Rolfe. A certain snappishness begotten by nerves characterized his daughter as it had his wife her mother; a certain flirtatiousness, too, gave Rumford pause. Once she set her foot upon it, she enjoyed the primrose path. Dalliance was a subject in which the Count had been expertly tutored, and he knew the ways in which young ladies lapse from spotless probity until they grow unchaste.

Flattered easily, she blushed. Cajoled, she flattered back. Sally had too little sense of decorum and mete modesty to let her father rest content while young men came to call; he himself had been a suitor and knew love's cunning ways. So he hovered in the drawing room and watched.

"Look at the floor," he told her, "not the wall. The well-trained eye is downcast."

"Yes, sir."

"Look at me when I speak to you."

"But," Sally protested, "you said I should not. I thought you said the modest glance . . ."

"With your gallants," Rumford said. "With all men but your father, girl. To me you raise your eyes and nod only in assent."

Thus he commenced to teach her the ways of the world. The legitimate result of long experience in fatherhood, the Count foresaw— what though he had been up till now an absent presence principally —would be his daughter by his side when he rejoined the court. Paternity was his new suit, and he dressed himself attentively in the raiment of protector. It was a universal preference and one he would adopt.

Now Bavaria required him; the wolves were at the door. They huffed and puffed and shook their bright sabers and threatened and complained and asked to be conducted through the gate. The French and Austrian armies, both, advanced on quaking Munich and demanded access and the right of unimpeded passage through the Elector's lands. From this to annexation was but a hair's breadth, blinked eye.

Karl Theodor sent messages to his Chamberlain in London. At first these were formal, unhurried, discoursing on the movement of the opposing troops. Then the Elector grew anxious and soon enough he begged the Count—without a day's delay, and by the most rapid route—to return. In spite of its proclaimed neutrality, things were disordered in Munich, and all governance collapsed.

As the Austrian army approached, the gates of the town had been bolted and the garrison placed under arms. The French army, too, drew near. These two opposing forces toyed with one another in the lethal game of war, and imperiled Munich was said to be the prize. Inside the city, Karl Theodor wrote, there was no one remaining to trust. The Elector's own confessor, Father Ignaz Frank, had died; so too had Charles Augustus, the Duke of Zweibrücken. The Count was most urgently needed, he must depart England at once.

So Rumford and his daughter, their servants, two carriages, a special English riding horse as a gift for Mary Nogarola, and their bags and baggage, left Yarmouth in July. Their route was planned through Hamburg, then down through Prussia to Leipzig, then Plauen in Saxony to Regensburg and the Elector's domain. The days were hot, the trip hard. They negotiated obstacles familiar to a traveler but rendered the more difficult because of nearing war, and they entertained, as traveling companions, discomfort and boredom and danger and uncertainty and heat. The food was poor. Where they slept they were attacked by bed bugs as large as land turtles and millions of starved fleas. Innkeepers were impertinent or lewd. "Your daughter, Count?" they asked. "Of course, of course. Congratulations, *Graf*."

Yet he took little pleasure in the girl, for she neither offered solace nor did she bring him peace. Under the guise of desiring instruction, she asked disputatious questions and hounded him with that very curiosity he had labored to instill. He had purchased a duke's *équipage* in London, and Sally pressed him on the wisdom of the choice: was the manner of their travel not what he called ostentation; was it not wasteful, vain? She thought eight horses four too many and wondered why he left the ducal leaves upon their carriage door; that way everybody assumed she was a duchess and charged twice as much. Does the additional speed and power of an eight-horse team justify the trouble and additional expense? Or is it not counter-productive; the time they spent while waiting to change relays seemed wasteful, did it not?

His daughter asked this in all seeming-innocence, yet it cut him to the quick and he endeavored to explain. A duke's carriage had been offered and was readily available; he had not had the chance, since they were in a hurry, to erase the strawberry-leaved insignia of rank. If those armorial bearings had visited upon them the tax of greatness, be it so; he had no need for ostentation; he simply thought to save time. Sally said she was an amateur with paint and brush, not greatly skilled, but would perform the operation of erasure, should he wish.

Outside of Leipzig the Count called a halt. He informed himself as to the movement of the troops, the French approaching and the Austrians retreating, the ill will festering between Count Morawitzky and General La Tour. All those who could depart the region had made haste to leave. When he stopped to visit his dear mistress Laura, Baroness de Kalb, her castle was closed up, and this was deprivation indeed. They were forced to board instead at an inn where his carriage was brought to a halt in the midst of an immense dunghill; impossible to descend. He had looked forward to a glamorous reception, and Laura's dimpling welcome and the pleasures of her bed. Then she sent word from Jena that she might meet him there that night, since she was passionately anxious for the sight of his dear face. He could not go.

Provisions were scanty, roads bad. The wide roads and good hostels had been commandeered by troops, and so they bumped and rattled south, hearing cannonade and musketry in the middle distance. One night the Baroness de Kalb passed by, rousing him from troubled sleep, and they spent hurried minutes together embracing in the second chaise; then she said she had to leave him and drove on.

The journey took three weeks. The comforts of paternity and the sustained proximity to this one single companion did little to alleviate Rumford's bodily requirements while the heat of summer waned. Often, for want of accommodation, father and daughter passed the night together upright in the cushions. The fair-skinned children and the elderly women they met when passing through a village were civil; at first sight of the carriage, they knelt. Sarah conversed with Anymeetle daily, acquiring the rudiments of local speech. Anymeetle averred that Saxons spoke the sweetest German you could ever hope to hear, and Rumford said he hoped to hear such music from his daughter soon.

Wass heisst 'Photometer?' What does it mean?"

"A photometer."

"*Dass isst's.* That's it, and what does photometer mean? *Wass bedeutet das?*"

"A device for calibrating light."

"*Wass heisst* 'Thermometer?'"

"Thermometer."

"*Genau.* Exactly. You see how similar the languages?"

"Yes."

"*Eins, zwei, drei, vier.*" The Count continued his numbers in German. "*Fünf, sechs, sieben.*"

"*Acht.*"

"*Achtung!* What does that mean?"

"'Attention.'"

"*Vorsicht!*"

"'Careful.' I'm trying, Father. Truly."

"Try harder," Rumford said.

Their welcome, arrived in Munich, was all that the traveler wished. His house had been readied, his staff in attendance, and they trotted grandly through the porte-cochere. The marble floors were polished, and the great mirrored stairwell gave his image back repeatedly—as if a single personage were multiform and various: eight noses, sixteen eyes. The brasswork and the silver shone; the furniture and pictures and the carpets and the tapestries were in their proper place.

And yet the weary traveler took no respite from the road. While Sally was being ushered open-mouthed from room to commodious room, invited to admire her apartments and the treasure there contained, the Count himself was closeted with Karl Theodor. Upon the hour he conferred with all members of the regency—not a moment to be lost!—for the situation was grave. Karl Theodor explained:

When the Austrian commander, General La Tour, first requested entry, he had been refused: he might proceed around the town but could not journey through. This decision had been taken under the guise of neutrality, as was right and proper, but the manner of refusal had been warlike and abrupt. To the eternal shame of the commanding officer, the trumpet sounded and the Munich troops were massed as if to charge. A cavalry detachment had defied the general—who was treated like a prisoner, not ally, and conducted at sword's point across the Isar bridge.

There the Austrians took up positions. On the surrounding promontories, furious, their army awaited the French. They threw up barricades and prepared for an assault or siege and, at the least sign of traffic with the enemy, the General swore darkly, would annihilate the town.

It was time to play for time. At ten o'clock next morning, Count Rumford composed a statement of apology—a pretty speech, a careful one—to General La Tour. Then he rode alone up to the hill where the General awaited him, attentive to his argument. To wit:

258

The Bavarians and Austrians were ancient allies, were they not, and it had been no one's intention to give the least offense; politeness as well as prudence require that all offensive language and unfriendly demonstration should have been avoided; this, the emissary regretted to admit, had not been the case. The offending officer—he who brandished his sword at the head of the Elector's cavalry—had been rebuked and dismissed. Such discourtesy could not be countenanced and would not happen again.

Yet the General must surely see how passage through the city would have been untenable, an abrogation of neutrality as such. And he might likewise rest assured that Munich would defend itself against the whole French army, should that prove necessary. Though some of the Elector's party might perhaps favor the French, he, Rumford, was against them and had been so from the start. Therefore the Austrian commander would have no need to shell the town and would be the first to know, from Rumford's own intelligencers, when the French approached, and he hoped that this sufficed.

It did. They smiled at each other, bowing, then talked of their mutual acquaintance, Maximilian des Deux Ponts, and in his honor drank schnapps. General La Tour's demand for satisfaction had been, at least provisionally, met.

Meanwhile barges had been loaded with the official archives and the art treasures of Munich; they were ready to be floated down the Isar to the Danube and thence to Passau. The Elector and his family were poised for flight to Dresden and safe haven there. The Electrice—for the first time in Rumford's acquaintance—bore herself with dignity, a composure begotten of fear. She failed to flirt or sim-

259

per and showed no desire to dance—betraying, in short, no principle but that of steadfastness in danger; she urged the Elector to flee.

"And what remains," Karl Theodor inquired, "if we retire?"

"But if we stay?" she asked him. "That hideous artillery. I hear it all night long."

"Nymphenburg has been secured?"

"It has, your Excellency."

"And what remains?" Karl Theodor repeated.

Violently, his consort shuddered. "Horror. *Shreklichkeit.*"

"Your subject's loyalty," said Rumford.

"What?"

"Your servant's loyalty," he said again. "Unaltered, that endures."

On August 22, at nightfall and having appointed Count Rumford his regent, the Elector left. The old man was near tears, his wattled face was damp, his nose rheum-encrusted and his pink complexion dim. He and the Electrice and forty hand-picked retainers stole out the western gate.

Now the Count took full control. This was the chance he'd dreamed of, the element he thrived on, the occasion for procedures at the municipal level and with the lives and livelihood of an entire populace at stake. His every operation was meticulously planned. He razed all edifices at the town's perimeter that could not be defended, and he was not a whit displeased that several of those buildings had belonged to his old enemies, those burghers of the council who had opposed him once. These were the very men that had refused to sign the proclamation in his honor years before. They had built buildings in his absence when in Switzerland and Italy, along the grassy verge of his beloved English Gardens. They would hate him the more cordially for such a precaution, he knew, yet he ordered these structures dismantled. They despoiled the view.

Now chaos once again came face to face with order, the two great principles contending on the field, and as he readied Munich for a siege its regent felt twenty years younger—the threat of present danger an elixir in his veins. A state of siege refines the random-seeming operations of a comity and renders them precise; it clarifies the mind. War had not been declared as such, but with the French advancing and the Austrians entrenched outside, the likelihood of a prolonged enforced neutrality was great. They would have to wait both armies out, and from behind locked gates.

Rumford's passion for sequence and detail proved suited to the time. His workhouse stoves and collective gardens served the embattled populace; he rationed heat and light. He dispensed bread proportionally, according to the size of a household and nature of its industry and need. He distributed clothing where the poor required clothing—outer-garments for the autumn and the coming winter's chill. The Count's military transport and his mobile kitchens kept his soldiers dry and full, and he maintained a perfect discipline on the streets and in the barracks. When the French appeared at last, taking up their assault position by the English Garden, Munich was prepared.

And this preparation sufficed, for French troops could not advance. They occupied the stable where once he quartered cows; these were safe within the city and could furnish milk and meat to the citizens of Munich but not their enemies. Those buildings that the Count had razed became armed fastnesses; the earthworks proved impassable. All provender had been removed.

From late August till the middle of September, the blue-suited soldiers camped cowering by his Chinese pagoda. Like a specimen impaled by those who would examine it upon a tray, the flower of the French lay pinioned there. The main body of their army was in fact in central Germany, and this detachment knew itself outnumbered. The Austrians sent volley after volley of their bomb-balls down, and the French were defenseless, exposed; in disarray, therefore, and in shorter order than the Count had dared imagine, the foreign troops withdrew.

Count Rumford watched. Standing on the city heights, he felt something of the same elation he'd known long years before when shooting at those waterlogged fleeing defenseless drowned colonials near the capsized bridge. Then he had been the hero of the engagement at swift Wambaw Creek; now he was Munich's master, and had preserved the town. Then he had fought a losing battle, though on the side and for the sake of order; now he won. He was older and above the fray, but the alarums and the wind-dimmed oaths and the smell of cordite acted as a cordial still; his blood was hot, pulse good.

They lost the weathercock on the tobacco factory and a portion of the roof in the veterinary hospital. That was the sum of the damage—that, and a few furrows in the potato fields. Soon after the French left, the Austrians also retreated, although General La Tour described his fleeing action as pursuit. The city had been saved.

"*Freude?*"

"Joy."

"*Und Friede?*"

"Peace."

"*Die Fremden?*"

"Foreigners," said Sally. "Strangeness." Her German had improved.

"*Wir bedanken Ihnen herzlich.*"

"*Doch, doch.* We thank you sincerely."

"It is time you start Italian," said the Count.

There was general rejoicing, jubilation in the streets; the people of Munich were grateful and well knew their savior's name. On a late September morning, bright and mild, Mary Nogarola rode sidesaddle to his door. The Countess had resumed her station as the Count's mistress of choice. Her children, Therese and Andrew, were with her husband in Mannheim—having been for safety's sake removed from nearing war. Her riding habit flattered her, and she flattered Rumford, and he flattered himself he deserved it; she said so grand a man, and one so grandly manly, must not be long permitted to languish unrequited. He had served the city bravely, unswerving in the storm of siege, and she would serve him too.

Mary and his daughter got along; she took Sally under her wing until, by the gentle pressure of such tutelage, rough edges were worn smooth. The Countess found his "little savage" charming and was charming in return. They huddled together, conversing; they could be found in corners and in whispered conference; they gave each other trinkets and tokens of esteem.

The Count on Fawn, his daughter on Lambkin and Mary Nogarola on her preferred mount, Tancred, formed a riding party often, touring the streets of Munich and the English Garden grounds. This day the three of them went out along the Isar to see what they could see. They were followed by two aides de camp, young Spreti and Count Taxis.

There had been a trifling incident at the excursion's start. Sarah, giving one of the grooms a look, had the horse destined for her brought forward. She skipped on with no assistance and almost immediately disappeared; not going far, however, for when the party passed the porte-cochere, she and her Lambkin were found perched at one side of it. This appeared amusing to the company, occasioning a general laugh.

But not so to Count Rumford. He frowned, and particularly so when he perceived the young lady's whip dropped, and the handsome aide, Count Taxis, dismount to pick it up.

All things went well thereafter, and would have without doubt continued so, had not the younger of the ladies, without due consideration, giving a whip to her horse, set out, soon losing sight of the company. Rumford, much frightened at seeing his daughter go off alone in unknown roads and winding paths, looked to his aide Spreti to tell him to follow her; but before the words could be got out of his mouth, the other one, Count Taxis, was on the gallop. The two horses raced pell-mell—one wild with sudden freedom, the other gaining ground. Where Sarah was erratic, the young Captain rode in control, pursuing her coolly and overtaking her at last and reaching out his white gloved hand to gather her limp reins.

"You have saved me, sir," she whispered.

"*Nein.*" His face was white, composed.

"And at such peril to yourself!"

"It was nothing."

"Not so, surely!"

"*Garnicht,*" he repeated. "Exercise."

"You are too modest, Captain. You put yourself at risk!"

"Not to my body, Miss Thompson."

"But?"

"But to my soul. *Mein Herz.*"

On arriving home in safety, and relieved of their riding-habits, they assembled as usual at the supper-table to take, each, a basin of chocolate. Sally made bad dinners, not being fond of foreign cookery; she declared herself, however, extremely fond of chocolate, and never had half enough. That most eligible of bachelors and elegant of cavaliers, Count Taxis, proffered his portion. She took it gratefully. Then, with her new-learned courtesy and increased command of German, she informed him she was doubly in his debt, and he said this pleased him to hear. "*Das freut mich zu hören,*" he said.

Her father gave her presents. She received a little shaggy dog—entirely white, excepting black eyes, ears, and nose. She called the puppy Cora and lavished affection on the creature, who seldom left her side. She met with Dr. Haubenal, her father's personal physician, who attended to Miss Thompson with a grave and proper mien. Sally fainted often; her diet was not good, but Dr. Haubenal was reassuring. He said the effect of her travels would quite naturally result in weakness and what he described as "systematic change." She must not excite herself and must not be concerned, yet he prescribed a regimen of exercise and a daily infusion of herbs.

She also received three teachers, who did not greatly please her and from whom she endeavored to escape. Mlle. Veratzy was hired by Count Rumford to teach his daughter music and French; Father Dillis, a Catholic Priest, was a professor of drawing. Her third and last professor taught the Italian language, and Sarah disliked him at sight. Signor Alberty had been judiciously chosen—for his appearance was an antidote to the softer passions supposed to be so easily inspired by the people of his nation. His stature was under the common size, but to appearance larger, from a great prominency of back and shoulders, so as nearly to hide all signs of a neck. His voice was not more fortunate, being harsh. His head corresponded with the prominency of his back; his nose the same, with sharp, fierce-looking eyes.

Summoning her fortitude, Sarah dismissed this trio, saying she would think of when to start her studies—but well-determined nonetheless to have nothing to do with them. Surrounded by people who spoke French, as did all the gentility of Munich, and knowing something of that language already, what was the use of her fatiguing herself with lessons? Music the same. She knew some music already and did not wish to know more. As to Italian, she had no desire to learn it, and from such a hideous mentor, for surely there was eloquence sufficient in her own English tongue? What she would study were sonnets, the rhymed declarations of love.

On their next horseback excursion they made the usual party, except that Countess Nogarola was kept back by a previous engagement. Sarah therefore rode Tancred, not Lambkin, and the horse proved troublesome. They were proceeding quietly when Tancred startled, reared, and tried to throw her. Count Taxis, frightened, said in English (which she did not suppose he knew and which, therefore, surprised her), "Take care, my dear!"

From her looking down and making no reply, he thought she was offended. He drew his horse near to hers and, looking Sarah archly in the face, asked her if she did not think that in learning English he learned pretty things. She told him it depended on their sincerity, and he assured her of the sincerity of his words and thoughts.

Sally had been indisposed for several days, but had said nothing about it; she was fond of horseback riding, and had had no wish to be confined at home. Now she felt faint at the young Count's protestations and decided to dismount. She slipped her foot out of the stirrup and took hold of the saddle to let herself down, but then her senses left her; so that when Taxis turned his head, it was not to see her on the seat but prostrate on the ground. The first thing Sally realized, on coming to herself again, was Taxis and the groom exceedingly frightened, lifting her; they had supposed her somehow to have had a fatal fall. But she opened her eyes and smilingly insisted on her absolute recovery; indeed, she told these gentlemen, there was nothing to recover from but embarrassment and shock. They rejoiced to hear her protestation that she was unhurt.

The groom declared he should never dare to see her father, had anything terrible happened to the Countess Rumford while in part under his care. The expressions of Count Taxis were, as may be imagined, more refined. Sally received his attentions that day with a maiden's proper mixture of pudeur, anticipation and reserve. He thought best to let the groom go in search of her father, who soon joined them, and they all returned safely together—Captain Taxis maintaining his hold on the reins, subduing her wild mount. He was lavish of kind looks.

On her father's birthday, as had been the custom now for years, a dozen of the workhouse virgins brought Count Rumford posies from their garden. They had a pretty manner of ornamenting flowers, of twisting them into letters and then words. Sally had produced a bust—improved upon by Dillis—of her father in his General's garb, and there was much applause and general rejoicing. The girls from the workhouse wore white.

At the head of their delegation arrived a child whose elegance bore no trace of poverty and whose bearing was both regal and assured. She swept into the drawing room as one who came there often, and with every certainty of welcome from her host. Nor was she disappointed, for the Count greeted this attractive creature familiarly, with marks of special favor, patting the chair at his side. She sat beside him gracefully, laughing the while, shaking her cascade of curls. They shared a private joke.

Sally, watching, was not pleased. She surveyed this happy scene with a degree of vexation, for the careless—even wanton—assurance of the girl could not fail to arouse a degree of jealousy in one who was not beautiful. Nor could on closer inspection Sally fail to notice the pronounced similarity of aspect between the man and child—a link-age, as it were, so manifest as to suggest the ties of blood. She asked Countess Nogarola, *sotto voce*, for the maiden's name, and Mary answered, "It's young Sophie. It's my niece."

"And her mother?"

"My sister."

"Oh? The Countess Baumgarten."

"*Ja.* Indisposed."

"And where is her father?"

In the ensuing silence Sally had her answer: the Countess smiled and nodded at Count Rumford in his chair. Thus the daughter from America first learned of the existence of her half-sister Sophie, the darling on her father's knee and by-blow of his wanderlust; thus did Sally first encounter the loose morals of the Munich court—her father's here on brazen show and foremost of the lot.

She fled the room. Her face was hot. It was as if, she told Count Taxis, the scales had fallen from her eyes and all expectation changed. If her father had expected her to be perfect in her conduct, why had he not been more so with his beautiful illegitimate? And given his behavior, his romantic indiscretion and close embrace of luxury, what was there in her conduct that he might disapprove?

Count Taxis poured her chocolate, sweet and steaming from the pot. She dashed the cup away. It broke. She kissed him on the mouth. "Oh, I say," Taxis said.

SALLY

She turned the page. And so, dear reader, have you and must I. Oh, I say, Taxis said. Days lengthen; the equinox nears. This morning I thought I saw buds on the trees, a light green haze appearing, and even though it snowed again the snow looked less serious somehow: mere transience, a dusting, a freeze that will thaw. The page turns, the world turns, the year does the same; affection heats or dissipates; my characters are fleeting and their author melts away.

But I like it that Rumford fell ill. It provides him a kind of humanity and makes him seem mortal, the son of a bitch. And I like it that he tried to care and follow the Elector's orders or anyway provide for unacknowledged children, and so I wrote a scene last night (a draft of a scene, not good enough, I need to know more about Gouverneur Morris) in which he states the case.

As also, trying to make sense of it, do I.

*On a bright winter morning, Gouverneur Morris arrived. He had trav-
eled from America, a visitor of consequence—and no one more persuaded
thereof than Gouverneur Morris himself. He carried with him greetings
from the Congress and the financiers in Philadelphia and Boston and New
York; he hoped for fruitful commerce with the Elector Palatine. He wanted
full and frank discussions and a chance to air his views. He had visited the
capitals of Europe—Vienna, Paris, London—turn by turn.*

*Morris was deep-voiced and earnest and proper and, by virtue of his
wooden leg, both dizzying in gait and in deportment grave. He clothed
himself entirely in black. He was well known to Rumford, although they
had not met before, and the moment seemed propitious to make welcome
such a guest.*

*They discussed the weather and geography and their respective healths,
as well as present circumstance in France. News had arrived from Paris,
and it was—as so often latterly—not good. The men did not raise old questions of alliance and allegiance but bowed and traded courtesies instead.
They spoke of revolution and its necessary consequence, the disruption of
market and treaty, the shifting alignments of state. The transactions we
envision will be—so Gouverneur Morris asserted—of mutual benefit, and
it is time to make of the Atlantic a corridor of trade. Disorder is abroad,
perhaps, but order reigns in Munich, and this was a pleasure to see.*

*"It would be my privilege," said Rumford, "to show you what we do
here. Those arrangements we have mustered in the interest of order."*

"Gladly, Count."

*So Rumford conducted a tour of the city, its palaces and squares; he
showed the halls and anterooms and guarded inner chambers of the Resi-*

denz. He walked the visitor down clean well-tended streets, discoursing the while on civil management, the advantages of supervision and the desire of the poor to elevate their lot. They strolled through the workhouse at Au, and Morris was impressed. Self-help, the men agreed, is best effected by benevolent instruction, and here we have an instance of just such a theory practiced—of assistance freely given to those requiring aid. As to whether they desired it, the question must be moot. Inertia keeps an object moving; so also it keeps it at rest. The task of the enlightened ruler is to alternate encouragement with discipline and whip with rein; Karl Theodor's subjects knew both. The poor of Munich, Rumford said, had been poised for forward motion like a horse above a hill, or—to alter and improve the figure—like a resistant block upon an inclined plane.

"Was there resistance?" Morris asked.

"A trifle to start with, perhaps."

"But overcome?"

"They are happy and productive. They are happy in being productive."

"And long may you be happy," said the American, "in having made them so. How charming it is here."

The children curtseyed, wearing white. They were used to visitors and organized display. They did their dance for Morris—six of them in sequence while the seventh played a flute. They offered him a posy, freshly cut.

Then the delegation toured the dining hall. Morris tasted Rumford's soup, appreciated it, and was full of high-toned compliment for all that he observed. The kitchen, he averred, was wonderful; the regularity, cleanness and economy of the house surpassed what he expected or had ever seen. They continued on their way, perambulating through the English Garden, and then they viewed the animals and waterfall and barns. The pagoda soared impos-ingly, and Morris found it no whit inferior to the Chinese Pagoda at Kew.

The telephone rings. I answer. It's the Republican National Com-mittee; they're grateful for my support. I tell them it's not mine, it wasn't ever mine. They want to know if I'd like to subscribe, if they can continue to count on my help, and I tell them no. They say, Now Mrs. Robinson, your husband has been a generous supporter of our organization for years. That was his business, I say, and mine is to inform you that he passed since the election, before the last election. Passed? asks the voice in the receiver, and I say yes, he's dead. Oh I'm sorry, says the caller, and I say I bet you are and then—slowly, linger-ingly, watching while the distance between telephone and table halves itself, then halves again—hang up.

Yet surface understanding puts a false face on things. As when a courtier adds pomade and lightly dusts with diamonds the wig that covers his bald brow, and bowing approaches a lady tight-laced and beribboned and thin-lipped and thick-rouged, the two of them pretending youth but led at eve-ning's end inexorably to that confessional where naked truth disrobes—for who would brightly scrutinize what is best left to shielding dark, and who prefers harsh certainty to yearning romantic surmise?—thus they were loathe to gauge the actuality of flesh.

Likewise soon or late politeness fades and fails to mask old enmity. As when a placid pool belies the rushing torrent underneath, its dangers and its treachery, so was their disagreement's depth disguised.

273

"I have come to understand," said Rumford at tour's end, "that the children of nobility require supervision also. We have a building for that purpose."

"Where?"

"Just here." The carriage stopped. They drew up at a steep-roofed mansion, its stone new-cut and windows veiled within the imposing facade. This building once entered proved spacious, and the appointments and the marble flooring and the tapestries attested to some luxury. A footman conducted them through the high hall.

"We built this," Rumford said, "two years ago, at the Elector's suggestion and as a public expense."

In the gardens young men exercised; they practiced with saber and foil. Catching sight of their protector, they stood stiffly at attention, raising blades.

"And who are these?" asked Morris.

"They are—how shall I put it?—flowers of the noble stock, yet grafted furtively. Their tutelage is shared, and the expense of maintenance is managed by subscription."

"I fail to understand you, Count."

Rumford smiled. He signaled that the athletes should resume what had been halted for his sake. "'Our by-blows of nobility,' as the Elector puts it. They require shelter as well as education. Those who exercise at fencing, there, will in all probability be soldiers and in any case may profit from a practiced ease with weapons once they undertake careers."

Young women of the latest fashion walked together, chatting. Their laughter and light gossip intermingled with the orchard's birds. Their plumage was alluring, clean and bright, and they nodded at Count Rumford also, and cocked fans.

"And these?" inquired Morris.

"Our daughters. They receive instruction in embroidery and music, in all domestic skills."

"How?" He frowned. "They live here also?"

"The ladies live here privately."

"A strong endorsement of unchasteness."

"No."

"But bastards on the public charge . . ."

"It happens in America, presumably. There too."

Gouverneur Morris, frowning, took umbrage. "And what do you refer to, Mr. Thompson?"

"You know me by that name?"

"Of Woburn. Thereafter of Concord. I do."

"In that case, sir, you know my firm conviction that this world of ours depends on simple principles. On a few fixed habits, and one of them—else who should ever prosper?—is parental concern. We care and must acknowledge it."

"A fine speech, sir," said Morris. "Yet thus you sponsor courtesans."

"Human behavior does not vary east or west of the Atlantic, I believe." So saying, and as if to mock by excess-imitation—to ape the disapproval of the self-important and too pompous, that righteous citizen so typical of what he fled from and once bade fair to emulate, had flourished in the absence of—Rumford clicked his heels and bowed.

Oh Christ, dear reader, so do and must I. A branch berates the window, and I feel very helpless, alone. You see what I mean when I said to begin with a person gets haunted by candlelit dark. Just scan it for the anapest and let me go to sleep; I've been sitting here since six o'clock and nothing—no single thing, not the gin or aspirin or breathing exercises or late night talk show—helps.

I wrote bodice rippers for ten years, pseudonymous, on contract, after Adriana left for Italy (*à la Mary Nogarola, Class?*), then moved to California and left me on my own. It's what I did for a living back then, two books a year of gussied-up prose and passionate attachments for my dime-store Scarlet Pimpernels or Heathcliffs on fake cliff and heath. I suppose I was missing my darling, suppose I was sending the Count in her stead where Adriana went in fact and sent back postcards: "Wish you were here. C.U. Soon."

She didn't mean it, of course. When she left she left for good. So that's what this story is, really (romance: a will-you, won't-you join the Morris dance?), though it's full of high-toned sentences: the flashing eyes, the prancing horse, the tale of nature's nobleman who furnished my last name. In that house of respectable ill-repute where the Elector's by-blows were lodged, might we by peering closely see the lineaments of gratified desire: grandad's grandad's beldam's baby, Sally Ormbsy at your several services?

Proceed.

✤ VI ✤

For Rumford these were halcyon days, the height of his career. When Karl Theodor returned, he was beside himself with gratitude, fairly dancing with relief. He clapped his hands and beamed and looked not a year over sixty; he insisted on a visit to that section of the English Garden where the French had been encamped. He walked the shell-plowed fields bare-headed and made his General repeat, down to the smallest detail, the particulars of conversation with General La Tour; he bronzed the shattered weathercock as a memento of war.

Nor did the Elector content himself with praise, but offered concrete proof of his esteem. Conveying a pension on his Minister for life, he ennobled Sally Thompson also, making her on her own behalf Countess Rumford and stipulating that their pensions would be paid no matter where they lived. He had a monument erected at the entrance to the gardens, with a portrait of Count Rumford and a legend carved in stone:

To Him
Who rooted out the most disgraceful
public evils
Idleness and Mendicity
Who to the Poor gave Succour,
Occupation, good Habits
and to the Youth of the Fatherland
So many cultural Institutions
Go, Stroller, and strive to match him

In spirit and in Action

And us

In gratitude.

Sally translated this. She had difficulty with the phrase, "*Lust-wandler, steh*," but her German had indeed improved and he commended her.

"I had excellent help," she confessed.

"From whom?"

"Count Taxis." She blushed. Where in other women the suffused cheek can be pretty, in his daughter such blotched color made her appear unwell.

"Are you all right?" asked Rumford.

"Yes. *Bien sur, certo. Gewiss.*"

"You don't look it, I must say. Your face is red."

"Papa," she said. "He helps me so."

"Who?"

"Your aide-de-camp, Captain Taxis."

Count Rumford was, not happily, surprised.

"And his manners are so, so excellent. Refined. And he comes from such a fine family!"

"Who told you that?"

She dimpled. He found it disgusting. She blundered on, displaying her Italian. "Young Spreti also, *non e vero?* You want only the nobility to serve you, *nicht wahr?*"

"And why?"

"Because the great master of Munich can have his pick of aides. The General selects his troops, the flower of nobility . . ."

"That's quite enough," said Rumford.

"*Dank stäerket den Genuss,*" she said. Her accent was atrocious. He would send Count Taxis off to fight the French.

When Sally was four or five years old, she had had two playmates about her own age, William and Elenora Green, and they were very fond of each other. They were sent to day schools in the same neighborhood, and were so much together that they were called the inseparables. They grew up in this manner in real love and friendship, knowing no difference from brother and sisters, except perhaps that Sally might have been more civil than a sister. For William was exceedingly pretty and engaging, and his mother, dotingly fond of him, led him to exact more from the young ladies than he otherwise might have done. Mrs. Green, the mother, was romantic in her character and dressed her son fantastically, keeping his hair—beautiful golden locks—always in ringlets, with belts of curious construction round his waist confining elegant dresses, a jockey cap with feathers on his head; and, more than all the rest, she bought him a fife, and had him instructed to play on it several little tunes. It was this fife particularly which Sally was obliged to hear, for Elenora would not.

William reveled in her praise. He played for her repeatedly—haunting highland melodies, sailor's chanteys, marching songs—and she always clapped. Taken away at a later period to other schools, he never forgot his first companion, seeking all the means proper in his power to give her testimonies of his friendship. His mother, knowing this, made proposals to Sarah Rolfe Thompson that their children should be married.

Half-jocular, wholly romantic, the arrangement was agreed to there and then. And often, in the years to come, Sally thought herself betrothed—not believing it, of course, and not entirely desiring it, but calmed and comforted to know that somewhere in some far-off place the playmate of her youth was thinking of her also, fondly, and planning to return. He would lodge his proper claim on her; he would play a courting-tune and ask for her white hand.

There were, therefore, four people in the present world that she held dear. After her mother's death she turned to Mary Nogarola; she had her father once again and, always, William Green, and now the young Count Taxis: these four formed her quartet.

However one gray afternoon she received a letter, addressed to her in Munich, by an unfamiliar hand. The article within had been composed in English, so she read: "Lost, being killed in a duel, Captain William Green, one of our most promising and beloved naval officers, barely attaining the age of eighteen. A duel said to be undertaken to vindicate the honor of a beloved sister. The sister is said to have had her mind deranged by grief at the death of her brother."

She knew that the fond mother of William, after he completed his studies, had put him into the navy; there could be no doubt who the officer was, nor of the identity of the troubled sister. Sally wept.

While she was thus bewailing the loss of her first suitor, mourning the brief brilliant passage of that bird of youth, there came a knock on the door. Countess Nogarola entered, stern and solemn, dressed in black. "My husband summons me," she said. "I must obey and therefore I leave in the morning."

"Do not leave me," Sally cried. Briefly, she related the sorrowful news of her letter. "I could not bear your going."

"Of course you can."

"I cannot face it," she sobbed.

"You too will learn obedience. You must bend to the cold wind, my dear. And fly with it, my dove."

"I cannot, I will not!" She buried her face in the pillow.

"There is worse news yet," said Mary. "And harder to endure."

She raised her tear-streaked visage, mutely daring to inquire.

"Your father sends Count Taxis packing. He leaves with his regiment on the hour, his suit has been refused."

Now everything was desolation: Sally stared. In ten minutes she had been deprived of all her wonted comfort: friends, amiable-seeming father, and her ancient and her dreamed of and desired fiancé. William Green was dead and gone and Taxis was dismissed. She had lost the four directions of her charted world.

Countess Nogarola spoke tonelessly: cold and calm. In her confidante's confident mien Sally saw how far she herself might be judged and found wanting, how little she knew of the ways of the court. "The negotiation with your father has not succeeded."

"No? Do not say so! No!"

"To end further importunities, the Captain and his regiment quit Munich as we speak. And I am sent to tell you."

Then Mary also left. The door remained ajar. The architect of her misfortune, the profligate seducer and most hypocritical of parents, the selfish, self-regarding fiend—for so she in that moment thought him—appeared; he came in with his stately military march and settled himself in the principal chair.

His daughter rose from her posture, taking Cora in her arms, and considerably abating in her great grief, or, rather, in the expression thereof.

Count Rumford said to her, "You seem very unhappy!"

For some time she remained quiet, then, thinking she had hit on a good answer, replied, looking at Cora, "You gave me this little beast. Is it your intention to take her away from me also?" Her father rose and quit the room, and Sally fell into a swoon.

His daughter's character, Count Rumford feared, had grown infirm. And he trembled at this all the more because it grew apparent that he himself had fostered such infirmity, having introduced her—albeit by accident only—to the courtier's wiles and ways. What to do with a fond child, so misguided and deluded as to dream herself betrothed to the young Captain Taxis—that trifler, that philanderer, that fool? How keep her by her father's side who longed to steal away? Rumford asked himself these questions and he asked of Dr. Haubenal—who, too, grew more concerned each day, wagging his thin fingers and long face—if the girl required bed-rest or diet or leeches or bleeding or might perhaps enjoy a change of scene?

The doctor commended this last. It had been his experience often, he said, and a subject of some interest with which he was conversant, that those whose minds are troubled by reflection on a grievous harm are best assisted by the act of bodily removal therefrom. There is benefit to be accrued from the simple alteration of locale. Thus the stimulus of repeated provocation is denied to memory, and by slow and, it may be, imperceptible yet definite degrees, the process of recovery begins—for who would choose to convalesce close by the site of injury when he might be withdrawn? Do we not retire the soldier from the field of battle in order to attend a gaping wound? Would we not pull the pinioned wretch away from fallen tree or stone before presenting that same patient to surgical table and knife?

Dr. Haubenal was not—the Count must understand him and need not draw back in distaste—comparing Countess Rumford to an injured soldier or a fallen wretch. Her injuries, if such they be, were of the softer, yielding sort and would surely prove susceptible to the kind ministrations of time. To the doctor's certain knowledge, there was no cure as successful for such a wound sustained.

Further, the cause of injury itself (here Haubenal arched his right eyebrow and smiled, a man among men of the world) had been removed. The offending party had been subjected, as it were, to the aforementioned knife. But nonetheless the doctor deemed it wise to warrant her removal and proposed a doubled distance between young Countess Rumford and the site of her so recent and such painful disillusion. Else she might suffer relapse. And this last—he warned repeatedly—must be prevented at all costs. It was therefore in the interests of the so admirably cautious and concerned sole parent to provide his daughter with the time-honored remedy of near and distant travel and that busy distraction: the world.

Rumford complied. He took Sally boating on the Isar River in a specially constructed raft, one of his own devising, and he showed for some few hours how the principle of buoyancy could be deployed. Then he took her to the mountains and paid a proper visit to Baroness de Kalb. While Sally lay on sofas in the library, staring at the countryside beyond the mullioned windows, he fucked his lovely Laura in the garden room. She uttered high-pitched cries. She bit her glistening lip. She enjoyed, she said, great variety in intercourse, and the regularity thereof was also of great consequence. Yet her husband's fond attentions had grown perfunctory and rare; he preferred the arts of silversmith and cabinet-maker to the art of love. For her own part, said Laura, she thought nothing more important on this earth. She rearranged her skirts. Then arm in arm they went across to the library, where Sally's tray of dainties had been left untouched.

Father and daughter remained three nights in the environs of Leipzig. They drove through ochre fields of grain, past peasants and their harvest of the high-heaped yield. The countryside was pacified because of Rumford's dealings; the Austrians and French—great armies both, withdrawing—had skirted her walled castle and had not breached the gate. For this he was amply rewarded by Baroness de Kalb. When she finished with her acrobatics, and left him spent in rumpled sheets, she descended to the daughter and they played piquet.

From time to time, while Sally wept, Count Rumford wondered at his conduct with the girl and examined his motives with care. Had he not preserved, beyond all else, her own best interests? Had he in any particular been wanting, as her attitude of injured innocence seemed coldly designed to convey? Was he not the very definition of the doting father, the exemplar of concern?

He was guiltless, he decided, and by himself reprieved. He knew the world, as young Sally did not, and was mired in it daily. Nightly he accumulated proof: there was neither faith nor hope nor honor in the dealings of women with men. Had he not at his right hand now, in lewd and winking Laura, a cautionary instance of misbehavior in marriage, the callous betrayal of vows? She squeezed his hand, then placed it on her thigh. Why let his darling daughter be subject to indignity (or, worse, to visit it upon a fond and foolish husband) when she might pass the coming years untroubled at her father's side?

He visited the mountains yet again. He took Sally to the glacier in the countryside near Chamonix and made careful observations of the site. He hunted for but failed to find that hut by Interlaken where he had cured his own disease and profited from chess. Rumford told his daughter, often, of the merits of those villagers, the quiet lives they lived and satisfaction reaped: the old man by the fireside, the old woman in the kitchen, white cows in the stable beyond. He discoursed on the benefits of privacy, the strength of paired rooks in a file, the enduring beauty and the mental challenge of chess.

Turning to the window, Sally yawned. She had set her face against him, Rumford knew.

"What would you have me do?" he asked. "What would you have me say?"

"Where is Mary Nogarola?"

"In Italy, perhaps, in Mannheim. Why?"

"I hoped to have letters."

"Regarding?"

"Our private business," she said, with cold composure.

"Oh?"

"I charged her with certain commissions."

"And what may those be? Or how might her whereabouts matter?"

"She was my friend," said his daughter, "and is my friend still, certainly. I believed her to be yours."

"Just so."

"Then where are her letters?" she asked.

In vain did he attempt to speak of friendship's nature and the harsh realities of transience on this earth. Countess Nogarola was his dear companion, yes, and nothing could dissever the bonds of their affection. Yet the intricate weaving of courtship, the warp and woof of passion, the very fabric of desire is foredoomed to fade. Or if repaired and often worn it can be—he smiled and shut his eyes a moment, remembering the Baroness de Kalb—to other partners transferred.

So Rumford urged his offspring to adopt his own procedures and find business sufficient to the day. She must not languish moodily expecting a reunion, nor a written explanation of some imagined slight; she should occupy herself the while, not mope and sigh and dream. Romantic entanglement palls. He had better things to do as outlet for his industry, and she might with profit follow his example—noting, as he did this day, how the glacier south of Chamonix changed color in the light.

Sally scrutinized the post. She attended it impatiently and waited for some signal from a friend.

I love the generous pride of an independant Soul, as much as I hate and despise Arrogance and Vanity in all their various forms and Combinations;

and have ever myself been much too ambitious of Applause and honorable distinctions to disapprove of that Ambition in another;—Beware only, my dear Child, that your Ambition does not carry you away from the path which leads to Happiness. Nothing is more natural to Youth and inexperience than the wish to shine in the higher Circles of Rank and dissipation; but believe me my dear Child, Disappointment is the least of the Evils that can happen to those who set their hearts upon such Objects. Rank is ever followed by Envy, Hatred, and Deceit, and Dissipation brings with it Corruption and Debility of Body and Mind, and an insupportable Ennuy or Discontent with every thing, which no Medecine—but that all powerfull one which Misfortune and want alone administer—can ever cure.

These few precepts did he copy for his daughter, intending to instruct her in the ways of the great world. She was, if not seduced by show, too readily impressed thereby—as though a young girl, openmouthed and watching while a conjurer performs. The hireling knots scarves, or forecasts cards, or makes an arrangement of rings, then pulls a cotton rabbit from a hat. To an attentive observer, the fellow is both clumsy-fingered and predictable: it is a trick done with mirrors and badly, but the child has scant discernment and sits rapt.

So too with the girl: she clapped her plump palms loudly, desiring both rabbit and scarf. No matter how he tried to urge that what she saw was sleight-of-hand, Sally said that she enjoyed the show and valued the performance. Therefore he warned her repeatedly: Be not credulous. *Dissipation* must endure those evils *Innocence* is spared.

On their return to Munich, near the blue shore of Lake Constanz, Count Rumford and his daughter took breakfast at an inn. As they were entering the carriage to pursue their way, having completed their meal and being prepared for departure, there was a nearing beat of horsehooves on the cobbles, a rumble of arrival and a shouted, "*Halt!*" Captain Taxis came up post-haste on horseback. Then he jumped down, spurs jingling, and strode to where they stood. Two minutes later, and they should have been gone. He had just learned, he said, of their arrival and their whereabouts; it was a happy accident, a chance proximity and encounter so wholly propitious that he had tracked them down.

The Captain bid them both hello, but in different ways. With the General a respectful bow and shake of the hand; with Countess Thompson, a paper privily left in her palm. It was a great event, for never had she before the honor of receiving a line from him or from anyone else, for a certainty, of that nature. As she already had had her ears boxed on account of this gentleman, she took care not to expose the letter. But how to wait till night before reading it?—for they were to make no other stop during the day. Her father watched her closely and did not leave her side. She was compelled to dissemble and had all day, in consequence, to ruminate on the subject of the letter.

Taking leave of friends being of a melancholy nature, Sarah took for granted the tenor of her letter would wear that impression. She was several times affected nearly to tears, to think what must have been the Count's feelings and how they mirrored her own. She only flattered herself that he attributed things to their right causes, and did not blame her. The countryside flew by unnoticed; her father's instructive discourse fell on unheeding ears.

But the moment did at length arrive for her to read the letter, and what was her surprise, on reading it, to find only a few gay fare-well lines, with neither regrets nor melancholy! Had he not himself pressed the letter to her hand, she should not have believed he wrote it. He commented on the excellent weather, the beauties of the lake, and wished her *gute Reise* and a most pleasant *séjour*. The main thing was, that the Countess Nogarola had required him to cherish the hope of their reunion, and that he looked forward to pouring both the ladies their hot chocolate once again.

She did not have further occasion to look upon this gentleman, and only learned years later of his unfortunate end. Both he and Lieutenant Spreti, Rumford's other aide-de-camp, lost their lives in Bonaparte's campaigns in Russia. The Bavarians at that time lost thirty thousand men.

Der Graf, what have we here?"

"The merest trifle. Nothing. An indisposition, merely."

"And how long have you suffered so?"

"I would not call it suffering."

"Count, we are old friends. I am your doctor, am I not?"

"*Gewiss.*"

"So, please, do not dissemble."

"I suffer, Dr. Haubenal."

"Where?"

"Here." He touched his index finger to his temple, then frowned.

"Is it a constant or a changing pain?"

"It fluctuates. Like my heart, it continues to beat."

"It is evenly distributed? Or on your right side only?"

"Only here."

"And how long have you had this, this indisposition? This complaint."

"*Ach*, Haubenal, you ask too much. How can I answer properly? We start to die, it is my firm conviction, from the moment we are born. Our first noise is a cry; we suffer as we breathe. This life is unremitting pain, and he who tells you otherwise is either a liar or fool."

"A fine speech, Count. Is there blood in your urine?"

"No."

"In your stool?"

He shook his head.

"You are able to sleep? You have dreams?"

He grimaced. His hand shook.

The more the Count considered it, the less he favored Munich as locale. His work in that city was done. The Elector was declining, in health and attentiveness and power, and his sponsorship of Rumford's cause was a mixed blessing now; nor did the Minister of War and Councillor and Chamberlain and Chief of Police have, if properly considered, still a pressing cause. There was nothing left to argue for or win.

His daughter's broken German and her preference for English reminded him acutely of how far he was from England or the land he had been born in and from which Sally hailed. She made Rumford yearn for home. Her voice held the accents of Concord, and he seemed to hear in it the happy burble of the Merrimac in springtime or the lowing animals in summer or the bright wind blowing off the summit of the mountains in late fall. When harsh and guttural—as was, alas, often the case when she spoke—her voice reminded him of labor: the wood-lot felled, cows milked, the pasture cleared. When soft, it was as though he were reprieved from chores. At times he half-believed he heard the chatter of the citizens in village green and Grange hall, the clatter of New England in the burr of Sally's speech.

This set the Count to thinking, dreaming, and he wrote Loammi Baldwin, his dear friend. He inquired—circumspectly at first, then more and more directly—what might be his reception in Woburn, were he to return. The answer was encouraging. To the best of Baldwin's knowledge, the Count was welcome back; he himself would offer surety and meet them at the boat or, awaiting their arrival, would light tall beeswax tapers in the windows of their house.

Next he made inquiries, of others, as to the Military Academy at West Point. His name had been proposed. The Military Academy required a commander, and he thought he might be just the man (given his experience of munitions, his military drawings, his long years of service at war) to fill the post. It seemed a good idea.

The American Ambassador to London, Rufus King, agreed. In addition to the Superintendence of the Military Academy, Count Rumford might expect to serve as Inspector-General of the Artillery of the United States. He would receive such rank and emoluments, consistent with existing provisions, and with what had already been settled upon the former of these heads, as would be likely to afford satisfaction. In Rufus King's opinion, he was the perfect choice.

This opinion, however, was not widely shared. While still Lieutenant-Colonel Thompson, he had fought against America in the uniform of King's Dragoon, and there were those who remembered. A German Count could not maintain that character at home, for resentment and the fierce self-vaunting sentiments of independence flourished yet amongst the colonials. He would be permitted to return without hindrance, perhaps, but must not look for any sort of diplomatic standing or advancement. To return to Woburn, Thompson learned, was to trade a distant exile for a near.

Do you miss America?" his daughter asked.

"Why so? Do you?"

They were standing in the hallway. "Not the town of Concord, no. Since mother's death . . ."

"Continue," Rumford said. "You should complete your sentence. A thought half-expressed is an act half-achieved."

"Sometime in the future—some months from now, perhaps, or years—I would, I think, if I were you, feel the desire once again to see my native land. Where once my heart and family . . ." Again Sally paused.

"The old familiar hearth, you mean?"

"I do."

"The source of fond renewal? Of heart and hearth and kin and kith and home?"

"Just so."

"Ridiculous," said Rumford. "You are not me. And your syntax is hopelessly garbled."

She flushed.

"Under the guise of compassion you confuse subject and object.

'If I were you,'" he mimicked. "Do not let the circumstance fool you, missy. 'If I were you' is nonsense. You are not."

"Why must we argue, Father? I asked if you were lonely."

"No."

"I'm glad. And very grateful, sir," she said, "for this chance to see the world."

She was lying, Rumford knew. She hunted the length of Bavaria for someone to steal her away, searching after Mary Nogarola or Count Taxis at each inn. If they changed horse and carriage, when they saw a file of soldiers, while they attended a ball—at every opportunity he watched her glance glide sidelong and her gaze beseech the eyes of others, as though his arm on which she hung were but a prison bar.

So he turned his thoughts to England and the prospect of returning there instead. He would put, if not an ocean, the turbulent channel between her and the prospect of escape. Since it lay within his power, he decreed his own position; he would give himself employment once arrived. He would travel to that kingdom with the Elector's blessing and as his representative; he had himself declared Envoy Extraordinary and Minister-Plenipotentiary-designate to the English Court.

Here was advancement indeed. This was a signal honor, a position to be prized! Old Count Haslang was retiring after many years of service, and Rumford would replace him in the lists. The Count would proffer papers to the court in London and, his credentials once reviewed, he would no doubt be received. There were those who warned him that the English looked unkindly on his years of absence—construing him a servant of their own crown, not Bavaria's—and would not make him welcome but call him renegade. Count Rumford paid no heed.

Once more he gathered his papers and possessions and bade his daughter pack. Once more he sought and gained permission to depart. Karl Theodor wavered, dithered, deplored his friend's decision, remonstrating feebly, and then at length concurred. He and the Electrice gave Rumford one last fête.

As Minister-designate to Great Britain, he traveled in great luxury. Sally joined him in the coach. Their journey was uneventful, a happy contrast to the rapid departure from London for Munich so many and such turbulent seasons before. He diverted himself through the long afternoons by regaling his daughter with stories, describing his experiments at Stoneland Lodge when he and the world had been young; he reported in meticulous detail as to the position of the target and the quantity of powder and monitored air—its constant temperature though incremental haze—within his lordship's barn.

In the course of this long narrative, he tailored his discourse to fit. The Count omitted, quite naturally, those piquant details of his intimacy with Lord and Lady and the daughters Germain that might have brought a blush to Sally's maiden cheek. That pale cheek remained averted, however, and she kept her eyes downcast. She did not seem to see or, seeing, greatly care to notice the beauties of the countryside and splendors of the road.

Nevertheless he persisted. He told her of his work while boring cannon in Karl Theodor's arsenal, and how the water boiled. He explained his understanding of the transmission of heat, then rehearsed his wars and stratagems, his unshaken faith in potatoes. He repeated his conviction that the poor are most deserving when industrious, and he discussed the nature of those industries in which they are most gainfully employed. He recounted his acquaintanceship with Gainsborough and Gibbon; he told her how he first met her mother and, thereafter, Governor Wentworth; he described his shipboard calculations and the nighttime stars. Omitting always and only those aspects of his history that might distress or oppress her, Rumford told his daughter the story of his life.

"I'm tired, father," Sally said.

"You are unwell?"

"Just tired."

"You wish to stop? To take some air? A light refreshment, possibly?"

"No."

"You wish me to stop? In the middle of the episode? Surely not!"

She sighed.

"Where were we?" Rumford asked himself. "Ah, yes. In the improvements at Au. We were dividing labor, were we not, between those who weave and those who knit and those who spin and those who card."

"Continue, pray." With a gesture so resounding as to be nearly audible, Sally shut her eyes.

When they reached London finally, it was as though the city were transformed; his stoves were all the rage and his recipe for soup was everywhere in use. They found a handsome residence and moved to Brompton Row.

His Most Serene Electoral Highness, the Elector Palatine, Reigning Duke of Bavaria had been pleased to appoint his servant Count Rumford to be His Envoy Extraordinary and Minister Plenipotentiary at the Court of His Majesty the King of Great Britain. Rumford so informed Lord Grenville by letter and awaited his reply. Hard on the heels of arrival, he requested of that Minister an audience wherewith to ratify his diplomatic post.

This was not accorded, for Lord Grenville proved unwilling to respond. He delayed and was detained and stayed away and strayed unavoidably far from St. James; Rumford arrived in September and cooled his heels all fall. His Majesty would not consent to receive the Minister in the character which had been assigned to him. It was, answered Grenville—when at length he condescended to furnish an answer—if not unprecedented, at least extremely rare and ill-advised to appoint a subject of the Country to reside at the Court of his natural Sovereign in the character of Minister from a Foreign Prince.

There could be no thought of the matter, no prospect of success. Should anything be said of the harshness of requiring the recall of a Minister already appointed, and actually set out for and arrived at the place of his destination, Lord Grenville was obliged to add that, had the usual notification of an Intention to appoint a new Minister to this Court been previously made, and the name of the person destined to his Employment mentioned to His Majesty (an attention which might reasonably have been Expected upon an appointment so unusual in its circumstances), His Majesty would then have been able to state his objection without risking any Éclat or appearing to compromise the personal character of the Gentleman whom His Majesty declines receiving.

That was the long and short of it: his business had failed. Sir Robert Keith and Thomas Walpole maintained their ascendancy, and in their eyes Count Rumford was the American-born British subject, Benjamin Thompson, spy.

So for the second time, and in the second country, there were those who set their face against him; he had been much maligned. Once again the Count was thwarted by persons pusillanimous and of understanding small. His appointment to the Military Academy in America had been refused, he was certain, by petty grudges and mean minds; his position as Minister-designate to England had been dealt with the same way. Since the idea of mere constancy was sacred to these folk of trifling consequence, they disparaged his career.

Yet what was that career, he asked himself, but a record of disinterested inquiry, of honorable and unceasing efforts to meliorate the lot of both high-born and low? How might he otherwise describe himself but as a scientist whose every breath—in fever, often, and often in pain—had been spent in the service of truth? That he had pledged allegiance to a series of employers was admittedly the case, but this was mere surface-adherence. His deep employment, Rumford knew, was always and unceasingly the proper advancement of man.

America, England, Bavaria—what might the names of nations matter, or the color of their flags? Why call a country constant when its boundaries are subject to such continued change? The history of Europe is the history of flux. As the wise man in the adage says, my home is where I sleep, my business my master's, and my master he-who-pays.

Mary Palmerston consoled him. She hated to be blunt about it but had to state the truth: he could lead a private life in peace but hold no public post.

Reader, what we have here is a cautionary tale. Do not leave your natal parish if you hope to call it home. Do not think yourself unnoticed when you report on others, and avoid amassing riches while improving the lot of the poor. He who wishes for celebrity must stand unmoved by accusation, since the celebrated man is everywhere accused. Kind critic, look on Rumford's work—those great sprawling edifices, the mighty schemes and verdant paths, the brilliant chevaliers and ladies, the pamphlets and machinery and battlements all come to dust—and ask yourself unblinkingly: how have I failed, how must I change my life?

He kept close quarters with Sally and retained her in the house. At intervals, however, it devolved upon the Count to attend a meeting or visit Mary Palmerston while the Viscount was away from town, or go out in society alone. At such moments he provided for his daughter, that she might not slip away unnoticed or in solitude repine. When Rumford was engaged in business where he could not take Sally, Sir Charles Blagden, one of his most intimate associates, would be invited to dine with her, *en tête à tête*. Sir Charles was a bachelor, not so old as her father, but not young. He said to Rumford privately that he liked the Countess well enough to make a wife of her, requesting that favor.

Sir Charles had hair in his nose. His eyebrows, too, were thickly thatched, and hair sprouted from his ears. His wig consorted ill with those white hairs, however, since he donned each morning the black perfumed ringlets of youth; stout-stomached and ill-favored, he believed himself a great romancer and, since the death of his parents, was rich. He admired the young Countess, he told her father over port, because of her good breeding and good lines. If Rumford were agreeable, and if the daughter did not mind, they might just as well make a match.

Rumford was ingenious. He asked a fortnight's notice and—employing in this instance a different strategy than that which had availed with Captain Taxis—prepared his case with care. His proceedings were thus: he would often turn the conversation on this gentleman, relating anecdotes not of a nature to enchant a young person. Then, once Sally was sufficiently affrighted, he spoke of Blagden's offer and asked for her response. She, of course, was shocked that the thing should be mentioned at all. When her father asked for her decision, implying it was hers to make, she told him, simply, "No."

This did not prevent the three of them being excellent friends, when they met again. Sir Charles told her one day he liked her better than he did her father, which she thought a great compliment and repeated thrice. Count Rumford was not jealous. He would say— smiling round at table, as his great friend and his daughter chaffed him while he masticated bread eight times and chewed each morsel thoroughly—they were a remarkable gathering and happy, were they not.

SALLY

Begat upon the housekeeper, *"d'un père absent,"* and raised above the garden room, Charles Francois Robert Lefèvre came wailing forth into this world at first light on October 13. In the year of our Lord, Class, 1813. The "absent father"—as you've no doubt already guessed—was my ancestor Count Rumford, grown old and soon to die. But Victoire Lefèvre, the mother, was young and fiercely determined; although she recognized that she herself might not attain a respectable station, she undertook to raise their son with a view to shared future security, watching his fortunes prosper and his venturesome spirit enlarge.

It was as though American blood predominated in his veins. She liked how he grew strong and tall and loose-limbed in his manner of walking; she liked how he availed himself—without so much as a by-your-leave—of fruit from the Helvetius orchard, and she encouraged by applauding them his free and easy ways.

His nose favored his father's, his mouth hers; he had Benjamin

Thompson's blue eyes. Charles was to be the pride and principal solace of her retirement, once she departed Auteuil, and while immured within its walls he proved her only joy. She herself would never marry, being left in some dubiety as to the condition of nuptial bliss, and being—as her suitors thereafter did not scruple by innuendo or gesture to remind her—damaged goods. That liberty she had enjoyed while in the employment of the Count did not survive his passing; the largesse with which the coachman or gardener treated her belowstairs had more to do with payment for services rendered than any deep-seated generosity, and equality and fraternity—those other two cardinal virtues espoused by Republicans since the all-leveling revolution—were available to the housekeeper only when supine or prone. Men rode her, in short, for their sport.

Nonetheless, and incrementally prosperous over the seasons—as the body's summer spent itself, and the warm days dwindled (cf. p. 118, *the honey-wind*, remember, Class?) and harvest-time yielded to winter, as her suitors grew feeble and few—Mlle. Victoire Lefèvre continued with our hunting trope and stayed the course. She hoarded both bijoux and francs. In the matter of her son's advancement she proved unremittingly watchful, a tigress for his interest, making sure that Rumford's legitimate daughter met with and approved of little Charles.

A *rapprochement* of sorts was effected between the two women, although this took careful management on the housekeeper's part. It must not seem that she ask anything for her own self, or that she presume too much, but she played with some success upon the tender feelings of her dead lover's daughter by suggesting that the two of them alone could understand Count Rumford's excellence and tend his memorial's flame. This was the import of her discourse, as in his wasting age it had become the theme—the principal subject, in truth—of the gentleman himself. In the wide compass of Paris there were none beyond these two who understood the magnitude of what the world had lost, she said, and little Charles might furnish them a daily and constant reminder of his delightful progenitor.

In her heart of hearts, of course, Mlle. Lefèvre believed the reverse. Count Rumford's presence in her life—so overbearing, brutal, and then so strangely passive as his illness advanced—had been less than kind. Or, to shift the figure, it sounded a mere overture, a prelude to the melody and soaring operatic presence of her son.

Nonetheless the lady dissembled; she sighed at the graven likeness of the dead Count now hanging black-wreathed in the parlor and let a tear fall in the presence of his legitimate daughter; she repeated that it eased her sorrow to witness the growth of their child.

"I look upon your *père*," said Victoire (whose English had not prospered, being seldom exercised, and whose pronunciation—never brightly fluent—had rusted from disuse) "as irremplaceable. And so too wiz ze fruit of his lions."

"His lions?" asked Sarah.

"*Mais oui.* Ze fruit of *votre* pear."

"Pair?"

"*C'est ca.*"

"We shall not look upon his like again," said Sally, and the housekeeper agreed.

For her own part, meantime, the Countess Rumford temporized. She had, at this late date and given the provisions of her father's testament, no reason to be envious of her impoverished half-sibling. Years earlier, by contrast, when first she looked on Sophie Baumgarten she had known the green-eyed monster and acted with asperity—finding fault in both her parent's action and the created result.

But where Sophie had been beautiful and clearly the Count's favorite, young Charles seemed a horse of a separate stripe. (A stripe, dear reader, or color?—would horses have stripes? Is it a zebra of separate stripe, a leopard of separate spots? I can't remember: *Hilfe. Aidez moi.*) The former was the daughter of the mistress of Count Rumford, who had been once also mistress of the Elector Palatine, the latter the son of a serving girl who fed on kitchen scraps. No one would censure Sarah now if she refused to listen to his mother's importuning and turned her upright back upon the youngster's outstretched hand. But by the action of contrariety so familiar to a student of human character, the very weakness of his claim for help elicited her strength.

Sarah Thompson was a woman of a certain age herself by now, with no further intention of marriage and no family to call her own; the French boy posed no threat. The Count had barely acknowledged his presence, it seemed, and her father's impatient lack of concern for the fate of his last by-blow—which she deduced by little hints, the low sighs of the housekeeper and her pinched and straitened circumstance—played on his daughter's compassion; it touched on and confirmed her own long-harbored grievances as to paternal neglect. She knew full well—no one better!—how Rumford could annihilate the self-esteem of those he purported to hold near and dear, and woe betide the slightest imperfection in the clear glass beakers reserved for his use. These alembics he dashingly broke. Therefore Sally could be generous, and when once she returned to Concord, New Hampshire, she forwarded cash and *cadeaux*.

In due time Charles became a soldier, and he married and had children of his own. He proved accomplished with the broad sword; he swore great rolling oaths *(Parbleu, Charognes des Gosses!)* and stood nearly two meters in height. By this period, however, Sarah Thompson the dowager Countess Rumford had resumed her old life in America and missed him in full manhood, nor did she meet his wife. From time to time she exercised her written tongue by sending a letter to wish the Lefèvre family joy of the *Nöel saison* or *Une bonne anniversaire, avec beaucoup des retours.*

The natural mother of the natural son responded in much the same fashion *(Harpy Berthday, Joyus New annie à vous and votres)*, being no more adept at writing English than her counterpart proved in French. Victoire was present at Charles's marriage to a draper's daughter in Paris, then the several accouchements that followed; in her declining years she liked nothing better than to dandle her young grandson and granddaughters on her knee. She played pat-a-cake and tickled them just where they liked to be tickled and, in the voluminous folds and pockets of her house-dress, hoarded sweets. She regaled them with wild improbable elaborate true stories about their grandfather's exploits, the way the Emperor Napoleon and their grandfather were great friends.

The boy was called Joseph Amedé Lefèvre, and he when three

years old was made a beneficiary of Sarah Countess Rumford's will, upon condition that he learn English and take the name of Rumford. She conferred upon young Amedé the lordly sum of two hundred thousand dollars, and when her lawyers and factors (an estimable profession, once practiced by my *père absent*) informed her both in person and by letter that she could not spare so much, she reduced the sum by half. One hundred thousand dollars seemed generosity more than sufficient, but ten percent thereof, in the event, crossed the wide Atlantic, and these ten thousand dollars—the lawyers and agents having availed themselves of their commissions—were thereby further reduced. One windy afternoon in May the surviving female members of the Lefèvre household—Charles's aged mother and his widow—were summoned to a counting house and handed a thin envelope of much-thumbed, meager notes. To their protestations and expressions of disappointment the gentlemen behind the desk had no answer to make but, *Hélas. La chaire est triste.*

Thus ended the affair. Young Amedé did not learn English nor take the name of Rumford, since the necessity of satisfying his father's half-sister's expectations had been rendered less imperative by her distant death. In simple reciprocity the quid-pro-quo of the transaction also was reduced. These two testamentary requirements and anticipated custom, reader (a name change, a facility with English), were thereafter honored in the breach.

Oh, Christ, I need a break. I walk to the door and stare out at the sky. It's not as clear to me now that I can do what I set out at first to do, or bring the past to book. Forty-two monosyllables all in a row, forty-five if we add in the breach. Or, to copy the response I gave to my dead namesake, *With a gesture so resounding as to be nearly audible, Sally shut her eyes.*

Young Amedé did take the cash, his own dear father having been unhorsed in the siege of Sevastapol and his grandmother, Victoire, grown enfeebled and distraught. From the news of Charles's death she would never recover, but sat in her chair by the window, warming herself in the pale yellow light and remembering the glory days of their long-vanished youth. A cup of hot coffee could cause her to weep, an apple set her reminiscing for what seemed to those who tended her a garrulous eternity, and the flower arrangements she contrived and rearranged were, to Mlle. Lefèvre, sacred: a bloom out of place, a bent stalk or discolored leaf might ruin the whole day. When finally she too succumbed to that remorseless reaper's blade (the same that had scythed the proud stalk of her son) those who sat at her bedside barely noticed or, noticing, wept. She had outlived her usefulness and will not grace this narrative again until Part III.

Now the track of my ancestry, reader, grows dim and fitful as the sight of old Victoire. The family tree sheds its leaves. Young Amedé grew up, grew old in his turn, and in his turn sired children. In 1870 the widow of his second son (who had fallen to the Prussian guns, in vain defending her native Alsace) booked passage for America. (*"There is nothing here to keep me. Where you go my heart goes with you."*) It seemed to her a desperate measure, although she had a brother who had traveled some years earlier to the French settlement of New Rochelle, their family being Huguenots, and he made her welcome so that—she retaining her accomplishment at piano, and having, as her listeners assured her and afterwards loudly proclaimed, the most melodious and piercing alto voice—in short but not surprising order (on March 2, 1872), Marie Lefèvre married again.

I have the photograph. The gratified suitor was called Roger Ormsby, and the couple faces the camera, she clasping her two hands together, his fist on the back of a chair. It is of course impossible to ascertain her stature, but Marie looks fair and slight and serious, maintaining her composure in spite of the photographer. Her lips are half-parted, eyes open wide, the pearls that ring her neck are not more white than is the flesh thereby enclosed. Her husband wears a cutaway that looks to be dove grey. Ormsby was to remain for all his life bedazzled by his wife's musical talents, her fine French lace, her upright yet somehow yielding posture and her sorrowful previous history in the war-ravaged city of Strasbourg.

You'll note perhaps, attentive reader, how our cloth begins to skein. How what we weave are similar strands, a darn good knit-and-purl yarn. How mention has been made of Ormsby my own mother's name and the city of Strasbourg where we've been before—Thompson strolling through the marketplace, sampling the coffee and *putains*, past soldiers and the squabbling geese, meeting Prince Maximilian des Deux Ponts (Zweibrücken when in Germany) raising a tankard (or is it a stein?) to the whole improbable ruck of incident, coincidence, sequence, consequence—and how soon enough, by extension, we'll all come home again. To an aging widowed lady who bears the great lost name. Oh isn't it wonderful, Class!

Except that things don't work that way, or only rarely and in books, and what I mostly need is sleep and what I mostly want to do is turn the page. The fact that I once had a sister, that I once loved a woman and in solitude beguile the time by writing Rumford's history—these seem to me more mere coincidence than echo of my ancestors. I had a friend who had a friend who worked in one of those hotels whose shtick is authenticity—where the bellboys dress up in waistcoats and the chambermaids don period dresses and they serve Savories and Dainties on ye olde pewter tray. After a while, it gets to you; you need to use the chamber pot, you make what Sally called a courtesy and hope to get it right. Ayup nope nope ayup.

Mornin', Miz Robinson."

"Thompson," says I.

"Cold enough for you?"

"It is."

"Well, what can I do for you?"

"Wood."

"Wood?" asks Alex.

"I'm running out of it. Running on empty," says I.

He studies me a minute, chewing on his lower lip. "How much would you be wanting?"

"How much will I need? Tell me that."

"Depends," he says.

"Depends?"

"How much you want to burn."

It takes me longer than it should have, perhaps, to understand this is a joke or that he means it as such. I stare at him. He rocks back on his heels again, bemused by his own brilliant wit.

"Two cords," I say. "Not face-cords, mind you. Two full cords."

"All right, Miz Robinson."

"Thompson," says I.

"Cold enough for you?" he asks.

⸙ VII ⸙

Meanwhile, Count Rumford deployed his great scheme. In Bavaria he had proposed a public institution and the ordered implementation of its governance, and now he did the same in the metropolis of London and by example thereafter—since improvement once made manifest is sedulously aped—all the world. The poor of England suffered while the means lay close at hand to meliorate their poverty; they languished in blind ignorance who might be taught to see.

Such suffering was needless and could be redeemed. Why should advancement be reserved for those who have no need of it or enjoyment be confined to those who have known it before? The commonweal must surely profit from penury's burden shook off. He, Count Rumford of the Holy Roman Empire, would take it on himself to found and fund an institution devoted to the cause of modern science and its practical effects. This would be his lasting monument and enduring legacy; from conception to lintel to capstone, it would ensure his fame.

Therefore he wrote a prospectus. He enlarged upon those procedures he had established at Au. The slowness with which improvement of all kinds make their way into common use, and especially such improvements as are the most calculated to be of general utility, is very remarkable, and forms a striking contrast to the extreme avidity with which those unmeaning changes are adopted which folly and caprice are continually bringing forth and sending into the world under the auspices of fashion. Yet the Count was undeterred. The Society for Bettering the Condition of the Poor had been established in England since 1796; now its real work might begin. In the present day and age, the benefits of science could be widespread—nay, ubiquitous—once a system of dissemination were properly in place. What he needed was a forum: that was all.

There comes a time in human tide when all things are propitious—when the conjunction, as it were, of favorable wind with favorable weather directs the vessel speedily to port, its sailors working with one will and one shared purpose, whistling. What might at first seem difficult and perilous becomes a rapid journey, where dark shoals give over to sand. And thus it was for Rumford with the Royal Institution; his captaincy unchallenged, he trimmed the lightsome craft.

The Count drafted a proposal for forming by subscription a public institution for diffusing the knowledge and facilitating the general introduction of useful mechanical inventions and improvements. It would also serve for teaching, by courses of philosophical lectures and experiments, the application of science to the common purposes of life. There would be lecture halls and demonstration halls and laboratories and pamphlets and a repository for working models and their various experiments displayed.

Next he undertook to answer the question of locale. On Albemarle Street, hard by Green Park and Picadilly, Rumford was shown and in short order acquired a fitting site where the work of renewal began. The pleasure inhering in renovation is both keen and costly, demanding close attention; what might otherwise have been discarded was instead improved.

The Count required money, and received it in abundance. He needed the enthusiastic sponsorship of those who could lend substance to and countenance the cause, so he went to the first of the land. In order to provide the pecuniary funds of the Society at its commencement, it was agreed that subscribers of fifty guineas each should be the perpetual proprietors of the Institution. Fifty-eight of the most respectable names came forward before the ink was dry.

"What are you doing, Father?"

"Work."

"What kind of work, I mean?"

"My life's."

"Then why so secretive?" asked Sally. "Is it some great state secret?"

"No."

"You tell me nothing, lately. You used to tell me everything."

"And did you listen?" Rumford asked. "In the carriage, did you pay attention?"

"They say you were a spy," she said. "They say your business is secrets."

"What?"

She dropped her voice. "'The secrets of the universe,' say I on your behalf. That's what my father studies—it's his work."

This was such arrant nonsense he could not forebear to smile. "Well, when I unlock them, Sally, you'll be the first one to know."

"Of this Royal Institution?"

"Yes."

"And is it truly royal?"

"The King is its chief patron, yes."

"Then I am *not* the first to know. His Majesty knows also."

"'The last shall be first,'" Rumford said.

Although his aspirations to the Ministry were dashed, in this at least he was not disappointed. He answered each objection and encountered none of note. There are few, very few indeed, who do not feel ashamed and mortified at being obliged to learn anything new after they have for a long time been considered, and been accustomed to consider themselves, as proficient in the business in which they are engaged; and their awkwardness in their new apprenticeship, and especially when they are obliged to work with tools with which they are not acquainted, tends much to increase their dislike to their teacher and to his doctrines.

Now lectures were prepared. These were to be delivered in the central hall, and on topics very pertinent and apt. Count Rumford's chosen list was long; he reckoned that the subjects must include at the very least those lectures that would treat:

Of Heat, and its application to the various purposes of life.

Of the Combustion of Inflammable Bodies, and the relative quantities of Heat producible by the different substances used as fuel.

Of the Management of Fire and the Economy of Fuel.

Of the Principles of the Warmth of Clothing.

Of the Effects of Heat and of Cold, and of hot and of cold winds, on the human body, in sickness and in health.

Of the Effects of breathing vitiated and confined air.

Of the Means that may be used to render Dwelling-houses comfortable and salubrious.

Of the Methods of procuring and preserving Ice in Summer; and of the best principles for constructing Ice-houses.

Of the Means of preserving Food in different seasons and in different climates.

Of the Means of cooling Liquors in hot weather, without the assistance of ice.

Of Vegetation, and of the specific nature of those effects that are produced by Manures; and of the Art of composing Manures, and adapting them to the different kinds of soil.

Of the Nature of those changes that are produced on substances used as food in the various processes of cookery.

Of the Nature of those changes which take place in the Digestion of Food.

Of the Chemical Principles of the process of Tanning Leather; and of the objects that must particularly be had in view in attempts to improve that most useful art.

Of the Chemical Principles of the art of making Soap; of the art of Bleaching; of the art of Dyeing; and in general of all the Mechanical Arts, as they apply to the various branches of manufacture.

Father?"

"Yes."

"You are unhappy, it would seem."

"Why? What makes you say so?"

"Nothing."

He returned to his book. The question of dissemination—of models and multiple patents—had still to be addressed, and there

314

were complicating factors to be noted and resolved.

"Only that I sometimes steal in here to trim the lamp, or when you do not hear me, and at times I think . . ."

"Congratulations. God be praised."

"Father?"

"For this unexpected evidence."

Her neck had thickened, her chin too. She revolved it towards him. "Sir?"

"That, at times, you think."

A year before, his cold retort would have been sufficient to have closed the case. But Sally had grown used by now to repartee, dismissiveness and scorn; she would not be deterred.

"That is unworthy of you, sir. You are unfair."

"I? *I?*"

"You need not hide it from me and need not grieve alone. I know you feel in exile here and how you weep in secret. And were it in my power, you would not be so solitary or without a friend."

He softened. A misery shared is a sorrow assuaged; he took his daughter's hand.

Sparing neither effort nor expense to put theory into practice, he made the house on Brompton Row his own. He altered and fitted up his house in so ingenious a way, and with such contrivances and arrangements, as to make it an attraction for many curious persons to visit. It was set some distance back from the great road that conducts one to the bridges of Fulham and Battersea; between the dwelling and the carriage road was a space planted with trees and sown with healthful grass. The windows had a double glazing, and the exterior made a three-sided projection, in which were placed vases of flowers and odorous shrubs. The table on which these vases stood was perforated, in order to furnish those plants of a hot-house character with the air necessary for vegetation. Accordingly, therefore, as one opened or closed the inner sash, one had these pleasant flowers within or outside of the room.

The house stood five stories high, including the offices which—as is routinely the case in England—were set below ground level. The arrangement was the same on all the stories: two apartments and a staircase. On the ground floor was situated the parlor, where Rumford received his morning visitors, and a dining room. On the first flight was a bedchamber, and a saloon for company; on the second the same arrangement; on the third, a bedchamber and a workroom for the Count.

He displayed his mastery of heat and cooking implements and stoves. The kitchen was a marvel of efficiency and skill. The mantelpiece in all the rooms was without projection, and there were cabinets on either side to keep the chimney from protruding in the room. Masked in summer by a border of painted canvas, it could be confounded with one of the panels of wainscoting—and many the guest who proved unable to discover its location in the wall. Those panels on the right and left of the fireplace were hung on sunken hinges, and Rumford raised one or the other, in the style of a table, when he chose to write or read near the fire.

The bedchambers likewise were disguised. He concealed the bed under the form of an elegant sofa, of which the seat was formed by one of the mattresses, and the other was constructed in a way to fold up as with a hinge through the length of the back part; thus the bed might be contracted by its doubled thickness to the ordinary size of an ottoman. Two cushions ornamented the two ends. Under the sofa he built two large and deep drawers which contained the bedding, coverlet and night-gear, and which were hidden by a fringed valance. In a few minutes, therefore, the sofa could be converted at night into an excellent bed, and in the morning the bed became an ornamental piece of furniture.

The dining room was both ingenious and convenient. Its area was changeable by means of a partition of window sashes with large panes. These formed a very large double door, which opened on the side of the casements for the sunlight, and by which also excess heat escaped in winter. When the folding doors were opened at right angles they corresponded with the windows, and the room could be to that extent enlarged; the same doors formed then two side recesses which answered for two sideboards, by which the service of the table was performed without the servants having to appear.

If Rumford wished—according to his mood or for the sake of privacy in discourse—to contract the room and to preserve its warmth by the effective agency of double windows, he had but to close the folding doors and, without depriving himself of light or the charming view of shrubbery with which the windows were bedecked, he sat protected from chills.

Father."

"Yes?"

"I'm very sorry, I did not mean to interrupt."

"And yet you do so."

Sally bowed her head but remained otherwise undeterred. "Sir."

"What is it?" Rumford asked.

"I meant to ask you . . ."

"Finish your sentence."

"I meant to ask you for permission."

"Yes?"

"To visit Mary Palmerston. She invites me to the country. She plans to go to Broadlands and says it must be very dull, with you forever in Albemarle Street supervising the improvements. "

"She says that, does she?"

Sally flushed but stood her ground. "Sir, she does."

"And for this you interrupt?"

"I stood in the doorway some minutes. You did not seem to be working."

"I was thinking. That is work. Were you to try it, daughter, you would apprehend my answer."

"Which is?"

"No."

He turned back to his desk. He dreamed his arching dream again, his great hall filled with scholars and those they would assist. There would be patrons also in the audience, nobility attending, and the gallery was stocked—nay, crammed and overflowing—with auditors both eager and alert. They waited for his every utterance as if it were true prophecy, attending to his words. It was the dawn of a new era, and he had ushered it in.

"I'll leave you for the moment then," said Sally.

"Yes."

"Supper is ready, when you will."

"Good."

"We have no visitors this evening?"

He shook his head.

"It will be just the two of us?"

He nodded. She withdrew.

Increasingly his daughter furnished just such interruption, and very little else. He wondered at the time it took to be a proper father, and if the game were worth the candle of her company at home. He had done his best to free her from the clutch of meddling suitors, to enlighten and instruct her in the ways of the great world. But she was twenty five now, with no adequate prospect of marriage, and a certain loud insistence that disrupted Rumford's peace. He who prayed for a silent companion was rewarded with a chatterbox; the bird he so lovingly caught and caged proved not so much melodious as shrill.

So he set himself once more to live alone. He proposed to Sally, offhand, on a wet spring day in Regent's Park, that perhaps she might prefer to spend the winter in Concord where the climate was agreeable. She had but to express the desire, said Rumford, and the wherewithal was hers; it would be a simple matter to procure a berth. He wondered—as he himself was certain Sally wondered daily—how his mother her grandmother fared.

"Will you come with me?" Sally asked.

"Not at this moment, no."

"But soon?"

"I have great employment here and must see it to completion."

"Yes. But will you come?"

"When you return to Concord, write me how you fare there. What you see."

"I shall be your emissary, father."

"My eyes and ears," he said.

This was one of their rare moments of agreement, and it troubled him that she should be so ready to depart. "Your obedient servant," she said. "I'll be your Northern spy, I promise"—and kissed him on the cheek.

Then for some weeks they were at peace, receiving guests and being guests together in the great houses of London; they went to Harrogate also, and took the waters there. To the admiration of observers, he and his daughter danced. Her manners had improved. No longer so entirely his savage, she was ornamental, almost, at his side; she spoke with some vivacity on subjects of some interest. Her crewelwork was acceptable, and—freed from the embarrassments of her atrocious German and incompetent Italian—Count Rumford regarded his daughter with earned paternal pride.

He was tempted to ask her to stay. He resisted temptation, however, and steeled his yielding heart. So in the autumn of the year she did indeed take leave of him—in a whirlwind of activity, a burble of farewells, a round of parties, dinners, the opera, tearful conjurations, Anymeetle Aichner clinging to Sally's neck, inconsolable, a new Niobé; then her trunks packed, fairly crammed with objects of intricate workmanship and interest to show the curious at home, with gifts of lace and finery and cameos and music boxes for his mother and seeds and cuttings for Loammi Baldwin and copies of his pamphlets for the broadest possible dissemination, inscribed, destined for personages of note back in America, and rare cut glass and clocks and Mary Nogarola's portrait for her parlor wall—and he remained alone.

Now he taxed his strength unceasingly and spared himself no detail of the task. The high-windowed building stood in disrepair—and in any case, for the Count's purposes, requiring that its interior plan be in every detail transformed. He supervised construction while the job was being done.

Mr. Swan was Clerk Assistant and Mr. Webster Clerk of the Works. They reported to Count Rumford every morning and again at noon; they provided an accounting every night at eight. Its progenitor accorded the Royal Institution such continued close attention that Mr. Webster protested, exhausted, and said there must be something left for him to perform who after all had been hired expressly for that purpose. The worthy Mr. Webster had been an architect and the sorting of papers and filing of plans in triplicate was, he urged, insufficient outlet for his skills.

Nonetheless the Count persisted. He had himself conveyed to Albemarle Street in the predawn dark, then left by the dark of the moon. At times the trip to Brompton Row seemed simply not worth making, and he slept beneath the eaves, having furnished a small suite of rooms. He ate his spartan repast there, drinking water from the tap. This was to be his crowning dream, his great and particular accomplishment, and had it been in Rumford's power to set the mortar for each stone, to mortise every joint and tenon, he would have done so gladly, then turned each piece of wood on the lathe.

He positioned the desks; he discussed the elevation of the podium and lights. He arranged separate staircases for his ingenious mechanics and for the necessarily discrete people of quality. He purchased the beakers and microscopes and devices and models and designed their installation; he determined the thickness of plaster and selected the color of paint. With Sally gone, and no one to restrain him, he worked eighteen hours a day.

Now in his temples, as before, Rumford felt a tell-tale throbbing and recognized the signs: he suffered a crisis of nerves. A smoky inhalation filled his nostrils where there was no smoke to smell; a continual nictation troubled his right eye. His legs and arms were weak. A whiff of cordite and his old familiar in the smoke—that spirit he first trafficked with in Concord—came to call. It would not let him be. His ears rang with explosions and his stomach—whether full or empty—ached. He was forty-seven now, and failing, and his micturition was painful and it reeked. When the Palmerstons invited him to Broadlands, to usher in the century, he accepted with relief.

Sweet Mary, too, had aged. Her daughters, Frances and Elizabeth, were grown and had departed the house. Without their noise and bustle it was as though their mother lost the source of her vivacity; she complained of scanty breath and leaned on Rumford's arm while walking on the terrace or surveying the prospect of hills. They were like a pair of old campaigners tending to their separate wounds— comparing *this* one gravely with *that* one, trading reminiscences of combat long concluded and battles long since fought. As when two warriors agree to sheathe their swords, lay down their shields and pause a moment, scanning the horizon, hands negligently curled to spears but with no warring purpose, so did their memories become a form of truce between them, a recollection of past exploits with no thought of starting over. They chaffed each other gently, fondly, and they were at peace.

He spoke to her of what he'd done and what remained to do. She heard him out. With such an audience Count Rumford felt encouraged to expand upon his aspirations for the race, the improvements he envisioned. There would be running water in each house, and heat and ventilation and efficiency in kitchens, and clothing would be durable and cheap; in the city of the future there would be nothing noisome: neither danger nor disease. Public conveyance, for example, would be rapid and noiseless and free. In 1800, he told Mary—who paid him close attention and lent a willing ear—there is much we take for granted that none imagined possible a century before; how then may we imagine the century to come? You and I, my dearest, will not live to see its midpoint, but the marvels of this era will be commonplace by then.

"Such as?" She put her hand in his.

"The practical effects of all our present study."

"Such as?" She pressed his palm.

"Mechanical advantage. Heat and light."

"But human nature, Ben! That does not change from year to year and will not be improved."

"I am," he said, "an optimist. I have great faith in improvement."

"And I in you," she said.

Such sweetness was a tonic to Count Rumford, and his stay at Broadlands proved in several ways restorative. He took daily exercise, sitting Viscount Palmerston's own horse. He admired the pictures in the gallery and the near and distant rolling hills and the prospect of the lake. Taking an interest once again in the night sky, he observed its constellations, and the spectrum of the eastern sky at dawn. He supervised the kitchen, concerning himself with coffee and the method of its preparation, greatly preferring that beverage to tea.

Mary visited his chambers, and he had free access to hers. Yet they did not kindle ancient fires or resume their old affair, for they had passed beyond the stage of bodily exertion, and their affection had become that of dear brother for sister. While Rumford read, she played the harpsichord. While Mary drew, he wrote. They continued with their walks, and as his strength returned these shared perambulations were of longer and longer extent. On New Year's dawn she sent him her chambermaid Millicent, with a silk bow tied around her neck and a note in Mary's handwriting that said, "Happy 1800. Undo me how you will."

The girl was shy in uniform but bold once he bade her disrobe. Rumford was greatly touched by Lady Palmerston's gesture—its saucy wit, its generosity, its abiding concern for his health—for Mary had been jealous once, and this gift of hers attested how even the sharp pangs and obdurate suspicions of green jealousy may fade. He used the wench with pleasure and returned her to her mistress with a note of heartfelt thanks.

For the rest of his visit to Broadlands the Count enjoyed Millicent's favors. As if in the Emperor's armory still, he rogered her till hot. Warming old bones in her youthful embrace, Rumford pressed his slack flesh to her taut. By fortnight's end he was himself again, restored.

It is an undoubted truth that the successive improvements in the condition of man, from a state of ignorance and barbarism to that of the highest cultivation and refinement, are usually effected by the aid of machinery in procuring the necessaries, the comforts, and the elegancies of life; and that the preeminence of any people in civilization is, and ought ever to be, estimated by the state of industry and mechanical improvement among them.

In proof of this great and striking truth, no other argument requires to be offered than an immediate reference to the experience of all ages and places. The various nations of the earth, the provinces of each nation, the towns, and even the villages of the same province, differ from each other in their accommodations; and are in every respect more flourishing and populous, the greater their activity in establishing new channels of industry. Successful exertions give courage to the spirit of invention; the sciences flourish; and, as the moral and physical powers of man increase, new methods of improvement become practicable, which in an earlier state of society would have appeared altogether visionary.

Who among the ancients would have listened to the extraordinary scheme of writing books with such rapidity that one man by this new art should perform the work of twenty thousand amanuenses? What philosopher would have given credit to the daring project of navigating the widest oceans? or the circumnavigation of the globe? or imagined the astonishing effects of gunpowder? or even suspected the useful and extended powers of the steam engine? These discoveries have nonetheless changed the course of human affairs, and their future effects can scarcely yet be conjectured! The men of those early ages, in the confidence of their own wisdom, might have derided them as impossible or rejected them as unnecessary; but, to those who enjoy the full effect of these and numerous other instances of successful invention, it surely becomes a duty to reason upon different principles, and to exert all means to give effect to the progress of improvement.

There were, as always, those who laughed. James Gilray drew a cartoon. Rumford saw himself in profile, beaming at the lecture hall, standing beak-nosed in the corner and surveying the proceedings there with evident delight. In this picture bald men ogled ladies with high feathered hats; there were puffs of smoke and anal eruptions and men drinking from beakers and a general air of noisy dissolution in the room. Once more he had to view the spectacle of himself in caricature, bare-rumped by the fireplace and warming private parts. Sir John Hippisley suffered the explosive effects of pneumatics while Davy held the bellows and Garnett tweaked his nose. The Count's own nose had sharpened as his cheeks wizened, chin dropped.

Others portrayed him in verse. It was not flattering:

> Lo, ev'ry parlour, drawing room I see,
> Boasts of thy stoves and talks of nought but <u>thee</u>
> Yet not <u>alone</u> my Lady and young Misses

The Cooks themselves could smother thee with kisses.

Long as thy chimneys shall thy praise endure;
Oblivion ne'er shall swallow Rumford's name,
Aloft ascending, lo, thy radiant Fame,
With thine own curling clouds of smoke shall rise
And sun-like give them lustre on the skies.

So wrote Peter Pindar, in his "Epistle to Count Rumford." Though he did so tongue-in-cheek, he touched a tender nerve:

I know they mock thee (in their laughter loose)
Because thou sweep'st a chimney with a goose;
I know the world a jealous spirit fosters
And christens thee the weakest of Imposters:
Stead of a war-horse, one of Folly's hacks;
The Prince, The King, The Emp'ror of the Quacks
Sir Joseph of the journals makes his sport;
Laughs at thy dinners, keeps thee from our Court,
Or long, long since had'st thou received commands
To come and lounge at levees, and kiss hands.

Yet in Albemarle Street things proceeded apace, for those who would not receive the Count as Minister now seemed disposed to make it up to him by the respect they showed the Royal Institution. The Lecture Theatre entered into use (Mr. Garnett proving helpful, Mr. Webster greatly so), and their shared enterprise enjoyed immediate success. From any corner of the room one heard without impediment; by dint of steam circulated in a large semicircular tube,

327

the hall in winter was warm. He had a sudden recollection, standing at the podium, of that day long years before when he had walked to Cambridge with Loammi Baldwin at his side in order to attend the lectures of famous Dr. Winthrop—how they had gawked and ogled and strained, from the hall's rear, to hear. Then Ben Thompson had admired the conduct of the gentry, their ease in the great halls of learning; now he himself was the cynosure of men's eyes. His models and machinery were everywhere in evidence; his apparatus gleamed.

A young chemist came to call, and Rumford gave him employment. Humphry Davy was self-taught, and he displayed a pleasing willingness to learn, so much so that Count Rumford perceived in this scholar something of his own youthful self when first he apprenticed to Dr. John Hay and set himself a schedule for each hour of the day. Where his inclination led him then had been to Abigail the nurse, and thence to that temptress, the world. But Davy slept beneath the eaves alone; he was a Cornishman and impervious to the flattering attentions of society. Susceptible to nothing but the beauties of experiment, he labored hard and long. He supervised the chemical laboratory and the journals of the institution; he was furnished with coal and candles and one hundred guineas a year.

Meanwhile, the coffers swelled. Count Rumford accrued those donations necessary for full funding of the enterprise; his subscriber's list increased. He established also—to be staffed by men of consequence and expertise—a Scientific Committee of Council. Through Evans Row and Dover Street and Vigo Lane and Cork, along Burlington and St. James Streets and Bolton and Stretton and Clarges, down Conduit and Warwick Streets and Bruton and Dover and Glass House and past Grosvenor Mews he made his daily way.

At times he asked himself wherefore this restless questing, this perpetual unease? Might he not warm his hands before the hearth of his own kindling and bathe in respectful regard? Had he not reason sufficient to retire from the noisome fray and pronounce with satisfaction that he and it were done? Would it not be seemly in a man of his increasing age to decrease his busy commerce with the world? Had he not had abundant cause to settle back upon his heels and wear his laurels gratefully and rest therewith content? Sally wrote announcing her arrival in America, and to say he would be welcome and ask if he planned to come home.

To this the Count made easy answer: no. He was born to ceaseless striving and the dream of inquiry; he had not found the moment when he wished to call a halt. His philosophical ambitions, far from slackening, grew taut-wound now; the desire for new knowledge raged unchecked. All else was various, he knew, but this in him was fixed. No permanence but mutability; no constancy but change. At midnight when he heard the bells—the great clocks tolling solemnly, the carillons unmuffled in the fitful London dark—what Count Rumford listened to was not the end of something, but the start of a new day.

Rumford, His Book

Part Three

The story of a life is long or brief as life itself; it will take time to tell. To fully represent a day one requires a day for the telling; an hour lasts an hour if entirely observed. For every hour there are minutes to account for and recount, and each of these may justly be considered to function as a fulcrum and serve both as cause and effect. In a minute there are seconds, and a second well suffices for consequential change. How wide the ramifications of, how various the import of the momentary act! The smallest interval contains both harmony and discord; in the blink of an eye or the beat of a heart whole histories may be composed. Thus a full and proper sequence will take a lifetime to report and still another to hear.

Yet who among us would endure that twice-told tale of life or suffer through each instant of the story? Such rehearsal is behindhand in its very nature; it partakes of repetition, not advance. It is echo, not originating sound. And were it possible indeed to see life steadily and whole we would report on sleep at least as much as wakefulness. The child, the growing and the grown are all alike in this. From the moment of birth to the instant of death—oblivions, each—we court the daily dark. We blink, we toss, we snore. We remember only fits and starts of that long night half-slumbered through, and when we wake to speak of it, what we remember is small.

Further, we exaggerate. The telling of an episode bears but a faint resemblance to the event as such. We describe as in retrospect crucial what seemed casual at the time; we are neither our own best witnesses nor trustworthy as judge. The very essence of an act may well escape the actor—since who can say for certain what he will leave behind? To ask a man to make his own accounting is to certify half-truths and half-evasiveness; the bubble reputation is for others to preserve.

And so it was for Rumford in the time to come. He was old in the young century, and his days entailed recurrence: much of what he did he'd done before. The years ahead appeared to him as though they were a mirror of the dark receding past.

He supervised the progress of the Royal Institution, but it went on without him when he left. He traveled to Bavaria to meet the new Elector and to secure his pension, then returned. In ten days, sleeping no more than five hours a night, he covered what he reckoned were eight-hundred twenty-eight miles, this time using public conveyance. He journeyed through Scotland and Ireland and installed his country kitchens and efficient fireplaces and his smoke-free stoves. He courted the favor of gentry and the favorable notice of their wives. He wrote journals, articles, essays and oversaw the publication and the distribution of these last.

His health was good. He lived alone, writing letters to his daughter and his American friends. He wondered, not infrequently, now he was free to marry, if he should do so again, but could not imagine—or, having imagined it, welcome—such change. Count Rumford lived his life in London as before.

Charles Blagden came to supper. He did so every second Wednesday, and on alternating Wednesdays served not as guest but host. He offered his opinion—and ventured so far as to call it conviction—that regularity in diet is of the utmost importance to the digestive process. The smallest variation ought to be embarked upon only when pre-meditated and as a calculated risk. The hazard of an ill-cooked chop, Sir Charles assured Rumford, was great.

So too were the uncertainties attendant on two dozen oysters, if there were salt in the stew. The oyster is a creature of salt water, and very sensitive indeed to saline consistency, as any excess of salinity will kill the thing outright. An egg, said Blagden, should not be eaten when younger than three or older than six days, whereas Stilton must sit for a year. He liked his wine well watered and he liked to hear of Sally's adventures in Concord—showing no regret at having retained independence, that life-long state of, if he might be permitted so to describe it, non-nuptial bliss.

"Mary Palmerston urges me to marry," said the Count.

"Nonsense."

"So I told her."

"Does she have a candidate?"

"Not to my knowledge, no."

"Why, then?" asked Blagden, looking up.

"Just a general conviction that a man is like a stallion. Better hobbled while he grazes. In winter, better stalled."

They laughed. They toasted Mary Palmerston and her delightful daughters. They toasted the prosperity of her eldest son, young Palmerston. They drank to that poor but genial Cornishman, Humphry Davy, and they discussed the nervous collapse of the good Dr. Garnett. They unbuttoned their waistcoats and stretched out their legs and agreed—this time at Blagden's—to meet on Wednesday next, for

Sir Charles expected salmon and a shipment of Madeira and would demonstrate the tactic of a bishop sacrifice in their game of chess.

The Count maintained his schedule. He exercised and wrote. He drank his evening sherry and his nightly port; he ate sparingly but well. He watched his garden flourish, then turn sere and wintry. He cultivated roses and rhododendrons and various flowering trees; he grafted shrubs. Pensive, he sat for hours in the top-floor study of the house on Brompton Row, or in the music room, when no one heard, tuned his violin. He conceived a desire—surprising in a man who had so often called it noisome—to visit Paris, France.

Arrived, he was enthralled. The town he had imagined poor proved rich beyond description; the sights he had thought commonplace were rare. Those structures he had once believed imposing seemed by contrast with these palaces mere painted dirt. Light poured down on the boulevards at night, and those he had conceived of as the denizens of murky deeps proved on encounter to be more properly described as *beati illumaniti* than the tenebrous reverse.

The river banks and tended parks held throngs of festive citizens; the buildings gleamed. Birds swooped and flitted everywhere above the soaring battlements and steep-pitched roofs; their plumage proudly crested the heads of chevaliers beneath.

The little Corsican was now the first consul of France. When presented to Napoleon—a privilege granted Rumford in the first week of arrival—the Count found himself much impressed. He had expected neither common ground nor reason to applaud. But, as he wrote Mary Palmerston, it is salutary sometimes to be proven wrong, to admit and therefore correct a misconception. As with the city, so the man; all that he had heard before was envy and divisiveness. Thus he had been misled.

No words can properly convey how admirable Bonaparte appeared to the American, how much a kindred spirit, or how greatly his demeanor belied his reputation. He too—for had not Rumford suffered through just such calumny and seen what envy makes of truth, what jealousy may muster in the way of false report?—was much maligned. The eyes were a tiger's, not ferret's, the posture ramrod-straight. The boots were good. The cheeks were smooth, not pocked, the stomach firm, not bloat, the forehead was capacious and the understanding quick. Bonaparte in all respects belied the tongue of rumor, for the manners of the consul were superb. He said, "You are most welcome, General," and in so saying signified that he had heard of Rumford's tactics in Bavaria while Munich had been under siege, and that he approved.

Briefly they discussed the Royal Institution and the munitions works at Mannheim and the Elector's Gardens and the quantity of food producible at Au. The first consul was attentive, and the wisdom of his plans and purity of his attentions proved on the instant manifest. "You must remain here, General," he said, "and visit as long as you wish. We will, I trust, meet again."

Rumford bowed, then straightened and withdrew. There were respectful whispers where he walked.

His reception thereafter in Paris was gratifying, truly, pure balm for wounded pride. In London he had been refused a ministry but in

Paris was accorded ambassadorial rank. Count Rumford's was a name for scientists to conjure with, and his welcome to the Institute of France proved flattering indeed. He was introduced by Jean-Antoine Chaptal, the chemist, to Pierre Simon de Laplace. The former wrote extensively on dyeing, viticulture, and the making of wine; the latter worked on probability and celestial mechanics. He met Joseph Louis Lagrange, Abbe Sieyes, and the famous Talleyrand—whose face was calculated, Rumford wrote, to silence prattling fools. These were citizens of rank and consequence, all pleased to make his acquaintance; what could be more inspiriting to the visitor?

Now for some time he drove about the city, establishing himself in the high circles of the realm. He met the Russian Minister—his old friend from Bavaria also newly come to France.

"*Ist das nicht der Graf von Rumford?*"

"*Doch.*"

"How good to see you, Rumford!"

"And you, my friend. And you."

"The whole world comes to Paris!"

"*Ja.*"

"*Entschuldigen Sie,* excuse myself, but in this town we must speak French."

"*Il le parait, oui.* So it seems."

"Or possibly Italian."

"Why?"

"For the sake of Buon-a-parte!" Stressing each of the name's syllables, the Ambassador touched his index finger lengthwise to his nose. Significantly, he winked.

338

They exchanged views for an hour on various scientific and political subjects. They had not seen each other for—the Ambassador counted on his two hands—nineteen months. The Russian seemed much animated and appeared to speak without the slightest degree of reserve. On returning to his rooms, however, Rumford discovered that this cautious negotiator, far from having committed himself in the smallest degree in their conversation, so rapid and so apparently unrestrained, had contrived to converse freely and with every sign of the most engaging confidence and animation without communicating to the Count a single new idea. In that respect, at least, he had the satisfaction to think that they had parted on an equal footing.

"My dear fellow," said the Russian. "You cannot imagine the pleasure."

"Do you remember," Rumford asked, "our happy times in Munich?"

"*Da.*"

"My daughter was convinced your servants were the tallest men. She believed that all your countrymen are giants on the steppes."

"I selected them for stature."

"So I told her."

"Here, however, the reverse is best the case. It would not do for excess height, it would insult our leader. Here my servants must be small."

The ladies all seemed fair, and their kind attentions gratified the Count. They were creatures of exquisite breeding who yet remained coquettes. Their manners impressed him greatly; he had not encountered the like. Madame Laplace received him in her bed dress and nightcap—well-worked and recherché. Everything about her displayed the charms of refined luxury, and she welcomed Rumford to her chamber without the slightest degree of embarrassment. On coming away he made many excuses to Madame Laplace for having kept her in bed until so late an hour; indeed he felt ashamed of his indiscretion.

Next week he met the celebrated Madame Jollien. Her bosom, which was moderately uncovered, was most beautiful, and her neck and shoulders fine, as were her hands and arms. Her skin was very white, uncommonly soft; her eyes were darkest black. She invited Rumford more than once to come and see her at her house, and he trusted he would have no reason to repent of his temerity.

Talleyrand's new mistress wore no wig. She had fine flaxen hair and was a divorcée, plump without appearing over-ample in the bust. She was nearly forty, and the Count could not determine if she had wit or no, since Madame Grand maintained, in his company, a perfect reticence.

He had an interesting *tête-à-tête* with Madame de Staël. She received him in her drawing room, in company, but they spent several minutes in private conversation. He fancied that he held a distinguished place in that Lady's good opinion; at least she gave him the strongest assurances that this was the case. She added that she was "a most loving mistress," and invited him also to return and put her to the test.

That day he went to visit Madame Pirony. She received him in the kindest manner, giving him a little air of her own composition. When she had finished singing, moreover, she surprised him with an affectionate kiss—for she had been sitting very near, and he had assisted her in holding the music. Luckily he was not put absolutely out of countenance but had presence of mind enough to return the compliment without hesitation.

Next he tendered his respects, for her murdered husband's sake, to the widow of the chemist Lavoisier. She was rich and of a certain age and no doubt had been a beauty. Her untimely loss, however, had dimmed lustrous eyes with weeping, then strewn ash on the rose of her cheeks. The Count was sensible, in her reception room, of melancholy artifacts displayed on mantels and in cases—those glass tubes and bowls and beakers with which the noble Lavoisier had pursued his art. Here, Rumford knew, great scientific work had been achieved. Here much had been accomplished and much had been destroyed.

By chance he had happened that day also to meet the contriver of the famous guillotine. M. Guillotin was a physician, and a very mild, polite, humane man. But the coincidence was not a little disconcerting to Rumford, who could not forebear to see on Madame's walls and shelves the shadow of love rendered truncate, the folly of learning brought low. She seemed to understand the perturbation in his breast and offered him a sympathetic smile.

Next morning he returned. He sat with her alone an hour and found her lively, witty, and pleasing in conversation. Outside, a bright sun shone and the shadow had been lifted from her brow. She laughed; she was cheerful and friendly and, he could not fail to notice, self-sufficient. Her air of independence was made plausible by wealth. He spoke of his philosophical pursuits and intended publications. Nothing amused him so much as to make experiments; nothing wearied him so greatly as to write them down.

"*Venez vous établir ici, et je veux etre votre sécretaire,*" she said. "Come establish yourself in Paris, and I will be your secretary."

"That would be charming indeed."

"*Vous travaillerez et moi j'écrirai.* You will work and I will write."

"You assisted your husband, did you not?"

"I did so, yes."

"And learned, I am told, many languages?"

"*Il le fallait.* It was necessary. And I wished always to be useful."

"Was it not hard for you? Demanding?"

"Greek, a little. Latin, no. The others"—she raised her eyebrows charmingly and made a moue of disavowal—"*ça s'arrange.*"

Primarily, they spoke English. He found her clever and good natured and uncommonly well informed. She had that way of substituting "s" for "th" that beguiles the auditor—or does so in certain inflections. "Zis soughtfulness of yours"—so Mme. Lavoisier expressed it—"I am vairy sankful for your soughts." What sounds like affectation in the mouth of old experience may be music itself on youth's tongue.

She was no longer young, in truth, but neither was the Count. And her "soughts" did make him think, indeed, and they gave him pause. There was something in her manner that reminded him of Sarah Rolfe, their fateful meeting by the garden gate in Concord thirty years before. Then too he had been nervous and had seized the day; then too he had advanced upon a woman both willing and frank.

The widow Lavoisier bore herself with much the same assurance—though her portion and her means were on an infinitely greater scale than that by which he learned to measure a provincial lady. His first wife had lived in comfort, Madame in luxury. Footmen hovered in her doorway where the great world—not schoolmaster and parson—came to call. She was the toast of brilliant Paris, no village emerging from mud.

Rumford had not stood so open-mouthed since he viewed busy Boston from Uncle Hiram's cart—for the munificence of Paris was, in truth, a shock. The marketplace at Strasbourg by comparison seemed empty, and rough manners of the countryside were nowhere in evidence here. Even the Elector's homes—the vaulting Residenz and Nymphenburg—seemed to our traveler in retrospect an innocent's conceit. Whatever he had heard before was but an overture. Whatever he had seen of fashion's heightened finery he saw now as rehearsal, a brave beginning only. The French men and their ladies were superb. There was nothing of democracy and everything of noble bearing in the way they rode, sat, dressed and danced; there were centuries of breeding in the way these *citoyens* conversed.

At the Opéra the Count offered his right arm to Madame Lavoisier. They attended a performance of *The Magic Flute*. The stage was well filled and the spectacle in all respects magnificent. There was one decoration—a momentary view of the Elysian Fields—which quite enchanted him: beautiful living figures draped in white were distributed among the trees, and the whole of the scenery was illuminated in the most resplendent manner by light perfectly white, the source of which was not seen. This most striking result, he conjectured, would have been achieved by Bengal lights placed on one side behind the scenes.

The shadows cast by gently moving figures on one another produced the desired effect. Yet the audience was not indulged with that enchanting view of Paradise for longer than a minute. The Turkish Ambassador, who sat in the adjacent Box, appeared to enjoy this particular minute more than anything else. It seemed indeed contrived (Madame flicked her fan at Rumford, smiling) to give that worthy an idea of what his religion taught him to expect in the other world. It was the only circumstance—maidens intertwined and dancing—that seemed in the smallest degree to disturb his secret meditations, or alter the solid gravity of his Excellency's countenance.

"You come here often, *il parait*. It seems the opera pleases you?" Rumford asked of his companion.

"*De temps en temps.* Not always, I confess it. But Mozart." She said this in the French fashion, with no "t" and a soft "z." "Moasare," she breathed again, "*Une telle génie!*"

"My daughter used to say," he said, "that she preferred the fiddle in a country barn."

"You have a daughter, General?"

He bowed.

"She is very young, of course?"

Again he bowed, then shook his head.

"But not *wiz* you in Paris, surely! She is married?"

"She is living in America."

"Ah! *J'aurais dit à Londres.*"

"The second act," said one of their party. "At this very moment, it begins."

What Rumford now considered were the procedures of love. He wondered, was it seemly that he should propose? It had been many years since—fleetingly, in Italy, with Mary Nogarola—he had felt that fierce compulsion poets write of and all schoolchildren know. In his chambers at the Hotel de Caraman he assessed the virtues of Madame Lavoisier: her wealth, her social standing and her house.

She had lost her father on the same day as her husband, both to the guillotine. This double outrage and ensuing sorrow aroused in our suitor the instincts of paternity as well as those of a more uxorious nature. He had been alone for nine and she for seven years.

He took breakfast with the lady on the morning of his planned departure; hers was the final farewell. Preparing himself with attention, the Count omitted nothing that might compliment his person— medals, a boutonnière of orchids and suit of watered silk. He carried his top hat and dress-sword and his military cape and wondered if it might prove possible she would return his regard.

Mme. Lavoisier received him formally, at nine. "So, *M'sieur le Compte*, it appears we failed to keep you."

"Yes."

"We were determined, Talleyrand and I." She smiled. At the corner of her eye a tear, or something very like it, shone. She flicked an invisible crumb. "You were not to be allowed to go."

"Madame, I will return, I promise."

"But when?"

"As soon as you command me."

"I?"

The look of glad surprise upon her solemn visage, the sudden blush upon her cheek and flush on her frank countenance to Rumford furnished proof. He reached for her right hand. "Your wish is my desire," he said. "*Votre voeux est mon désir.* You have but to say you wish it and the wanderer returns."

"Come, come," she said. "You mock me."

"On the contrary. I mean it."

"More tea, *mon Général?*"

"No, I must go. My carriage waits."

"We shall *sink* of you *wiz* pleasure."

Rumford looked at her significantly over his gold cup.

"You have made many friends in France."

"But only one of consequence. I believe I may venture to say," he said, "that no private individual was ever received in any country with more marked attentions, or more flattering proofs of esteem and respect."

Again she blushed. Again the color that suffused her cheek was, to Rumford, happy confirmation.

"What 'flattering proofs of esteem,'" asked Madame Lavoisier. "Which 'marked attention and respect?'"

"The kiss with which I leave you."

"Count!"

Here he suited his action to words.

In the middle of each road there are crossroads and alternatives; we cannot know till followed where the track we travel leads. We cannot tell till landed if the shore will prove hospitable—if the soil be fertile or exhausted or brown chalk. There are turnings and detours and well-trodden traps; there are highwayman waiting to waylay, Samaritans willing to help; we do not see what watches us from trees.

So too must each encounter ramify in import. A casual or offhand meeting will soon enough prove consequential, as the Count more than once had occasion to note. A ten-minute conversation may result in generous preferment or ten minute dalliance transmit the fatal pox. Had Rumford not engaged to traffic with the English once, he might have prospered in America, living in affable domestic honored obscurity not five hundred yards from the Merrimac. But he was doomed to wander and call no nation home.

In London there was little now to keep him; he knew it on the instant of return. His heart was elsewhere lodged. He had felt himself years younger in Paris—a youth again when at the widow's side. Yet in marked and chilly contrast to his welcome on the continent, the members of the English court looked at the Count askance. The French and English, after all, were ancient enemies, and war was being bruited once again. Count Rumford to his peril had trafficked with that enemy and there were some who called him traitor, twice. The King would not receive him nor converse in amiable tones—as did Napoleon Bonaparte—of the scientific future of the nation, the improvements to be marshaled in the time to come.

So at the Royal Institution he retained her image; through the dark of London's winter she furnished a beacon of light. She flitted like a lovely wraith from lecture hall to laboratory, remaining at his side. Above his furrowed brow or floating near his shoulder, she displayed her kind concern. Here was the assistant Rumford dreamed of when he dreamed. With such a lady near at hand, what might he not accomplish; what achievement could remain beyond his reach?

There was sleet on the paving and slush in the rose beds, a continual gray dampness in the sky. It snowed; then the snow turned into rain and then it froze. This drear weather invaded his soul. The English character—once so impressive to the Count, so much the model of an equable correctness—now seemed merely pinched to him, a blossom too ruthlessly pruned. As when a gardener prepares to stunt the growth of some rare shrub by cutting it, and by continual labor transforms a tree from full to dwarf, so had the English been diminished by centuries of caution. There are those who may admire such control and call it the triumph of nurture; there are those who in their nature hate constraint.

Now he coursed again through dark primeval forests, the wilderness of flesh. Rumford hired doxies of a certain age and dressed them in what clothes he could that copied Paris fashion. Then he reduced them to their practiced play and, pronouncing French endearments, sported through the night. He burned brightly with his passion for the Widow Lavoisier, and he did not wish to trim that flame or behave with due propriety; he ravened through the hallways of the house at Brompton Row.

At two in the morning, alone with his whores, he asked himself what kept him in London, why should he not depart? Society was dull. The Royal Institution was established and on solid footing and decreasingly his creature and in any case a bore. If England were to shut him out—for at this juncture, cravenly, even his publisher demurred, suggesting that his treatise on fireplace management might not attract sufficient audience to justify a second pamphlet—he too could turn away. Lord Palmerston had died, and Mary mourned her husband at Broadlands and would not come to town.

Her heartfelt grief had in it somewhere an aspect of reproach. She refused to be consoled. She recognized only after his death how often in life she had tried her dear consort's affections, afflicted him with her amours and been merry in his absence. Now she was sorrow itself. Perhaps she also sensed how Rumford reveled elsewhere, how she had been supplanted, as for the first time in their liaison and after a suitable interval she would be free to wed. This was so manifestly not the Count's intention—at least not with this particular widow—that Mary Palmerston grew angry. The familiar green-eyed monster took possession of his mistress; she taxed him with ingratitude and said he was fickle, unfeeling.

Charles Blagden too was restless and ready for a change. He suggested that they journey to the continent, stopping at Paris and Munich and Rome. It seemed a good idea. In the spring of 1802 the Count made inventory of the contents of the house, and he caused that inventory to be detailed and particular, including even one rat trap and one rope mat in the belowstairs store room. It was his expectation that, should he require an item, his housekeeper Bessie would know just where to find it and precisely what to send. He had his carriage readied with his own and appropriate crest. He walked through Chelsea on the dawn of his departure, watching the Thames run softly, and breathing the thick air; London had been home to him but now he longed for France.

"You'll come back, Excellency."

"Bessie, yes."

"And do you have a notion when?"

"Not yet. I will keep you informed."

"Of course, sir. Very good, sir. We will miss you, Excellency."

Her tears were genuine and flooded the red delta of her cheeks. When Rumford departed Brompton Row and set sail from Dover, however, it was without regret. He would not see the white cliffs and green tended valleys and black streets of England again.

The story of a life is difficult to tell in due and proper order when disorder rules the day. A decision may be taken in the blinking of an eye. How give sufficient emphasis to that emphatic moment when everything must change? The tyrant, time, is undermined then overthrown by memory: a year may be forgotten while an afternoon endures. Nor should we measure by the clock the likelihood of lastingness; a minute can well matter more than does a week.

Now once again the wheel revolved and he was Fortune's fool. Whilst the receding and approaching coast were both obscured by rain, he leaned upon the railing, inhaling wet salt spray. "*Alea iacta est,*" said Caesar, when confronted with the Rubicon to ford. The die was cast for Rumford too—who had no legions with him and no enemy across the water except a waiting widow and the prospect of her arms.

He did not note the beating waves beneath his beating heart. He did not know what he might find but knew he had to seek. The tumult of a channel crossing on a storm-tossed vessel was equanimity itself by contrast with the wild and passionate uncertainty within his pilgrim breast. Without a thought of Palmerston or Blagden or Laplace or Lagrange or Talleyrand or Bonaparte or any of the secondary actors in the drama of his suit, he planned a clattering assault on Paris, that citadel of love. Reaching her high stone house at six and passing the doorman unannounced, heedless of his mud-stained cloak, he ran up the marble stairs.

The Count flung wide the door. She sat alone. The widow Lavoisier was neither startled nor alarmed. Her gaze spoke volumes to him, her smile of fond welcome was sweet. He hurtled headlong to her side and prostrated himself at her feet.

The hours of a life are difficult to illustrate when darkness intervenes. What secrets did they share or endearments whisper on this night of their private embrace? Who bathed the traveler and laved the red dust of the road? Who first confessed to whom a hot desire for cool sheets and tremblingly unlaced restraining ribbons, silken stays? Who lifted which black garter from white flesh? Who traced which scar, then touched what wound, exchanged which sweating vow?

Some matters are appropriate to study; for others it is mete we trim the lamp. The practiced back-and-forth of libertine and lady bears no attentive scrutiny when both are past the prime. A seemly canopy should cover the exertions of this aging pair, a curtain shield their copulation from the light.

Count Rumford closed his eyes. So did the widow Lavoisier. So too should we who witness turn aside.

SALLY

_⸻∞⸻_

And now we come to New Rochelle and the home my great-grandfather caused to be built on upper Beechmont Drive. The Ormsbys
were prosperous people, and very conscious of a certain—how should
I express it?—position, a certain standing in town. In the 1880 portraits they look grim. Stout, too: sober bürgerliche types who unbuttoned themselves over port and cigars, whose women tippled and
had fainting spells and were sent to Saranac or Lake Otsego for the
healthful waters, then carried off by what was called consumption or,
later on, TB.

Great-grandmother Marie's husband Roger Ormsby took his
civic duty to heart. He subscribed to local charities and had breakfast
every other Friday with the mayor, and he helped to build a tennis
club and concert hall and keep the Tom Paine cottage nearby from
what would have been at that period not so much the wrecker's ball
as torch. These Huguenots had a sense of community, and of their
importance as pillars thereof. "It's an eyesore," my great grandfather

said—so my mother remembered him saying—"but an eyesore we need to be proud of. And one we must maintain."

The more I think about it the more I wonder if he recognized how Tom Paine and Ben Thompson would have been sworn enemies. Though in fact I doubt they ever met, they would have hated each other on sight: the one born in England and come to America, the other the reverse. *The Rights of Man* and *Common Sense* asserted so loudly, so resoundingly and rowdily by Citizen Paine flew in the face of what Thompson held dear: a respectful silence in the presence of one's betters and a fixed polite obedience to the ordered arrangement of things. They both were pamphleteers and inventors; they both died outcast and alone, but there all resemblance ends. Poor Tom and my rich Ben.

Whether great grandfather Ormsby understood how the Paine cottage he helped to preserve would constitute a mute reproach to the mansion he built us on Beechmont Drive—a street of mighty spreading elms (*stately*, is it *stately*, Class; isn't the oak tree the one we call *mighty* and the chestnut *spreading?*)—with its slate roof and mullioned windows, its brass knocker on the door and brick turrets and painted half-timbers and servants' quarters and the stone circular driveway with, of course, a porte-cochere, this Victorian *folie* and adaptative corruption of Elizabethan style, a mighty stately spreading *Victorethan*—or whether he thought the two were interchangeable I never could decide. If the abode of Citizen Paine—a humble home, a small producer's garden—and its overarching neighbor were meant as conscious irony, I can't figure out to this day. Yet it all seems so ponderous, so much a declaration, a castle built out of alphabet-air as is this paragraph. My family, I mean, with its sudden prominence and equally sudden disgrace may be construed as, reader, a cautionary tale.

Old Ormsby must have known as much, knowing what he built with other people's money was a house of cards set in cement; he must have worried privately that sooner or later the structure would crack. He pursed his lips and stroked his side-whiskers and studied the contracts by lamplight. In silence and in cunning he feared that his whole edifice, from rooftree to root cellar, would come tumbling down.

In my imagination there are tables heaped with food. There are candelabra and bright silver stirrup cups and thick embroidered linens, gardeners and parlor maids and, in time, electric lights and cars. Great-grandpa sports top hats or bowlers and has the inherited ancestral Thompson fondness for a white cape and white gloves. He likes lawn tennis, possibly, and diamond stick-pins and gold-headed canes, but is not, I think, a crook. He was wealthy and then he went bust.

It's not so much a skeleton or secret as something we didn't discuss; my mother would have told me if I'd asked. So what I imagine is Ormsby at work: the office on New Rochelle's Main Street with its busy hum of commerce, its messengers and telegrams and office boys and ticker tape machines. Ormsby & Ormsby, Ltd. dealt in property and railroad bonds and bottled drinks; it had satisfied partners and investors, and everyone shared in the profit while the old man alone shouldered risk.

Yet now his fortunes fluctuate, proving Newton's law once more: what goes up must come down. It happens far more often—these speculative bubbles bursting—than we are encouraged to think. First there's a failed investment or perhaps an over-enthusiastic or over-rapid expansion; next there's incautious excess in the guise of speculation, the attempt to recoup all one's losses in a single masterstroke, a calculated gamble, and then comes what partners and auditors will in retrospect describe as unsound professional practice and the tell-tale request for a loan at excess—great-grandfather called them exorbitant—rates. Soon enough there's the hint and suspicion of fraud, and then the irate inquiries and suggestion of incompetence and finally the bill collectors and closed shutters and locked doors.

But this is not his story, gentle critic. It's his daughter who suffered a nervous collapse, remaining at Lake Otsego till the hospital where they sequestered her was burned and shut down in its turn. There were many financiers before the Great Depression—witness dear Ormsby—who crashed. The house on Beechmont Drive went up for sale and what was profit turned to loss.

I don't know why or what made him a bankrupt or caused the third-floor window to be so invitingly open—whether he jumped, I mean, or was pushed, whether he was killed or killed himself, thereby saving his creditors trouble and time (remember the defenestrated *Maréchal* Berthier, old Boney's pal, p. 12?)—but do know that my mother went from being cosseted by parlor maids and tutored privately at home to a young girl on the public charge with no father (killed at Belleau Wood, digging out an ambulance) and dead burned mother with a kind of rapidity reserved in our fables for the reverse. The American dream is an upward-rising one; you are supposed to find, not lose, the pot of rainbow-gold.

Our family fortunes declined, and my mother's declension was steep. Yet she never tired of reminding us how our living rooms in Patterson or Stamford were smaller than the bathroom of the third upstairs New Rochelle maid. Let's call it an X-pattern: the way that the first of our line once ascended rung after rung of society's ladder is no more precipitous than the Ormsby decline. *In through the window and out through the door, arrived to see the maiden who's ne'er a maiden more.* For every man like Benjamin Thompson who grows up to become an authentic grandee there are ten thousand citizens whose grandiose imaginings will come to nothing much. I think perhaps what really happened (for this too constitutes inheritance, a kind of unearned transmission) is that great grandfather—with his fits of temper, his sudden absent-mindedness and blithe forgetful generosity—went mad. We would call it Alzheimer's now.

Once burned, twice careful.

"Is that the expression?"

"Twice burned, thrice cautious."

"I don't think so, no."

"Thrice burned, a fourth time prudent."

"You're talking to yourself again."

"Not so you'd notice."

"We hear you."

"No."

"An old person's habit, that's what it is. Like an open book, Sally, we read you."

"Except I'm not talking out loud."

My mother used to tell me that I read too much, too late. She warned me that I'd strain my eyesight after light's out with *Heidi*—the goats, the snowbound chalet—or *The Swiss Family Robinson* and my Eveready under the tent of the sheets. My beautiful sister had gotten her beauty-sleep always, she reminded me, and woke up well-rested and ready for whatever the morning might bring. *Yes, and look what it brought her,* I wanted to answer but never quite dared to: *marriage, death.*

So to complete this lineage we have: my mother née Ormsby who married William Thompson, a C.P.A. from Bridgeport, Connecticut, who believed that what he'd plucked was not merely a "Rose" but bouquet. That was how he put it, Class: I got me a whole greenhouse when your mother tied the knot. When I got her to consent to be my blushing bride. It was his single trope, his one rhetorical device, and like my husband a generation later he repeated the same saying often: *My rose is a bouquet.* Cf. p 148.

I mean by this that Thompson is my father's name, of "the antient and respectable Family of Thompson," and that he married whom he married and I'm therefore the Count's baby—what would you call it, reader, his dependent, his subscriber?—twice. Descended in this warp and woof from both sides of the knot. Young Ben was fanciful, and he gussied up his history in order to escape the confine of the middling sorts—but I've gained nothing from my ancestor but grief: the work of words, the heavy load of invention it's my duty to shoulder and bear. He stares at me mutely, his heart on his sleeve and his hat at his chest. I didn't ask for this, I tell him, I didn't choose it, you chose me instead; it's not my preferred felicity to tell your story right.

Charles Blagden and Count Rumford went together to the theatre. They were presenting Shakespeare's Hamlet, Prince of Denmark, *and the performance was good. The ghost looked incorporeal and smote his breast with the most engaging hollow resonance—produced, the Count inferred, by thin metallic sheets beneath his robe. Ophelia, too, engaged his sympathy; her mad-scene was convincing, and she tore at her clothes with persuasive abandon, bringing tears to the onlooker's eye. The squabbles of the courtiers and the schemes of those in power spoke directly to the Count; he himself had been to Wittenberg and endured just such indignities as Hamlet had to suffer from false friends.*

The prince, however, was too fat. When he complained of "solid flesh" and wished that it would melt, he had good reason so to hope; he fairly split his hose and could not close his vest. When he spoke in the famous soliloquy of taking arms against a sea of troubles, and by opposing ending them, he barely raised his arms. Hamlet's duel with Laertes was sham; he stood stage center, revolving, while his adversary pranced. Although the prince labored and panted, those who brought him to his poisoned fate did not raise a sweat. Had Hamlet spent more time at exercise, said Blagden, he might have proved a proper man and come into his kingdom's crown and lived to tell the tale.

Count Rumford disagreed. The truth of Hamlet's history is inescapable: we die when we are meant to die and live how we must live. The fall of a sparrow, it may well be argued, obeys not only nature's law but that of gravity. Who takes away my honest name takes from me what might otherwise endure, since history is written by the victor not the vanquished; were Fortinbras to have decreed that Hamlet was misguided, a

mad renegade, we would not hail him now. So they speak of me in Boston
as a traitor, I am told. So they celebrate old Franklin, who copied—nay,
purloined—my stove. It is the fate of exiles to be everywhere reviled.

One of my boiled pots was titled *Burning Sappho*; I wrote it in three
weeks. There were girls like Adriana and phrases like "soft inside ob-
late of knee," the Isles of Greece, hysterical punning and *hysterica passio* throughout. But I remember thinking then that someday I might
try again, how the heroine with a ripped bodice might grow up and
learn embroidery and tell us what she knew. Consider how the au-
thors of all those early novels didn't hesitate to interrupt and lay claim
to a kind of omniscience or admit what they didn't quite follow: why
X behaved badly, Y well.

I have Count Rumford's essays, reader, and the letters too. The
ribbon they were tied with is the ribbon I untie. As the daughter of a
father who, as far as I remember, sent me nothing written, ever; as the
mother of no offspring of my own, I study them, trying to decipher—
through the faded ink and how and where the paper folds, the blots
and spots and ornamental penmanship and watermarks—some clue
to what Sally made of it all: his paternal injunctions and confessions
and instructions and advice. It's clear that Ben Thompson wrote to his
daughter, clear that she did answer back.

But her letters are lost or were destroyed; his own she kept carefully, bound with this velvet. I sit here and read them. I ask myself *why*.

Paris 1804, July 2

My Dear Sally:

This letter which will be intirely devoted to very serious and important business will no doubt obtain your serious attention.

In order to be able to compleat, in a legal manner, some domestic arrangements, of great importance to me and to you, I have lately found, to my no small surprize that Certificates of my birth, and of the death of my former wife are indispensably necessary. You can no doubt very easily procure them, the one from the town Clerk of Woburn, the other from the town Clerk of Concord and I request that you would do it without loss of time, and send them to me, under cover, or rather in a letter addressed to me, and sent to the care of my Bankers in London.

As an accident may possibly happen to that letter I beg you would at the same time send another set of these certificates directly to Paris addressed to me, Rue de Clichy No. 356.

I should imagine that the certificate of my Birth might be drawn up in the following form,

This is to Certify that Benjamin Thompson, now Count of Rumford, of the Holy Roman Empire, the son of the late Mr. Benjamin Thompson of Woburn in the County of Middlesex in the State of Massachusetts, Yeoman, and of Ruth his wife was born at Woburn on the 26th of March, in the year 1753.

The other certificate might I should suppose run thus.

1., N.N., Town Clerk of Concord in the State of New Hampshire do hereby certify that it appears by the public Records of this Town that Sarah the late wife of Benjamin Thompson Esq. formerly of this Place, now a Count of the Holy Roman Empire, died at this place on the   day of the   month of

  in the year

  in witness whereof &c.

If these forms should be objected to, you will send me such as you can procure.

To the above two certificates which are indispensably necessary you may as well add a third, which may be useful, That is to say a certificate from the Town Clerk of Woburn of the Death of my father, and the time when it happened.

The new French civil Code renders these formalities necessary.

As by that Code the consent of Parents is necessary in order to make a marriage legal I desire you would procure for me the consent of my mother, expressed in the form hereunto annexed, neatly drawn up, and neatly and properly signed. You can give your personal assistance to that business.

Two like copies of that consent must be sent with the two copies of the certificates, and no time must be lost in procuring and sending them.

I recommend the inclosed letter to your particular care, and I desire that you would deliver it with your own hands, and as soon as possible.

Give my best compliments to Col. Baldwin, and to all my old friends.

I do not yet dispair of seeing America once more.

So he informed his daughter of his plans. By then all Paris knew. It had been a lengthy courtship, and a complicated one, for the affair was not as manageable as he at first assumed; whim and hesitation proved the order of the day. The widow was unready—although, the Count was persuaded, not unwilling—to be wife.

She had been so steadfast in the memory of Lavoisier that in her present circumstance she found herself inconstant and, by one of those conundrums that define the female character, came to delight in change. Now arbitrary moods were less the exception than rule; variety described her pleasure who had been fixed in grief. The creature he believed domestic proved wild and hard to tame. For twenty-three years married and seven years a widow, she behaved like nothing so much as a schoolgirl while Rumford pressed his suit.

One morning she received him graciously, endearingly; next day her door was shut. One evening she caressed him with every mark of favor, but next night was not home. Her approbation and regard proved less entirely certain than the Count had reason to expect or as fond future husband wish. Had he not crossed the channel for the sole intended purpose of matrimonial conjunction, and could he rest contented with any arrangement the less?

She said neither no nor yes but blew, he complained, cold and hot. She wanted to be Madame Lavoisier forever, then someone else entirely, then Madame de Rumford, then both; she wanted him to move into the Rue d'Anjou, or to join him at Clichy, or to take a third and separate residence. She thought he should leave Paris at once, then that she should flee instead, then that both of them should travel and, when abroad, decide.

They settled on this last. They planned a journey together to Switzerland and, thereafter, Italy—those regions where love flourishes in landscapes strange and wild. He offered his service as guide and, since he could properly describe himself (though disinclined to boast) as expert in the country and that role, they studied maps and made arrangements and he told her of the glacier with its colors in the moonlight, the secret spot by Interlaken that was his heart's true home. Their itinerary followed in its outline the trip he had taken from Munich when near to death ten years before; this time also the Count hoped—indeed, he planned, nay confidently expected!—to be once more reborn.

Meantime she entertained and thrice weekly held her soirées. She enjoyed a reputation, she told Rumford, as hostess, and it would be unsuitable to close her house to company because now she had discovered—she dropped her eyes—a single companion of choice. So the Lavoisier mansion stayed gay. He was very welcome at her evenings and might play or, rather, practice for the part of host.

The widow entertained around the fire, after the English fashion, though he disdained how the fireplace smoked. At eleven o'clock, on one uncovered mahogany table, she caused refreshments to be served: these being soup, a hash, jellies, orgeat, fruits and compotes and cakes, with a bottle of wine; on another, contiguous, the whole apparatus of tea. Marie Anne Pierrette Lavoisier made and then presided over an excellent bowl of punch. Ten or a dozen men routinely joined the company, with perhaps one other woman present in the room. Rumford went from group to group, making sure they wanted nothing, and conversed.

It was in this manner he first acquired the suspicion that, since the great chemist's murder and in the widow's affections, he had not been the first. His predecessor was in all respects a worthy man to follow, and the loving assistant of the one would surely be an expert helpmeet of the other. But Rumford did not like to think that the chevaliers of France—those ten or a dozen here assembled, not to mention those at present elsewhere in the city, not to mention foreigners—had soothed Madame's grief heretofore. Hers was a great sorrow, but it had been assuaged.

She wore ostrich feathers in her hair. She smiled and rubbed her cheek. She lifted naked arms. The openness of manner that once gratified the Count now came to seem a troubling freedom of behavior. Between license and licentiousness is a small space to cross, and when that line is nightly blurred, that distance traveled readily, the censorious may whisper and the scrupulous must pause.

He was not alone, perhaps, in having been accorded the privilege of consolation. Nor had been his alone, perhaps, the opportunity upstairs to help Madame forget. She was too familiar with too many to lay such suspicions to rest. That intimate glance she vouchsafed him from her white chair by the fireside fell, he was constrained to notice, on several others equally, and there were those who smiled back.

So Rumford assessed his position and, as when defending Munich, took stock. He grew less sanguine weekly as to the prospect of her hand and, this denied, looked coldly at the prospect of her body in the sheets. What silk and satin can enclose is nakedness improved, and without the widow's dower, her bower held few charms. The ample portion of the lady had rendered more enticing the ample provider thereof. There were many as lovely in Paris, though very few as rich.

When he turned his attention elsewhere, however (escorting Madame Pirony to *Les Mystères d'Isis* and having a delightful entretien with her thereafter, lapping champagne from the incomparable goblet of her bosom and anointing his own manhood with the sorbet of her choice), the widow Lavoisier grew restive and, in her turn, complained. She warned that if he came to France for mere indulgent dalliance he might as well leave her alone. She asked if he were serious and he said, "Madame, never more so. Your servant to command." She accused him of inconstancy who was constancy itself, then inquired what he wanted, and Rumford said her hand.

My dear Sally:

I shall withhold this information from you no longer. I really do think of marrying, though I am not yet absolutely determined on matrimony. I made the acquaintance of this very amiable woman in Paris, who, I believe, would have no objection to having me for a husband, and who in all respects would be a proper match for me. She is a widow, without children, never having had any; is about my own age, enjoys good health, is very pleasant in society, has a handsome fortune at her own disposal, enjoys a most respectable reputation, keeps a good house, which is frequented by all the first Philosophers and men of eminence in the science and literature of the age, or rather of Paris. And what is more than all the rest, is goodness itself.

She is very clever (according to the English signification of the word); in short, she is another Lady Palmerston. She has been very handsome in her day, and even now, at forty-six or forty-eight, is not bad-looking; of a middling size but rather en bon point than thin. She has a great deal of vivacity and writes incomparably well.

It was possible—nay, probable, the Count decided, examining himself with close attention in the mirror and having completed his morning toilette—that Madame Lavoisier, when faced with the chill prospect of his disaffection, found her own affections kindled and, by the very breath of his attention rumored elsewhere, fanned into hot flame. When he fornicated with Madame Jollien and Mademoiselle her daughter (for so it had been bruited by the wagging tongues of Paris), the widow Marie Anne Pierrette may well have taken counsel with herself and chosen to mend headstrong ways.

She was, after all, not young. He was, after all, not poor. His fame, if hardly equal to that of the late Lavoisier, was nonetheless considerable, and he wore its mantle while alive. The news of his success with other ladies of the city would ratify his value if she doubted it before. She had in front of her the prospect of a slow then steep decline into unattended age; she needed him at least as much if not more than he her.

The widow did indeed—as she had promised him when first they met—prove expert with the pen. Now she sent him letters, delivered by her coachman daily: scolding letters, soothing ones, seductive *billets doux*. She baited and hooked him with praise.

This gratified our suitor and strengthened his resolve. He had decided he would marry, and the wealth of Madame Lavoisier proved a strong attraction and endorsement of her candidacy; it made her a suitable wife. Then too, she urged him on by writing, in her fine flowing hand, endearments so graphic and particular he was once again enthralled. She who was propriety itself in utterance used phrasing in her letters that would make a sailor blush.

The moral excess of this attitude might properly have caused the Count concern, for although from time to time and in the spontaneity of passion he had elicited such language from the mouth of bawd or mistress, he had not read the like. But it was him she wrote to, after all, his parts she praised so lavishly, her honor and fortune she offered and unblemished reputation set at risk. These letters exhorted the Count, as it were, to scale her body's fortress with grappling hook and battering ram, with leathers and chain-mail and cannon, all the mechanical contrivances appurtenant to amorous siege. She described the plans she had and arrangements made for pleasure in the evening soon to come, and urged him to make haste. Thus fortified, and with the warming assistance of brandy, he returned to Rue D'Anjou in her provided carriage and administered to Madame Lavoisier the saving emollient of love.

When they went to Switzerland they did so in one coach. For old time's sake he took the route through Nancy, Strasbourg, Mulhouse, crossing thence to Basel and to Berne. In Strasbourg he described to the widow his meeting with Maximilian des Deux Ponts. It was not a little curious, indeed was food for fruitful thought, that his history might be assessed as altogether altered by the seeming-accident of casual encounter; from Maximilian to the Elector Palatine, in retrospect so fateful and foreordained a sequence, had been in prospect for Ben Thompson then no more than mere inconsequence. He had not known, at Strasbourg's muster, whither he would travel next, but followed the favoring breeze. Yet his fame and the world's favor ensued from that chance introduction, and it was no doubt—when closely considered—not chance. So too, said Rumford, do I count my meeting with you, dearest; if we had not met that afternoon we would not be here now.

Thus they discussed the problem of free will. They might choose what fate they wished, but was that process of election truly a free choice or instead long fated by the web of circumstance; had not their threads been twined? Were not their fortunes part of the same whole, was not the knot ready to tie? What choice do we have, dearest—Rumford smiled at his companion who wrested her gaze from the window—though we flatter ourselves that we are competent to choose. So a man may pick a chicken and reject a goose.

I do not like the comparison, said she. "*Je n'aime pas ça. Ce n'est qu'une bêtise.*"

"Forgive me," said the Count. "I did not intend the metaphor. I would not compare you to the fairest of the fowl."

"*D'accord.*"

"My point was merely, dearest, that the range of selection available at market predicates and to a degree predetermines the nature of the purchase."

She turned from him again. Undaunted, he continued. "In every important respect that man who makes his decision has been led to do so by the wares available, the time of day, the season, the money in his pocket and so forth. Yet he deludes himself with freedom, believing himself to possess the opportunity of choice."

"Your point?" said she, with what he construed at the time as pardonable—indeed, in some degree fitting—impatience, but should have recognized instead as contrariety.

"You were speaking of alternatives."

"We have none."

"No?"

"We must marry in the fall."

Paris, Rue d'Anjou

December 20, 1805

My dear Sally:

I gave up my lodgings on quitting Munich, and managed so as to settle all concerns of business. I flatter myself I am settled down here for life, far removed from wars and all arduous duties, as a recompense for past services, with plenty to live upon, and at liberty to pursue my own natural propensities, such as have occupied me through life—a life, as I try to fancy, that may come under the denomination of a benefit to mankind.

I brought all the Aichners with me, two of their boys excepted, who are placed in the army—one as corporal; the youngest, George, about sixteen, as a drummer. The little girl named for you and the Countess, Mary Sarah—you two being considered God-Mothers to her—is very small of her age, considered a dwarf. But she is very clever and interesting, and excites universal attention. Madame seems to take quite a fancy to her, allowing her to dine with us at a sideboard when we have no company. The whole family of Aichners, consisting of six, with Father and Mother, are so good, and those of an age to work so industrious, they cannot be considered a burden, and will ever be a comfort to me, being, as it were, my family. And next, my dear, I hope to get you. But next spring we are going to travel into Italy and the South of France, to be gone two years, so you must patiently stay where you are for the present.

You will wish to know what sort of a place we live in. The house is rather an old-fashioned concern, but in a plot of over two acres of land, in the very centre and finest part of Paris, near the Champs Elyssees and the Tuilleries and principal boulevards. I have already made great alterations in our place, and shall do a vast deal more. When these are done, I think Madame de Rumford will find it in a very different condition from that in which it was—that being very pitiful, with all her riches.

Our style of living is really magnificent. Madame is exceedingly fond of company, and makes a splendid figure in it herself. But she seldom goes out, keeping open doors—that is to say, to all the great and worthy, such as the philosophers, members of the Institute, ladies of celebrity &c.

On Mondays we have eight or ten of the most noted of our associates at dinner. (Then we live on bits the rest of the week.) Thursdays are devoted to evening company, of ladies and gentlemen, without regard to numbers. Tea and fruits are given, the guests continuing till twelve or after. Often superb concerts are given, with the finest vocal and instrumental performers.

The weather held propitious and the season fine. As when a calm belies a storm, the blue sky preceding clouds, so did their honey-month make sweet what caution might instead assess as over-ripe or sour, and the remainder of the journey gave him unalloyed delight.

If Madame wished to acquire a peasant rug or a brass bowl or great stinking cow-bell for her pleasure, why then he purchased it; if Rumford chose to play piquet, she partnered him, and well. Her conversation was spirited and information sound. She made learned allusions to Tasso and St. Augustine and the process of molecular transferal and that ancient foolishness, phlogiston, while they toured the Alps. She called him her sweet Hannibal, her brilliant mountaineer; she called him her enormous knight, her small cauliflower, her dear. They enjoyed themselves so thoroughly they scanted Italy, postponing that shared pilgrimage until the war was done.

For some time the lady seemed docility itself. Those of her habits when at home that had provoked his censure—a negligent attentiveness, a promiscuous regard for the well-being of her other guests, an imperial assumption that the house, once hers, was hers alone—all vanished while on foreign soil and on Rumford's arm. She leaned upon it lightly and fluttered her bright eyes. At night, again with brandy's aid, she implemented in their rooms those complicated procedures she had written of by day.

She continued in this custom though they traveled side by side. By slow degrees, moreover, her letters (still handed to him on the silver salver by their coachman in the morning, her maid at lunch, his valet at tea) shifted tone. What began as *billets doux* became a frank discussion of marriage contract law. The widow's language now was not so much speculative or hortatory as grown business-like, matter-of-fact. Describing her assets and requiring he list his, proving in this the daughter of her father—a collector of rents due—she drew up the terms of marriage and requested he assent.

He was to obtain the necessary documents from Woburn and from Concord; they were to marry in private and in Paris in the fall. She would not relinquish the great name of Lavoisier but, on the contrary, regarded it as her sacred duty to keep that name preserved.

She would be thenceforth known as Madame Lavoisier de Rumford, and she had no fixed objection to making the acquaintance of Sarah Countess Rumford but neither did she wish his grown and spinster daughter to reside in Rue D'Anjou. Next she settled on him—so that he might spend without constraint—one hundred and twenty thousand *livres* in the five percent French funds. This was to go to the survivor of the three: herself, himself, or his daughter. At the widow's age, of course, and in spite of their exertions, she would furnish her new husband with no additional heir. An income of six thousand a year out of her own property was secured to Madame Lavoisier, and her house in Paris, as well as the Count's at Brompton, was to revert to the survivor of the two.

Further, he was to settle on Sally three hundred pounds a year. The girl had her pension from Bavaria of two thousand Florins, and he had his own. In recognition of his newly married state, and the expenses thereby entailed, the Elector conferred an additional four thousand Florins on the Count's annual sum. They plighted their troth in Paris, in private, on October 24. Thus Rumford was amply provisioned, and his daughter the Countess provided for in time and times to come.

I have never been so happy, Count."

"Nor I," he assured her. "Nor I."

"It is, how do you say, formidable."

"*Formidable*," he agreed.

"Zis bliss," she said, "zis rapture. We must make an announcement and inform all our friends."

"Of what?" the Count inquired. "Of these financial arrangements so successfully completed?"

"*Et pourquoi pas?* Why not?"

"They are our little secret, *non?*"

"I have no secrets," she said.

In this they were at odds. If Mme. Lavoisier made a profitable investment, or when by contrast she forfeited notes, if she enjoyed a *blanc mange* or romantic consummation or whispered confidence, she wished the news broadcast to all; when she acquired a picture the world must come and see. The Count was reticent by contrast, quiet in his pleasures, and she chided him not so much for his dissemblance as restraint. Her passionate chatter produced in him a monitory silence; her enthusiasm served to make him circumspect.

"You are too critical," she said.

He begged leave to disagree. "It is possible," he said, "to be private in these matters. To hold privy counsel, my dear."

"They warned me."

"Of what, Madame?"

"Precisely zis. They told me you would be zis way. So secretive in everything. So guarded."

"And who were your informers?"

"Those who serve—as you do—secret masters, *mon ami.*"

"Because I do not wish to broadcast what we arrange by contract you believe me a traitor? A spy?"

"I have never been so miserable. So unhappy in my life."

⸺⁓⁓⁓⸺

As in private, so in public: the world order changed. The news that reached our couple, interrupting their enjoyment, grew daily more imperative and rife with rumored war. There were alarums in a fortnight and excursions in a month.

Napoleon—since none other could do it for him, holding prior claim on that title—had declared himself the Emperor of France. In Notre Dame Cathedral, he wrested his crown from the pope. The Count and Madame Lavoisier were, by having eaten a rabbit in blood sauce, indisposed, or else they surely would have watched, attending the great spectacle and in the vaulting apse and arching nave have joined the reverential throng to hail apotheosis on this earth. The Count remained the Emperor's man, holding firmly to Bonaparte's cause. King Francis II of Austria proclaimed himself Emperor also, however, and there were new alliances and ever-mounting threats.

Then these bellicose conditions invaded hearth and home. It grew difficult if not impossible to savor in wartime the pleasures of peace. The dove that Rumford married proved, once his wife, a shrew.

No sooner had he brought the Aichners to their lodging—sweet and gentle folk, without exception trustworthy and obedient, hardworking—than the servants of the widow lodged complaints. *There is no extra space. The Germans are unclean. Their ways are not our ways.* Such were the lies the widow's staff (no doubt jealous of preferment and the entry of those who were wont to serve him) now swore to as plain truth.

Her French cook was corrupt. Her maids and gardeners and footmen failed to make the Aichners welcome in the service of the Count.

Escaping all chastisement, they vilified their counterparts and would not take them in. Nor did the widow, as would have been proper, correct this cruel impertinence and turn her servants out.

His ancient and honored retainers were given nothing to wear. Bitterly he complained of this, but when he said they were not safe in Munich, she said, less so in France. He said they knew his chosen ways, and how to mend and prepare his clothes, and she said what they ought to mend was not clothing but behavior; when he called them wholly loyal she called them faithless spies. He said little Sarah was an expert at the sideboard, and she disagreed. The family Aichner were given the most menial of tasks, the rooms behind the alley, the table-scraps and slops and offal one would hesitate to feed—for fear of infection—to dogs. When he ordered Madame Rumford to make restitution, to apologize to his dear friends and dismiss her venal corrupt insubordinate Parisians, she answered, simply, "No."

Sally:

The newspapers will acquaint you with the other particulars of this Peace, which will occasion a great change in the political state of Germany, as in fact, of all Europe. I hope that I shall not, and I do not think that I shall, lose by any of these changes. At all events, the Elector, or rather the new King, has just written me a very kind letter, giving me hopes, rather than suggesting fears of any thing of a disagreeable nature. But dependencies like mine can never be otherwise than uncertain, as I feel it, notwithstanding my marriage. I may make a change, after all, but never certainly to the disadvantage of anyone. Between you and myself, as a family secret,

I am not at all sure that two certain persons were not wholly mistaken, in their marriage, as to each other's characters. Time will show. But two months barely expired, I forebode difficulties. Already I am obliged to send my good Germans home—a great discomfort to me and wrong to them.

Charles Blagden comes to Paris."

"And?"

"And I would have him stay with us. He has much to tell, he writes, of England's attitude. Of its readiness for combat and its present disposition with reference to Bonaparte."

"No."

"No?"

"No again."

"I did not hear you, surely."

"Surely, *M'sieur*, you did."

"Your reasons, Madame? Presuming, of course, that you have them."

"I have my reasons, sir," she said.

"And I have the right to inquire."

"Go see him in the garden, if you must. Install him in the cabanon. He does not set foot in this house."

"*Our* house, I might remind you."

"So you believe."

"My old friend comes from London, my close associate. And you refuse him a roof?"

"The English do their best to drive us all from shelter, sir. It would be a mere stupidity—even a form of, how do you call it, *trahison*—to give him freedom here."

"He would not abuse it."

"No?"

"I knew you willful, Madame, but did not think you unfeeling."

"Charles Blagden is not, I repeat, welcome here. *Je le rêpete.*"

"What has he done, or failed to do, that could possibly affect you so? Or is it the impertinence of believing himself my—and therefore yours also, *our*—excellent friend?"

"He believes himself a lover," said the widow Lavoisier.

"And?"

"And was here before you, *M'sieur.*"

"And?"

"You force me to speak ill of him, you force me to speak frankly. You insist upon chapter and verse."

"If I were to refuse acquaintance to those men here before," he said, "as you so delicately phrase it, Madame, I should deny half the world."

My very dear Sally:

In answer to your inquiries respecting myself, I can only tell you that my health continues good. But while making a paradise of our situation, affluence, and all the advantages of a good reputation well earned, the esteem and even united applause of mankind, can not make amends for disappointments. If I have earnestly wished to hear of your being comfortably settled in America, it is because I have no hope of seeing you happy with me in my present situation.

It is not always in my power to render my house agreeable to my particular friends, a disagreeable restraint upon me.

Now indeed he was a prisoner in Paris and his house. The Emperor made war, it seemed, on the whole universe. At Ulm and Austerlitz he slaughtered Austrians and Russians in quantity unparalleled; it was rumored on December 10 that twenty thousand soldiers died between red dawn and dusk.

Count Rumford attempted to maintain an equilibrium, to swallow—as his daily portion—insult and indignity. Though successful in much else, in this he failed. The meetings of the Institute were few and full of contention; Laplace was no longer his friend. French hatred of the English was equaled only by their hatred of all things German, and he found himself doubly excluded from the corridors of state. Those who had received him when he first arrived in France now pretended to forgetfulness or remembered to forget.

Such perfidy is commonplace, he knew. The common aspect of the world is dark, though from first breath till deathbed we may believe it bright. The Count continued (bravely, he asserted; boringly, Madame complained) with his Conjectures respecting the Principles of the Harmony of Colours, and his Experiments on the Relative Intensities of the Light emitted by Luminous Bodies. When the pleasures of the drawing room and bedroom have turned capricious and sour, there is nowhere so sweet as the laboratory, a focused nightly labor in a studio alone.

Therefore he spent long hours on scientific inquiry. He turned all his attention to efficient single-wick lanterns, employing a diffusing

378

cone of unpolished glass, and then designed and drew receptacles for oil. While engaged in doing so he could not avoid the melancholy reflection that, scant months before, he had imagined the widow's assistance in his every task, her promised support both as technician and scribe. Had she not offered, early on, to act as secretary, to play for him the helpmeet's part as once with Lavoisier? Yet Rumford worked in solitude and with a double burden: the door he bolted from within was not one on which she knocked.

That kind of illumination which is most favorable to very distinct vision is not that which is most agreeable; nor is it the most favorable to the beauty of objects in general, or to human beauty. Lines strongly marked are always hard, and some uncertainty is necessary in order that the imagination may have room to play.

Madame Lavoisier de Rumford insisted, per contra, on brilliance. Hers was a visage both pointed and plump, and she labored under a continual misapprehension of its quality, having been flattered too long. She believed those compliments that he had felt compelled to make and, mistaking his diplomacy, thought expedient praise sincere. Now, however, it was time to tell the truth. No decayed beauty ought ever to expose her face to the direct rays of an argand lamp, nor should she ever look at her glass with her spectacles on. That mysterious light which comes from bodies moderately illuminated is certainly most favorable to female pulchritude, and ought on that account to be preferred by all persons who are wise. The harsh accuracy of an undiminished glaring beam upon her face, therefore, far from any sort of compliment, was to the lady cruel.

Out of loving kindness Rumford said so to his wife. Concerned for her best welfare he explained in dispassionate detail why the lamp should be silk-skirted and her reflection dim. She did not take it well. She said that he could shine his light instead on Madame Pirony, then broke his apparatus with her stick.

Paris, October 24, 1806

My dear Child:

This being the first year's anniversary of my marriage, from what I wrote two months after it, you will be curious to know how things stand at present. I am sorry to say that experience only serves to confirm me in the belief that in character and natural propensities Madame de Rumford and myself are totally unlike, and never ought to have thought of marrying. We are, besides, both too independent, both in our sentiments and habits of life, to live peaceably together—she having been mistress all her days of her actions, and I, with no less liberty, leading for the most part the life of a bachelor. Very likely she is as much disaffected towards me as I am towards her. Little it matters with me, but I call her a female Dragon —simply by that gentle name! We have got to the pitch of my insisting on one thing and she on another.

It is possible that, had the war ceased raging, and had we gone into Italy, where she is dying to go, and with me too, she having heard me speak much of the delights of that country—she having been very happy, too, in travelling with me in Switzerland—it might have suspended difficulties, but never have effected a cure. That is out of the question. Indeed, I have not the least idea of continuing here, and, if possible, still less the wish, and am only planning in my mind what step I shall take next—to be hoped more to my advantage. Communication with England is prohibited, and it makes me sad.

❧ III ❧

Paris, Rue d'Anjou

24th October, 1807

I can do no more, my Dear Sally, than simply give you the anniversary of my marriage, for I am still here, and so far from things getting better they become worse every day. We are more violent and more open, and more public, as may really be said, in our *quarrels*. If she does not mind publicity, for a certainty I shall not. As I write the uncouth word quarrels, I will give you an idea of one of them.

In the first place, be it known that this estate is a joint concern. I have as good a right to it as Madame—she having paid rather more in the beginning, but I an immensity of money in repairs and alterations &c, &c, besides a great deal of my own time and care spent while we have been here.

I am almost afraid to tell you the story, my good child, lest in future you should not be good; lest what I am about relating should set you a bad example, make you passionate, and so on. But I had been made very angry. A large party had been invited I neither liked nor approved of, and invited for the sole purpose of vexing me. Our house being in the centre of the garden, walled around, with iron gates, I put on my hat, walked down to the porter's lodge and gave him orders, on his peril, not to let anyone in. Besides, I took away the keys. Madame went down, and when the company arrived she talked with them—she on one side, they on the other of the high brick wall. After that she goes and pours boiling water on some of my beautiful flowers.

His flowers, his beautiful blossoms! His roses nonpareil! His dahlias and his peonies and lilies in a row! How could she trample on his flowerbed, though trampling on his heart! His amaryllis scalded and his tulips stripped! Her cloven heels in wanton boots so brutal to his buds!

The Count was inconsolable and married with a witch. His wife was Jezebel, a harridan, who did him grievous wrong. He had bound himself through vows and civil contracts and honeyed promises of duty to a fiend. He—the very definition of fidelity, of trust and sweet confidingness!—to his eternal sorrow had compacted with a slut.

He had leisure to reflect on this, and how it came to pass. Love's melody had turned for him to discord, contrariety and sheer unlovely noise. How painful to a listening ear, how cacophonous and mournful sounds the instrument ill-strung; how bitter and unpalatable tastes the sweet draught staled!

It was no small irony, he knew, that this his second marriage should thus replicate his first. That he who so prized ladies and had been so often prized by them should twice have been so terribly mistaken was a shock. What had he done or failed to do to merit such a fate? Of all his glad companions—his amours and affairs beyond counting— only these two caused him sorrow, only his wives gave him pain. The widows Rolfe and Lavoisier had this in common: him. Whatever he had done, he knew, he did nothing to deserve that pair, a punishment outstripping any crime.

When he reflected on it by himself, he was by himself absolved. So modest a suitor, so amiable a consort had not been found in Paris in these seven years! When he tried to make of their abode a fit and proper place to work, she summoned her old lovers in to play. While he attempted reason, she was illogical in argument and in discourse rude. She screamed and kicked and bit. When he suggested affably that she might moderate her howls, she doubled their volume instead.

So Benjamin Thompson, Count Rumford, went down on his knees by the wall. The iron grating of the fence and brickwork of the gateway, the porte-cochere and porter's lodge each signaled his imprisonment, his friendless captive state. His glorious flowers, his darlings, his buds!—she boiled them, one and all.

Nonetheless he held the keys. In truth the Count made certain that his fits of rage and outbursts of temper were by the servants witnessed, since he wanted them afraid. The porter was obedient and rushed to do his master's bidding, for he had seen the Count when furious; if the lady had no scruple and would rave and shriek in public, why then so might the man.

He practiced with his sword once more and, in the walled garden, fired both side-arms and musket. His hand shook; he grew weary. Yet he swore great English oaths and muttered imprecations at the air and generally contrived to give the impression—witted, schemed—of witlessness and danger where he walked. He was not without a plan. Though their mistress proved intractable, her servants were easily cowed; he had but to wave his pistol at them and they reformed their ways.

When he locked her in her chambers, she pounded on the door; when he hid the keys from prying eyes she cursed. Count Rumford stopped his ears. While she blasphemed and hissed at him he returned to his experiments with clothing and coffee and light. Unabashed and resolute in these his high endeavors, he need brook no interruption from a sequestered wife.

Thus he continued with improvements in the house. He had the brickwork taken down and the fireplace constructed to his own preferred design. He had the ancient kitchen implements destroyed, then replaced with his own. Madame's chairs and sofas and carpets he ordered removed to the cabanon, where she might lie with Blagden in the future if she chose. She rutted in her room, he knew, with all who could gain entry, so why not in the garden on her own new-shredded sheets? These he draped over trees and swathed across shrubs, and since nothing in his garden grew he planted her fine china and the shards of splintered glass. When she wept and moaned and wailed for help he played the violin. He did so beneath her high window and, when she shut the window, at her keyhole in the hall.

There he took up his position and remained on the qui vive. Soon enough her tactics changed. She cajoled him, entreated him; she leeringly suggested he might enter and be welcome, thus promising contrition and the pleasures of surrender. She tongued the bolt and fastened knob and pressed it, she said, to her breast. She said if he undid the door he could undo her altogether, do with her what he chose. She used, in short, all those devices of seduction that had worked on him before, the lures and wiles and stratagems that magicked him when first in France. But now like their deviser they grew old.

Armed only with her key and lock he waged his hard campaign. It lasted for nine days. Provisioned with saber and pistol and violin and sandwich the Count pitched camp by his wife's bedroom door and kept the servants back. Those menials who had driven off the

Aichners, adding injury to insult, now cowered when the Count approached and did his bidding rapidly. Drinking coffee from his field-pot, he made certain the aroma wafted in to her, its appetizing fragrance filling the passageway morning and night. He cancelled her Tuesday soiree. He cancelled Thursday lunch. He told her, through the keyhole, of those dinners and dances and parties he had cancelled in advance.

By Monday noon all resistance collapsed and Rumford, relenting, made peace. She yielded, yielded utterly, and he unlocked the door. Her room smelled rank and foul. Her hair was loose, her teeth were out, her slop-pot overflowed. He handed her the papers and the pen, and when she agreed to his terms and conditions as set forth hereinafter he set the creature free.

Paris, Rue d'Anjou
St. Honore, No. 39
April 12, 1808

After what you know, my Dear Sally, of my domestic troubles, you will naturally be anxious to learn the present state of things. There are no alterations for the better. On the contrary, much worse. I have suffered more than you can imagine for the last four weeks; but my rights are incontestible, and I am determined to maintain them. I have the misfortune to be married to one of the most imperious, tyrannical, unfeeling women that ever existed, and whose perseverance in pursuing an object is equal to her profound cunning and wickedness in framing it.

It is impossible to continue in this way, and we shall separate. I only wish it was well over. It is probable I shall take a house at

Auteuil, a very pleasant place with the Seine on one side and the Bois de Boulogne on the other, about a league from Paris. I have seen a very handsome house there which I can have—rather dear, but that matters little can I but find quiet. It would be truly unfortunate, after the King of Bavaria's late bounties joined to former ones, if I could not live more independently than with this unfeeling, cunning, tyrannical woman.

Little do we know of people at first sight! Do you preserve my letters? You will perceive that I have given very different accounts of this woman, for *lady* I cannot call her.

Now, my Dear Sally, as soon as I get settled, enjoying again independence, I shall wish you to join me.

In the mean time believe me Your Affectionate Father.

ITEM: I, Marie Anne Pierrette Lavoisier de Rumford, do hereby agree and solemnly swear not to trouble my husband with parties or unwelcome guests. In the case of entertainment at our home on Rue d'Anjou, No. 39, whether planned or improvised, whether morning, noon, or night, I will submit to him for his prior approval a full list of invitees. Each and all such persons shall be subject to his veto, which veto I declare is absolute.

ITEM: I, Marie Anne Pierrette Lavoisier de Rumford, née Paulze, confess to grievous error in my treatment of the workroom of Benjamin Thompson, Count Rumford, hereinafter referred to as my husband. It is his, and his alone. It no longer in the least pertains to or contains the apparatus of his predecessor in this place, Antoine Laurent Lavoisier.

ITEM: I will not enter the aforesaid laboratory or permit the members of my household staff to clean its walls and floors and any appurtenant objects on the sofa or tables or chairs without express permission on my noble husband's part. Further, no member of my household nor the undersigned will enter his workroom unsupervised and without previous notice. I recognize the value of his work.

ITEM: I confess and admit that I have been destructive thereunto by troubling his peace, his concentration, his nighttime labor by my lewd insistence that he join me in my bed. I shall await his invitation and offer none of my own.

ITEM: I shall perform my wifely duties when and wherever he wishes, and at his command. I shall let him, if he so chooses, use me on all fours.

ITEM: Most truthfully and absolutely and irrevocably I certify and promise that none other, boy or gentleman, retainer or guest, old friend or new shall in the aforesaid manner enjoy me or find access to my chamber or welcome me elsewhere. That this has been the case before I shamefully acknowledge; that my shameless ways are mended I declare. In this as in all else I have my husband to be grateful to, sole master of my passions and ruler of my soul.

ITEM: Those valuables expressly set aside by contract remain in my possession; all others I convey freely to my husband, Benjamin

Thompson, Count Rumford. I confer on him my rubies, my emerald bracelet, my pearls. They are but outward tokens of my inward fealty; would I could offer more! Had I twice as much to give him it would be but a moiety—nay, tithe!—of what I owe.

ITEM: This paper signed, and my release secured, I will resume the part of docile helpmeet and obedient spouse. I will not again raise my voice in anger or my clenched fist in violent display. That I have been a shrew I yieldingly admit; that I have driven from my bosom all such misbehavior and hot shrewishness I pray. The harbored grudge I do renounce and the compact with rebellion disavow. I am in this as in all else entirely remorseful and reformed. When my husband asks a favor—be it difficult or easy, great or small, in public or in private—it will be my greatest pleasure to comply.

ITEM: I will not converse with strangers at the gate.

ITEM: I will not be familiar with the Porter in his lodge.

ITEM: I will handle no hot water by the flowerbeds, nor no oil.

ITEM: Should it come to pass that, in spite of these my declared good intentions, I prove unsuitable as consort to my husband and cause him further grief, I will in no way impede his desire to establish and thereafter maintain a separate residence, furnished with what hangings, pictures, household implements and articles of furniture &c. he in his wisdom may select. Should that house be distant I will defray the moving costs; should his rooms be proximate, I will visit only when and if he asks.

ITEM: I will not speak till spoken to, nor sing unless requested. I will, when so instructed, bathe.

ITEM: I promise graciously to honor and gravely to make comfortable those guests my husband may elect to entertain at home. I will not call them bores. I will not shut them out. I will in no way—by behavior, word or attitude—make them feel unwelcome in the house. If my husband chooses to receive the Members of the Institute, they will be happy here. If he prefers to entertain a lady of his choosing, it shall be my desire to assist with his.

ITEM: I renounce all animosity to others of my sex. I shall embrace his daughter, if she comes to visit, and endorse her as my own. I particularly disclaim all thoughts of jealous suspicion with reference to Madame Pirony, Madame et Mademoiselle Jollien, Madame de Staël, the chambermaid Sarah, and others it shall please or once have pleased my husband to approach; they are as sisters to me, and welcome in the house.

ITEM: This document is sacred and a truthful attestation made in private. I shall not refer to or describe it when in company; it shall be our little secret, man and wife.

Item: I will speak to no one in the avenue or boulevard or park.

Item: The argand lamp is his. The calorific theory is his and his alone. In witness whereunto, and of my own free will, I herewith set my pen. *Marie Anne Pierrette Lavoisier de Rumford, née Paulze.*

Paris, November 29, 1808

Peace dwells no longer in my habitation. I breakfast quite alone in my apartment. Most of our visitors are my wife's most determined adherents. Three evenings in the week she has small tea-parties in her apartment, at which I am sometimes present, but where I find little to amuse me. This strange manner of living has not been adopted or continued by my choice, but much against my inclinations. I have waited with great, I may say unexampled patience for a return of reason and a change of conduct. But I am firmly resolved not to be driven from my ground, not even by disgust.

A separation is unavoidable, for it would be highly improper for me to continue with a person who has given me so many proofs of her implacable hatred and malice.

Now he breakfasted alone. He supped alone at night. He could not tell his daughter all, nor write her in sufficient detail how her father grieved. His document so lovingly prepared, so carefully composed and legally attested, was by his wife denounced! His truthful declaration she falsely and wholly ignored, his hope of amiable commerce and dream of loving kindness she cruelly denied! No sooner signed and by him freed than Madame broke their covenant, tearing and shredding his signed text. No sooner did she emerge from her room than she destroyed its locks.

What Rumford next endured took all of his endurance, and it broke his spirit. Methodical, unfeeling, and with a malign inventiveness, she gainsaid every item on his list. She fertilized his flowerbeds with salt and fitted the house with new keys. She kept these hidden from him so his workplace and experiments and essays might not be secure. At times he doubted of his sanity and feared for his frail health. No sailor ever was by siren-music so betrayed, no wanderer by Circe more entirely translated into beast; her treachery redoubled and perfidy increased.

She fomented in her servants the habits of discourtesy, turning his allies away. She intercepted his mail. Having encouraged in the foolish French their distrust of his English ways, she hinted his bluff honesty was but a spy's disguise. Inviting her rabble, refusing his friends, she swept into or past his laboratory unannounced. Far from choosing to reduce their scale of entertainment, she gave parties daily, nightly, and just outside his door.

In vain did Rumford reason with her and in extremis plead. She laughed at him, snatching her emerald bracelet back and festooning her neck with rubies and pearls. She pranced nakedly in front of him while he bent to his book, or spread her legs and licked her lips and encouraged him to look.

To the Count's shame, he complied. He was after all her husband and had his needs and expectations and his conjugal rights. She knew perfectly, suggested his wife, how best to give him pleasure and submit to his hard probing and endure his stiff resolve. She wiggled her white rump at him until he was enflamed; then, when he also kneeled, she jeered at him and stood.

Therefore he made his escape. In pursuit of some protected domicile, some shelter from this inward storm, Rumford abandoned the house. His association with the halls and rooms was more than he could meekly bear, and he set himself to make a separate home. He followed where his fancy led, wandering the avenues and through the frozen parks. So revolted did he feel by female wiles and wanton ways that he took consolation once again in the silent concurrence of boys. Their downcast eyes and slim-hipped frames were sweet to him, inexpressibly a comfort and often—without urging, of his own unforced volition—Count Rumford augmented their fee. At last he found a place most suitable for his retirement: surrounded by gardens, adequately private, and in the charming suburb of Auteuil.

Madame, I leave you."

"*Entendu.*"

"I expect no compensation."

"And would not get it, *M'sieur.*"

"What though I labored long and hard on the improvements in this house. What though I spared no expense of spirit, time, and expertise. I expect nothing, no."

"You will not be disappointed, then."

"My disappointment—if that is the word to describe it, that understatement of the case—resides elsewhere."

"Where?"

"Here," Rumford said and smote his breast. "In the region of the heart."

"You are making *plaisanteries,* a pleasantry, yes? You mock me, *non?*"

"On the contrary I mock myself who came here hoping for so much and leaving with so little. Who had such happy expectations and departs so sad."

"The house in Auteuil: it suits you? *C'est convenable, on m'a dit.*"

"*C'est assez convenable, oui;* it is sufficient, more or less."

"And adequately furnished?"

"Modestly. A few good things."

Madame appeared to soften. "I shall visit you, perhaps."

"Of course. You will be welcome."

"I would like to meet your daughter when she comes."

"Yes."

"I was greatly looking forward to ze pleasure of her acquaintance."

"She will help me in my privacy. In my absolute retirement."

"Kiss her for me," said Marie Anne Pierrette Lavoisier de Rumford.

"Certainly, Madame, I will."

"May she serve your purposes in your *retraite.* May she prove, in her filial duty, obedient. Submissive."

"*D'accord.*"

"May she help you in your projects as, *hélas,* I from time to time have failed."

He reached for her. She raised her hand. Her fingers were, the Count observed, bedizened with new diamonds.

"Then tell her when she needs to leave—when she is tired of your treatment, wholly furious and beaten and imprisoned and insane, brutalized and begging to escape, completely and utterly sick of you, sir—she will be welcome here."

With which she left him smilingly and returned to her roomful of guests.

> Sally:
> I find myself relieved from an almost insupportable burden. I can not repeat too much how happy I am—gaining every day in health, which from vexations had become seriously deranged. I am persuaded it is all for the best. After the scenes which I have recently passed through, I realize, as never before, the sweets of quiet, liberty, and independence. My household consists of the most faithful, honest people, attached to me, without dissension, bribery, or malice. And, above all, that eternal contradiction. Oh! happy, thrice happy, am I, to be my own man again!

I, Benjamin Thompson, Count Rumford, acknowledge principles of order on this earth. They have been my unrelenting study and my greatest consolation in this vale of tears. I shall describe those principles hereafter; it is my sole, my best remaining work. I continue making notes. I experiment ceaselessly still. I prepare and publish essays:

On the order of sovereignty.
On the nature and justification of faith. On recognition earned.
Of the Salubrity of Warm Rooms. Of the Salubrity of Bathing.
On the ethics of merit, its rank.

ITEM: The public in general, and more particularly those Tradesmen and Manufacturers whom it may concern, are requested to observe, that as the Author does not intend to take out himself, or to suffer others to take out, any patent for any invention of his which may be of public utility, all persons are at full liberty to imitate them, and vend them, for their own emolument, when and where, and in any way which they may think proper; and those who may wish for any further information respecting any of those inventions or improvements will receive (gratis) all the information they can require by applying to the Author, who will take pleasure in giving them every assistance in his power.

On the order of gardens, both vegetable and flower.
On vehicular conveyance, its advantages.
On the order of the arts, their hierarchical sequence.
Of the proper compass of a life.
On the poor of several nations, their characteristics.
On house-maids in Ireland and Scotland, their charm.
On portraiture.
Of the management of Light in illumination.
Of the propagation of Heat in various Substances.
On frigorific rays.

ITEM: Saucepans and other kitchen utensils which are very bright and clean on the outside may be kept hot with smaller fire than such as are black and dirty; but the bottom of a saucepan or boiler should be blackened in order that its contents may be made to boil quickly, and with a small expense of fuel.

Of the Management of Fire and the Economy of Fuel.
Of my great and grievous wrongs, their perpetrators.
Of the eventual and undoubted triumph of my cause.

ITEM: I am even sanguine enough to expect that the time will come when open fires will disappear, even in our dwelling-rooms and most elegant apartments. Genial warmth can certainly be kept up, and perfect ventilation effected much better without them than with them. And though I am myself still child enough to be pleased with the brilliant appearance of burning fuel, yet I cannot help thinking that something else might be invented equally attractive to draw my attention and amuse my sight, that would be less injurious to my eyes—less expensive, and less connected with dirt, ashes, and other unwholesome and disagreeable objects.

On exile and imprisonment.
On the benefits of travel.
On the perfidy of wives.
Of the excellent qualities of coffee.
On the art of making coffee in highest perfection.
Of food, and particularly of feeding the poor.
On wit, its use and limitation.
On disobedience, its value; of obedience, the same.

And so he was alone. And so, at fifty-five years old, twice disappointed in marriage, no longer young and hale but sick at heart, the Count became a bachelor once more. With characteristic perversity, the French, he knew, called his condition that of a *célibataire,* yet no description could have been farther from the truth. Celibacy is simpler far, and more readily embraced, within the marriage bed. He who chooses chastity is safer wed.

From sheer relief at his release, he rioted nightlong at table; he seized what remained of the day. When reminded of Charles Blagden, and disregarding all advice, he ate his chops in sauce. He ate oysters in excessive brine and drank not claret but champagne and preferred, to Stilton, Camembert or Brie. He indulged in an orgy of eating while, outside, Paris starved. When he looked in the mirror he saw to his shock the painted grinning face of ancient George Germain; when he brought his boys down to their knees and watched them at their playful work he saw Sackville's reflection in the clouded glass.

He settled in Auteuil, in the house of Madame Helvetius; his landlady was a widow and, for the most part, clean. She told him that she much admired men of science from America. She had been a friend of Franklin's, and the name of Benjamin was sacred in her memory; she was gratified to welcome yet another of that learned cadre, *les Americains.*

"Helvetius. It is a Swiss name, surely."

"Yes."

"I greatly admire the Swiss," he declared.

"Of course you do. *Évidemment.*"

"And why should that be evident?"

"All practical Americans desire to be Swiss," she said. "It is part of your training, your birthright."

"And you think me an American?"

397

"But absolutely, *M'sieur Le Compte. Ça va sans dire. Ça se voit.*"

"If it goes without saying," he said, "then why am I unwelcome here? There is an ancient amity between our nations, *non?*"

"*Mais si!* Since Lafayette."

"Then why do they think me a German—or, worse, a British—spy?"

"That is not a matter, *mon ami,* of where you have been born. It is rather a question of, how do you call it, allegiance."

He hazarded his question, "To what, Madame, do we owe our allegiance but the truth?"

She touched his sleeve—a gesture less coquettish than compassionate. Where the powder on her neck had flaked, the skin seemed raw and red. "But what I ask myself, *M'sieur,* is whom has purchased you and to who you owe your business. This is the critical question, always, regarding a man."

He bowed. "You are too clever, Madame Helvetius, to distort your grammar so. Or to believe me an informer."

"*Non.*"

"No you do not believe me, or no you are not clever?"

Charmingly she tossed her curls. "*Ça m'est égal.* It's all the same."

"And might I ask you why, Madame?"

"I am not, any longer, addicted to belief."

He leased a side wing of the house, giving out upon the river. There was a statue in the garden based on the Buonarotti that earlier he'd seen in Rome; he scanned the stern face of Moses, a reflective visage

398

that gathered birds would perch on and, preening, defile. He hired a housekeeper and coachman and gardener and valet and four upstairs maids. With these few servants he prepared to weather the encroaching famine and the coming storm.

Mary Nogarola died; he learned of it by letter. Count Rumford mourned her exceedingly and would not be consoled. The dear companion of his youth—that changeable mistress and aunt to his child, that accomplished rider and excellent wit—he could not believe her gone. His grief was sharp, omnivorous, and it consumed him quite. Now everywhere that Rumford looked was betrayal, desolation, a lined red ledger of accounts and totality of debt.

His daughter Sophie, he learned, was married and unhappy and deserted and by all reports insane. His legitimate daughter booked passage from Boston, then prepared to sail. Before she came to France, however, he decided to see Munich one last time; he planned to close his domicile there and visit Mary's resting place and water that cold earth with his hot tears.

The Emperor his benefactor was fighting on all fronts. Again, all Paris whispered, for Bonaparte seemed ill. Having borne so much upon his broad shoulders he stooped; he had a crisis of the liver, then the spleen. The Marshals and Lieutenants and Generals and cavalry that rode past Rumford's window appeared to signal wearily how far the mighty had fallen—their happy prospects shattered and their high ideals corrupt. The legless and the lame were everywhere in evidence, pressed into service nonetheless and sent limping on.

The Count watched from his study, gazing down. Concealed behind the curtains, he stared at the processional where men filed lurching by; they had lost their limbs in battle but waved their bloody stumps, or wielded crutch and cane. He who had fought so often and so valiantly watched cannon fodder marching past or lifted in their comrades' failing arms. He hated it: the carnage, the embargo, the forked flickering rumors of peace.

Auteuil
24th October, 1809
Dear Sally:

The Mentor arrived some weeks since, when I was expecting you. Without doubt the reason you did not come was owing to your not finding proper protection, and in these terrible times of war you cannot be too particular. This unfortunate war chains me to the spot, for I am so situated between the three governments that I am obliged almost to turn into a cypher. It is England where I want to go, but dare not risk it. And it is there I should much prefer receiving you than here.

By the date of this letter you will perceive it to be the anniversary of my wedding-day with Madame Lavoisier, today four years. I own I make choice of this day to write to you, in reality to testify joy; but joy that I am away from her, as has been the case for the last six months. It would be difficult to describe what I suffered there for the last year. I often wished you, but am now exceedingly glad you did not come, as it would have made you unhappy and perhaps done me no good. I was made quite ill at last, but now, thank Heaven, I am recovering my health and spirits fast. I am like one risen from the dead. Adieu, my dear child. You will hear from me soon again, and I hope to see you soon. I have some pretty rooms prepared for you. I had one of the Aichners to come and wait upon you, but she did not exactly please me, and I sent her back again. My old servants, her father and mother, are nicely established, owing to mine and the Elector's kindness, at Munich, and are very happy.

SALLY

It isn't true; the Aichners were unhappy and their master ill. Count no man fortunate, not even if he be a Count, until you know his end. And while Rumford's end draws near—as must our telling of it, reader—I find myself more sympathetic to our boy. He thinks better of himself, perhaps, than do those of us who study him, but he's sinned against at least as much as sinning in old age.

Es ist Vollbracht! It is finished, or nearly so, and he begins his magnum opus, an essay to capstone his long life's long work. He does this in Auteuil, where he lodges in great pain. Renting a side-wing of her house from the widow Helvetius—once Franklin's mistress, so they say, and a beauty in her time and prime, but now like the Count in the sere—he dedicates himself to what such worthies before him as Aristotle, Linnaeus and her *caro* Buffon had attempted to do, making sense of the visible world. He has decided what to call it, this *chef d'oeuvre*, his crowning achievement and labor: *On the Nature and Effects of Order.* And that's our subject here.

I myself labor night after night. With my magic Macintosh, my variation on the theme of the Baldwin Apple, at the touch of a button I scroll through these last stages of his age. Against his near-oblivion I have amassed the files, the folders, and they leap into existence at my mouse's tapped command.

For Count Rumford has grown weary, and the autumn light is fitful, and the work requires more attention than he proves able to give. In fits and starts, those herky-jerky memories that come to us when half asleep, or not as yet entirely awake, in bursts of brief illumination that remind the modern viewer—this one, at any rate—of early films, the hand-held camera and television set reduced to snow, in white spasms of precision and from present to past tense our hero recollects: his life. His principles. The two being one and the same. The old cock detumescent, the old mind ghost-forsaken, sinking to its havoc, the half-remembered melody and near-forgotten tune.

Perhaps you've noticed, reader, that I'm older now, at sixty-nine, than was our boy in his *retraite,* which argues both the virtue of contemporary medicine and increased life expectancy in our great republic. Also it's possible his genes were weak (dear dad died young); also what I think is maybe he had syphilis. Could it have been the devil's compact, a disease contracted long before and left untended till too late, the third stage of it overtaking him not gently now but fast? So what he remembers while writing is what I imagine while writing it down; what he composes disrupts my own rest.

But when he does compose—scratching out his testament on Order in the house—he uses, I ask myself, what sort of implement: a fountain pen, a quill? Would he, as with the Murphy bed and coffee pot, have predicted present usage with a device of his own making: a ballpoint possibly? Does he strap it to his palsied hand or use someone for dictation; if so, who?

These nights I know the answer: I am being *written*, reader, at least as much as he.

The phone rings. I answer it; no, he's not in. No, he won't be back. It may have been an annual pledge but the man who pledged it has moved on and left me with no forwarding address. My husband, Mr. Robinson. This is his widow, yes. I'm sorry, you're welcome, he's dead.

Long years before, when journeying to London from the continent, Thompson had his papers stolen while enjoying a short dalliance with a purchased wench. She had approached him saucily in Calais, asking if he wished some private pleasure before he went on board.

Cf., Class, p. 245.

The ship was being loaded but he need not hurry and there was sufficient time for her to faire la veuve. At that very moment, in fact, he had been reminded of the channel crossing north to south where once he stood disconsolate with Edward Gibbon by his side; his stomach churned within him queasily as though on deck, as yet untested, leaving England on his first such voyage, and to quiet its roiling vexation he unlocked his carriage door and bade her join him there upon the bench. Her name was Lizzie, or such was the name that she gave. Her aspect was both pert and coy and he found himself aroused by the near-total absence, when she opened her mouth, of teeth.

So Rumford closed the curtains and lay back while she serviced him, rewarding himself as was only right and proper with satisfaction along the hard route. Soon the traveler noticed a jostling above—but his attention had been fixed within and there was no altercation sufficient to require his buttoned and buttressing presence without: only laughter, a rocking, its motions difficult to disengage from those he himself was engaged in. For while the toothless creature smacked her lips, encasing him, her accomplices outside regaled the driver with a stirrup cup; they set the fool to cackling, then snoring where he sat.

The Count said, "Very good," and pulled up his trousers and reached for his purse. The slattern wiped her lips. He noticed how she cocked an ear for what was transpiring beyond, and though he believed it then only the ruckus of lading, the signal to his driver that they might commence to board, what she heard from her confederates was sufficient to inform her that she must detain him yet.

"It's better the second time, Excellency," simpered the drab. "Better, I promise, the second time 'round. When you ain't in such an 'urry."

And again she bent to him to furnish sweet relief.

Cf., Class, p. 171.

What munificence his must have seemed, a veritable pasha lying there among the silks! What a vision of salvation to the poor damned Lizzie, so briefly in luxury's lap! She was full-figured and empty-headed, or so it appeared, and with no purpose to her ardent sport but the coins he had offered, and she made a graceful courtesey when at length she left.

The Count resumed his embarkation, boxing the ears of the coachman, and strode aboard the vessel, breathing deep of salt sea air. It had been his fixed intention to publish those essays in England which would consolidate his reputation and secure the good opinion of intelligent persons every-

where. He felt a pleasing weariness, a depleted sensory longeur, and he idled to observe the sailors by the mizzenmast, their trained and concerted endeavor; while he ruminated on their knowledgeable practice with ropes he swallowed sherry to steady the nerves, then at a certain point arranged himself upon the deck in blankets, wearing his white cape to keep out the chill.

When they disembarked at Dover, he discovered he'd been robbed. Now Fortune's Wheel had turned again, his papers all were gone!

Cf. p. 93.

To the query "Where and how?" Thompson made no immediate answer; he racked his brains for explanation, tracing minutely the day's operations and questioning the driver and all persons involved in the lading and stowage and arriving at the conclusion —reluctantly, inescapably— that he had been outsmarted by a whore. While he lay back in the cushions and gave himself over to Lizzie's attentions the gang that she consorted with had been busy robbing him, bearing off his essays in the padlocked trunk. Under the assumption that there were furs and jewels contained they lifted the case full of writing, and it afforded the Count small consolation to imagine their foul shocked disappointed faces when they found mere language inside. They impoverished him utterly, whose treasure was his prose.

He posted a reward and hunted high and low. In time the trunk would be returned but there was nothing left within—not one of the thousands of pages he had so scrupulously composed, nor any of the drafts and tentatives on which he'd been engaged.

For all his time thereafter he was certain of a plot, the purchased compliance of Lizzie and those hirelings who had displayed her on the prim-

rose path. Following instructions from the legion of his enemies—and well aware beforehand, no doubt, of his planned route for England—they took advantage of his momentary distraction, expecting to make off with gold, or encoded military orders and consequential dispatches and matters of state. Not so. They found only his life's only work.

Possibly they burned it or tore it into shreds. Probably they wiped themselves with his clear diagrams and proofs. No doubt in noisome den or ditch where they forced the padlock open his papers, rotting, still repine; they line the nest of magpies, squirrels, or barn swallows wattled with mud. The wind lifts them fleetingly, drops them again. The illiterate cutpurse is dead.

Well, shit, he deserved it, says I. He got what was coming to him. But did some bits and written scraps remain, some charred residual survive, and do I have it here to hand, or am I inventing this also?

Old Sally Robinson sits in her chair, rocking and watching the clock. Hickory dickory dock.

For time is the great healer, and over time he healed: our hero started again. Pox-raddled, ponce-addled or no, he bends to his table and scratches out prose: *On the Nature of Order*, etc. And now the point I need to make is that this second time around Count Rumford takes precautions: no further dalliance, reader, nor distractions in his project. All day in the one chair and paying no attention to Bonnet the coachman and taking only intermittent notice of Victoire Lefèvre, he works.

He works.

He works.

For how can he guess what his Sally will do when once she reads the pages; how could he know that the fire he claimed to have mastered will stake its own claim finally and establish hot dominion?

She burned it, she burned what he wrote.

Ben imagined his reunion with Loammi Baldwin. They would embrace and reminisce and enlarge on their shared history. They would embroider plain cloth of the past; they could forgive each other, surely, what nonetheless they were unable to forget. Then they would laugh and clasp each other's hands and fondly allude to the exploits of youth, the stinking fish Loammi cleaned, their long earnest rambles through town. They might remember problems set and puzzles solved, the Committee of Safety outwitted: his narrow escape from the gang who would hang him but failed. Instead they raised a barn. For this the Count had Loammi to thank; he did so, heartily.

"What crops this season?"

"Wheat."

"What further?"

"Barley. Turnips. My own strain of maize."

"Let me commend potatoes, friend."

"Why so?"

"In order to break stony soil. To serve as first planting, none better."

"At your service, Major Thompson."

"Good."

"Do you remember Mt. Pleasant?"

"Yes. Its prospect, anyhow. The hope we had of scaling it."

"I did so, later."

"Lucky man!"

"It seemed so, yes, and I smile to remember the exploits of youth. For it beggared expectation—the cliffs, the trees, the waterfall."

"Were you alone? What expedition did you lead? Who joined you as companion then and furnished the rest of the party? How long did you explore it and how long ago?"

To all of this he heard no answer. The candles flickered, faded, and with them faded also the vision of his friend. Count Rumford shut his eyes.

Evening, Miz' Robinson."

"Evenin'," says I.

"And how are we feeling tonight?"

"Better, Doctor Allen."

"Good, that's good."

"A bit of trouble, maybe, breathing."

"Oh?"

"Headache. A migraine, that's it."

"The 'fire in your head'—that's what you called it, correct?"

"Correct," says I. "You remembered."

"Don't you think, maybe"—he offers this carefully—"you're working too hard at that uncle of yours?"

"Uncle?"

"Your ancestor, what was his name?"

"Thompson," says I.

"Right. Benjamin Thompson."

"No."

"No?"

And then I repeat it: no, Doc, I'm not working hard enough, and he says well, if you say so, and I remind him how nobody in Concord or New Hampshire or the whole remorseless continent can under-stand: if Ben had been Benjamin Franklin instead they'd raise a statue here. Or name a park in his honor, or an avenue or postage stamp or dollar bill or whatever we do in America to commemorate our dead. Don't you remember, I ask him, that Franklin Roosevelt said the three most interesting men, the three most impressive minds in our coun-try's history were Thomas Jefferson, Ben Franklin and my ancestor Ben Thompson?

That so? asks the Doctor.

It is. But because he picked the losing side, because his sympa-thies were Tory and history gets written by the stay-at-homes, it's as if the Count didn't exist; I am, says I, the despair of the would-be-forgotten, and he hoped to be remembered, so it's my duty, clear as clear, this old lady knows what she's doing.

All right, he says, I was just asking, and I say don't ask.

He bends above me where I sit and studies my nose, then my throat. Say Aah, says he; I, *Aah*.

But I don't want to be ungenerous, he's one of a fine dying breed, the kind that makes house calls, that come when you phone, and something in his watery eye, his pink scalp in the lamplight when he leans down to take my pulse—the tape wrapped on his stethoscope, the stale emanation that rises from his suit, its cuff frayed, two sleeve-buttons missing—makes me want to reach out to him also: two old codgers in this cold house, in the foregathering dark.

So I cough when he tells me and breathe when he asks and hold and breathe deeply and hold and exhale; I let him peer into my ear.

"Spring's coming," I tell him.

"Not yet."

"It's coming," I tell him. "It is."

"We'll have another storm or two. It's freezing now. Outside, I mean."

"Did you have trouble getting here?"

He shakes his head.

"Don't think I'm not grateful," I say.

He pulls out his prescription pad and licks the pencil's point. If you don't mind repeating it let's do a little history, OK? Is there diabetes in your family; did either of your parents, to your knowledge, ever have a heart attack?

When I tell him no, he asks cancer?

I tell him no, not to my knowledge, but let me ask you something doctor, do you think it was syphilis, and then he cocks his head at me, that right eyebrow rising, that slight hesitation before he responds so I believe I've got it right: the Count was paretic, he died of a dose.

What are we discussing, asks my visitor, what?

The clap, I say, the pox.

I haven't heard that word in years, he says. If you don't mind me asking, who?

The Count of course.

Ach, Haubenal, you ask too much.

There's sleet at the window. We hear it. All right, it isn't spring.

411

Dr. Allen packs his things meticulously, he swallows a cough drop and snaps his worn black leather bag's lock. I see him to the door.

Not impossible, he says—*fire, fire*—although it's more likely, Mrs. Robinson, from the symptoms you're describing, from everything you tell me what your ancestor had was a stroke.

On the Nature and Effects of Order

In the course of a long life, and one which has been filled with in-structive encounters, I have come to the conclusion that there is and always has been and forever will be an organizing principle behind the random-seeming nature of events. Few men have seen as much. Few men have done (I write this in due modesty, but am beyond that point in age where false modesty persuades) more. That which seems an accident to the untutored witness would have been predictable— nay, inevitably consequent—to the schooled observer. That which may appear surprising should come as no surprise.

For years—for decades now—I have been engaged on a course of study tending to an answer to the single question: Is there or is there not a pattern in the vicissitudes of circumstance? Do we or do we not describe uncertainty as mankind's lot; is there a form of certainty belying, as it were, our ignorance thereof? A tree felled in a forest makes noise albeit unheard. The undiscovered waterfall is nonetheless a cataract and will be charted soon. So it has been my constant care to ascertain an answer to this question: is there a natural order, and what are its effects?

It will of course be objected that the unseen hand of our Creator represents just such an organizing principle, and that we may lay the inquiry to rest by describing the one as the other. Some are content so to do. Some think it contravenes the natural humility of our position to attempt to comprehend it, and that the enterprise must surely be foredoomed. But I submit our Creator would not have wished and did not during the procedure of Creation tolerate such a result. His method is exemplary of the very spirit of rigorous inquiry, of trial and error acknowledged, that we scientists construe intrinsic to our work. Experiment, it may be said, is the stuff of existence itself. It is thus reverence, not blasphemy, to light the dark of Genesis and pierce Maya's veil.

My inquiry must be perforce partial and divided. The subject is a large one and the discussion long. I have divided it, accordingly, and for more palatable digestion, into three parts, as did great Caesar with Gaul. The first is focused on order and disorder in the physical world; the second takes as its topic order and disorder in the spiritual or unseen universe; the third, as is fitting and proper, reconciles the two. Philosophers since time out of mind, and in the same disinterested speculative spirit, have raised these very questions and sought these very answers—but they have not availed themselves of the great strides made by science. They show no understanding of recent discoveries on the nature of matter, of light and of heat. I do.

That I have found an answer cannot be denied. That it is persuasive will no doubt be gainsaid. The history of progress has—to its shame and discredit!—a history of concomitant detraction; there are always doubters, mockers, scoffers close at hand. The world was flat until proved otherwise; the sun went round the earth until a wise man demonstrated the reverse. Disorder rules, insurrection succeeds. Brute chaos gains adherents daily and would seem to hold the field. Yet it is my strong contention that *order*, not its opposite, resides in the deep sense of things—that a universal truth of being may be described both in and as its systematic nature. I propose to prove as much: the earth goes round the sun.

My career has concerned itself primarily with the practical nature of science; those monographs and essays I have previously published are cumulative evidence, as the reader is no doubt aware, of unstinting labor in the service of such inquiry. Others may in time to come stress this or that component of the whole; some may well winnow and glean. Yet their author cannot in conscience do otherwise than commend these pages in their entirety to the public's sustained attention. It is time for a full listing of accounts. For want of a nail the shoe was lost, for want of a shoe the horse, for want of a horse the battle was lost, for want of a battle the war. Thus it is not my proper business to pick and choose, to cull and select and reject amongst the many thousand pages that comprise Count Rumford's oeuvre; I would instead suggest the reader read them all.

That done—a reading project of some days, mayhap, but arduous years in the writing—he should approach the second of my topics: the nature of things unseen. Here too, although less visibly, the problem of order pertains. The use of science is so to explain the operations which take place in the practice of the arts, and to discover the means of improving them; and there is no process, however simple it may appear to be, that does not afford an ample field for curious and interesting investigation.

If the writer may allow himself a brief digression here, it is surely worth remarking that in this wintry time for France bright spring delights America—that those who starve along the Seine might gorge themselves instead beside the Hudson's freshets. There is war in Europe everywhere and peace across the sea. Not forty years ago the opposite condition was the case. Not forty years ago a man who hoped to prosper would have been well advised, as I myself can well attest, to flee the shores of battle-scarred New England; now, were it not for house arrest, he might instead desire to quit beleaguered France.

The child is father to the man—so goes the ancient saying. What we sow we reap. We begin in darkness, wailing, and end in the deep dark; the sons of men are doomed to labor, their daughters to labor in pain. Though there be laughter and amusement in the first acts of the drama, the final action is a tragic one: so writes the philosopher. What is certain in this vale of tears is hunger, uncertainty, death.

Yet what of seeming-chance? How explain the sudden bounty, the unexpected windfall, the fortuitous encounter? How best describe those twists and turnings on life's journey that for good or ill bemuse a traveler? We meet, it may happen, a beautiful stranger or highwayman; we meet with great good fortune or catastrophic accident or fail to have a meeting because we set out on our way ten minutes early or late. We are driven from our homeland or forcibly removed from those very fields we planted; what we sowed we do not reap. Others profit from the harvest, laying claim to our inventions and arrogating for their use the bed we occupied.

This is the way of the world. But is such alteration the action of insensate chance, or rather that of history? Is there and may we discover a pattern to this constancy in change? The Emperor who roamed the continent must prowl tomorrow instead the narrow final confine of a jail. The most beautiful of ladies (*Mary, Mary, Mary, Mary!*) dies abandoned and alone. That we live with contrariety all thoughtful persons acknowledge; in our end is our beginning, so too with the reverse.

Therefore at this present moment and in this commodious house, I declare myself prepared; what is the present, after all, but the past's future arrived? I am convinced of death, wholly reconciled to its approach, yet wholly ignorant of when and in what guise the messenger will come.

Bienfaiteur de l'humanité
Grand sans effort et sans envie,
Il n'a déployé son genie
Que pour signaler sa bonté.

Paris, 14 January

My very dear Michael:

I have just returned from visiting Count Rumford, as the gentleman now styles himself, in his retreat at Auteuil. It is not a happy scene. He is set upon by sycophants and does not seem to notice; age and illness have increased his unthinking acceptance of praise. He is childlike in his pleasure at a compliment; he claps and smiles. His servants feed him sweets. The great head lolls, he drools. Yet that former tendency of his to bridle at all criticism—a tendency we both often remarked—has been, I would venture, increased. So the members of the household approach their venerable master with feigned respect, with deep salaams, then laugh behind his back.

I had hoped to talk with him of his theory of caloric, for there are certain details that remain to be discussed. His expertise was real, his experience unequalled, and it seemed to me still plausible that, on the matter of heat transfer, he might help. But all such expectation faded on the instant of arrival; brain fever has undone him quite; he cannot speak. He endures a waking sleep. He deludes himself, apparently, with the scribbled certainty that he composes his *chef d'oeuvre*. He is writing his memoirs.

There are beggars in the street. They gather in his kitchen garden, awaiting daily bread. At noon each day the window is flung open, and the rabble of Auteuil rush to the trough. It is a vicious spectacle; they snuffle and jostle and fight each other fiercely for his scraps. The leavings of a salad, the peelings of potatoes, the breadcrust and the gristle and the boiled bone and the bits of fat—these furnish Rumford's charities, his feast.

He waits propped on the settee all day, facing the garden, nodding. His first wife as you know is dead, his daughter gone abroad. He and the present Madame Lavoisier de Rumford are, if rumor may be credited, not now on speaking terms. He lives alone. His landlady, the widow Helvetius—a charming woman still, and conscious of her tenant's history—retains the larger portion of the house. She it was who let me in, then shewed me out; Rumford's porter, it would seem, was elsewhere occupied. From the kitchen I heard sounds of laughter, music, drunken revelry. The Count did not appear to notice or, noticing, to mind. It was, let me assure you, a pitiable spectacle—and calculated to unstring the hardest heart.

I sometimes think that this our present age—so remarkable for the expanded nature of its knowledge, so busy with invention and improvement everywhere—has paid too little heed to inward understanding and what the ancients called self-knowledge. "Know thyself," at any rate, is not a counsel our poor Thompson took to heart.

He urged us to be prudent but was prodigal himself. He was born to straitened circumstance, yet flourished mightily. His knowledge of the world was wide, yet it is my conviction that—in these final years, at least—he mourned his exile keenly, desiring nothing further than permission to go home. To be honored at a distance and dishonored close at hand is bitter mockery. I hope you do not think me over-clever in Thompson's defense, since he and you and I will each be judged by standards that we cannot hope to measure and jurors whom we cannot sway, but the boy I used to know is father to this man.

He shivers in the heat. He makes no noise. Even his enemies—and they are legion nowadays, and you yourself have sometimes been counted among them, not wholly free of rancor—must take pity on the fellow. He communicates by blinking. Then he coughs. This was the sum and substance of our interview; I left no wiser than I came but sadder, infinitely. Forgive him, Michael, if only for my sake and the sake of our old friendship; he did not know what he did.

Lacrimae rerum. It is the only comfort I can offer or moral I derive: the sorrow inhering in things. A single flower may reward our close attention as well if not far better than the grandly framed bouquet. But I was never certain that he knew me or even that he understood (cheeks damp, tears coursing down them, eyes wide) he wept.

Believe me, my dear colleague, your very faithful and affectionate,

Etcetera

Why should I not mention even the marks of affectionate regard and respect which I receive from the poor people for whose happiness I interested myself, and the testimonies of the public esteem with which I was honored? Will it be reckoned vanity if I mention the concern which the poor of Munich expressed in so affecting a manner when I was dangerously ill? that they went publicly in a body in procession to the cathedral church, where they had divine service performed, and put up public prayers for my recovery? that four years afterwards, on hearing that I was again dangerously ill at Naples, they, of their own accord, set apart an hour each evening, after they had finished their work in the Military Workhouse, to pray for me?

Will it be thought improper to mention the affecting reception I met with from them, at my first visit to the Military Workhouse, upon my return to Munich—a scene which drew tears from all who were present? and must I refuse myself the satisfaction of describing the fête I gave them in return, in the English Garden, at which 1800 poor people of all ages, and above 30,000 of the inhabitants of Munich assisted? and all this pleasure I must forego merely that I may not be thought vain and ostentatious? Be it so then; but I would just beg leave to call the reader's attention to my feelings upon the occasion; and then let him ask himself, if any earthly reward can possibly be supposed greater, any enjoyment more complete, than those I received. Let him figure to himself, if he can, my situation—sick in bed, worn out by intense application, and dying, as everybody thought, a martyr in the cause to which I had devoted myself—let him imagine, I say, my feelings, upon hearing the confused noise of the prayers of a multitude of people, who were passing by in the streets, upon being told that it was the poor of Munich, many hundreds in number, who were going in procession to the church to put up public prayers for me—public prayers for me! for a private person! a stranger! a Protestant! I believe it is the first instance of the kind that ever happened; and I dare venture to affirm that no proof could well be stronger than this that the measures adopted for making these poor people happy were really successful; and let it be remembered, *that this fact is what I am most anxious to make appear,* in the clearest and most satisfactory manner.

My blue-eyed Ben, my darling Ben. He never knew his father, that explains it, really. That's the reason why he ran away from home. That's the reason, really, he never would come back.

Let me take a single instance of the universal process: love. Love is widely construed to be a phenomenon of great consequence, as tending to define the interaction of the species—whether of child for parent, parent for child, partner for partner, master for slave. Romance is a principal topic in discourse and story and dream. Argument and hatred, too, may be viewed as the absence of love. Poets sing of it and playwrights put it on the stage and painters represent its practice; there are few topics as common and none, it may be, more so: the desire of two entities to commingle and conjoin is, one may fairly claim, a condition of existence as we know it, a *sine qua non.*

Yet who has studied that condition with microscope and rule? Who with telescope and caliper has charted its course and arrival; who can explain its origin or predict its course; who may measure this abstraction except by its effects? What we know of love, or think we know, has long been written down in manual and guide book; the

421

procedures and their etiquette have been minutely described. And it is of course a relatively simple matter to measure the physical action of love—the blush on cheek, the flush on brow, the upright nipple and distended member and, in pleasure's climacteric, the curled toe.

What will strike the curious observer as far more curious, however, is the order that such passion necessarily entails—the sequence, as it were, of stimulus and subsequent response. These are various and many: as numberless, it may be urged, as the forms of love itself. A partial catalogue must once again suffice:

Four partners at one time would seem, to the discerning practitioner, most satisfying. All else is superfluity. In this arrangement the mouth and hands and sexual organ each have their proper function and their place. Some subscribe further to the theory of the gratification of feet, as being yet another extremity, and that the plausible limit of partners in congress mounts therefore to six. But the attention wanders perforce; the perfect focus of engagement is diffused by sheer extension, and though one may commend a gallant for his acrobatics, this is not the same as ardor: it is excess and consequent waste.

For reasons heretofore adduced, three partners may prove sufficient; this is according to taste and leaves the right or left hand free to dangle emptily or be elsewhere employed. The rectangular arrangement is as satisfying and rather more symmetrical than the pentagonal; the triangular (two additional partners) may claim its adherents as well.

If we love without requital it is unrequited love. If we love in perfect harmony it is as an instrument tuned. If we love in disproportion it is comic where not sad—as when, say, a man plights his troth with a tree or woman vows fidelity forever to a crow. The old enamored of the young engender derision if wealthy, scorn if poor. The young enamored of the old and not of their possessions are few and far between. Brutality runs rampant in alley and kitchen and wood. Debauched exhaustion and satiety must also be considered; the Duc d'—, I am informed, had more mistresses than shoes, and of the latter he could claim three hundred pair. Fewer women would engage in sex if they might receive compliments standing; the soft flattery of courtship is best delivered prone.

But however strange or foolish the predicament of lovers seems to those untouched by Cupid's shaft, the stricken party to himself seems sane. It is this that Plato meant when speaking of the shadow self, and this the poet wrote of when he writes of scars sans wound. What does the suitor seek to find if not a sense of order; what do we in that lovelorn state require but requital, as of particles made whole? The numberless varieties of love in this regard look similar: there is a tremor of expectancy, imbalance seeking balance, unrest portending rest. All else is merely detail, divergence and diversity within the common ground. All else is fireless smoke.

I give and bequeath, I give and bequeath, I give and bequeath . . .

Let us examine next a preliminary instance of the problem posed by order in its incorporeal guise. I refer to those alarums and excursions, those arrangements and alignments occasioned by national pride. We recognize effect here though we may well question cause. The patriotic impulse is, this writer must confess, entirely alien to him in its common form: my country is the world. The excellence of men and institutions knows neither boundary nor border; likewise their stupidity honors no frontier. Men die and shout while dying that they do so for their nation; their sons are raised to honor this same shibboleth and to avenge past wrongs.

Thus we may safely say that the sins of the fathers are visited unto the third and the fourth generation; he who speared the father bears, should his adversary prosper, a grandchild to be spitted on the sword. So year by decade and city by nation the argument endures. More women and their children are sacrificed to empire than any other cause; no sickness is as lethal as the furled banner, hoisted flag.

But whatever one may think of such behavior, that it has grown ubiquitous cannot be denied. This century was born in strife and seems likely to continue in the martial mode. Even the biblical famine and plague, the pestilence and locust swarm endured but seven years; we surpass that number now. I was born long ago and in another country, but all my life I have been in or near the thick of battle; it has been waged unceasingly and will not, I fear, abate.

What causes men to fight if not for the dream of peace, a boundary extended and preserved? Why do we squabble and bluster over additional ground? How argue with conviction that a few feet of territory requires bodies piled on it in order to establish that abstract thing, dominion, and that the names of city-state or nation need perforce be writ in blood?

All such furious wrangling derives from a single fallacy: that men have been created equal and may be so described. This widespread and pervasive faith is wrong. It was useful for the Declaration signed by my old countrymen and composed by that same Jefferson who once was stationed here—but even he no doubt apprehended that what he wrote was wishful, the ideal and not the actual case. Both common sense and scientific inquiry repudiate equality as an organizing principle; hegemony in nature is not the exception but rule. Domination and submission may be everywhere observed.

My first wife was born in Rumford, Massachusetts, and raised in that same village, later called Concord, New Hampshire. The peaceful resolution of a disputed border gave rise to the glad name of Concord; the river ran equably past. No inhabitant was murdered and no enmity aroused. Why should we not or could we not in times to come (as I have done in matters personal, taking my own title in honor of that agreement and not, I flatter myself, vainly) pursue just such procedures and agree? What's in a name but reasoned collective convention: this is a table and that is a chair, here a sofa, there a stool. What keeps us by contrast bellicose but habit, old arguments remembered and resumed? The man who hates his neighbor must perforce extend his neighborhood, ridding it of what he finds unwelcome. Thus he who claimed the meadow claims the hill. From hill to mountain range is but ambition's enlargement, and so we pass from treaty into war.

The Americans despise the British, the British the Bavarians, the Bavarians the French. In their turn the French profess allegiance to the idea of equality, and in the name of liberty lop off fraternal heads. All thoughtful men must surely see that this way madness lies. Yet I—who have been privy to the hopes and dreams of common folk, to

425

the enlightened aspirations of their leaders, who moved with knowing ease from barnyard to villa, schoolhouse to palace, who knew the function of 'prentice and master—have been denied by all. I who cast my lot with government am but an outcast now.

He's a pretty boy, no doubt of that, a very pretty boy. He studied philosophy too.

My daughter Sarah Thompson, Countess Rumford, arrived here from America of late. For the last years she has been prevented equally by circumstance, disposition, and desire from joining me in France. She is a simple creature though she thinks herself complex and would seem to the discerning eye to represent in her sole self those contrarieties and contradictions named above. I shall avail myself therefore of the paternal privilege and describe her situation in some detail: both order and disorder may be therein clearly seen.

Like many creatures of her sex, she wishes to seem fair. But fairness and equity are, alas, two separable notions; the doubling usage of the term misleads. To be "fair" as in "judicious" may well require wizened age; the most beautiful of creatures proves often in temperament foul. Nor can my Sally—though pleasing enough in demeanor—be truly described as attractive; she was never pretty except to a fond father's eye, and those who sought to make their fortune by arrogating hers.

I have ever been her partisan and always wholly loyal. I expect nothing less in return. So imagine my surprise when, hard on the heels of arrival in France, she hastens to make the acquaintance of that Jezebel, that creature of the lower depths who styles herself my wife. Of all the denizens of Paris this lady is the worst. Mme. Lavoisier de Rumford is both the most perfidiously charming of women and the least to be believed. Were it not improper to speak ill of the noble dead, I should accuse my predecessor—the great chemist Lavoisier—of posting to his fate relieved, since surely a brief encounter with the guillotine one afternoon would prove less enduringly painful than a series of encounters with so sharp-toothed a consort at night. She was his wife; she is (I write it to my shame), at present, mine.

We have reached and settled on a parting of the ways. I live here by myself. The consolations of such solitude are few, and I had every reason to expect my visitor would succor me in exile, taking her father's side. No matter how erratic in her judgment heretofore, it was permissible to hope my spinster daughter had with age grown wise.

That I have quit the world is evident; it does not come to call. That the glittering soirées at Rue d'Anjou may possibly beguile a girl desirous of gay company I also if unwillingly accept. I am an old, fond man who permitted Sarah on request to visit the lady in question, of whom I had written her often and to clear effect. I wished the girl to see the confines of my prison, the visage of my jailor, the lubricious ways of Paris, so that she might apprehend the reasons for my flight. A thing abhorrent is, once understood, a thing abhorred. So I sent her to the party with detailed and precise instructions: not to be taken up or taken in.

But I may have underestimated, as to my peril earlier, the cunning ways of women, their deep guile. Madame Lavoisier de Rumford made my daughter welcome in the house. She received her with all marks of approbation and respect, speaking kindly to her, soothingly; she admired her plain costume and heard the dull recital of her travels and travails. They kissed and hugged and wept. Madame served her famous punch. Then, smoothly pouring poison, she asked if Sally knew I am to be a father yet again. She had heard it, she said, on the street.

That I take comfort in the servants here is true. That one of them was rumored pregnant is the case. But when I tell my daughter not to pay attention—saying this is pure conjecture, this is calumny, mere supposition and envy—she answers that the brazen Madame too urged disbelief. Good my wife refused to think it possible I could get a woman with child. *Incroyable, incapable,* quoth the fiend. So I am damned if I accept the blame, twice damned if I refuse.

Then Madame, it would appear, proceeds apace. For the next hour, *tête à tête,* she spews forth falsehood and bile, inventing her own history, omitting nothing that might do her credit or diminish mine. And the credulous ignorant Sally, sitting at that witch's feet, accepts her version of the story, her recounting of imagined injuries and woes. She accepts as a token of friendship the very ring I gave milady when we were betrothed.

All this I learned that evening when my daughter returned from the dance. She was flushed, excitable, having drunk a quantity—no doubt an excess—of wine. The tell-tale redness of her nose and constant wringing of her hands informed me, or should have, of that precarious condition she all too often enters: imagination enflamed. I conducted her upstairs and showed her to her room. I turned—without a word of censure, be it noted, with no smallest hint of reproach!—to go. My own bed warmly beckoned; it was late.

"You monster," Sally cried.

"I beg your pardon, dear."

"Cruel, unfeeling monster!"

"You'll feel better in the morning."

"Never!"

"Of course you will. Now go to sleep."

"I won't!"

Next, pouring forth a torrent of abuse salted with weeping, my daughter told me what no father ought to hear. She has hated me, she said, since first she came to London, and hated me in Munich and hated me on both sides of the ocean all her life. I have made of it unending misery; I have driven her dear mother to an early grave, have abandoned friends and country and thwarted her few hopes.

Some women are made lovely, tearful; she was not. I turned once more to go; she screeched I should not leave. She needed to recite her woes and needed me to hear. With inexpressible reluctance, standing in the doorway, I remained. According to poor Sally, I have denied her suitors, have disabused and driven them away and even had them killed. I have made over-much of my beautiful illegitimate Sophie, giving her the choicer slice of cake. I paraded my lovers in front of my daughter, outraging her virginity, fondling paramours in carriage and in castle, routinely forbidding her all such solace as I routinely take. Further, I disdained her accent, her education, her attire; I am neither proud of her nor patient enough with her nor comfortable as companion; I have caused Madame de Rumford sorrow and she, Sally, is ashamed.

In this vein she continued for some time. The list went on. I cite these few particulars in order to suggest the whole, the *hysterica passio* of a maiden lady deranged. That I am willing to repeat such lies is surely proof of their impertinence, their utter irrelevance here. I heard my daughter out in the most patient way conceivable, more troubled by her troubled mind than by its fabrications. I suggested, as before, that she might ease her careworn state by the expedient of travel. I reminded her—considerately, cautiously—that she had been insane before, and Dr. Haubenal her faithful friend had then prescribed the Upper Engadine as cure. She might be well advised, I said, to take that cure again.

My daughter's rage abated. She turned white. "But I have only just arrived," she said.

"And look how unhappy already."

"I want to stay in Paris."

"It excites you," I averred.

"Not so. Not tomorrow, I promise!"

"It may prove fatal to your health."

"Please let me stay here, Papa. On my knees I beg you. Please!"

Nonetheless I made arrangements and she went.

An ingenious young man, Doctor —, a physician who resided in London, made a long course of experiments on himself several years ago, with a view to determine the relative nutritive powers of those substances which are most commonly used as food by mankind; and he found that sugar was more nourishing than any other substance he tried.

He took no other food for a considerable time than sugar, and he drank nothing but water, and he contrived to subsist on a surprisingly small quantity of sugar. If my memory does not fail me, it was no more than two ounces a day.

It is much to be lamented that this interesting young man should have fallen a sacrifice to his zeal in promoting useful science; but his health was so totally deranged by these experiments, which he pursued with too much ardor and perseverance, that he died soon after they were finished. All the resources of the medical art were employed, but nothing could save him.

I am not unacquainted with the manner of the age. I have lived much in the world, and have studied mankind attentively; I am fully aware of all the difficulties I have to encounter in the pursuit of the great object to which I have devoted myself. I am even sensible, fully sensible, of the dangers to which I expose myself. In this selfish and suspicious age it is hardly possible that justice should be done to the purity of my motives; and in the present state of society, when so few who have leisure can bring themselves to take the trouble to read anything except it be for mere amusement, I can hardly expect to engage attention. I may write, but what will writing avail if nobody will read? My bookseller, indeed, will not be ruined as long as it shall continue to be fashionable to have fine libraries. But my object will not be attained unless my writings are read, and the importance of the subjects of my investigations is felt.

Persons who have been satiated with indulgences and luxuries of every kind are sometimes tempted by the novelty of an untried pursuit. My best endeavors shall not be wanting to give to the objects I recommend, not only all the alluring charms of novelty, but also the power of procuring a pleasure as new, perhaps, as it is pure and lasting.

How might I exult could I but succeed so far as to make it fashionable for the rich to take the trouble to choose for themselves those enjoyments which their money can command, instead of being the dupes of those tyrants who, in the garb of submissive, fawning slaves, not only plunder them in the most disgraceful manner, but render them at the same time perfectly ridiculous, and fit for that destruction which is always near at hand, when good taste has been driven quite off the stage.

When I see, in the capital of a great country, in the midst of summer, a coachman sitting on a coach-box dressed in a thick, heavy great-coat with sixteen capes, I am not surprised to find the coach-door surrounded by a group of naked beggars.

Antimony, silver, arsenic, bismuth, cobalt, copper, tin, iron, manganese, mercury, molybdenum, nickel, gold, platinum, lead, tungsten, zinc; les molécules simples et indivisibles qui composent les corps.

From this account it must be hoped the reader comes to understand those difficulties the writer faced in attempting to subordinate disorder to its opposite—in attempting, as it were, to bring some systematic peace to a continent and household racked by constant war. Whether martial or civil, outward or inner, such strife is testimony to the omnipresent threat of chaos and the countervailing claim of order: the hard-earned habit of beneficent control.

My daughter wept; I shed no tear. She crawled; I did not bend. In vain she raised her salt-streaked face and her beseeching palm, then tried her ancient stratagem of promised reformation, of obedience in my presence and complicity abroad.

But all of this was shopworn now, transparent in its purpose. Sally wanted to remain, I knew, only to torment that poor unfortunate housekeeper she called "the woman with flowers" and refused to call by name. She was jealous and vindictive yet again. As a lesson in the practice of humility, I suggested to my daughter that she wash the feet and knead the weary shoulders of this member of my household, signifying thereby how the last among us shall be first and none should cast a stone. I acknowledged that the lady even now awaited me, and that I could not wait. I said I feared all contact with Madame Lavoisier de Rumford as though it were contagion, and that Sally herself might well be infected, then suggested that she pray. I promised her conveyance out of Auteuil in the morning, with a view to Switzerland and its bright glacial prospect. I extinguished the lantern and left.

In regard to the most advantageous method of using Indian corn as food, I would strongly recommend, particularly when it is employed for feeding the poor, a dish made of it that is in the highest estimation throughout America, and which is really very good and very nourishing. This is called hasty-pudding, and it is made in the following manner:

Lime, baryta, magnesia, alumina, silica.

Paris, June 6

Tres chèr Jonathan:

I write you in the French fashion, since it has grown incumbent on me to acquire French. A peculiar language, this, and one it will be, *je vous assure,* a pleasure to forget. I have just completed an interview with the daughter of our colleague—Sally Thompson, now the Countess Rumford. Since I myself have been unable to visit with the man (they keep close watch on me here, and I cannot travel freely), I must rely on hearsay and opinion as report. *Tant pis.*

She seems troubled in her spirit and unquiet in her mind. She spoke with great vexation of her visit to Auteuil. The *matter* of our conversation follows: the *manner* of it, however, is not easy to convey.

She wrung her hands; she blew her nose and said repeatedly she fears her father is unwell. She hinted at poison and plots. She is disappointed with him, yet there is an element also of filial concern. She believes him half a prisoner, and in this is half correct. Of the mass of her reproaches and her accusations, here is the digested remnant: make of it what you will.

When she came to see her father, she stood waiting in the hall. He kept her there. It is not so much discourtesy as the absolute absence of manners; Count Rumford has his system and it does not change. He had prearranged his schedule and could not make the time. *Would* not was more like it, Sally says; he simply doesn't care. He cannot be bothered. He is busy with his memoirs, his inventions, his roses, his lawsuits, his letters and grievances and what she calls his naked outrageous courtesan and his recipe for soup. It is always someone, she complained, *something,* there is always a new reason to insult her, a fabricated excuse. He has an appointment with Napoleon, with Lafayette, with the exiled Duke of some unpronounceable kingdom in a mountain range she hasn't even heard of and never could find on the map.

How much of this is accurate I find it hard to assess. The habit of betrayal, once engrained, runs deep. Quite possibly the Count no longer knows to whom he owes allegiance; he has served many masters and not all of them are dead. So what shall we make of this man; how describe him plausibly—how separate the traitor from the fraud? Well managed, he might still prove serviceable, Jonathan; ill managed he may do considerable harm.

The charitable impulse is in his case abstract. He seeks to help the poor and the downtrodden with a systematic program that has no hint of kindness, case by particular case. In similar fashion, I fear, he no longer thinks himself a subject of His Majesty—nor, for that matter, of the Holy Roman Empire—or citizen or *citoyen* but simply a man of the world. And these are most dangerous of all, these hirelings to the high bidder, these self-styled intellectual patriots in service to mankind. *Tout court. En bref.* We must assess this carefully; we must proceed with care.

In the meantime, please believe me your very constant and devoted—though in this instance and for fear of scrutiny, your nameless—etcetera.

We began with the assertion that the physical and unseen world will be here reconciled. It is neither a simple proposition, nor brief. When I was young and poor I understood the ways in which to serve the old and rich; I knew what I must offer in exchange for what they gave. My great friend Leigh instructed me that the bent knee need not entail submission, though there are always those who see corruption in pure amity and call patronage improper. Long since we had such commerce, but it did prove useful then and has remained most pertinent. We learned how to flatter, obey and command; we expect now no less in return.

Yet revolution is the system of the time. Disorder and disruption seize the day. The Emperor was driven back, defeated by those Mongol hordes who breed and prosper mightily across the frozen steppes. Meanwhile, we starve. Mendicity abounds. Beggars flourish everywhere; they throng the streets of Paris, but there is no workhouse, no work. The nature and effects of order would seem ever more elusive, not to say illusory. Nor can I write with conviction that I see the end of all this wrangling, for the brotherhood of man so confidently proclaimed in America and France has turned wholly fratricidal: we kill and kill and kill.

I continue with my notes. I do so with a heavy heart, and weary shaking hand. The mob ignores my soup. They disregard my coffee pot, my invention of the floating bridge, my double boiler and my convertible sofa. I am set upon and vilified no matter where I look. Laplace denies my prior and original conception of the argand lamp. Lagrange rejects the calorific theory: a fool by fools thought wise.

They laugh at me in Paris when I take my constitutional in winter wearing white. My carriage has broad wheels. So too will the wheels of the world one day be ample and broad-based and sheathed. In time I will be proven right and everywhere acknowledged and revered. The patently absurd procedures of the present age will be by my methods improved. There will be rapid distribution of food and fuel and wealth. There will be equitable allocation of the land. But till that time (and who may now with confidence assert that it is soon to come?) we are constrained to narrowness and lie here in thrall to confusion. We fail to take advantage of the frigorific rays.

I have lived my life, it may be said, in the service of mankind.

I have suffered mightily to gain what knowledge I have gained, to learn what things I learned.

I have not been content with personal advancement; I hoped to help the poor.

My peace is gone, my heart heavy. I won't find it ever again.

Il ne leur a fallu qu'un moment pour faire tomber cette tête, et cent années peut-être ne suffiront pas pour en reproduire une semblable. It took only an instant to sever that head, and a century will not suffice to produce an equal one.

For I did not take as seriously as perhaps I should have, and as others surely do, the notion of countries, nations, borders, of absolute distinction between peoples: war on war.

In time to come, however, there will be multitudes to celebrate my name. They will walk the English Garden and delight in green allées. They will harness power as I have done and improve munitions greatly and, in so doing and for fear of brutal consequence, make battle obsolete.

The light of science shines. It will illumine man and nation both.

Stay awhile: *Verweile doch.*

For I have understood the nature of gunpowder, of the calorific theory and what we may call nuclei, of the transmission of energy, heat of the sun, the excellence of coffee.

The variety of clothing and propriety of pigment in.

Yet mourn my native country with a keen abiding grief.

I would have, had I but the chance.

On this and other subjects, a great deal remains to say.

⸏ V ⸏

The light is fading, westerly; the garden will go dark. He has been waiting since five. At the stroke of six Bonnet will come, who was his coachman once but now serves as valet. He also keeps the gate. Nobody visits; none call. Call him coachman, footman, valet, drunk or idiot; it makes no difference to Bonnet who cultivates indifference like a garden plot. Discourtesy is this year's weed: rank, rank.

Count Rumford licks his teeth. His tongue finds the socket and probes. Pain is his familiar—in one form or another has proved his *fides Achates*, a faithful companion for years. In his youth pain was explosive, in middle age expansive, but now in his old age barely protuberant and as a swelling lanced. The upper left quadrant flares, fades.

There are those who hold—although he knows them credulous— that we live several lives: the Baron may have been a bull, the bull a carpenter, the carpenter an ant. The hero of the moment may have been a coward, and the saint a scapegrace long before. All things are interchangeable, and he who wields the pruning fork might once have been a bush. According to this theory, the warrior was earlier a carrot and the courtesan a rock, for time is not a line but circle: the sun now setting in the west is rising elsewhere also, and advance entails retreat.

So too with a career. He has been a teacher, soldier, diplomat. He traveled like a meteor, they say, ascending out of anonymity to fame. From Benjamin Thompson of Woburn, he grew to be Sir Benjamin Thompson of London and then Count Rumford of the Holy Roman

Empire. He has discovered much. There are principles of nature he has learned to recognize: order and disorder and their various effects. He was a scientist, philanthropist, a courtier and informer and a meliorist and fool.

Bonnet will enter as the first bell sounds and depart after the last. Five beats are three too few. In summertime he seems to linger, in wintertime make haste. At six o'clock on winter evenings Bonnet makes both his entrance and his exit by the clock, and does not alter pace. The hangings are white silk. It is better to have servants who accommodate variety than those who cannot vary their routine.

Rumford shuts his right eye, then the left; the room, adjusting, moves. The light is not a constant, nor the shadow of the leaves. No day repeats entirely the pattern of its predecessor nor anticipates the next. He coughs. He wipes his mouth. These summer days so brief, so brief—he sits in the one chair from lunchtime till the too-rapid arrival of dusk.

There comes the first faint whirring of the clock, the door slides smoothly open, then the chime. Reeking of anise, Bonnet appears. No change of temperature ensues, no sudden draft in the grate. The Count exhales. In how many countries, in how many houses great and small has he felt uneven heat, a fever by the hearth yet palpable chill by the wall? I have, he thinks, built well.

The valet limps perceptibly; the cuff of his right sleeve has come undone and shows linen less than spotless where he draws the curtain cord. His hair requires trimming; his buttons have gone dull. Bonnet could certainly have closed the curtains in five beats, but his actions would in that case have been hurried and his gestures rash. Capillaries flower in the desert of his cheeks.

"*M'sieur le Compte,*" he asks. "Is everything acceptable?"

Rumford makes no answer.

"May I bring you coffee?"

Non, he shakes his head. So doing, he displaces air, its volume rearranged. He has had small appetite this afternoon, scant thirst. He has had two wives, both widows, and one daughter from the first. His serving man bows and withdraws. The Count reminds himself— making a note of it, writing it down—to remind Victoire: a room is not a stable; he who curries horses cannot curry favor with an ill-groomed coat. It is not a matter of fashion but attention: Have the barber attend to Bonnet.

It had been Rumford's habit to maintain strict working hours, and this is imperative still. Once, such commerce as invades a house did not deflect attention; the clatter of petitioners (though whispering in his ear, though kissing his hand, embracing his knees) had proved no disruption. Claimants and counter-claimants took soon or late their leave; then twenty might arrive for supper, fifty or a hundred for a dance. When he lay ill in Munich many thousands had convened to mourn his departure from or—once recovered and triumphal—cheer his return to town. The women and their children would frolic in the nursery and make a joyful fuss. His colleagues would foregather to admire and debate. Yet with an assiduity bred of strong conviction the Count continued working; he worked in his carriage, on ship's deck, all night at need in the foundry. Once, he could work all day long.

Now his head feels like fire, feet ice. Again he licks his teeth. He cannot see that garden he so labored to make lovely, sees only the curtain, then wall. The moon will rise. It will traverse the oak, the lombardy poplars, the elm; he shivers not from cold but sympathy: wind, wind.

His daughter is in Switzerland and will reach this country soon. She must remember his concern when she promised to visit him earlier and did not arrive. He is, it may be, over-fond; he is too much afraid. Yet surely he could claim the prerogative of a father's fond anxiety, learning the particulars of her arrival together with an accounting of those who aided and assisted her, who joined in the overland journey and brought it to conclusion. She has had, he trusts, an easy voyage and a proper welcome and accommodations both commodious and clean. Nonetheless she fails to write. It would have comforted him mightily to hear from her, and to receive however cursory a line; Sally answers her provider with a perfect inattention born of scorn.

Had he the inclination, he could tell his daughter truth. Her sympathy is limited, her ignorance complete. She obeys too piously the standards of comportment; she lets opinion weigh too heavy on the scale and believes the tongue of slander and has quit him for that reason, some will say. She should have been less pious and more dutiful, he thinks.

Knight of the Orders of the White Eagle and St. Stanislaus; Chamberlain, Privy Counsellor of State, and Lieutenant-General in the Service of His Most Serene Highness the Elector Palatine, Reigning Duke of Bavaria; Colonel of His Regiment of Artillery, and Commander in Chief of the General Staff of His Army—he has been all these things, and more, but now his footman reeks and his tooth aches and from the corner of his right eye self-pity leaks away like watered ink.

When young, Count Rumford had enjoyed the most robust of constitutions—a vigor attendant on hygiene and exercise, a fortunate conjunction of nature with nurture that favors some men in their prime. He thought nothing of twenty-mile walks, then cut the winter's wood. He sat his horse all day and hunted game or the King's enemy—riding to the bugle or the trumpet, turn by turn. His sight was clear, aim steady. Often there was dancing, and many the night he rode till dawn in that sweet contentious saddle and the glad combat of love.

It has its proper place. It too is exercise. But now he is no longer well and his nights are entirely quiet; he has quit the world. It is not hard to quit.

With his left hand, carefully, he rubs the cramped bent fingers of his right. He coughs. What we take from Peter we use to pay off Paul. He, Benjamin Thompson, Count Rumford, never took out patents on his work. He made his own designs available to the public, for the comfort and improved condition of the poor. No matter how they vilify, calumniate or question him, the profit of humanity has been his one reward. The process of invention is the progress of ideas. What country he resides in is which language he employs.

This house is warm. The heat is regular and evenly distributed and does not vary by more than six degrees from room to room. He has overseen improvements. If not perhaps as thorough as those changes wrought in Brompton Road, or his first house in Paris—that temple of misguided pleasure on the Rue d'Anjou—the modifications remain adequate to his purpose, and it is unlike those nests of infection once believed wholesome, where the fire roasts and stairwell freezes, where the excess and absence of comfort contend with one another. Here one encounters no draughty hallways, no abrupt shifts of temperature by the stove or window or the garden door. There is no residue of soot or discernible odor of smoke, and all that man may reasonably marshal for convenience waits at hand.

Yet he plays at billiards and cannot hold the cue. He scarcely keeps it level while he aims. When he bends across the chessboard lightning darts along the pawns—a curious phenomenon, as though the ivory burns. When he blinks, the pieces change. He shuts his eyes; they flame. He studies his next move and the board is rearranged. For this reason, evenings—since he entertains no company—he plays against himself. He is his own opponent: self-indulgent who was worthy once, upon a time accomplished, now inept.

What though he gave up soldiering he did not give up travel. Often, his daughter came too. With proper nutrition and ventilation the frailest plant takes root and brings forth both flower and fruit. It can indeed be argued, by anyone who cares to verify such matters, that the risk of mortal illness is greatest in childhood, of mortality when young. What then may we not make of sturdy stock? Those who live, as he has, past the campaigner's season should expect with equanimity a long autumnal respite from the storm.

For there have been occasions, as Sally must remember, when the fever racked him, when too much work and too brief rest robbed him of his strength. Twice the typhus came. Once in Bavaria he thought

444

he would not live and had no hope for further life and hoped indeed for surcease from unremitting agony. He remembers days that felt like weeks, weeks months, months years, when the pillow was his sole companion and the fevered sheets. Then, little by little, he healed. All such seizures pass, are transient if not terminal; we may remedy the system's failure by an admission thereof.

Now the Count endures no sickness from which he can recuperate except this wasting disease: long life.

He blinks. There is no profit to be found in an account of loss; he will amuse himself this evening; he is sixty-one years old. It is time to call Victoire.

As if in answer to his unvoiced call—the door pivoting noiselessly on its oiled hinges—she comes. The clock strikes and he blinks again by way of signaling welcome, for she bears a tray with cakes, a spray of violets, coffee, two cups. Mlle. Lefèvre deposits the bright serving tray on the inlaid table and, with a fluid motion that he does not tire watching, turns up the two lamps. She sits, then smoothes her dress. And now the displaced air is welcome, not unwelcome; her scent is that of flowers, her perfume an enhancement, not—as with Bonnet—disguise.

"*Ça va?*" she asks.

He smiles.

"*T'as faim? T'as soif?*"

He has tried to teach her English, and she could have asked if he were hungry or thirsty in English instead. She reads it well aloud. But the pleasure of intimacy, the gift he gave her this calamitous New Year,

1814, of the second-person familiar—the chance to call him "Tu," who is nonetheless her employer—delights Victoire, therefore him. "*T'es bien réposé,*" she says approvingly. "You've had a rest, a nap."

At a certain age it is impolitic to inquire too closely as to age; she might have been twenty-seven, thirty, thirty-two, for she is one of those women who blossom and then hold the bloom. When he asked her she said twenty-five, and he let it go. Since October and her *accouchement* she has resumed that ripeness he first noted and approved, not of excess but sufficiency: taut, trim.

Mademoiselle Victoire Lefèvre has been in his service two years. She applied to be a table maid and entered his employment sight unseen. It was the custom of the Count to supervise such matters, since the nature of a household is determined by its staff. The master is reflected in the man. But he must have been absent that morning, or preoccupied; he would not, he is persuaded, have forgotten such an applicant. Madame Fleury conducted the interview at the porter's lodge; Fleury the porter was present then too. He could not remember the name of the girl she replaced.

One morning she was simply there, in his household uniform, in the entrance hall. She had been arranging flowers. The basket was full, the vase empty, and she chose with deliberate caution, stripping excess leaves. She turned each bud attentively, searching for discoloration in the light, and pinched and stroked and sniffed. For every flower chosen there were three rejected or at least set aside. In contrast to that ruthless treatment afforded his dear blossoms by the harpy he had married and had latterly escaped from, this scene was doubly affecting. How sweet the girl, how lissome her long neck!

446

The Count dawdled, appreciative, watching; she did not know he watched.

"'Rose girl, rose of a girl,'" he can remember reciting. "'What will you sell me? Your flowers? Yourself? Or both?'"

When she turned to notice him she dropped the basket, shocked. He told her not to be afraid, he had not meant to startle her. It was a poem, simply, a translation from the Greek.

"I am so clumsy," she said. "The Count must think me clumsy."

"No, not in the slightest, *mignonne*. Your name?"

She gave it.

"In this first skirmish," he said, "you have proved victorious."

Victoire had curtseyed, coloring, and bent to her armful of blooms.

That had been two years ago, of an April morning. Much has happened since. Sally sailed from Boston and arrived and disapproved and left again. Soon enough, she will return. She—so adamant and barren—could not tolerate the sight of burgeoning Victoire. For now there is an infant son, Charles Francois Robert Lefèvre, born last October 13th. At the registry they list the father as unknown, "*un père absent.*"

The Count made arrangements, however, dealing with French lawyers and his friend the banker, Baron Delessert. The girl herself made no demands and continued uncomplainingly with her former tasks. She placed her trust in providence and noble generosity and, she has assured Count Rumford, in his paternal concern.

Often he has questioned her, cajoled her into offering her version of events: how she came from Normandy, looking for advancement and what she called the large horizon, leaving the village behind. She had traveled with her sister, Sophie, and their young neighbor, Thérèse. The three of them had shared such hopes, such improbable dreams of marriage with farmers, drapers, vintners, chandlers, and— the connubial state once attained—homes of their own!

They presented themselves at the gate. They learned from Fleury's nephew that the Count (recently installed at Rue d'Auteuil and establishing his household) might require help. Yet she had no expectation that the distinguished gentleman would be so kind, so amiable, and so much alone. Victoire had confided all this later—little by little, haltingly, offering her scraps of history like someone at confession, whispering in the hot dark her litany of sins.

T'as faim?" she asks again. "You would like something to eat?"

He chooses to extend by postponing his pleasures, the coffee and the cake.

"This apple tart is excellent," she says.

There is both seemly and unseemly haste; the former we call competence and the latter greed.

"You are unwell?"

He shakes his head.

"You would enjoy it if I read?"

He smiles. He picks up his essay on coffee, newly bound though two years old. The binding of tooled leather bears his crest.

"To please me," says Victoire, "first have a bite of apple tart."

"Apple sweet," he wants to say. "That's what my friend Loammi said. He was always planting apples. Grafting stock." But the pun would have been lost on her, *sweet tart*, and he last had seen Loammi Baldwin before Victoire—whether twenty-seven, thirty-two, or older —had been born.

"One bite," she repeats. "The tart is *impeccable*. Sweet."

He leans back.

"It must be in the air," she says. "Charles too, this afternoon refused to swallow, he took nothing, the poor child. *Le pauvre.*"

Again, she arranges the light. He blinks.

"You should have heard him fussing. You should let me bring him to you."

Rumford does not wish to see and does not wish to speak of Charles. He is encumbered enough.

"Some coffee anyhow." She pours. The blend, the pot, the procedure are of his own devising; he takes neither sugar nor cream.

Her hands are soft yet shapely; so too her arms. He approves of how she pours, then positions the two cups. Her hair is auburn, her skin fair, and though he is a tall man she holds herself so proudly that their eyes meet on a level; hers are green-flecked brown. The quarter hour sounds, and therefore she undoes the button at her throat.

"Better?" she inquires.

He nods.

"*T'as faim?*" Victoire repeats, undoing lace.

He nods.

"You wish a drink first, possibly?"

He has forgotten his tooth. He puts his finger there. Then, as

449

before, as always, heart-stoppingly as if for the first time, she comes towards him yielding and brings her white breast to his mouth and, offering the nipple, permits the Count to suck.

But ah, the arching reach of it, the intricate equivalence of child in bed to man in chair, with sixty years between: the span of time, the mirroring arc, the way what Rumford has been once a continent and world away becomes again what now he is—a mewling helpless bundle to be fed and stroked and washed. It is time for truth-telling at last. For, truth to tell, he has not always been without ambition or vainglory, has not been wholly free of pride in each of his transactions on this earth.

"*Tiens*," she says. "*Mon Général.*"

He has been, he confesses, abrupt. He has been imperious and watched with satisfaction the effect of his greatness on others. Nor did he always take sufficient notice of his daughter or his mother or his old friends or wives, for he enjoyed the jealous whisper and the admiring glance.

There is nothing so wasteful as the attempt to heat ovens and boilers by heat drawn off laterally from an open grate. He has fashioned an experiment to demonstrate this point. Two legs of mutton were cut from the same carcass and of equal weight; he roasted one in his contrivance and one on a spit. After being cooked the joints were weighed again. It was found that the one from the Rumford Roaster was six percent heavier than the other; it was also pronounced—by cooks kept ignorant of the meat's provenance—to be much more juicy (the juices having been retained, not squandered on the open flame) and to have a better taste. There was, in addition, a greater weight of inedible fragments from the spitted joint.

"*Le pauvre*," says Victoire.

The future will redeem him, will release him from this vale of tears, will fix him in a gathering of scientists and colloquy of engineers and meeting of philosophers and men of excellent attainment. It is his rightful place. It is where he belongs. He has been ever mindful of the unrewarded poor. He has labored till he broke his health in the interest of others, always selfless, self-effacing, and in the commonweal. Could he but see his mother once, could he but make this clear to her, could he explain to his dear daughter how he strove unceasingly for the sake of that high purpose and illustrious ideal—could he find pen and paper, wielding the former, spreading out and by means of sympathetic ink devised by an infusion of extract of nutgalls, covering with his bold and certain hand the latter.

To have been young in Woburn and old now in Auteuil, to have traversed such distances and sit immobile here, to choose the side of order and watch disorder rampant, to drink so deeply of sweet wine and finish so bitter, so parched—Rumford sighs. To be maligned who wanted praise, ignored who deserved recognition—he coughs. Napoleon, they tell him, is incarcerate on Elba now, and this comes as no surprise. He will escape, no doubt, and fight again and be defeated and returned. It is how to pass the time. With his test-tubes and armies and wheels. With his biscuits and muskets and eels. With Josephine lifting her heels. And thus the brilliant Emperor; *Vive l'Empereur!*

The scarecrows in the western wind, the crows in trees, the skeletons who bivouac then break their camp and march and fight and starve and pitch their tattered tents and groaningly at night combat the daily dead again—all, all fling caps in air and dance the pegleg jig and chorus, "*Vive l'Empereur.*"

He's sleeping now," declares Victoire. She pats at the pillow that cradles his head.

"*Peut-être,*" says Bonnet.

"He's sleeping, I tell you," she says.

"I don't see any difference, *moi.*"

"You don't know how to look."

"*Je m'en fiche,*" declares Bonnet.

"Help me move him, you. He's very heavy when he sleeps."

"*Il dort toujours,*" the coachman grumbles. "He sleeps, he always sleeps. As far as I'm concerned, he's dead weight all the time."

"*Tais-toi.* He may be listening."

"I thought you said the master sleeps."

"I said that, yes."

"*Alors?*"

"He might wake up, he could hear you."

"Let's put him to bed, then. I'm thirsty."

"Tell me something," says Victoire, "I don't already know."

"What you don't know won't bother you." Bonnet wipes his hand across his mouth and carelessly, with the ease of old habit, puts it between her legs.

"Don't do that, you."

"Why not?" He mimics the Count. "I'm thirsty, I'm dying of thirst."

"Not now."

He opens his mouth and waggles his head and lets his tongue loll free. *"Je meurs de soif."*

Victoire removes his hand. She did not sleep with him last night because she worried over Charles, his cough, his fever, and by the time Charles truly slept Bonnet had been too drunk. He can be violent on gin, and she is sick of violence, has had enough of it, has seen enough of it to last this lifetime and the next, and therefore stayed out of his way.

"He's sleeping," says Bonnet.

Out of darkness then, the night endured, the drifting sift of hours and his history rehearsed, he wakes to universal pain—that ache and stiffness everywhere that signifies, since life is grief, renewal and dawning alertness (a rooster, a susurrus in the eaves, his caged birds uncovered to greet the new day), and thus by slow yet certain stages the future becoming its own present too. He can tell it, can foresee it, can imagine how his name will ring and signify to generations yet unborn, how an old woman in Concord will report his story, writing it, and day by month and month by year recover what he feared was lost, how the poor will sing his praises, foregather and be grateful and release themselves from straitened circumstance by means of his inventions until the crack of doom. They will offer up thanksgiving in his name. Those who laugh at him in Paris—who joke that the Count's workmen have been blinded by the light of his hand-lantern and, taking a sample home to display, wander all night in the Bois de Boulogne; who complain they detest the potato and bread-crusts in soup; who call a bad meal dining *à la Rumford* and cackle at his carriage and the way that he wears white—will be but dust.

The French are fond of jokes. He too enjoys a joke: his detractors and critics must die. Everywhere the wide carriage wheel and the coffee pot will triumph, the clothing industry flourish, the houses and the kitchens of the poor be properly arranged.

Humphry Davy comes to visit. So does Baron Delessert. So does Daniel Parker. Yet his daughter does not come. She is being sent for, says Baron Delessert. She will arrive in time. She will be in Paris soon. Daniel Parker is his friend. He lives in a great house in a great park. He owes Count Rumford nothing but is owed in turn by every man in France, the richest American there.

Count Rumford is not poor. He suckles on the swelling breast of his housekeeper, Victoire. His house in Auteuil is not poor. It has first-rate windows and a view of the river and trees. Madame Helvetius the owner had a reputation as coquette. She was, the Count has been reliably informed, a woman who rode the cock horse. She must have been a woman of considerable charm. Ben Franklin had proposed to her along the winding drive. But that is nothing new, of course; Franklin propositioned every third lady in Paris and called it a proposal. Sometimes he met with success. Sometimes he rogered his dog.

So Humphry Davy traveled. He left Cornwall for London and then he left London for France, arriving from Banbury Cross. He tells his old employer of the lectures and experiments that proceeded nowadays apace in the great Theatre, sir. Rumford yawns. I refer, your Excellency, to the lecture hall you built. He yawns again. But Davy has a certain candor nonetheless. I am grateful, he assures the Count, for all that you have done. I owe you my career. He has admitted as much.

When they play at billiards, he cannot hold the cue. When they play chess together, he does so by himself. His feet feel like fire, head ice. Outside his roses bloom, his brilliant white varietals, his fragrant yellow beauties, his multitude of loves. He pawns his queen, then takes his own rook, arranging a forced mate in three. A false-faced man and trickster, someone who dons another's garb—was this who he became? The wind may change, and its direction, and to the distant witness he might well appear inconstant. Yet like the steeple's turning cock he sits nonetheless rooted and firm: a boy again, Ben Thompson, who fouls his fresh-washed pants.

Beau temps," Bonnet repeats. "A pleasant evening."

"Speak for yourself," says Victoire.

"It will be hot tomorrow, though. *Un temps atroce.*"

Lifting her shoulders prettily, she shrugs. "He's getting a bit better. Charles."

"And the old one. *Le vieux?*"

"He seems all right. No worse, at any rate."

"His daughter is supposed to come."

"I've heard that before," says Victoire.

"No, truly, she's *en route.*"

"Yes?"

"The Baron wrote: great Delessert. He told her that she better hurry, if she intends to see him."

"*Ça m'est égal,*" she says. "It's all the same to me."

"*Et moi,*" he says, "I don't give a shit. *Je m'emmerde.*"

Beyond, the dark is absolute and Rumford turns to see. The Count blinks his right eye, then left.

As if a magic lantern cast its shadows on the wall, as if he closed his eyes and saw on the bright screen of his shut lids those scenes where he had been an actor once, the parts long played (the prologue and the several acts and epilogue remaining), the tumult and vivacious fuss of youth in its salt prime, then manhood, then maturity, then old age and incontinence and now in voiceless steep decline himself refracted in a silver pot—by the inexorable geometry of his reflection rendered comic, bulbous, noting also (and this is better, this is earned improvement, this is what he wanted and deserved) above him that beautiful nipple, its liquid streaming—he sees:

Himself in Woburn, milking cows, the barnlight falling whitely from the haymow and good Uncle Hiram somewhere in the middle distance, clucking, humming, jostling the pails;

The slate and chalk and ruler; forgetful Mr. Fowle;

Himself in Salem, bent above the workbench, measuring powder and saltpeter and pretending concentration while Mary Appleton flounced past, her skirts a purple glimmer at the doorway to the street;

Himself in Concord, on his horse, the Merrimac below them and bright Blaze reined in, explosive, the trout and buzzing mayflies and high lethal wheeling hawk;

Loammi Baldwin with the kite; John Appleton, Merchant, with ticking and leather and buttons and tweed; the red-headed stammering suspicious Hopestill Capen at the till; then Abigail above him in Dr. Hay's garret, her bed;

The tent of her hair;

There should be a round hole, about a quarter of an inch in diameter, near the end of the handle, by which the saucepan may occasionally be hung up on a nail, or a peg, when not in use. The cover belonging to the saucepan may be hung on the same nail, or peg, by means of the projection of its rim.

The continual astonishment of her ankle, calf, knee, thigh;

The monstrous child in brine;

Patriots; the barn he took his refuge in, lumber, axe and saw, the sugar maple and the lengths of oak he split;

Himself escaped, at sea;

Lord George Germain and his great seal of office, the pomade and brilliantine and powder at his lordship's temples, the long nervous fingers drumming with impatience, the yellow, carious teeth;

Himself in the stable at Stoneland, firing, taking measurements, waiting for the air to clear, then firing again;

Himself in the ox-cart, post-chaise, curricle, the ducal coach, the Elector's personal and imperially provided carriage—his broad-rimmed wheels, his horses impressively matched;

Paul Rolfe his student, dribbling gruel;

The pudding is then eaten with a spoon, each spoonful of it being dipt into the sauce before it is earned to the mouth; care being had in taking it up, to begin on the outside, or near the brim of the plate, and to approach the center by regular advances, in order not to demolish too soon the excavation which forms the reservoir for the sauce.

Sarah Rolfe Thompson, his wife: her pink bolster, the applejack brandy with which she regaled herself secretly, the pinch-lipped disapproval, the holier-than-thou insistence on her station and estate;

Salt sea again, the waves;

Forked lightning and the thunder and the drenching wheeling freezing spume, the tilt and pitch and misery and wind;

The bread he baked on tombstones and served rebellious locals, their fathers' and grandfathers' names incised on the burnt crust;

For vengeance is mine, saith the Lieutenant-Colonel;

The pudding is to be eaten with a knife and fork, beginning at the circumference of the slice, and approaching regularly towards the centre, each piece of pudding being taken up with the fork, and dipped into the butter, or dipped into it in part only, as is commonly the case, before it is carried to the mouth.

Target practice at the river, its red bank;

His own face caught by Gainsborough when young;

The nose, its intricate turnings, its nostrils and its nostril-hairs and the unblemished spatulate arrangement of the down-turned tip, the absolute precision with which he remembers its size and color and consistency, a single powdered ridge of bone, its shape, saving only the question of whom it belonged to—a parent, total stranger, child, friend, corpse, or someone he had barely met but watched with some intensity?—he could not tell; he could not remember even what he wished to tell, or what it ought to signify, or why;

Himself alone;

Lithe double-dealing insubordinate Jonathan Leigh at sword's point, parrying, thrusting, lunging, smiling, not breaking a sweat;

Bright fire in the hearth;

J'adoube. With your permission, dear friend, I adjust;

The pleasures of a garden well planted, carefully tended, then harvested, then cooked;

Bishop to king's bishop four;

The Merrimac, the Thames, the Isar River, Rhine, Rhone, Tiber, Arno, now the Seine;

Humphry Davy; Michael Farraday; Lagrange; a man called Johann something that he met while in the English Garden—directing his soldiers there how to build earthworks, where to channel through the swamp and make of it a meadow—this young poet of some breeding and promise and, the Count was told, distinction, with a housemaid on each arm;

Wer immer strebend sich bemüht; a snatch of song; *Den können wir erlösen;*

His solitude; a flute;

Mary Nogarola with her chocolate, Mary with her nougat; Mary on horseback, on the balcony in Italy; Mary with her dark eyes fixed on him reproachfully, Mary with her marzipan, Mary laughing, Mary dead;

Himself with a lantern, a roaster, a greenhouse, a portable kitchen, a candle;

Young Captain Taxis sent packing; Spreti too; Charles Blagden disabused;

His exile state, his enemies, his forlorn perseverance and wholly undeserved and total isolation;

The banners and standards and bloodied torn flags and ridiculous slogans the people chant, marching, marching, saluting, credulous, about to die;

Great China, where the few benevolently govern many, where the wise instruct the foolish and make law;

Himself in Munich, at the Marienkirche at dawn, the beggars everywhere, their leering importunities, their hands;

The potato; the vats of good soup;

The potatoes are then added, having previously been peeled with a knife.

That half-stifled shivering encouragement of Lady Palmerston; the screams of Baroness de Kalb, the gasping hot-breathed high-pitched shudder of Mademoiselle Jollien;

Himself abandoned, ill;

His books, his charts, his maps, his military drawings, his inventions and improvements by the score;

Heat; light;

Fat bald squint-sighted Ambassador Franklin with his pious regimen and inefficient stoves;

The flashing eyes of the Electrice, her tongue, her skipping heels;

Tancred, Lambkin, Fawn;

The perfect acoustics in Albemarle Street, the Repository and the theatre and the storage room he slept in with the white snow blowing past;

The black magician in his cave; great force for good and yet the devil's compact; Marie Anne Pierrette Lavoisier de Rumford, bitch;

His long and bootless battle for redress;

And first of all, the throat of the Chimney should be in its proper place; that is to say in that place in which it ought to be.

America—bright vision of the future, that refuge of the huddled poor and harbor of the persecuted faithful, that shore of rock, upstanding birch and ash and black walnut grove and meadow where the laborer might take his ease, the hills, the mountains and the plain, a land-mass so extensive he can but guess its farther shore—a beauteous new-mapped continent now fading, receding behind him;

Harry Modiste, you beak-nose;

The comforts of imprisonment at last, this circumstance that even addle-brained he knows is house-arrest, the Emperor's benign neglect, the doubling and the trebling certainty of night-time watch, his servants bribed, his every action marked, described, set down in triplicate for England, Bavaria, France;

Sir: Please to give the Nature, Essence, Beginning of Existence, and Rise of the Wind in General.

Count Rumford licks his tooth. Once more the quadrant flares. He welcomes in this instance, since it proves him not insensible, the pain. He hears the shuffling mutter of Bonnet behind him, and Victoire there somewhere also, and her fond approval of what is surely some new antic of young Charles. He does not turn to look. He cannot share their joke or enjoy their shared grunting mutual encouragement and brief sharp panting laughter. The wise man waits in the one chair, for where is the advantage of attending to what he cannot remedy or halt? Victoire cries out once, loudly, and then they go quiet again.

Now the astonishment, flame in his head, the absolute implosive shock, and what was space is lack of space, and what was time is lack of time, and what was bright vivid remarkable life is not.

Him can we save. Woburn, the dear dream of home.

SALLY

Lüstwandler, Steh. Stroller, halt.

When did our Johnny Faust announce enough's enough? And tell the passing moment, stick around, you'll do just fine. For it must be clear by now that Faust's our great original and who Count Rumford flatters by unconscious imitation: Western Man, the mage himself. Note his habit of study and life-long restlessness, his ceaseless hunt for satisfaction and the pregnant serving-girl, his devotion both to luxury and the simple life—remember that couple in Switzerland, Class? With his reclamation project for the Isar river-bank, his travels and fire and boiled witches' brew, our boy's the very template of the turning world, the Enlightened and Romantic worthy rolled up into one. We'll miss him, won't we, when he's gone; we'll stand before Gainsborough's portrait in the Fogg Museum or we'll go to the English Garden and grandpa's farmhouse in Woburn and read the citation and plaque.

That Holy Roman Empire he styled himself a noble in—already at the time a long-outmoded dignity and ceremonial title (and is it possible Karl Theodor, the sly Elector Palatine, knew he could purchase Thompson's loyalty with only a handful of silver, mere wampum and ribands to put on his coat?)—is over now. *Fertig.* Gone and forgotten: *Vollbracht.* So even while acquiring it he gained a name foredoomed to fade, and there's something halfway comic in his vision of entitlement. *They laughed at him. They watched him pass.* Et seq.

Yet Roosevelt did mean it when he praised Benjamin Thompson's intelligence, saying it rivaled Jefferson's and Franklin's as one of the three finest minds in our country's history; had he not been a turncoat he'd be celebrated still. Like Benedict Arnold he picked the wrong side, but it was a coin-toss; he *could* have chosen otherwise and been by schoolchildren admired. What was missing in the man, I think, was any degree of awareness that he might be in the wrong—that saving grace, uncertainty, without which we as characters and as a nation are doomed.

Damned. The stroke of midnight, now.

And what of the woman who sits here eternally, scribbling? What of *le souscrit,* reader? Who also plans to close the book and put away her childish things: the leather-bound edition of the Essays, the baking powder cans with the profile of Count Rumford and copies of his letters to his daughter my ancestor, the photograph of Rumford, Maine, its factories and river, the portraits and the diagrams and pencil drawings and military commissions of Andrew MacMillan and Thomas Stickney and muster roll of what such soldiers wore in Concord, and the translation from its formal French of his great friend the Baron's funeral address.

Ayup ayup nope nope.

Morning, Miz' Robinson."

"Morning," says I.

"What can I get for you?"

"Potatoes," says I. "Dried peas. Chickpeas. Bread."

"Whole wheat?" asks the grocer's boy, Daniel.

I nod.

"That all?" he asks. "That everything?"

"A sack of onions. Black-eyed peas."

"You cooking for company?"

"Not today."

He tilts his head towards the hill. "Been having visitors? Family?"

"Well, yes." I plan to give him Husband's watch. I'll bequeath it to him, anyhow. "In a manner of speaking."

"Still with you, are they?"

"No."

EPILOGUE

1814

Address pronounced over the grave of Count Rumford
By M. Benjamin Delessert, on the 24th of August, 1814.

It is permitted to me, my friends, as a member of the Administration of Hospitals, to be the medium of expressing our sorrow at the loss of the distinguished man who was pleased to honor me with his friendship. I leave it to more eloquent voices to speak of the productions of his rare genius; to boast of his numerous discoveries in the sciences, and his ingenious methods of penetrating to the secrets of nature; to describe his theory of heat, his experiments upon light, his observations upon combustion, upon steam, upon gunpowder; and to commemorate him as the founder of the Royal Institution of London.

I wish here and now only to recall to your minds those of his most directly useful and beneficent works which have made his name known in every part of Europe. Who is ignorant of what he has done for relieving the scarcity in food; of his multiplied efforts for making food more healthful, more agreeable, and above all, more economical; what service he has rendered to humanity in introducing the general use of the soups which go by his own name, and which have been so invaluable to so many thousands of persons exposed to the horrors of the prevailing scarcity? Who has not been made acquainted with his effective methods for suppressing mendicity; with his Houses of Industry, for work and instruction; with his means for improving the construction of chimneys, of lamps, of furnaces, of baths, of heating by steam; and, in fine, with his varied undertakings in the cause of domestic economy?

In England, in France, in Germany, in all parts of the continent, the people are enjoying the blessings of his discoveries; and, from the humble dwelling of the poor even to the palaces of sovereigns, all will remember that his sole aim was to be always useful to his fellow-men.

Alas! death has snatched him away in the midst of his labors. Pitiless death has removed him from those to whom he consecrated his existence. But his spirit survives on this terrestrial orb. His genius, smiling over us, lifts itself heavenward, and he goes to take one of the high places prepared for the benefactors of humanity.

When Sally arrived he was dead. She did not believe it at first. The woman, his housekeeper, wept, but she was often tearful; she had been taught discourtesy and had grown too familiar with the Count and had, Sally knew, presumed. Those that we encourage to shrug off the yoke of virtue must live with the burden of vice.

Baron Delessert had written her in Switzerland in August and warned her to make haste, returning, if she wished to see her father. They did not expect recovery, nor could Count Rumford speak. He had been in failing health for years but, since his recent seizure, matters had grown worse. He waited, wrote the Baron, like a prisoner for pardon, and only a filial visit might procure him his release.

She did proceed to Paris and hire a conveyance but did not arrive in time. It had been raining heavily. The body was prepared. The nose was improperly pinched. He had died on Saturday, surrounded by his roses and the caged birds in the parlor, sitting, as had been his custom, upright on the couch. The coachman and the porter and the porter's wife kept watch; all others had forsaken him or, with the silver, decamped. He was buried at Auteuil.

On the 24th of August, at eleven o'clock in the morning, with Sarah Countess Rumford at his side and the housekeeper wearing black, with a contingent of foreigners present, the Baron delivered the funeral speech. He and Sally then consulted on the wording and dimensions of the memorial stone. It was of marble, six feet wide and six feet high and three-and-a-half feet thick. Its citation was in French and when carved it claimed, inaccurately, that the Count was born in Concord and that his labors for the poor would make him in perpetuity cherished.

They read the will. The bulk of the estate was designated to three beneficiaries: she herself as Rumford's daughter, and also Harvard College and the Military Academy of the United States. Included in the bequests were a plain gold watch for Humphry Davy and a gold headed cane and gold-enameled watch, with the gold chain and seals attached, to Daniel Parker. To Benjamin, Baron Delessert, the Count left a gold enameled snuff-box, set round with diamonds, this being the same as had been given him by His Majesty Frances II, Emperor of Austria.

In her New Hampshire drawing room the daughter hung oil portraits of her father's particular friends—the ladies he cared for most dearly: Mary Nogarola, Countess Baumgarten, Baroness de Kalb. Further, she hung a pastel likeness of herself when young. She hung portraits of Benjamin Thompson at several stages of his age, and landscape studies of Bavaria, in chalk. By the parlor door she hung a Kellerhofen portrait of Karl Theodor, the Elector Palatine.

Then Sarah burned the majority of her father's scolding letters and his salacious scrawled notes: those lists and scraps and earnest maunderings he had assured her were his magnum opus. Long years before, when traveling from Calais to Dover, he had been relieved of papers that he planned to publish and, being desirous of celebrity, loudly bemoaned the theft. His more recent writing would, the Count was certain, ensure his reputation for centuries to come. More likely, she feared, it would do the reverse—so she tore up his *Essay on Order*, its nature and effects.

Upon repeated tearful application and having taken counsel with her conscience, the Countess permitted the Lefèvre woman to stay in the house in Auteuil. She conferred on the Lefèvre boy a portion of her father's wealth, providing he and his family assume the name of Rumford. Then he too became a soldier, and died in the Crimea, and there were none beyond young Amedé to call her proper heir. This she did, with stipulations—that he maintain the cherished surname and learn English to pronounce it in—but by the time this legacy had crossed the wide Atlantic she could not follow to insure it nor determine to her satisfaction if Amedé complied.

My great great great step-grandmother Sarah survived for nearly forty years after her own father's death, bitterly, and saw Napoleon sequestered after Waterloo and Charles Blagden dead and buried and Kings and Generals and Presidents and Emperors undone and the beautiful Sophie her half-sister gone wholly mad, a suicide, and Loammi Baldwin, too, decline amid his honors and die while drinking soup. She sat with him at table that final night in Woburn; he went first red, then white. Loammi shook his head at her as if he disapproved of something—the cream perhaps, or pepper—then gargled and spat. His mild gaze blankly fixed on her while he fell forward to his plate held the promise of instruction or, perhaps, reproach. She did not care to distinguish. She repudiated both.

She painted and did needlework and rode. She traveled to the continent again—avoiding, however, Auteuil. She refused the desultory suitors of her parish and lived by her own preference alone, preferring also, when in company, to converse in French. The dowager Sarah Countess Rumford left her large house and land in Concord, and her considerable fortune, to charity. She died on December 2, 1852, when seventy-nine years old. To the son of Joseph Walker,

Charles, for whom she entertained sentiments of affectionate regard, she left a French Bible, an alabaster block, and a gold-wrought clock. She gave away the furniture and medals; she gave away the landscapes done in chalk and the portraits in oil and watercolor, together with their frames.

To her church she gave a violin, to her village school a length of rope. She had two favorite causes, and she endowed them by bequest: a home for parentless children, and the New Hampshire Asylum for the indigent insane.

Author's Note

The usual disclaimer affidavit here applies; this is a work of fiction not scholarship. Nonetheless, and to the best of my ability, I have been faithful to the facts of Benjamin Thompson's strange eventful history. If I name a date or place, the data does exist. So too with the bulk of the characters here, although I did take liberties when weaving story-yarn. Dr. John Hay, for example, is an actual historical personage—but Abigail his servant was created for young Thompson's pleasure then pain. Edward Gibbon crossed the English Channel in the same vessel as Thompson, but what he said I made up. Rumford did conceive of and in part compose an essay on "The Nature of Order," but it has been lost; its animadversions are mine.

Most of what transpires in the life of Benjamin Thompson, Count Rumford was reported by that man himself. Some of the language I copied verbatim, as in his letters to his daughter and Loammi Baldwin, his disquisitions on gunpowder and mendicity, his plans for kitchen implements and the Royal Institution. Indeed, the five volumes of Count Rumford's *Collected Works* provide a near-inexhaustible wealth of material. My own edition is the first American, printed from the third London Edition in 1798; the most recent text was published by Harvard University Press, (1968–1970). Had I yielded to the strong temptation to paraphrase these writings in their entirety, this book would be five times as long.

Like my invented narrator, I have been "haunted" by Benjamin Thompson's candlelit ghost for more than twenty years. Like her, I once owned a house with a shallow fireplace and learned how it best yielded heat. (The man who taught me how to use it, however, was not a local real estate agent but the late Thomas Irvine, a Rumford aficionado to whom I owe a great deal.) Way led on to way. I was helped in my researches by the staff of the William Clements Library of the University of Michigan, the Houghton Library at Harvard University and, most notably, the Baker Library at Dartmouth College. The excellent collection there was in large part established by the late Sanborn C. Brown, whose *Benjamin Thompson, Count Rumford* (The M.I.T. Press, 1979) remains the definitive study of Thompson's life and work. This was my principal source-book, and sufficient to the day.

Other volumes proved useful, of course. A smaller "science study" by Sanborn C. Brown appeared as *Count Rumford: Physicist Extraordinary* (Anchor Books, 1962). There are fanciful books (*The Countess,* by March Cost, The Vanguard Press, 1963) and utilitarian books (*Rumford Complete Cook Book,* published by the Rumford Chemical Works in Rumford, R.I., its cover claiming "More than 5,000,000 copies in use"); there are articles that focus on his physics or his military exploits or experiments with heat. The English author W.J. Sparrow wrote *Knight of the White Eagle: Count Rumford of Woburn, Mass.* (Thomas Y. Crowell, 1964), and there is an invaluable if rather more fanciful account "published in connection with an edition of Rumford's Complete Works by the American Academy of Arts and Sciences in Boston in 1871." This *Memoir of Sir Benjamin Thompson, Count Rumford, With Notices of His Daughter* was compiled by George E. Ellis, and it is from his sizable text—more than six-hundred and fifty pages—that I derived the language of Sarah's romantic imbroglio with Count Taxis, her education in the etiquette of curtseys, and so on.

I have visited Thompson's birthplace in Woburn, Massachusetts, the statehouse in Concord, New Hampshire, the Royal Institution in Albemarle Street, London, the Englische Garten in Munich and many other venues of his much-traveled life. Everywhere his adepts made me welcome; everywhere I saw the same half-mad and wholly-committed glint in my interlocutor's mirroring eye: Come along, they seemed to say, admire this roaster, study this portrait, touch this medal, you must be one of us. It has been a great gift, truly, to talk with physicists, historians of science, taxicab drivers, art historians, masons, bakers, booksellers, editors who have in common principally their interest in this half-forgotten man. So many helped me in so many ways that I have decided, perversely perhaps, to name no particular names; my gratitude is general, and all-encompassing.

Some fifteen years ago, I published two pieces of my own on the subject of Count Rumford. They are "Rumford: His Book," an essay in the *Michigan Quarterly Review,* Spring, 1992, and "Rumford," an article, in *American Heritage,* Volume 44/Number 5, September, 1993. Chapters 1 and 2 of Book I of this novel appeared in somewhat different form, respectively, as "Rumford: His Book," in the *Southern Review,* Fall, 1993 and "Rumford, His Book," in *New Millenium,* Spring & Summer, 1996. An Account of "Rumford and Sally" was published in *Shenandoah,* in the Fall of 1995, and I anthologized our hero as "Benjamin Thompson, Count Rumford, on the Nature of

Order and Love," in *The Book of Love*, (eds. Ackerman and Mackin) W.W. Norton & Co., 1998.

Then, for a decade, I let my narrative steep. At some point the notion of a living witness entered in, and Sally Ormsby Thompson Robinson arrived whole cloth. As she observes—and as I also suggest in the epistolary exchanges between those who spy on him in the penultimate chapter of Book III—the problem posed is that of self-knowledge; few men have written so extensively about their own achievements and with so little awareness of the human cost entailed. His life spans, in effect, the end of eighteenth-century meliorism and start of the Romantic period—the transition from outward-to-inward facing consciousness. The protagonist of a long novel fairly requires some self-awareness, however, and it was not until I stumbled on the notion of point-counterpoint (Sally's authorial commentary) that the Count took fictive shape. Whether he emerges vividly is not for me to say—but like Baron Delessert I dare to hope "his spirit survives on this terrestrial orb." R.I.P.

About the Author

NICHOLAS DELBANCO is a British-born American who received his B.A. from Harvard and his M.A. from Columbia University. He currently directs the Hopwood Awards Program and is the Robert Frost Distinguished University Professor of English at the University of Michigan. An editor and author of more than twenty books, Delbanco has received numerous awards—among them a Guggenheim Fellowship and two Writing Fellowships from the National Endowment for the Arts.